Down Undercover

Maggie Matheson
Down Undercover

ISBN: **9798849002095**

Down Undercover

The story so far...

In the first book about Maggie Matheson – *The Senior Spy* – Maggie, at the age of 81, is lured out of retirement and back into her beloved Secret Service by her great-grandson, Joshua, for 'one last case'. The prospect of making contact with the son she gave up for adoption as a baby is an important factor in her decision, but, quite honestly, so is the prospect of not having to spend another afternoon in front of the telly watching programmes about antiques. She is not disappointed by the excitement her return to the fold brings, as she is whisked off to Mainland Europe to tackle a cyber gang, intent on bringing down the largest of international organisations. There, many exciting events occur, not least of which Maggie discovers some interesting facts about her family and those she had worked with.

For those who have not read the first book – and as a reminder to those who have – there follows a short cast list that explains some of those connections and introduces a couple of new characters that appear in *Down Undercover*.

Of course, if you are into spy books, you probably already have the wherewithal to work it all out anyway.

Main Characters in Down Undercover

Maggie   Grandmother, great-grandmother, tea-drinker, bridge-player, spy.

Bill   Maggie's son (Peter) who she was forced to give up for adoption, now reunited. Bill is a nickname. He is also a spy.

Ben   Husband of Bill, Not a spy, though he would make an excellent one.

Joshua   Maggie's great-grandson, Bill's grandson from a previous marriage. The youngest spy in the British Secret Service.

Sharon   Maggie's daughter, sister of Bill. She lives in Australia with her husband, Sean, and Maggie's grandchildren.

Dingo Derek   An old friend of Maggie and Maggie's husband, Frankie. Lives in the Outback.

Tina Sheldon   Maggie's former boss who Maggie helped put in jail for cybercrime and other nefarious activities.

Emanuel Taylor   Arms dealer and diamond thief.

To our dear friend, Wendy

Down Undercover

~ ~ ~

Chapter 1

The flight attendant was incredibly helpful. Maggie was, frankly, a little embarrassed by all the fuss; she had not expected an upgrade or even asked for one. But the attendant had insisted she turned left as she boarded the plane into Business Class, leaving Joshua to turn right, happy, he said mischievously, to have some peace and quiet for the duration of the flight.

Neither had she asked for special assistance, but again the airline had been adamant. It was the least they could do after the problems in the transit area, put down, they said, to a mixture of 'staff cuts' and 'an unprecedented systems failure', the like of which they had not seen before. Even now, as she settled down into her extra wide seat and gratefully took the glass of champagne offered to her, she did not fully know how she had ended up actually *on* the baggage reclaim belt. This had been much to the amusement of other passengers, and to the amazement of Joshua who had been expecting her to meet him outside Costas. Still, she had got what she had been asked to get. That was the main thing.

'How are you feeling, Mrs. Matheson?' asked the kindly-looking stewardess.

'Oh, I'm fine, dear. This is all rather lovely. I don't suppose there is any space for my great-grandson here, is there?'

'I'm afraid not. It was fortunate we had this seat available.'

'Well, it's nice anyway. Thank you for having me.'

'You're welcome. It must have been traumatic for you on that luggage carousel.'

'I was quite comfortable really. The case I was sitting on was soft and I had my knitting to amuse me. The only dodgy bit is when you go up and through those plastic flaps. You don't quite know what's going to be on the other side.' *At eighty-two, Maggs, it might not be that long before you find out.* Travelling up the belt in the darkness towards the light, it had felt almost spiritual. 'It was quite a relief to see it was just a reclaim area and that I wasn't a prize on the Generation Game.' *Home croquet set, cuddly toy, George Foreman Grill, elderly Secret Service spy...* 'Maybe you're a little young for that TV show, are you?'

'A little, maybe. How did you end up in baggage reclaim, Mrs. Matheson, if you don't mind me asking? Singapore is a transit stop for you, isn't it?'

'That's right, dear. We're off to see my Sharon in Adelaide. We started at Heathrow.'

'So you had no cases to collect?'

'No, but I think I misread the signs and took a wrong turning. I can get a bit muddled.' The stewardess nodded sympathetically. Maggie got a lot of sympathetic nods these days. She did not mind; they were always well meant and usually an indication the person might be helpful. 'Apparently, none of the security alarms are working, otherwise I would have been stopped before then. It's very interesting backstage, as it were. I thought it would be full of people hauling luggage from one place to another. I didn't see a soul.'

'No, it's mainly done on bar codes now, fully mechanised.'

'How clever! So, I wandered around for a bit through these corridors, and then it opened up into the area where all the cases were. It was quite dark and then I spotted what I thought was my case. I realise now it wasn't, of course, because that was being taken from one plane directly to our next one. I tried to get it off, but couldn't. The next thing I knew was that I'd joined it on the belt.'

'Well, thank goodness you're okay, Mrs. Matheson.'

'I'm fine. Cor... this bubbly's lovely!'

'Glad you like it. Let me know if there's anything else you need.'

'Thank you, dear.'

Maggie put her glass down in the holder and started to fiddle with the onboard entertainment screen. This involved switching it on, muttering at the picture of the tiny airplane hovering over Singapore, and then switching it off again. Several times. Inside the sleeve next to her seat, she found a smart brown, leather zip-top bag marked, *Sing Airlines Amenity Kit*. As she began to unpack its contents, she concluded that travelling in Business Class compared to Economy had to be a lot more traumatic an experience, if all these things were needed. Apart from the eye mask and ear plugs – which she always asked for on flights – there was a lip balm, made using the wax from bees that pollinated the manuka bush in New Zealand; three different types of moisturiser, one of which was for her feet (how much walking she was likely to do stuck in a metal tube over the course of eight hours for her to need to keep them moist, she had no idea); a hand-wrapped mint, fashioned by descendants of the Sicangu band of the Lakota Sioux; and a bar of fancy soap, the origin of which remained a mystery because she could not untie the fancy gold ribbon knotted around it. She was in the process of reading about the benefits of having a flannel made of bamboo when she felt a tap on the shoulder. It was Joshua.

'Getting past the Rottweiler patrolling the entrance to Business Class is harder than breaking into Kim Jong-un's summer residence,' he said. 'These hostesses have a dark side to them, don't they?'

'They were all perfectly pleasant to me when I came through.'

'That's because you had special permission to be here. They're not so keen on us Economies.'

'I'm sure you had no trouble sweet talking your way in.'

'I just said that I had to remind my great granny not to take her laxatives until we arrive in Sydney and, for some reason, they let me straight through.'

'Cheeky bugger!'

'Anyway, did you get it?'

'Of course.'

'Slightly dodgy you ending up actually on the luggage belt. It was a good job you weren't sitting on Taylor's case. That would have been a bit too obvious.'

'I've said it before: the more conspicuous you are, the less conspicuous you seem.'

'Hmm...'

Maggie reached into her handbag and pulled out a tissue, inside of which was a very large diamond. It glinted briefly as her overhead light caught it before she wrapped it up tightly inside the bamboo facecloth and passed it to Joshua. It was the size of a plum; large enough for her to feel it inside the sock in the centre of Emanuel Taylor's suitcase, small enough for it to have been given to him on a walk-past in car park three at Heathrow Airport fourteen hours earlier, without anyone noticing. Unless you were specifically looking out for it, which Joshua's team had been.

'I've still no idea how you found it so quickly and easily, Maggie. When I go away, I struggle to find my toothbrush inside my own wash bag.'

'We both know that's not true, young Joshua. You're very well organised and meticulous. I don't know what it is but I have a nose for diamonds. Must have been those three years I worked the South African mines.'

'You've never been to South Africa, Maggie.'

'Oh well, maybe it's all that bling I see them sell on the TVQ shopping channel.'

'You obviously did the swap?'

'There would not have been much point going through all of that if I didn't, would there? Mr. Taylor won't notice anything until he tries to sell it later.'

When Joshua persuaded Maggie to be involved in the case, he had described the job as 'something to do to break up the long journey.' She had previously insisted that despite the kick she had got out of the case that had recently brought her out of retirement involving her corrupt former boss – 'The Sheldon Shenanigans', as she had named it – she would not be repeating her exploits. For a start, she had had a lot on her mind.

Her family had suddenly expanded with the revelation that Joshua was her great-grandson and Bill, Joshua's grandfather and one of the other agents on the Sheldon case, was her estranged son, Peter. Having given him up for adoption at birth, she and Bill had years to catch up on. During the case, she had established that he was a very capable agent indeed. His dad, Frankie, would have been so proud. She was so proud. But getting to know Bill as a son was a different matter. There had been a barrier there around the guilt she felt in giving him up – in her mind, if not Bill's who had been so gracious and understanding. Building a relationship was a work in progress, work she was determined to continue.

And then there had been the planning for this visit to see her Sharon, Sean, and the grandchildren in Adelaide. She had been looking forward to it for ages, especially the moment when Bill would meet his sister for the first time. Bill and his new husband, Ben, were following along soon after for what she was sure would be a special occasion.

However, this little diversion had been a real tempter. That shot of adrenalin as she did the swap...

'Thanks so much for doing this, Maggie,' said Joshua. 'When Taylor's contacts realise he's apparently dealing in fakes now, they'll cut off all his financing at source. It should have a massive impact on his ability – and those connected to him – to supply illegal arms in the Middle East. He'll be persona non grata for some considerable time. Hopefully, it will allow the diplomats to get in there and do their jobs.'

'Worth a few quid, that diamond?'

'Several million, I would think.'

'Well, I'm glad I could help. It paid for my air ticket and it's all worked out nicely with my upgrade. Plus, I've always wanted to have a go on one of those conveyor belts.'

'You didn't get on it on purpose, did you, Maggie?'

'Me?' Maggie tried to look shocked. 'As I told the air hostess, it was a complete accident. Now then, do you know how this thing turns into a bed? I've seen them do it on that programme where celebrities pick an airline to test out the perks. One of the criteria they look at is how flat the seats go.'

Maggie pressed a button on the side and pushed her head and shoulders against the top of the seat in an attempt to force it back. It did not budge and her head just ended up bouncing back and forth.

'You've switched the reading light on, at least,' said Joshua. 'I know how much you love technology, so I'll leave you to explore. See you when we land in Sydney. Don't go off without me, will you? We need to get a taxi to the hotel before we get the internal flight to Great Auntie Sharon's in the morning.'

Great Auntie Sharon... It made her little girl sound so old! *To think you're the mother of a great aunt too, Maggs!*

The attendant came by and showed Maggie how to operate the seat. An hour after takeoff, stretched out (very flat), and with several glasses of champagne and a tender sirloin steak nestled comfortably inside her, Maggie was fast asleep. She did not wake up until just before they were due to land in Sydney.

~ ~ ~

Chapter 2

'What time is our flight in the morning?' Maggie asked.

She and Joshua were wide awake and sitting in the hotel lounge. It was three a.m. local time and, try as she might, Maggie had not been able to get any sleep at all after they had checked into the hotel the evening before. She was now regretting sleeping so much on the leg over from Singapore. She might have suggested they check out some of the Sydney sights, but the hotel's location, though handily placed for the airport, was not so convenient for the city centre.

'It's already the morning. We need to check in by nine,' said Joshua. 'There's a shuttle every twenty minutes from here which takes five or ten minutes. I've booked us onto one for eight to be sure.'

'Definitely not worth going to bed then,' said Maggie rather grumpily. She felt tired but was past the point of sleep.

'It takes a few days to get over the jet lag. Maybe you can catch up a bit on the next leg to Adelaide.'

'I'm not good with these time adjustments.' The previous occasion she had been to Australia was three and half years ago, and she had only stayed ten days because that was the deal with the flights. 'I'd just got over the jet lag last time I visited and I had to come straight home again. That's why I prefer Sharon to come and see me with the girls; it doesn't seem to affect them as badly,

16

though it's hard for her to get a lot of time off, what with being so busy on the newspaper. Sean's got his plastic surgery practice.'

'We could have done with using his skills on the Sheldon case for your nose job, instead of you trying to break it yourself in the back of Voigt's car.'

It had been just over a year now since that case. Chris Voigt – the original target – had pleaded guilty to attempting to defraud governments and other organisations, and had been sentenced to eight years imprisonment, a lengthy stretch that reflected the seriousness of the crime. His lawyers had appealed and were awaiting a trial date. Maggie had spoken in Voigt's favour, both as a character witness and to validate Voigt's role in securing Sheldon's arrest and saving Bill's life, mitigating factors the trial judge, Maggie felt, had ignored. Maggie had had her concerns about that judge's impartiality. She had no proof, but she suspected strongly that he was under Sheldon's influence and was acting out of revenge. Maggie would not have been at all surprised if the judge was one of her 'sponsors' as Sheldon called them, furious that his share of the proceeds from the operation she had set up to take over Voigt's cybercrime enterprise had been prevented. 'I can tell from his eyes,' Maggie had told Bill at the original trial when asked to justify her theory.

There were hopes that Voigt's sentence would be cut on appeal to a third of the original, which meant, with a good record in jail, he could be out within eighteen months. Sheldon had no such hope of an early release. Maggie was pretty certain that her trial judge, Justice Jane Blackman, was a true, independent thinker, far too honest and genuine to be corrupted. 'I can tell from her eyes,' she had told Bill again. Sheldon's best efforts to lie and squirm her way out did not help her case and the jury unanimously found her guilty. Justice Blackman gave her the harshest sentence available to her – life – with a recommendation that she served a minimum of fourteen years.

Up until Joshua had just mentioned it, Maggie had barely thought about Sheldon. For her, it was in the past. The small diversion en route to Australia notwithstanding, she was set on devoting the rest of her life to Bill, Sharon, and Joshua, along with their other halves and families. It was a pleasant thought...

… turned totally on its head by the text that came through on Joshua's phone.

'What do you mean Sheldon's escaped? How on Earth in this day and age does that happen?'

'I don't know, Maggie. She was in the maximum security wing of Tarmore jail.'

'Where do they think she is now?'

'No idea. Leave it with me. I'll make some calls, but I need a better internet connection. You stay here while I speak to the night porter to get something sorted. They might be able to find me a quiet room. You won't go anywhere, will you?'

'Where can I go at three o'clock in the morning on an industrial estate outside of Sydney?'

'Why would that minor detail stop you doing something you shouldn't do? Promise you won't move? I won't be long.'

Maggie watched Joshua go over to speak to the porter on reception. As they disappeared round the corner, presumably to a room where Joshua could work, she felt suddenly anxious. It was silly really. So what if Sheldon had escaped? She would no doubt be captured again quickly. The days of criminals going on the run for long periods were over, weren't they? In any case, the news had only just come through to Joshua, which meant Maggie was on the other side of the world, thousands of miles away from the problem. Even if Sheldon wanted to hurt her, she could not do anything from there.

The fact that thought had gone through her mind shocked her – *if Sheldon wanted to hurt her…* Why would she want to do that? *Why wouldn't she, Maggs?* Muggie had been instrumental in thwarting Sheldon's lofty ambitions to make billions of pounds; instrumental too in putting her away in prison. Maggie was also to blame for exposing her lover's infidelity, and she had befriended Sheldon's ex-husband, Carlos, helping to reunite him with his – and Sheldon's – children. Sheldon wouldn't like any of that. Besides, she had always hated Maggie's guts; she despised anyone that stood up to her, and Maggie had done plenty of that when she had been working for her in the Service.

So, plenty of reasons to think Sheldon might want to seek revenge, but plenty of reasons not to worry about it from over ten thousand miles away. She could relax, for now, maybe even grab some sleep. This was exactly what she did next…helped by a dose of Rohypnol placed on a rag and smothered over her face.

~ ~ ~

Chapter 3

Maggie's first thought as she woke up was not, 'Where am I?' which, when she looked back on it later, it should have been. It was, in fact, 'I wish someone would shut that door. It's so chilly!'

It was a frustrating sign of the way her brain worked these days that sometimes a lack of urgency was absent at times when maybe it should not have been. On the one hand, that laissez-faire attitude helped her deal with potentially stressful situations in a relaxed way. Situations like the lack of kiosks at the local cinema in Frampton, which meant she now had to get her tickets from the confectionary area and stand behind people who spent ages making decisions about what sauces to have with their nachos. On the other hand, it sometimes meant she got distracted at a time when she really should have been thinking about how to deal with a pressing problem.

And she certainly had a pressing problem now. She realised that as soon as she looked down.

Looking down also explained why she was feeling chilly.

In different circumstances, she would have loved the panoramic view she had. The reds, oranges, and yellows of the early morning sky provided an amazing backdrop to the silhouetted sails of the Sydney Opera House. The harbour water was calm, just a few gentle waves mixing the sunrise's palate into a melange of colours that any Italian ice cream seller would have been proud to have on their stall. It was a picture postcard scene, instantly recognisable to anyone from around the world. Maggie knew it very well too. She had seen almost that exact view three and a half years ago when she and Sharon had tackled the Sydney Harbour Bridge walk as her treat for her birthday. It concerned her why she was seeing it again now.

Fifty feet below, a party of tourists was enjoying the view too. They were harnessed safely to the wires that ran up and down and along the bridge walk. However, they had more freedom to move than Maggie did. She was sitting upright on one of the bridge's great horizontal struts with her legs tied straight out in front of her, and her back hard against a ladder that led up to the last uppermost section. Her hands were bound to the bottom rung. She could see the people below, but it was unlikely they could see her because of the angles of the struts. She was about to call out when she noticed the handwritten note pinned to her skirt. The message was clear:

Give us back the diamond or your grandchildren will be joining you up here… without the ropes.

Taylor! It had to be him. Somehow, Emanuel Taylor had discovered her involvement and was on to her. *So much for your 'conspicuous and inconspicuous' theory, Maggs.* But it was an extraordinary response if indeed it was him. How had he got her up here? She was off the tourist trail of wires that she could still see the party following below. Whoever had done this had gone to a huge amount of effort to haul her up, possibly putting their own

21

lives at risk. How had they got on to her so quickly and organised such a stunt? Uppermost in her mind, though, was the threat to her family. Was it legitimate? Were they really at risk?

She became aware of a low groaning noise directly behind her. There would have been a time when she could have flexed and twisted her body enough so that she could have got a glimpse of who it was, but those days were long gone. She had not retained the hearing implant used on the Voigt case, but she had invested in a very good hearing aid which helped her now identify the source.

'Joshua? Joshua… are you okay?'

There was another moan and a few incoherent words before Maggie could make out, 'What… where…?'

'Joshua, it's Maggie. I'm right behind you. Don't move.'

She knew she was tied on and secure for the moment, but she had no idea how their captors had left Joshua. He may have been left to his own devices, for all she knew.

'Maggie? Where… where am I? Where are you?'

'We're on top of the Sydney Harbour Bridge, dear. Don't make any sudden movements.'

'What? On top of… Whoa!'

'Joshua! Are you okay? Don't move, whatever you do.'

'I can't. I'm tied on.'

'That's good.'

'Good? How is being tied to the top of a bridge good?'

'It means you won't fall off.'

'Well, that's something, I suppose. How did we get up here?'

'I've no idea.' Maggie read out her note. 'It's pinned to me. Do you think it's Taylor?'

'Hang on, let me think.'

'Take your time. I'm not going anywhere.'

'Okay, right... well, I don't see how. We had agents eyeballing him throughout; he spent the whole time in the first class lounge. His bag was sent on to him by the airport staff. Even if he discovered the switch when he reclaimed his baggage, it would have taken something to get this organised. Oh... my head hurts. Does yours?'

'Everything hurts if I'm being perfectly honest.' Maggie took another look around. She was normally okay with heights, but balanced rather precariously on a beam was confidence-sapping, to say the least. 'You said that diamond job would be straightforward. How have we ended up like this? And, more importantly, what about that threat to my grandchildren?'

'I agree, that's a worry. They obviously have some resources behind them if they've got us all the way up here.'

'Where's the diamond now?'

'Stored.'

'Stored where?'

'I don't know. I passed it on as soon as we arrived in the airport in Sydney.'

'They want it back, Joshua. These people are serious.' She looked down. The group she had seen earlier was making their way along to a viewing point where they could take pictures. She knew from the visit before that all their cameras and phones would have to be secured safely onto their persons to prevent things from being dropped onto pedestrians and traffic below. Anything else would not be allowed on the bridge. She had not been allowed to take her handbag for that very same reason; its whereabouts now crossed her mind before she dismissed it as another silly worry in the context of their current situation.

'What are we going to do, Joshua? I've been in some scrapes in my time, but this has to be up there as one of the most challenging.'

'We'll have to get the attention of that group climbing up,' said Joshua.

Maggie looked down and could see a new group slowly making its way up one of the ladders about hundred feet below. 'Will they be able to hear us? This wind is pretty lively.'

'Someone will.'

'The note… what about the threat to Sharon and the kids?'

'The sooner we get down, the sooner we can deal with that. Start shouting, Maggie.'

Maggie did. But it was not the noise that got the group's attention.

Maggie had abseiled part of the way down a skyscraper when she was on a case in New York. She had also been hung upside down from the roof of a warehouse by sets of chains attached to her feet in a remote town in former Czechoslovakia. And, just for the hell of it, she had bungee jumped into a canyon as part of her sixtieth birthday celebrations. All of those things had been absolutely terrifying and had got her heart thumping. But none of them compared to dangling three hundred feet in the air on a winch from a rescue helicopter. She loved every second of it.

The first thing Joshua did when inside the safety of the helicopter was to show the I.D. on the tag around his neck. He used it to persuade the pilot to patch a call through to Bill who he told to make arrangements to get Sharon and the family out of their house immediately to somewhere safe.

At this stage, he was reluctant to involve too many people, local officials included, as he explained to Maggie: 'Someone has access to a lot of resources, including the ability to drug two agents, transport them onto a famous Sydney landmark, and make specific threats to family members, all within several hours of what we thought had been a successful operation in Singapore. Now, until we get more information, I suggest we keep our cards close to our chests. No details of what we know; just our names, Secret Service number and, when the officials ask, make up something innocuous about the purpose of the visit.'

Back on the ground, the post-mortem of the incident by the police was brief, much to the dissatisfaction of the investigating officers.

'I'm here for pleasure,' Maggie had answered when asked why she was in Sydney. It drew a sceptical look from Sergeant Cappelli, the case officer based in 'The Rocks' area of the city. He had played back the recording of Maggie's rescue in the hope that it might encourage her to realise the seriousness of her position.

'Look at my face there,' Maggie had countered as she watched herself being winched in. 'It's got pleasure written all over it!'

25

By referencing their Secret Service jobs – nothing more – Joshua hoped it would be enough to get them released quickly. Maggie was in her element; she had made a career out of saying plenty while giving away nothing. Sergeant Cappelli might have thought he had broken every lowlife and con artist who had crossed his path in his fifteen years working in downtown Sydney, but he had not come across anyone quite like Maggie. Of the two of them, it was she who came out of the interview feeling far more informed as they parted company.

'Well, it was very nice to meet you, Sergeant Cappelli. I hope I get to meet your wife, Sandra, someday. She should definitely go back into teaching now that your two children are older. They sound adorable! Make sure young Mat keeps up with the violin – you never know where that might lead him. And Shauna sounds like she is such a promising athlete. What was the name of that athletics club again?'

'Avalon Hawks,' Sergeant Cappelli sighed.

'That's right, you did say.' She drew him to one side and whispered in his ear. 'Get that prostate checked too. You're a bit young for anything nasty, but it's probably better to be safe than sorry.'

'I will, Mrs. Matheson. You have my card if you feel you can open up with any more information at some stage.' He nodded at his colleague who came out of one of the other interview rooms with Joshua. 'Nothing from him either, Paulie?'

'Nah, Serge.'

'Right, you two. We've spoken to the foreign office and they've advised we should release you without charge, based on the background checks they've done. I have no idea what you were both doing up there, and neither of you will say. However, I must advise you that it is a public disorder offence to climb any part of the bridge without being part of the official tour or without permission from the port authorities. Is that clear?'

'Yes, Sergeant,' said Maggie who was about to comment that she was hardly likely to have climbed all the way up to the top with her great-grandson, tied themselves up, and then asked for help to get down, all on her own volition, when a look from Joshua stopped her.

'Oh, and I understand these belong to you, Mrs. Matheson,' said Sergeant Cappelli. He held out a plastic bag. 'These are your dentures?'

Maggie examined them. 'They certainly look like them.'

'They've been washed. Apparently, they bounced off the bridge guide's first aid kit on her back and down into the Japanese woman's jumpsuit. The guides are trained to have a good look up and all around when things fall, otherwise, I'm not sure they would have found you so quickly the way the wind was carrying the sound away.'

'I agree that was lucky,' Maggie said. 'I shouldn't shout so vigorously. I must apologise for my rather gummy expression during the interview, Sergeant. You must think I look like an old woman without them in.'

27

She took the dentures out of the bag, turned away, and pushed them back in her mouth.

'Can we go now?' asked Joshua.

'Yes, you're free to go.'

'Thank you, Sergeant,' said Maggie as she made her way through the door to the reception area. She turned to shake his hand. 'Oh, please apologise to Mrs. Takahashi.'

The Sergeant looked astonished. 'How did you know her name?'

'Your constable told me when you got me a cup of tea.'

'I was only out for a minute.'

'Yes, well, you've all been very nice. Anyway, it must have been quite a shock to poor Mrs. Takahashi to have my gnashers disappearing down her front like that. Good job she didn't fall. Please pass on my thanks to Danielle.'

'Danielle?'

'The guide.'

'Oh, yes. Course. Will do.'

Maggie and Joshua left the police station with directions on how to get to the British consulate, plus ten dollars from Sergeant Cappelli's own wallet for emergencies which Maggie, despite his protestations, had insisted she would pay back.

On the steps, she turned to Joshua. 'Such a nice man that Sergeant Cappelli. To give me money like that.'

'I expect he wanted to make sure you didn't have reason to come back.'

'I wasn't too hard on him, was I?'

'Put it this way: of the two officers that interviewed us, my one looked like he could still finish his shift.'

'Oh dear. Well, he deserves a break.' Then she added seriously: 'You're sure Sharon is safe, Joshua?'

'Bill spoke to her and they've gone straight to Sean's cousin outside Adelaide.'

'Will they be okay there? If it is Taylor who's behind this, it sounds like he has a lot of influence.'

'Bill's onto it. We're sending security staff from the consulate in Adelaide. I have a contact there. They may well be moved on again for security reasons.'

'You really don't think we can trust the police? Not even people like Sergeant Cappelli?'

'I'm not sure who we can trust at this stage. We need to be very careful.'

'I had not realised Taylor was such a big fish.'

'He's a crucial cog in that whole arms dealing setup in the Middle East, which is why we had to stifle his financing by swapping the diamond.' Joshua paused. 'But I don't think it's just Taylor who's behind this.'

'If it's not Taylor, then who is it?'

But Maggie knew the answer to that before she had finished the question.

~ ~ ~

Chapter 4

At the consulate, it soon became apparent that Joshua was right to be cautious. The usual lines of communication to the Service were 'dodgy', as he put it. He phoned the hotel, but all their belongings had gone, along with the receptionist who had been so willing to help Joshua with his private room (and by implication, must have been in on the bridge stunt). He obtained a new phone for him (Maggie was rather offended that he did not offer her one – she would have declined in any case, but she felt affronted not to be asked) and a credit card to help buy things they might need.

Maggie was grateful for the help of the consulate staff. There had been many a time as a spy when she had been stuck in a country somewhere with nothing other than the clothes she stood up in (and on one rather embarrassing occasion, not even the clothes) and it had been incredibly difficult to source what she needed. The backroom staff had always worked miracles to do what they could. Nowadays, it seemed you just had to flash an I.D. tag and within an hour everything was sorted. Rather reluctantly, she had to concede that it was probably modern technology that made the difference. Clearance checks took less than a minute and the rest… well, it seemed to Maggie, just appeared.

'3D printing helps, of course, in terms of providing tricky documentation such as false passports and credit cards,' said Joshua when she remarked how impressed she was. Having never even got to grips with 2D printing, Maggie was reluctant to enquire any further. An hour later though, while waiting in the airport lounge for their flight to Adelaide, she was perfectly happy to use the credit card to shop for a new handbag, travel case, toiletries, and clothes. It was a big relief to be heading off to join Sharon and the family so soon after their unexpected delay.

Had she actually got onto the plane, it might have been an even bigger relief.

'It's gone blank,' said Joshua.

'My mind has too,' said Maggie who had found a discarded copy of *The Sydney Times* and was busy not getting any of the clues in the cryptic crossword. 'Completely blank. They're far too fancy pants for me in this paper. I'll stick to *The Lady*. More my level. Some of this one's missing, too.'

'No, the board. It's gone blank. All the flight information has disappeared.'

Maggie peered over the new reading glasses she had bought in the shop. She was already missing her bifocals which she had left in her old handbag. She was convinced she had got the wrong strength – it was a major flaw in those off-the-shelf displays, she felt, that you needed reading glasses to read what strength reading glasses they did – but even she could see that the board was, indeed, blank. She looked around for another board.

'Maybe that one there is okay,' she said pointing to one by the departure gates which was starting to flash. She was just about to get up to take a closer look when Joshua stopped her.

31

'It's okay. I can see from here. Hang on, though. That's strange. It's not giving the flight information.' He sat forward. 'It's coming up with some sort of message.'

Maggie watched as a message, in big letters, scrolled across repeatedly:

We're going to make your life hell, Maggie... We're going to make your life hell, Maggie...

'Well, I've heard of personalised service, but I'm not convinced their P.R. department has got this one right,' she said. 'It doesn't make me want to pay extra for a window seat. What on Earth's going on?'

'I'm not sure,' said Joshua grimly. 'Someone's hacked into the airport's systems I would suggest.'

'Well, let's go and find the announcer's little room and ask there. Maybe they'll be able to help.'

'I'm not sure there is a little room as such, Maggie. It's all done remotely somewhere, I should imagine, and whoever has done this is likely to be very remote indeed.'

'All done inline, you mean?' said Maggie whose only response to plugging the gaps in her computer knowledge exposed on the Sheldon case had been to buy herself a tea towel with humorous computer jargon on it. It had hung on the wall in her kitchen until she had got fed up with trying to work out why the jokes were funny. Normally very fond of wordplay, it was all too literal for her – *I remember when a Hard Drive was a difficult journey into the*

32

office. 'Well, of course, if you have a difficult journey into the office, that could very well be as a result of a hard drive,' she had moaned to Bill – so she had used it to wrap up the Smartphone Joshua had left her and popped it into the bottom drawer of the lounge sideboard.

'I don't like the look of this at all,' said Joshua anxiously. 'Wherever we go and whatever we do, they're onto us.'

'She's onto us, you mean, don't you? Sheldon.'

Joshua rubbed the back of his neck. He suddenly seemed ten years older. 'I can't discount that as a viable theory. I can't discount the Russians either.'

Of course, the Russians. The memory of the girl in the restaurant where the Sheldon Shenanigans had all started. There had been talk – nothing proved – that the girl might have been working for them.

'How it's being done, I really can't say, but whoever is behind this must have access to some serious malware functionality. It's an amazing feat of technology.'

Maggie had long given up nodding knowledgeably when Joshua came out with expressions like 'malware' and 'functionality'. She opted now for the vacant expression she used when people insisted they tell her all about how wonderful their grandchildren were. None of them were anywhere near as wonderful as her own, so what they were telling her was not only uninteresting, it was also factually incorrect.

A notification pinged on Joshua's phone. When he looked up this time, she could have sworn he had aged another ten years.

'What is it, Joshua? What on Earth's wrong?' Maggie adjusted her glasses as he showed her the text. It read:

We're not joshing joshua hand back the diamond

'That's a brand new phone. I've only transferred a few key contacts. No one else has got that number, apart from a select few in the Service. I've only just downloaded WhatsApp.'

Maggie, of course, had no idea how these things exactly worked, but she was savvy enough to understand when security had been seriously compromised. It pinged again:

Now!

'Right, come on,' Joshua said decisively. He grabbed her hand, pulled her unceremoniously to her feet, and headed towards the exit.

'What about my new wheelie bag?' Maggie protested. 'My new clothes?'

'Leave them.'

They passed a cleaner busy mopping an area cordoned off to the right of the check-in desks. He had a trolley with two bins on it with lids. As they passed, Joshua lifted one of the lids and threw his phone in.

'Wow! A teenager without a phone,' said Maggie struggling to keep up. 'Won't you get withdrawal symptoms?'

'I won't need it where we're going.'

'And where is it we are going, exactly?' she panted, as they arrived at the taxi rank.

'Off-grid.'

'Off-grid?'

'Yes, at least from an I.T. point of view. Somewhere safe. Somewhere they can't connect to us. Somewhere without mobile phones, computers, internet, nothing that can connect us to the outside world. Off-grid.'

'Well, if it's off-grid you want, then I'm your man.' Maggie closed the door to the taxi he had just opened for her. 'With all due respect, Joshua, being away from anything computer related is my area of expertise. Come on, I know just the person to help.'

This time, she grabbed hold of his hand and wheeled him around. They headed for the trains.

~ ~ ~

Chapter 5

Maggie and Dingo Derek went back many years. She had first met him the day after Frankie's fortieth birthday meal whilst on holiday at a rather beautiful cliff-top resort in Tenerife. Technically, she had met him at the actual meal; that is if you call witnessing a scolding in front of a packed restaurant a meeting.

Dingo had been on the receiving end of several heads of large, grilled prawns, propelled by an attractive young lady who Maggie later found out was his (soon to become) ex-girlfriend. The woman had followed up the crustacean attack by then throwing everything else she had access to on their cosy table for two, some of which had hit their mark, but most of which landed on various other diners sitting at their own cosy tables for two (it was that kind of restaurant). The tapas mainly all used up, the woman had then stormed out, leaving Dingo sitting there with very little ammo with which he might have retaliated (had he been so inclined) and with even less dignity than the hapless prawns.

He left the restaurant soon afterwards, only to be stunned at the doorway by a particularly well-aimed small terracotta bowl of butter beans in garlic and tomato sauce which the woman had found from somewhere and returned to throw at him.

Maggie bumped into Dingo the following morning when she left Frankie to sleep off a hangover and gone for a stroll. He was sitting on a wall overlooking the harbour, with his back to the sea. She might have walked straight past him had it not been for her uncanny knack of never forgetting a face; particularly one that had a terracotta bowl-shaped bruise on its cheek and, on closer inspection, several large, grilled prawn antennae stuck in its eyebrows. Maggie, being Maggie (and being a spy), was naturally inquisitive, and had struck up a conversation with him during which she found out two key facts that immediately made him even more interesting than the fact he stank of prawns.

Fact one was that he was a farmhand on holiday who usually worked on a remote sheep station, 300 miles west of Sydney.

Fact two was that he was not the son of a billionaire media mogul. His ex-girlfriend had discovered that too, moments before inflicting the tapas carnage.

There was an additional fact which Maggie found out as they began to chat, which was that she liked him very much. Despite his attempts to impress the girl with his false back-story, Dingo was a down-to-Earth man, lonely and fed up shearing sheep in the middle of nowhere, and just someone who was in need of a little excitement and attention. Maggie and Frankie took him under their wings for the rest of their stay and she had kept in touch, via letters, ever since, even after Frankie died.

This Maggie explained to Joshua on the train. 'He will help us. Trust me.' It was a brief conversation because she ushered him off at the next stop with herself and the rest of the crowd, before pushing him back on again two carriages down, just before the doors closed.

'That was the first step to getting out of the city.'

'Out of the city? Where are we going?'

'To the outback.'

'Specifically?'

'The outback, Australia. Now, stop fussing and do as I say. In a moment, I want you to go down the far end of the carriage. We need to split up temporarily, get a few bits and pieces and then join up again. Where's the next most central stop with shops?' She looked up at the map above Joshua's head while he reached into his pocket. 'You were going to check it on your phone, weren't you?'

Joshua nodded rather sheepishly before turning round to join her in studying the map. It was straightforward enough. 'Central Station it is then,' said Maggie. 'Between here and there we go in opposite directions along the train. Mingle and change carriages when you can. If we're being monitored, it should put them off our scent.'

Joshua objected. 'If they're able to hook into the airport departure boards, they'll be sophisticated enough to do the same with CCTV. They will be all over us, Maggie. Might not all be in live time, if we're lucky, but they'll be able to track our movements historically at the very least.'

'Joshua! I might not know everything there is to know about CCTV, but I do know how to make myself scarce. Believe me; I've had enough practice with that back home avoiding Celia Sharp's attempts to recruit me for flower arranging duties at church. I went along with it once and deliberately put the gladioli in upside down to discourage her from asking in the future. It didn't; she sees me as some sort of creative genius now.'

'With all due respect, Maggie, you were, and still are, brilliant at your job. But things have moved along in the world of technology.'

'Watch and learn, young Joshua. Watch and learn.'

Maggie had some reservations about the next part of the plan. Stealing was not something she condoned, but this was a desperate situation. She had no money, no cards, no means of identification, and now that she and Joshua had split up, no one with her. Crucially, she had to change her appearance to avoid being identified by cameras. To do that, she was going to have to resort to theft to get hold of some sort of disguise.

Besides the prospect of having to steal, she had some other major concerns. At the forefront of her mind was the safety of Sharon and the family, but that was out of her hands for now. She just had to hope they were okay. Next on the list of things to worry about was whether Dingo Derek was still where she thought he was. She had not heard from him for a while and, for all she knew, he could be dead. That was definitely a negative aspect to her plan, but the fact they had not been in contact was also a positive. The last time they had communicated was by letter. Dingo, like Maggie, was a part of a mythical 'club' she called *BAFTA*. The B and A stood for 'Ban All' and the 'T' and the last 'A' stood for 'Technology Acronyms'. The 'F' in the middle stood for 'Flippin' or if she was having a particularly bad day trying to work out how to contact someone regarding her pension other than through online chat, something stronger.

She had told Joshua to be on the 07:10 the following morning to Brisbane via Coffs Harbour. That gave them the rest of this day and the night to ensure they were both fully disconnected from anything that could be used to trace them. Together they were a liability to each other, so Maggie had been explicit in her instructions: 'We don't speak or look at each other if we see each other on the train. After we've got off at Coffs Harbour, turn right when you leave the station and keep walking until you come across the first pub. I'll meet you in there.'

If Maggie had known then what she would have to go through to fulfil her own instructions, she might well have preferred to risk standing naked on the top of the Opera House with a banner saying, 'I'm not Maggie Matheson. Look elsewhere.'

~ ~ ~

Chapter 6

'The barman won't serve me alcohol,' said Joshua sliding back into his seat. 'Says I'm underage. I've got no I.D. to prove otherwise.'

Maggie opened one eye and looked up at her great-grandson. Joshua was dressed in a pair of bright red jeans, a black polo top, and a pair of white Adidas trainers. His hair was cut really short all around, except for the fringe. It had been dyed red and gelled up to form a small tuft. His eyebrows had been plucked and shaped, making him look permanently surprised. The yellow contact lenses he was wearing made him look very strange, as did the dangly earring with a bright white skull that hung from his right ear. It matched the buckle on his snakeskin belt. The man bag he carried – Prada, Maggie noted – hung from his right shoulder. He had casually laid his hand on top of the zip, showing off an array of five different rings, all of them black and all of them chunky. Maggie was not sure whether the tattoos of a beautiful girl surfing on his right arm and a row of red roses on his left were real or not, but they certainly looked it, as did the scar on his right cheek and the pencil-thin moustache. It was a remarkable transformation. She had barely recognised him when she had walked in the pub five minutes earlier.

Maggie sighed. 'You could have made an effort with your disguise,' she mumbled sarcastically before putting her head back down onto her arms which were on the table. The rest of what she

41

said was not intentionally directed at the beer stains, but she was too tired to keep her head up any longer.

'If you want something alcoholic, you'll have to get it. He said he'll only serve me soft drinks.'

'Nfnfnfnf.'

'What was that?'

Maggie forced her hands to move and get her fingers into a 'T' position.

'Tea? I'll see if he can do that.'

She could only have been asleep a few minutes because there was still steam coming from her mug of tea when she finally managed to lift her head. Joshua was sitting opposite her chomping on crisps, a pint of coke with two brightly-coloured, curly straws in front of him. 'What?' he said in response to her nod towards the straws. 'It's all part of the image I've created.'

'Wacky teenager who gets dressed in the dark, you mean?'

'I've taken my cue from the mistress of mystery. You always said that the more conspicuous you are, the better the disguise. I'm hiding in plain sight.'

'Did I really say that?' Maggie took several sips of her tea before leaning back against the hard wood of the booth they were sitting in.

'Yes, you did. Anyway, I've got here, haven't I?'

Maggie nodded slowly. 'As have I.'

'Yes, as have you. Both without being followed.' Joshua took a large glug of his coke before asking, 'And shall we talk about your outfit, Maggie?'

42

'Must we?'

'Official briefing, please, Agent Matheson.'

Maggie forced herself more upright, took a couple of hefty sips of tea, and immediately began to regain some semblance of normality. She was always amazed at the healing effect of the drink. She defied anyone to ask for one without using the words 'nice' and 'cuppa tea' in the same sentence. (Unless you had your head down on a stinking table in a remote bar in Australia after one of the more challenging nights of your life, in which case, she decided, you could get away with, 'Nfnfnfnf').

She allowed a moment to compose herself before she responded. 'Okay... if you insist.'

'Oh, I do, Agent Matheson. I do.'

'I'll tell you as soon as you take that smirk off your face.'

Joshua put down his drink and made a show of passing his flat hand down over his face, settling his expression into one of neutrality, surprised eyebrows and all. Maggie harrumphed before beginning her story.

'After we split up, I was faced with a dilemma. My plan was to walk into one of the charity shops, choose something a bit old and drab looking, take it, and walk out again.'

'What stopped you?'

'Two things: one, I'm not keen on stealing from a charity shop – even if it is for a legitimate cause – and two, everything in there looked almost exactly the same as what I was wearing at the time and, in fact, what I wear all the time.'

43

She ignored the noise that came out of Joshua's mouth which she assumed was an attempt to suppress a giggle. 'So...' he said.

'So, I decided to go into one of those smart boutiques in the mall. I had less qualms about taking something from there, and I figured by going upmarket, it would have been more of a contrast, along with the wig that I planned to acquire.'

'Yes, can we discuss the wig you're wearing?'

'Cheeky bugger! I couldn't find one.'

'That's not a wig?'

'No. I'll come onto my hair in a moment. Anyway, I went into this posh shop and started going through the racks. I planned to select a few things, change, and either sneak out the back or make a dash for it.'

'A dash for it...'

'Well, you know. Walk out and hope no one stopped me.'

'So that didn't work?'

'Goodness, I can tell why you're one of the Service's top spies! Of course it didn't work. Was it my grubby pink boiler suit that gave it away, or the wellington boots?' Maggie waited for another sarcastic comment, ready to pounce on it, but Joshua remained silent as he waited for her to go on. 'Anyway, I was in the changing room, stripped down to my underwear, and about to try on a natty two-piece outfit and blouse, when the fire alarm went off. I had one leg in the skirt when this assistant yells out from right outside the curtain of the cubicle, that it wasn't a drill. There was an actual fire in the apartment upstairs and we all needed to get out immediately. The alarm was bad enough, but her shouting out like that took me

44

by surprise. I was off balance with the left leg in and the other one out, so much so that not even my infamous Hokey Cokey skills could save me tumbling through the curtain and onto the floor right by her feet. The whole curtain came down on top of me. The assistant was very nice, helped me up, and suggested we wrap the curtain around me to protect my dignity, and then she starts to escort me out of the shop. On the way, we get caught by the automatic sprinklers that have come on and both get drenched. We eventually get out and then there we were with the other customers and staff waiting for the fire brigade and police to turn up. Well, I couldn't hang around; I remembered what you said about trusting no one at the moment, even official, so at the next opportunity I sneaked away.'

'Soaking wet, in your underwear, with a curtain wrapped around you?'

'Yes. What other choice did I have?'

'This is your idea of going off-grid, is it? Of being inconspicuous? Walking through a busy shopping mall wearing a curtain. What colour was it?'

'Bright green with daffodils dotted around. Not my favourite – would have clashed with my shoes, if I'd been wearing any.'

'You were barefoot?'

'Well, I had tights on. I was getting changed, remember? Navigating my way through the hole in a skirt is hard enough at my age without having the additional problem of putting shoes through it too. Mine are very clumpy. They're like those black rubber bricks people throw into swimming pools during lessons.'

'Weren't you cold? Yesterday wasn't the warmest of days.'

'Bloody freezing. I walk around the corner and try to go into another boutique. This time I'm determined to sneak out the back way, conscious that if anyone is still watching on CCTV, I might have got their attention.'

'You reckon? What was it you were most worried about? The curtain, the wet hair, or an eighty-two-year-old woman walking barefoot through the shopping mall?'

'I never realised that my great-grandson could be as sarcastic as this.' Maggie took another slurp of tea whilst eyeing up the row of optics behind the bar. If she had had the energy, she would have got up and ordered something strong to make her nice cuppa tea even nicer.

'You won't be surprised to learn that I was not welcome in any of the boutiques. Some of them have security guards on the door, most of them perfectly pleasant. One of them even gave me a dollar out of sympathy. In the end, I decided that my approach wasn't working and something more radical was required. I came out of the mall and found myself in one of the seedier parts of town. Don't ask me where; I have no idea. The great thing about the seedier parts of places is that they have nooks and crannies and – best of all – no budget for security cameras.'

'That sounds a sensible area to head for in the first place. It wasn't your plan A to do that then?'

'My original plan A would have worked if it had worked. How was I to know there would be a fire?' She paused for breath before adding, 'I'm not a novice, Joshua. I've done plenty of this sort of thing before, you know.' Maggie was feeling slightly annoyed, mainly with herself, and it showed in her tone. Joshua waved an apology, but it did little to dampen her frustration which was born mainly out of embarrassment about what she was wearing. She turned away briefly and was horrified to find herself staring into a large mirror that was hanging up amongst various sports memorabilia. This mirror had the words 'Sydney Swans', a reference to the Aussie Rules team, decorated gaudily along the top. Usually, Maggie might have been mildly distracted by the tackiness of the design, but this time she was diverted by something far more shocking – her own reflection.

The pink boiler suit was not the worst part. It was far from flattering, but its impact was lessened by the fact that it was partly covered by the yellow high-vis jacket she had draped over her shoulders. It was her hair that horrified her the most. The expression 'being dragged through a hedge backwards' fleetingly crossed her mind, but she decided it did not do the look justice. Being dragged through backwards, rotated 180 degrees and the process repeated many times, might just about have clinched it as an apt phrase, but only if it was a particularly thorny hedge. Her face was even more weathered than she could have imagined. Dirt had got into every crevice, it seemed, and the bags under her eyes contained at least half the potato stock belonging to 'Big Bert's Bonza Spud Bonanza' she had seen advertised in one of the TV shops in the mall. Her hair was black, rather than the usual grey, so the boot polish that had been smothered on had worked from that

47

point of view. But the angles it had been moulded into were truly something to behold.

She heard Joshua cough politely. 'So, you said it's not a wig.'

Mesmerised for a moment, Maggie dragged her eyes away from the mirror. 'Where would you get a wig that looked like this?'

'Um, a joke shop? Or one of those Goth places?'

'No, Brenda did it for me. Brenda the Bag.' Joshua's face was a picture of patience so she continued. 'Remember, it had been a long day. I was feeling pretty tired by this stage. I went down an alley, found this old deck chair next to a skip, and before I knew it I had dozed off. When I woke up, this woman was staring at me.'

'Brenda the Bag? So-called because...?'

'She's a bag lady – lives out of several bags. She's deliberately dropped the 'Lady part.'

'Because she's homeless and being called a Bag Lady is a stereotype?'

'No. Brenda the Bag is hardly any less stereotypical, is it? She's dropped the Lady because she doesn't want people to associate the lady part with the fact she has a title. She owns a penthouse in Melbourne and half of Dorset.'

'A lifestyle choice then?'

'Sort of. Anyway, she starts accusing me of nicking her deckchair. I manage to calm her down, give her the seat back and it's then we both get placed into the skip...' Maggie raised her finger and called across to the bar. 'Excuse me, please. Could I have a large gin to go with this tea?' She stood up and stretched her back before self-consciously lowering herself down again as she

48

became aware that the three other occupants of the bar were all staring at her.

'You'd think they'd never seen an octogenarian before in a pink jumpsuit and high-vis jacket with her hair covered in boot polish.'

'Did you say you were placed in the skip?'

'Yes, and I'm being quite specific about that. We were both picked up and lowered – not thrown – lowered into the skip.'

'Why?'

'Brenda says it's always happening to her. Some lunatic's idea of cleaning up the streets, possibly, but she's not too sure. They're very gentle about it and I was far too tired to put up any sort of a battle. They even handed over her bags afterwards. Anyway, it's quite steep, this skip, and empty so we can't get out. I bang and shout, but either no one's around or they're ignoring us. Brenda wasn't too bothered. She said she felt safe in there. It's getting quite late by now, so we have no alternative other than to make a night of it. Fortunately, Brenda the Bag has useful stuff in her bags, including...'

'... a pink jumpsuit and a bright yellow jacket... plus wellies of course.'

'Not wellies! Why would she carry wellies around with her? Nor a high-vis jacket.' She glanced up, thanked the barman for the drink he had brought over, and took a glug. 'Ahh, that's better. Lovely drop of gin, that. It was comfortable enough in the skip. Carrying your home around with you has its advantages. She had blankets, and the jumpsuit fitted perfectly. I didn't sleep much to start with, though. I kept worrying about having been spotted on

49

CCTV, even though I kept telling myself I would have been caught by then if I had.'

'How did you get out?'

'This is where my newly adapted plan A really started to work. Eventually, I'm so tired I zonk out. I'm woken up by a loud clunk. I look up and one of those massive chutes is being lowered into the skip from the scaffold above. You know the sort of thing. The ones they use so they can work up high and dump rubbish directly into the skip?' Joshua nodded. 'I yelled out because I could guess what was coming next. Brenda wakes up and we both start shouting. Fortunately, the foreman is on hand and hears us. Not a particularly sympathetic man, but he arranges help to get us out. We are then the laughing stock, of course. One of the men cracks a joke about health and safety and how next time we should wear high-vis jackets, and tosses one of the jackets in my direction. I go along with the joke and put it on. It gets us both a cup of tea and biscuits, plus a pair of wellies when they see I'm shoeless. By this stage, I'm getting worried about missing the train to meet you, so Brenda and I head off towards the station.'

'And the hair?'

'So, by now, I've explained to Brenda that I need to get to Coffs Harbour to meet my great-grandson. I don't explain why, of course. Brenda has this idea to raise a few dollars for the train fare. I agree to that rather than risk being thrown off. It would only draw attention to myself.'

'Maggie, you're in a pink jumpsuit and...'

'I know! Let me finish. There are benches outside the station. She suggests I cover my hair in boot polish, stand on the bench and become one of those living statues. She has friends that make a fortune out of it.'

'But what statue were you supposed to be?'

'I'm buggered if I know. Is it ever obvious what any of those people are supposed to be? Whatever I was, it worked. I stood as still as I could and waved every now and then. Within twenty minutes I had raised enough from commuters and tourists to get me here and for Brenda to get herself a lunch.' Maggie sat back, exhausted. She raised a cautionary finger when Joshua started to ask another question, before alternating drinking her tea and gin. She was quite pleased with the peace and quiet when he went back to drinking his coke and eating his crisps.

It meant that she could have a moment to enjoy anticipating the look of surprise he was going to have any minute now.

~ ~ ~

Chapter 7

'Is there a Kate Middleton in here?' The barman called across, just as Maggie finished her gin and was contemplating whether to have another. She nodded and put her finger up. 'Yep, that's me.'

'Kate Middleton?' Joshua whispered. Maggie raised an eyebrow in response.

'You're Kate Middleton? Fair dinkum. The wife's just called down to me to say Pam had a text from Joanie saying that Barry had phoned her last night. He saw Don up at Kookama Creek yesterday afternoon. Don had just spoken to Darleen, Tezza's wife, who had bumped into Posty. He'd been out delivering mail out at Boolinga Ranch. Anyway, the upshot of all that is there's a message for you.'

'Thanks. What is it?'

'It says they'll be here by four.'

'Right, thanks.' Maggie looked at the clock on the wall. It was 15:55. 'Any time now, then,' she said to Joshua.

As she said it, there was a screech of brakes outside and a loud honk of the horn.

'Come on, Joshua. Pay the man – I assume you have acquired some money from somewhere since you are so pleased with yourself and so mocking of me – and then let's go. I may be a little unconventional in my methods, but we've both got here safely, and I can guarantee we are off-grid. Unless they're looking for

52

someone in a pink jumpsuit and boot polish in their hair. Which they won't be.'

He sighed and followed her lead of sliding out of his chair. 'After all that, you're probably right. And I assume that car outside belongs to Dingo Derek?'

'Dingo Derek? No, he lives miles from here and never comes into Coffs Harbour. I told you he's a bit of a loner. This is our lift to his place.'

'Who's in the car, then?'

'You'll see.'

Maggie was right about Joshua having some cash as she watched him leave a twenty-dollar bill on the bar. She nodded her thanks to the barman as she and Joshua walked outside together. She should have felt a little guilty about enjoying Joshua's reaction as they stepped out of the pub. After all, he was her great-grandson, a very capable agent and not one, normally, to lose his cool.

'You'll trip over your jaw if you let it drop any lower, Joshua,' she said, feeling no guilt whatsoever. As she approached the large pickup truck parked outside, she waved and smiled at the two faces leaning out either side. 'Afternoon, Bill. Afternoon, Ben. How's it hanging?'

The pickup truck had a high chassis and Maggie needed a leg up from Bill to get onto the back seat. She was aware that her pink protruding backside must have been quite a sight as she clumsily clambered in. Once settled safely on the seat, she was mightily relieved to see that, being out of season, the streets of Coffs

Harbour were pretty much deserted. Her face dropped a little, though, as they drove off and she saw the three customers from the bar with their noses pressed up against the window. Were her and Joshua to be traced to this point and enquiries made, she was pretty sure it would not take much for the three men's memories to be jogged. However, the convoluted message from the barman about the lift had been deliberately made to divert attention away from their actual destination, should such an occurrence arise. Boolinga Ranch was a thousand miles away from where they were heading.

Bill had climbed in on the other side, while Joshua joined Ben in the front. Maggie gave Bill an affectionate pat on the knee followed by a peck on the cheek. Every moment she spent with this man after being apart for so long felt precious. It was hard to resist the urge to make up for all the days of love she missed by hugging him and never letting go. Still a strange situation for both of them, she was conscious he might need time and space. *Early days, Maggs. Early days.* When they did come together, she was always grateful for his calm steady influence. She needed that from him now.

'Before we say anything else,' she said, 'I need to know whether Sharon and the family are okay.'

'They're fine. They've been moved to a holiday home a hundred miles outside Adelaide. It was the middle of the night, but someone went over immediately and squirreled them away. They will be in complete communication lockdown though.'

'The girls won't be happy about that. Youngsters are on their phones all the time.' Maggie heard a sympathetic grunt from Joshua in the front.

Bill reached over and gave Maggie a comforting squeeze of the hand. 'They'll be okay.' Maggie nodded bravely. 'Nice outfit, by the way. You planning to start up your own 1980s retro band?'

'If I did, I wouldn't have any of you three in it. Joshua looks like he's been abducted by aliens and then thrown out the spaceship for being too weird, and you two look like a couple of lumberjacks.'

Bill laughed. 'So you don't like our checked shirts? This is what they wear in the outback. We're posing as rugged sheep farmers.'

'I'm pretty sure rugged sheep farmers don't bother to iron creases into their jeans.'

'Good point. Come on, Ben, step on it. We've got a long drive ahead. Let's get on the road and then we'll find a quiet spot where Maggie can clean up and get changed.' Bill opened up the bag that had been on the floor in the well by his feet. 'There are some spare clothes in here, a selection of toiletries – I've no idea if you still like *Eau-de-kangaroo pouch,* but that's all they had – and the bottle of Scotch for Dingo Derek.'

'Very efficient. Thank you. I'm looking forward to getting out of this boiler suit.'

'There must be a suitable cactus you can duck behind somewhere in the outback,' Ben chuckled as he took a left turn and headed out of town.

'Can I ask something here?' Up until that point Joshua had, apart from the earlier grunt, said nothing, maybe content, or bemused enough, to go along with the ride.

'Of course you can, Joshua dear. What can we help you with?'

'What on Earth's going on? How did Bill and Ben get to here so quickly, Maggie? I thought Bill was at home when I phoned him.'

'Ah, now, that's a tale. There are ways and means. I told you that being off-grid is my area of expertise. It's what I do all the time. How do you think I survive at home without a mobile phone? I eat, pay my bills, go out, get hold of a plumber when I need one. All of them without having to even flick a mouse.'

'Click not flick. I get that, but how...?'

'There are communication alternatives. Pigeon carrier, for example.'

'Maggie...'

'It's an Australian bird we'd need rather than a pigeon,' interrupted Ben. 'And bearing in mind the country's more liberal approach to gays these days, I could make a joke about how I much prefer a cockatoo...'

'But you won't, will you, Ben?' said Bill. 'That would be in bad taste.'

'No, apparently, I won't.'

Maggie could sense Joshua's frustration building as he waited for an explanation. 'Well, Joshua, it was quite simple really. When I was in business class on the way from Singapore, I got them to patch a call through to the boys, asking them to cancel their later flight and get on the next one to Australia.'

'What made you do that at that stage? We had the diamond and everything seemed okay.'

'Call it instinct. After the diamond switch, I had a funny feeling something might go wrong. I didn't know about Sheldon escaping

56

then, but I just had this knot in my stomach. Your great-granddad swore by my knot. I got it on the first case we ever did. It was just the two of us and it ended up with a frantic car chase through London. We'd spent weeks pursuing these three Czech agents across Europe and we nearly had them. I fired a shot out of the car window into the suspects' back tyre. That impressed Frankie.' Maggie smiled to herself. 'It forced them off the road and into a car park barrier. Frankie dragged them out of the car and got them to lie face down on the tarmac. I helped handcuff them and then the backup arrived.'

'That's impressive, Maggie,' said Ben. 'So what about the knot in the stomach?'

'Well, at one point we had lost them in the traffic. We came to a T-junction and had to choose left or right. Frankie started going left, but I stopped him and told him to go right. I had this knot in the stomach, see, and it just felt the right thing to do. Just like I knew I had to phone you two.'

Joshua turned round to look at Bill. 'How'd you know to come to Coff's Harbour?'

Maggie answered on their behalf. 'I phoned Bill from a phone booth using that dollar the security guard gave me.'

'On his mobile?'

'Yes,' said Bill. 'Maggie knows all our numbers off by heart. We were in Brisbane by then. Soon as Maggie told me you were going off-grid and where you were meeting, we did the same and got rid of the phones. I put mine in the back of a truck heading north out of Brisbane.'

'Mine's on board a fishing boat, God knows where,' said Ben

'Well, I'm impressed,' said Joshua. 'Really, I am. I can see I still have a lot to learn in this game.'

'You're doing just fine, believe me,' said Maggie. 'At your age, I barely had the confidence to speak to anyone. You're not out of your teens yet and you've already led several major investigations.' She felt a burst of pride at how good both he and Bill were at their jobs. Spying definitely ran in the family. Frankie would have loved it knowing their legacy was so successful.

'So we're still off to Dingo Derek's?'

'That's the idea,' said Maggie.

'Then what?'

'That's to be discussed and decided. I need to catch up on my sleep first.'

Coffs Harbour was over two hours behind them when Ben pulled in at a service station. The scenery had changed from the lush green of the coastal areas to the more arid and plain scenery that was more typical the further inland they went. It was not quite the outback yet, but as she came round from her nap, Maggie was beginning to get a feel of what sort of environment her old pal, Dingo, might be used to. She had discarded the yellow jacket, although Bill, on a particularly long stretch of barren landscape, earned a slap across the arm for suggesting she hang on to it in case she was needed for lollypop lady duties.

The service station was at the leading edge of a quintessential one-road remote Australian habitation. Maggie could see the other end of it as they got out of the truck. Between them and the miles of nothingness again in the distance, there were maybe four or five shops and a few dozen houses, all of them bordered by brown dirt. The wind had got up and was whipping small clouds of dust across the road. Two dogs lay asleep on one side of the garage forecourt, oblivious to any cars that might want to use it, and apparently unconcerned by the brown dust coating they were receiving. Maggie heard a door clang open and an old grizzled figure limped towards them from an even older grizzled hut. She had to stifle a laugh as she realised he was wearing the same shirt as Bill and Ben. He lit up a cigarette as he unhooked the nozzle from one of the two pumps that made up the entirety of the station. The other one, unleaded fuel, had a piece of paper stuck to it which flapped violently in the wind with 'out of order' scrawled on it.

'You want diesel, mate?' he said to Ben who was making a good show of taking on all driving-related responsibilities.

'Yeah, mate,' Ben replied. 'Nice servo you've got here.'

Bill and Joshua had gone to see whether there was any food for sale in the hut. The chances of that were remote according to Maggie's finely tuned inbuilt retail-opportunity-location-detector. The hut was more like a shed kept on an allotment to store, not owners' precious gardening tools, but the manure they were too ashamed to put on public display.

Ben joined Maggie at the back of the vehicle where she was sheltering from the worst of the dust and wind.

'Ben, did you just speak to that man like an Australian might – and I stress *might* – do?' Maggie asked.

'No, of course, I didn't.'

'You did. You called him mate and said, and I quote, "nice servo you have here", whatever that means.'

'Jeez, did I?'

'You're doing it again. Can I remind you, Ben, that you're from a village just outside of Matlock in Derbyshire and not from some made-up suburb in Melbourne?'

'Oh, I loved *Neighbours*!'

'And my Frankie loved *Star Trek,* but he didn't go around speaking Klingon.'

'Sorry, Madge.'

'Madge? Look, you're on dodgy ground here. Keep your voice normal otherwise it will look suspicious.'

'But you're still in a pink boiler suit? Isn't that suspicious?'

'You've made a fair point, Skippy, and I will change it just as soon as I find somewhere suitable. Which probably won't be here, judging by Bill and Joshua's faces.'

Bill and Joshua joined them after what was a brief exploration of the facilities.

'No food here,' said Joshua.

'Dare I ask if there's a toilet?'

'Couldn't see one.'

'Scuse, mate,' said Ben calling over to the attendant in a broad Anglo-Australian-Derbyshire accent. 'Is there a loo here?'

'A what, mate?' The man removed the nozzle and held it up ominously close to the cigarette which still hung limply from his mouth.

'A toilet,' Maggie intervened. 'Washroom, W.C., privy, latrine, restroom, gents or ladies, a bathroom.' The man took a large draw on his cigarette and stared blankly at her. She watched in horror as a piece of smouldering ash dropped off and hit the hand holding the nozzle.

'Bugger and fuck,' the man cried out as he shook the burning ash off his hand before, much to Maggie's relief, putting the nozzle back onto the pump. 'I'm always doing that. What d'you say again?'

Maggie decided his choice of language required a more colloquial approach. 'Is there anywhere to take a shit?' she said.

'Maggie!' Ben said, astonished.

'Ah, you want a shit? There's a dunny behind the shed. But be careful of the funnel webs. They'll bite yer fuckin' arse, and I won't be suckin' any poison out of it if they do, I'm tellin' ya. Anyway, what are you wearing, Sheila? You look like Dame Edna Everage auditioning for a part in Charlie's fuckin' Angels!' He started to laugh uproariously before doubling over in a coughing fit.

The others turned to Maggie to watch her reaction to the insult. Most of her friends back home were unlikely to wear a pink boiler suit, she knew, but if any of them ever did, they would have been offended by the remark and even more offended by the robust way in which the man delivered it. Not Maggie. She knew a good line when she heard one, and burst into laughter, joined by the others.

The man eventually got his breath back enough to take Ben's dollars and tell them that a funnel web-less toilet could be found in

61

the small diner further up the street on the right. For some reason, Maggie felt the need to apologise for Ben's poor attempts at the Australian accent.

'Oh, is that what he was doin'? Didn't understand a bloody word he said.'

It was not far. The diner was empty save for two members of staff, but it looked clean and welcoming, as did the toilet facilities. There was even enough space in there for Maggie to change. She cleaned her face and had a go at washing out some of the boot polish from her hair in the sink. She got the worst of it out, but it made quite a mess which she cleaned up with some paper towels. By the time she came out, the others were sitting down and tucking into plates of steaming hot food of various kinds. Maggie had ordered a lasagne which she found surprisingly good. They chatted while they ate, avoiding the main subject which Maggie knew they would have to get on to eventually, namely what they were going to do once they arrived at Dingo Derek's. She had no idea yet – her priority had been to make sure the family was safe and she and Joshua got away from immediate danger. That step seemed to have been achieved, at least for now.

Bill reckoned they were still some three hours drive away from Dingo's. They had more than enough diesel to get there, but it would be getting dark by the time they arrived.

'That takes us into another day, obviously,' said Joshua who had made a fist of returning to normality by ditching the jewellery and straightening his hair. The yellow contacts had come out and he had rubbed off the scar and moustache. 'Having no phones lessens the likelihood of us being traced, but it does limit our options to do background research.'

Maggie was surprised they seemed to think that the fact they could not access the internet would somehow limit their ability to do some research. Surely, there were other means still? An image popped into her head of them driving a thousand miles to the local library and then looking for information in the 'International Bad Guys' section. A bit extreme, even for the 'good ol' days', but intelligence was collected and evaluated back then – without the internet.

She had to admit the case involving Sheldon and Voigt had exposed her Luddite ways. Since then, she had made an effort not so much to actively ignore technology, but neither had she actively embraced it. So, when something like a gas bill came through which asked her if she would be happy to switch to paperless communication and use email instead, she always resisted the temptation to scrawl all over the form: 'Why would I bloody well want to invest in hundreds of pounds to use something I don't know how to use, just for your convenience and not mine? And by the way; I pay a fortune already,' and instead just ticked the 'no' box.

'I appreciate that you all might feel cut off,' she said, 'and wanting to find out more. But can we establish what we do know and use that? I know more than anyone the importance of good information – without the backroom staff in the Service, those of us out in the field would not have been able to do what we did – but let's just imagine this is forty years ago. That's not hard to do. Two of you are dressed like people from a Monty Python sketch and Joshua – well, I'm not sure what era your outfit comes from, but even I can see it's not the latest thing. That old boy at the petrol station only took cash, the pumps were older than he was, and when I pointed out that a lit cigarette at a petrol station surely breached health and safety, his reply of, "Health and bloody what?" did not inspire confidence.'

'Or he was just choosing to ignore the regulations,' said Joshua.

'Joshua, he's from another time. He offered Ben free picture cards of Aussie athletes from the Commonwealth Games because he had spent over sixty dollars.'

'I'm pleased with these,' said Ben holding up six cards. 'Brisbane, 1982. They could be collectors' items.'

'I'm not saying everyone round here is living in the past as much as that man, but I bet things are done at a different pace in the Outback. They rely on more than the internet to get by, just like many of us back home. That's why I wanted to get to Dingo's.'

'Can he really help and, if so, how?' asked Bill.

'He's a man of many resources, believe me. If anyone can help us get to the bottom of what's going on here, he can. Joshua has made it clear that Sheldon and or Taylor is behind this and they've got inside the Service somehow, either through manipulating people or...' Maggie stopped as she struggled to find the right terminology. 'Or...'

Joshua helped her out. '...through accessing internal networks.'

'Exactly. Now, Dingo won't understand about the last bit, but he's very good at understanding people and their ways.'

'That sounds useful, Maggie,' said Bill. 'But we are going to need to get around the technology at some point. If he can't help with that, well...'

'Bill, he's got a fallout bunker stacked full of provisions to survive for many years in a post-technological age, along with some weaponry should anyone unwelcome try to take it over.'

'I apologise. I can see now why he could be a useful man to know,' said Bill.

'Yes. He told me all about it in one of his letters. He also has what he believes to be the most powerful shortwave radios in the world.'

'Now they could come in handy,' said Joshua.

'So we've just got to get there, explain our situation and decide how he can help us,' said Bill. 'Is there anything else he has access to, do you think?'

'I don't know,' said Maggie starting to tuck into her lasagne with relish. 'Let's finish up, get there, and find out.'

The countryside became more barren the more they drove towards the centre of the huge country. They were only a fraction of the way in from the east coast but since that last stop, they had not seen any other towns, very few cars, and, disappointingly for Maggie, no kangaroos. Very occasionally, a huge freight lorry with two or three trailers attached would thunder past in the opposite direction. It became noticeably hotter, even though the evening was drawing in, and Maggie was relieved when Ben turned up the air conditioning. It was modern technology she had no qualms about accepting.

'We're close by,' she called to Ben from the back. 'Look over there. I remember Dingo writing to me that he lived near the only bump in the landscape for a hundred miles in any direction. It's hardly Uluru, but it stands out, doesn't it?'

The rock they could see to their right was a lot smaller than Uluru, but impressive nevertheless. As they drove past, just like its huge counterpart in the centre of Australia, it shimmered with hues of orange through to red as the sun bid its slow farewell to the day. It distracted all of them except Ben who said he was keeping his eyes firmly fixed on the road ahead.

Which was why he was the first to spot and point out the airplane making a sudden sharp descent and landing on the road directly in front of them. He was also the first to point out, rather more loudly and in a much shriller voice, that unless he pulled off the road sharp-ish, there was going to be a collision.

It was difficult to assess the speed of the plane from Maggie's position in the back. She could see it was a light aircraft of some sort and had a wide enough wing span for her to understand why Ben would be concerned. Avoiding it was not going to be a problem – it was not as if there were other vehicles, pedestrians, or buildings to be worried about, only scrubland that they could easily run on to – it was just the shock of seeing a plane heading towards them. The concern was further compounded by the fact that someone seemed to be leaning out of the side of it and gesticulating with their arm. Well, that was her first thought. Then she realised, as the plane veered off to the side, that the pilot had been actually signalling for the plane to make a right-hand turn. She smiled broadly: 'I think I can guess who that might be. Follow that plane!'

It was a slightly surreal experience driving behind Dingo Derek's plane down the long, tree-lined drive into his large property, and it was not just the fact that they were following a plane. Each side of the drive was littered with an enormous amount of dilapidated vehicles. Cars of different models, shapes, and sizes were interspersed with motorbikes, vans, and trucks, some with trailers still attached. One truck and trailer lay dead on its back with wheels in the air doing a passable impression of what could be any one of the oversized beetles found in Australia. Maggie could not be sure, but to the right of the house at the end of the drive it looked like there was a tank. An unusual sight, but then again, this was Dingo's place. As they approached the low flat-roofed house, Maggie saw her old friend –unmistakably Dingo – lean out once more, look behind at them, and mouth something.

'Open your windows, boys, and let's hear what he's saying. I bet he's surprised to see us!'

Ben and Joshua pressed their buttons and the windows came down. As they did so, Maggie could hear snippets of Dingo's familiar broad Australian drawl filter through. She quickly got the gist of it.

'Who the fu... 'ell are y...? Gerroff m.. fu...in' prop...ty!'

Eventually, the plane came to a stop just outside a small wooden building to the side of the house which Maggie assumed to be a makeshift hangar. The plane door opened as they drew up nearby and a pair of dirt-covered shorts appeared, supported by two hairy tree trunks wearing red socks and enormous walking boots. Their owner rather clumsily slid down off the plane wing, obviously in a hurry to deal with his unwanted visitors.

Red-faced and topless, Dingo Derek stomped towards Maggie and the others as they got out of the car. Before he had a chance to repeat his earlier requests from the plane, Maggie stepped forward. 'G'day, Dingo. How are ya?'

'And you thought my Australian was bad,' Ben whispered to her sullenly.

Maggie ignored him, instead headed towards the huge Australian who had stopped in his tracks, his angry demeanour evaporating in a second.

'Maggie? Is that you? Well, I'm jiggered!'

Maggie continued her march forwards, her arms open. Within moments, she found herself picked up and wrapped in what felt like a hug from a giant doormat with arms.

'Ow, Dingo! I am over eighty, you know. Bit of respect for an old lady.'

'You're not old, Maggie. You've not changed a bit.' She found herself being lowered gently to the floor. It seemed to take a good while to get down. 'Let's have a look at you.'

While Dingo cast his piercing blue eyes over her, she took the opportunity to examine his face in detail too. He was just over nine years younger than her and still looked in great shape for his age. The last time she had seen him was twenty years ago when he had paid her and Frankie a surprise visit in the UK. Then, she remembered, his hair was greying, but now it was totally white. He wore it long, down to his shoulders, and it would have been quite luscious, even beautiful if it was not speckled with grit and dust. The fact he had probably not brushed it for many days added to what was a complete mess, not helped by the ends which looked like they had been used to dip engine oil. If he had been fronting an advert for shampoo, the slow-motion toss of the hair look would have been replaced by the not giving a toss whatsoever look.

What his hair lacked in presentation, though, was more than made up for by the rest of his features. She had always thought of him as a handsome man, a fact that she had openly admitted to Frankie who had agreed with her. The girl in the restaurant all those years ago may not have got the son of a billionaire she wanted, but she had missed out on the opportunity to spend more time with an impressive physical specimen. His beard was still mainly black and, surprisingly, well kept, bearing in mind the lack of attention to detail elsewhere follicly. His most notable feature was his high cheekbones which set off his 'just right' nose perfectly. His skin had taken a bit of a beating through age and countless hours in the sun, but it gave ruggedness to his features which Maggie still found attractive. And those eyes.... well... All of that, and the fact that he was six foot six with the frame of a fifty-five-year-old Arnold Schwarzenegger, made her heart flutter in a way it had not fluttered since a Hugh Grant lookalike switched on the Christmas lights in Frampton a few years ago. (In reality, he had looked nothing like Hugh Grant, but it had not stopped her from giving credit where credit was due).

'What do you think, Dingo? Do I still cut it?'

'Maggie, you cut it better than a wombat's knob slices through a pack of butter.' Even by Australian standards, Dingo's use of metaphors was unusual. It drew a laugh from Ben and the others.

Dingo looked over her towards the pickup truck. 'Now, who are these blokes with you here?'

Maggie did the introductions and watched them wince as Dingo gave them each a firm handshake. She briefly explained their connections to her. He lit up when Bill was introduced as her son. 'Frankie's and Maggie's boy, is that right? Well, I never. That must have been a shock for you, Maggie. Don't get me wrong, Bill, a pleasant shock. I know how much your mum and dad regretted losing you... I mean, giving you up... ah, shit, sorry... the adoption thing, if you know what I mean?'

Maggie knew exactly what he meant and sympathised with Dingo's clumsy way of vocalising it. She struggled to understand herself – let alone explain to anyone else – why she succumbed to pressure from the Service to allow their son to be adopted all those years ago.

'It's fine, Dingo,' said Bill. 'We're making up for lost time.'

'Sure are,' said Maggie with somewhat false joviality. 'Still won't call me Mum, though.' She softened the rebuke with a gentle nudge in Bill's ribs. 'Refers to me as Maggie.'

'Well, you call me Bill and him Ben. They're not our names. And now everyone calls us Bill and Ben because of you.'

'And what do you call each other?' Maggie retorted with a playful wag of the finger.

'Bill and Ben, but that's not the point!'

The banter brought a low chortle from Dingo. 'The main thing is that you're together. That link between a parent and their kids is precious. Hang on to each other for dear life now, won't you?' Maggie thought she spotted his eyes saddening a little – a regret that he had never settled down and had children, she wondered – before brightening up again. 'I'm chuffed. How did you find each other?'

'Now, that is a story I'm going to have to leave for later, Dingo,' said Maggie, 'but I promise I will tell all. Just as soon as you've invited us in for a cold beer.'

'Jeez! Where are my manners? Of course, come on in.'

He set Ben on his way towards the house with what Dingo might have thought was a gentle guiding hand, but what looked like from Ben's stagger forward as if he had been whacked across the shoulder blades by a cricket bat. On the way in, Dingo bent down to whisper in Maggie's ear. 'That other one's your great-grandson, you say? Why is he dressed like a cross between that weird kid from the Munsters and Danny La-Rue? And why the fuck's he got a handbag?'

'It's a man-bag.'

'A what?'

'A man-bag. He's in disguise.'

'Disguised as what? A fuckin' parrot with a dodgy haircut? And what's with the surprised-looking eyebrows? He looks like he's just seen the poms beat the Aussies in a test match.'

'Say what you think, Dingo. Don't hold back, will you?'

'Have I ever, Maggie?'

71

Within a couple of minutes, Maggie found herself sitting on an old, worn chair on Dingo's veranda, looking back out the way they had come in, and enjoying a can of Tooheys. There was a beautiful sunset and she was tempted to imagine that the rest of the world was like this: safe, secure, peaceful, and, importantly after a long drive, relaxing. Then she was reminded of why they were there.

It was daunting if she thought about it. They were, effectively, on the run from people in an organisation that had remarkable resources at its disposal. They seemed to have control of, or at least access to, major systems, judging by the messages they sent through at the airport. They knew enough about Maggie to make specific threats to Sharon and her immediate family, and they looked like they may have infiltrated the Service unless Joshua was overstating that particular worry. It would not be the first time that had happened, as she knew full well from the double-crossing that went on in Voigt's case. It had the hallmarks of Sheldon's grubby hands all over it. Yet, Sheldon had been in Delton Park maximum security prison up until 48 hours ago. What influence could she have had from there? The other main suspect was Emmanuel Taylor, whose diamond she had taken in the transit hall in Singapore. Her understanding was that he was a significant player in the arms supply industry, but would he have the savvy and backing to have pulled a stunt on them like this? From what Joshua had said about him, he was more of the gangster type. Surely, if he just wanted the diamond back, rather than kidnapping her and Joshua and going to all of that trouble of tying them to the top of

72

Sydney Harbour Bridge, he would have just demanded it back from them more directly, no doubt with plenty of menaces. All of this was going through her mind again as Dingo brought out some bread and cheese, and put it on a small table next to Maggie.

'The plate's for you, Maggie. I only need the one with me here all on my own. You blokes will have to make do with your laps and fingers.'

'Is that a hubcap y'all put it on?' said Ben who, in an apparent effort to lose his Aussie twang, now sounded like a hillbilly.

'I recycle and use what I can.'

Maggie wanted to question him further about the tank she had see but was interrupted as Bill and Joshua, who had been deep in conversation at the other end of the veranda, came over to join them.

'That looks great,' said Bill taking the lump of cheese which Dingo offered him and tearing off a piece of bread.

Joshua caught Maggie's eye and nodded in Dingo's direction as if to say, 'Come on, you brought us here, what are we going to do now?' By the looks of things, he and Bill had been bouncing around their own thoughts and ideas, but Maggie was acutely aware that the ball was in her court. She felt responsible for what happened next. Could Dingo really help them? She felt for the knot in her stomach, but experience told her it was never there when she deliberately tried to reach for it. They were there because she knew Dingo was an expert in cutting himself off from the world. Hopefully, it meant he knew how to get stuff done without swiping or clicking anything. If he could not help them, who could?

A thought surprised her – *You're not here because you just wanted to see him then, Maggs?* – which she decisively shoved to one side.

She put her plate and beer down and started to stand up. It was one of those chairs which were incredibly comfortable, and one she would not usually have sat in unless she was planning to spend the night in situ. Her usual rule of thumb was to avoid anything where her backside ended up lower than her legs. The only way to find out, though, was by committing herself to the seat, by which time gravity normally did its thing and, if she had made the wrong call, she would end up looking upwards at her kneecaps. From there, her eyelids usually joined in with the whole 'downward momentum' trend and she'd invariably fall asleep. On this occasion, though, she was determined not to succumb to tiredness because she wanted to get some earnest discussion going. Dingo was on hand to help her out of the chair.

'Thank you,' she said, wiping cheese and crumbs off the new skirt Bill had acquired for her. 'And thank you for the beer and food.'

'Pleasure,' said Dingo. 'You'll stay the night?'

'That would be appreciated, although this isn't a social call, Dingo, as you may well have worked out by now.' To her annoyance, she found herself blushing at the thought of socialising with Dingo. Just the two of them, on the veranda. But what would Frankie think? *He'd probably say, 'Go for it, Maggs'.* He had never been the jealous type when he had been alive, and he would never have wanted her to be on her own after he had gone. She coughed

74

in the hope that it would divert people's attention away from the heat she felt rising in her cheeks. It didn't.

'You alright, Maggie?' said Ben. 'You've gone very red.'

'I'm fine.' She straightened her skirt and then found herself adjusting her hair. *Great work, Maggs. All you need to do now is look coyly in Dingo's direction, giggle, and simper.* 'We would... ahem... like, or rather... ahem... we need your help.' She managed to avoid the simper but not the coy look and giggle as she added, 'Please.'

'Of course, Maggie. Anything for you.' He took her hand and patted it before letting it drop by her side again.

If she had had a fan, she would have likely placed it in front of her face and averted her eyes. She just about managed to not say, 'Oh, Mr. Darcy... you are too kind,' before she got herself together and continued. 'We're in a spot of bother and it's going to take quite a lot to get out of it. I am... we are... being hunted down.'

Dingo looked indignant. 'Hunted down? Who by?'

'We're not entirely sure. Look, I'll get Joshua to tell you what's happened so far, and then we can have a think about what we can do about it.' She looked at Joshua and Bill. 'If that's ok with you two?'

They both nodded. Joshua gave an update, during which Maggie spent the whole time trying to pretend Dingo's hand was not resting comfortably on her shoulder. He added some information that Maggie had not been aware of. It had come out of the conversation that he and Bill had had a little earlier. Bill managed to do a few discrete checks before arriving in Australia.

Nothing conclusive had been revealed, which Joshua said was a worrying sign in itself as it meant avenues were being closed off by someone from within the Service. Emmanuel Taylor had left the UK under his real name on the pretence, no doubt, he was on a valid business trip. But there was no record of anyone with that name ever passing through Singapore immigration control, something he would have needed to do to enter the country. Now, with no record of his name on any of the passenger lists that were held leaving Singapore, he no longer existed in terms of an audit trail. No surprise there in many ways as, if he wanted to disappear, he would undoubtedly have false documentation. But it did suggest that Taylor had discovered Maggie's diamond swap fairly soon after it was done.

'It was possible,' Joshua said, 'that he was tipped off that it had happened.'

'So we were set up?' Maggie said.

'We can't be certain,' said Joshua, 'but we can't discount it. The hotel receptionist was in on our little jaunt to the top of the bridge. That stunt would have taken some organising, too much to have just been a reaction to Taylor discovering the switch when he was supposed to have done, i.e. when he tried to sell it to his contacts. It would have needed time and planning, people with the expertise and the means to get us up there without anyone noticing...'

'Or pretending they hadn't noticed,' interrupted Dingo.

'Exactly. Insiders to help them gain access to the bridge.'

'So, if the diamond swap was organised from within the Service by people in cahoots with whoever, it suggests it was never a

76

proper job.' Maggie had not meant to sound bitter, but she could not help herself.

Joshua seemed to take it as an implied criticism of him and his role in getting her involved. 'It's my fault. I should never have persuaded you to do it. This was supposed to be a trip to reunite the family, not a chance to work.'

Maggie took a hard line. 'Listen, Joshua dear. If I didn't want to get involved, I would not have done it. Don't assume you can make me do anything I don't want to do. Now, stop blaming yourself, and let's get back to thinking about how we get out of this mess.'

'You have an idea, Maggie?' said Bill.

'I have the outline of an idea, but it will need to start off with Dingo taking us on a little tour of his facilities first. Do you still have that hidey hole you wrote to me about, Dingo, and is it still well stocked?'

'Yeah, I do and it's stocked up like a fat koala at a eucalyptus tree sales convention.'

Maggie could see a look of puzzlement on Ben's face in reaction to Dingo's latest comparison to ram home a point. 'You'll get used to these quirky metaphors, Ben. It's a Dingo thing.'

'Yes, but I just want to understand. Surely,' he continued slowly, 'the salespeople wouldn't take actual trees to a convention, would they? Maybe some leaves or saplings but not enough to make a koala fat.'

Maggie knew that Dingo was not the sort of man to take offence at Ben's pedantry. Maybe it was the amount of time in solitude that made him more easy-going when people did eventually turn up. It could quite easily go the other way with some people who might be more sensitive, driven mad by their own company. Besides, Ben said it in such a way that it was in no way a challenge or criticism.

'Good on yer, Ben. I take your point. Look, imagine that this here sales convention is for salespeople who sell whole eucalyptus trees by the acre. They tour around various people's eucalyptus orchards, sipping good wine and doing their deals. The fat koala follows them around, see? Plenty of leaves for him to stock up on.'

'Do eucalyptus trees grow in orchards?' said Ben, who remained unconvinced.

'Yeah, course they do,' explained Dingo, giving Maggie a quick wink before ushering them all off the veranda. 'How else would the koala get so fat?'

It was quite dark now. Maggie could hear all sorts of unusual noises, near and far, as a variety of nocturnal animals made their presence felt. Dingo led with a large flashlight as they made their way along the side of the house. There was no moon to light up the sky which made the stars filling the heavens all the more impressive. She was familiar with the Southern Cross, having had a quick astronomy lesson from Sharon's husband, Sean, on her last visit, but struggled to get a handle on any of the other constellations The universe had always fascinated her, even more so as she got older. Sukie, back at the Italian restaurant in Frampton, had rather poetically pointed out to her that people had that connection because their bodies were made up of materials that came from the stars originally. Maggie liked that, although the analogy was ruined somewhat when Sukie pointed out that her age meant she would almost certainly become stardust again years and years before any of the other diners in the restaurant.

'Right, we're here,' said Dingo, stopping about a hundred metres away from the house. He shone his torch around. Maggie caught sight of the tank she had seen earlier before the light settled on a patch of dirt.

'This is it?' Maggie said.

'Yep.'

'You told me you had a bunker. I expected it to be underground, but surely you have to be able to get in it, otherwise what's the point?'

'That's what I'd hoped you'd say. Look, I know this sounds selfish, but if there is a nuclear or asteroid strike followed by Armageddon, I don't want every Tom, Dick, and Sheila coming in. It needs to be hidden.'

'From who, exactly?' asked Bill.

'There are people around who would want this if the time came to it.'

'Maggie said you lived miles from civilisation,' said Ben.

'I do. The nearest house is ten miles away and the nearest shop is even further. That's where I'd been when you arrived. I fly to get my shopping.'

'If people are living that far away, then, surely, no worries,' said Ben, reverting to Aussie-speak. His attempt to correct his slip by adding 'mate' in an English accent, only made it worse.

Maggie's scowl at him was lost in the dark which was a shame, she thought, as it had been a good one. A tired face with traces of boot polish and her slightly mad knotted hair had the potential to make for a very effective scowl.

'Better to be safe than sorry where folk are concerned,' said Dingo. 'Come on, I'll show you what's inside and you'll see what I mean.'

Dingo walked the few metres over to the tank and fiddled with something under one of the tracks. There was the sound of a double bleep and a hatch opened up right where he had been standing moments before, lit up by a strip of lights that went below ground. Maggie peered over the newly formed hole. 'You want me to get down that ladder, do you?'

'What'd you expect, Maggie? A lift with a bell boy? Come on, we'll help you if you need it. It only goes down fifteen foot or so. Are you scared of ladders or something?'

'Not as such. Just scared of falling down them.' She took a deep breath. *Come on, Maggs. You've faced a lot worse than this.*

'You go down first, Joshua,' said Dingo. 'Three steps down, you'll see a button tucked away on your left. Press it and that opens up the inner hatch. I'll go next, followed by you, Maggie. I'll guide you down. Bill, go last after Ben. Press that button there, Bill,' he indicated a small green button just under the lip of the hole, 'as you step down. The top hatch closes sharpish, so mind yer bonce.'

They all did as instructed. The climb down was not as bad as Maggie had anticipated, and she soon found herself with Dingo and Joshua at the bottom which opened up into something she had not expected at all. In her mind, she had imagined a small room, maybe a couple, with a few beds, a table, somewhere to go to the toilet (the most important facility), and an array of provisions stacked around the place. Admittedly, she could see various containers and boxes which, presumably, held the stock Dingo had said was plentiful. But this space was far from small. It was a large natural cave, and as she walked around she could see more rooms and tunnels going from it. As she approached one tunnel, it lit up and she peered into it.

'How far does that go?' she asked.

'Not that far. Ten, twenty yards maybe. Then there's another room a couple of spaces down there, similar to this one. They need their privacy as much as the next person.'

'Who do?' she asked. 'Who's this for?'

'Look, this isn't really for me. I'm getting on. Why would I want to survive something like a nuclear strike or a meteor? It's for the locals.'

'The locals?'

'Yeah, the *Iwelongas*. Indigenous: been here forever, their people. We have an arrangement. They've spent their lives being turfed off their land. The land above isn't strictly mine, although I paid a hefty whack to some property company for it. It's theirs, as is everything else round here. They allow me to live on it in exchange for them using this as a haven and a passageway into other parts of the bush where they can hunt and live fairly freely. Every now and then they come back into this western world, as it were.'

'Is coming back a spiritual thing?' asked Ben.

'Nah. They need to earn some cash. They enjoy the occasional ciggie, beer, and pizza as much as anyone. They come back to help out on the farms when they're needed. You can't pay for pizza with kanga testicles.'

Joshua appeared through an entrance to one of the tunnels. 'I didn't even get to the end of that one. So this is where people will go if anything drastic happens?'

'Yeah. They're a superstitious lot, the Iwelongas. They believe that the upper world has had its day and the future of mankind is destined to live underground for a decade before it re-emerges. I figure, what with the crazy stuff that's going on in the world at the moment, they're not wrong. All I've done is help them build a little steel protection on top of these caves in case something bad does happen. That's why there's all that scrap metal about the place. They can scoot down here and live comfortably for years. There's a freshwater source down that tunnel that comes from way deep underground. I've taught them how to test for and deal with any contaminations. Enough food to last them a good long while here, too.'

'Might they not be out in the bush when a nuclear strike or similar happens?' asked Ben.

'That's possible, but it's here if they can get to it, which they will be able to if they've got their prediction right.'

Maggie had been trying to ignore the knot in her stomach – a worry knot, rather than the helpful kind – which had come to life and been nudging her ever since Dingo had mentioned the name of the tribe. She asked rather hesitantly, 'And their prediction is what and when ...?'

'The world will end at a quarter past four pm, a week on Tuesday,' said Dingo, rather too matter-of-factly for Maggie's liking.

'That's very specific.'

'Yeah. I've suggested they get here by 3:55 at the latest, just in case.'

'How many of them are in the tribe?' asked Bill.

Dingo had barely opened his mouth before Maggie answered for him. 'Sixty-seven, or at least that was how many there were as of last July.'

~ ~ ~

Chapter 8

They were back at the house, inside now, as the cold desert air had made it too chilly to be outside on the veranda any longer. Joshua and Bill were checking the two handguns that Dingo had said they could take away. There were no weapons down below, Dingo had explained, since the tribe did not believe in using guns. He had no such qualms. Hopefully, the secret bunker would stay secret, but he did not trust his Australian neighbours, 'more than I would trust a platypus in a feather boa trying to gatecrash a ducks-only party' as he put it. He could spare the two guns, particularly in the hands of experts. He had also brought up the portable shortwave radio which he was in the process of setting up for a demonstration.

Maggie was deep in thought, trying to make sense of the note that had been pinned to her skirt at the top of the Sydney Harbour Bridge, and, in particular, the piece torn off from the bottom. At the time she had paid little heed to it, being too concerned about the part she could see which was the direct threat to her family if she did not give back the diamond. Now, though, she was wondering if there had been something important on it that had been deliberately removed. Why would someone go to all that trouble of taking two people to the top of a bridge, tying them up, and then make threats on a scrappy piece of paper? Whoever had done that was far too professional to do that, surely? *Unless they were deliberately trying to make it look like an amateur job, Maggs*? No, that didn't figure out. It did raise the possibility that whoever was making the threats was not necessarily in synchronisation with those who were delivering them.

And then there was the article. As soon as Dingo had mentioned the name of the local tribe, *Iwelongas,* Maggie could see the article from the Sydney Times supplement in front of her with that name specifically in it. Before she had tried (and failed) to complete the crossword at the airport and just before the warning messages started coming through on the arrivals board, she had read the start of an article titled, *Diamonds Are Not Forever.* It had caught her eye, for obvious reasons, but what had particularly intrigued her at the time was the links it made to beliefs by some Australian Aboriginal tribes that when the last diamond was removed from the ground and taken off Australian soil, the world would end. She had not been able to finish the article because, frustratingly, the bottom of the page had been torn off of it, and she had been left wondering when the end of the world was predicted to be. As interesting as the article was, she had thought nothing more about it then. Events had somewhat taken over from that point, but now there were too many coincidences happening to ignore. It was time to share her thoughts.

'Can you boys stop playing with guns; you, Dingo, stop fiddling with the radio, and Ben....' She looked across at Ben who was sitting quietly on a sofa flipping through the pages of a book. '... and Ben... don't talk in an Australian accent anymore.'

'What? I wasn't...'

'I know, Ben love. It's to save me time telling you off later. Now this plan of mine has just taken a bit of a turn. My original thought was that we could take some guns, fly somewhere in Dingo's plane and then arrest the culprits.'

'That was your plan, was it?' said Joshua. 'Bit vague, if you don't mind me saying.'

'Well, I did say it was just an outline, but that was the gist of it. Still is, to some extent, except that we need to factor a few more things in. There's something else going on which we had not considered. I don't know what it is yet, but let me explain my thoughts. To recap: first of all, I am called in for a mission to do a swap of diamonds for an international arms dealer. Simple enough in itself. We think it goes okay, and then we find someone's onto us. We get kidnapped and a message is left on a torn-off piece of paper. Torn off piece, please note.'

'You think that's significant?' said Joshua.

'I thought it was a bit strange at the time, but not overly so. I think it's more significant now because I was reading an article about the *Iwelongas* just before we went off-grid. That's how I knew how many were in the tribe. It didn't click that they were from round here, though. That information was probably torn off too, as was the additional information about when they think the world is going to end. Literally, a section cut out in the magazine I was reading, which was a bit odd, now I look back.'

'That's no coincidence,' said Joshua.

Bill nodded in agreement.

'Did the article talk about the fact they believe the world's end is linked to diamonds?' said Dingo.

'Yes. So we've got links here; diamonds plus two pieces of communication fed to me with missing information – the note on the bridge and the article. Remember that too: fed to me, or at least withheld from me, which is just as important.'

'Did you know about the article, Dingo?' said Bill, rather suspiciously, Maggie noticed.

'Nah, not a clue. And before your investigative mind goes into overdrive about whether I'm somehow wrapped up in all of this, let me stop it right there. I had no idea you blokes were coming. Besides, Maggie and I go back a long way. I loved your father like a brother. And I love your mum like a sister.'

Maggie had mixed feelings about the last sentence, but she agreed with the sentiment. There was no way Dingo would be behind any of this, of that she was sure. She said as much and Bill backtracked with an apology.

'I'm sorry, Dingo. I have to explore all eventualities.'

'I get that, mate, but I want to reassure you that I'm fully behind you and your mum with all this. I wanna help.'

'It's appreciated,' said Joshua with a nod of thanks.

'So,' Maggie continued, 'the other thing we have learnt as being significant is a date: Tuesday week. The day the Iwelongas think the world will end. 4:15 pm.'

'That's November 24th,' added Bill.

'So you think someone's out there is playing a game of Cluedo with you, Maggie?' said Dingo.

87

'Yes, I do. Either someone is trying to warn us something is going to happen, possibly on that day...'

'... Or they're setting us up,' finished Joshua.

'Exactly.'

'Whichever one it is, we have to go along with it. If we run away, nothing gets sorted, and the risk to us all remains. We use the advantage we have of being off-grid to find out what we can, but at some point, we may be exposed.'

'I recognise that date for another reason,' said Ben. 'It stuck out in my mind because I remember thinking it would serve her right to be in jail the week after she was sentenced when she should be celebrating it. It was read out in court. The 24th November is Tina Sheldon's birthday.'

They had been sitting in virtual silence for a good ten minutes, mulling over what these latest thoughts and events meant before Maggie realised Dingo was not with them. How she had missed him leave, she had no idea; he was not the sort of man you lost easily in a room. However, he was soon back with news.

'That's sorted. I've spoken to Sid.'

'Sid?' said Ben.

'Yeah, Sid. He's the nominated leader of the Iwelongas this week. They take it in turns on a rotational basis. It's Sid's fortnight. His wife Nelly's peeved because she's only going to get a part week when the world ends.'

'Sid and Nelly: they're not very, how can I put this, without sounding condescending or racist,' said Ben, 'um... the names are not very...'

'Long?' suggested Maggie mischievously.

'No... um...'

'Short, then?'

'No... I mean yes, they are quite short names but... they're not very... um...'

'Modern?'

'No, er...'

'Suitable for black people?'

'No! That is racist. Well... yes. I suppose I do mean that in a way. What I mean is that they don't sound very Aboriginal.'

'Plenty of Aussie Aboriginal people take what might be deemed Western names,' said Dingo levelly.

'Yes, I know... well, no, I didn't know, actually, because I haven't met any Aboriginal people here, but I guess I sort of knew that. I guess I thought that the Iwelongas would be more...'

'Traditional?' said Maggie.

'Yes! Thank you! I thought, because of where they live and their beliefs, they might be more traditional.' He glanced at Maggie who was smiling. It probably was not the best time for a windup, but she had enjoyed it anyway.

'They're abbreviations of their whole names,' said Dingo. 'Sidakoora, which means hunter of the great white wallaby that dances in the night, and Olanelle which means woman who plays host to the delighted pack of possums.'

'Really?' said Ben.

'Nah, mate. They really are called Sid and Nelly.' Dingo grinned. Ben looked at him and then he too smiled as he realised he was the butt of some gentle ribbing. Maggie chuckled; if she thought Ben could not take it, she would not allow anyone to be so 'cruel', including herself. It was one of the many things she loved about Ben; he could take a joke... and give as good as he got when he wanted to.

'Anyway,' Dingo continued, 'I wanted to let you all know that we're sorted for the next thirty-six hours or so in terms of them looking out for us. They'll post people around the area and get a message to us if anyone comes within a cockroach's shit of a hundred miles of the place. That's what that big hump's handy for nearby – a great place to watch over a very flat area. And they have excellent night vision, the Iwelongas.'

'That's great. Thanks, Dingo,' said Joshua. 'I don't suggest we spend too long here anyway. We need to keep on the move.'

'I expect they might not want to commit a huge amount of time to looking after us,' said Ben. 'If you think the world's going to end in ten days or so, you would want to spend your last days and hours contemplating and reflecting on life.'

'Nah, not really. They would have been happy enough, except there's a two-for-one Pizza deal at Big Alfonso's in Delaka Creek. Next bus there leaves the day after tomorrow.'

'Well, it sounds like we're safe for the moment, so thank you, Dingo,' said Maggie. 'I've got a lot of thinking to do, as have we all. Can I suggest that overnight we all contemplate life, as Ben suggests, but on our own, and think about what all this information that we do and don't have means. It will affect what we do next.'

'Just remember, my plane is at your disposal,' said Dingo. 'The shortwave radio is bloody useful and virtually undetectable if you know the right frequencies to use. If there's anything else you need apart from the guns, let me know.'

'Perfect,' said Maggie. 'Now, where shall we sleep?'

Following a much-needed shower, after which she felt and looked much more like her usual self, Maggie clambered onto the only bed in the house – Dingo's – while the rest slept on a combination of sofas, cushions on floors, and chairs. It was agreed, with the exception of Maggie (despite her protestations that she should be included on the rota), that they take it in turns to stay awake should any warning come through from the Iwelongas. Ben asked whether they had an unusual animal call or something else they should listen out for.

'Yeah,' Dingo replied. 'They usually do the sound of the wayka-fuckup bird.'

Despite her tiredness and quiet relief that she would not be on lookout, Maggie found it hard to drift off. Her spy brain was trained to make judgements based on the best information available. The information she had so far was sparse and required quite a lot of conjecture. The best theory she could come up with at the moment was that Sheldon was going to do something significant on her birthday and that she was toying with Maggie. The messages she and Joshua had been sent supported that last idea, as did the newspapers being left about, pointing her in one direction without giving the complete picture. For all Maggie knew, Sheldon might even be behind Brenda the Bag lady's antics in helping Maggie to get the train to Coff's Harbour and onwards to Dingo's place. She hoped that was not the case, but she could rule nothing out.

Then there was the question of motive. If Sheldon was involved, why all this *malarkey*, as Frankie would have put it? If revenge was her driving force and she had such control, she could have had that manyfold by now. She was an evil witch, but this was a lot of trouble to go to. No, there was something more to this that Maggie was missing. The most worrying thing for Maggie was that every choice she was making was somehow playing into Sheldon's hands. Maybe, whatever Maggie did along the way was integral to Sheldon's wider aims? *Are you that predictable, Maggs? You never used to be.* Maybe predictability came with age. Being old and predictable was a depressing thought.

Then she reminded herself where she was; in the middle of nowhere, as safe as she could be for now, with a strong and capable bunch of people around her. That had to count for something, didn't it? With that positive thought, eventually, she drifted off to sleep feeling somewhat easier...

... and pretending not to be disappointed that Dingo had given up his bed and not offered to share.

~ ~ ~

Chapter 9

Maggie awoke with a start. She had been dreaming that she was on board a floundering ship with klaxons sounding out urgent warnings. She had had the dream before, and she usually tried to stay with it on the off chance that she ended up having the sinking feeling mitigated by Leonardo DiCaprio's warm hands around her waist. At her age, she was used to taking the rough with the smooth. A one in ten success rate of an embrace with a famous heartthrob was enough to risk the unpleasantness of drowning the other nine times.

She quickly realised that it was not a klaxon that was disturbing her sleep, but someone, or multiple someones, doing a darned good impression of one. She had been sleeping on top of the bed, put off from getting in it by a splatter of engine oil on the bottom sheet. Dingo had assured her the sheets had been washed that day but, even so, she did not want to risk ruining the new dress that Bill and Ben had got for her. A blanket had kept her warm enough in the chill of the night, but she threw it off now as she realised something was going on. At the same time, Bill came rushing through the door.

'Quickly, Mum! We've not got long to get out of here.'

Maggie had had the foresight to leave her shoes – selected by Bill and Ben, and sensible flat ones, she was pleased to note – by her bed, for exactly this scenario, and she was in them within seconds, commenting as she grabbed her bag and followed Bill out, 'Blimey, Bill. It must be serious if you've called me Mum.'

'Yes, well. Thought it was more likely to get your attention. Come on; the others are in the kitchen at the back of the house. This way.'

Maggie was led into what she would describe only loosely as a kitchen. It was not part of the main internal framework of the house, more of a lean-to on the back; a rather dilapidated lean-to at that. There was a large metal sink on the left with crude wooden benches on either side and a concrete barbecue on the opposite side, similar to the public ones available in many of Australia's open spaces. It brought to mind socials she had attended with Sharon and Sean, with the blokes showing off their bush skills as they vied to be the first one to light their tinderbox-dry barbies in thirty degrees heat using only a can of petrol and a flamethrower.

Bill flicked off the inside light as they stepped through into the lean-to. The klaxon sounds had stopped, and she became aware of some distant voices not too far away. As Bill switched on his torch, she could see Joshua standing with Ben by the opening. He had a gun in his hand. Bill had one too, she realised now, and he replaced Ben in keeping lookout. He indicated that Ben should stand next to Maggie by the back door of the house. With only wooden walls and plastic windows for sides, Maggie felt slightly exposed and vulnerable – she had seen Wendy houses that offered more protection than Dingo's lean-to – but she assumed Joshua and Bill's actions were precautionary and there was no immediate threat, otherwise they would be safely back inside.

'What's happening?' she whispered to Ben.

'Dingo's out there talking to one of the Iwelongas. Some vehicles have been spotted stopped by the roadside a few miles north of here. There are at least another two cars east on the road we came in on, roughly the same distance away. Dingo's trying to find out more. It's suspicious. He says only truckers tend to use these roads in the middle of the night.'

There was the sound of footsteps nearby and then Dingo ducked under the supporting beam of the outer frame to join them. He looked quite different. In the dim light of his torch which added to the one that Bill held, Maggie could see that he had probably showered. His hair, now tied up in a neat ponytail, was no longer the tangled mass of earlier and she wondered, rather guiltily, whether he had made the effort for her.

'Oh, Maggie, good that you're up and awake.' His voice had a tension to it she had not heard before. 'So, Sid thinks there are four, possibly five, vehicles out there, spread out on all the routes around. The lookouts reckoned they arrived about the same time, five minutes or so ago, and they all switched their headlamps off within a few seconds of each other.'

'Definitely co-ordinated, then,' said Bill. 'Are they stationary?'

'At the moment they are. Harder to see people if they're travelling on foot now.'

'It makes no sense,' said Bill. 'I don't get what they would want to achieve by attacking us. As we said before, if they've tracked us this far, they could have got us ages before now.'

'Unless,' said Joshua, 'as Maggie said last night, it is someone playing a game. Sheldon would enjoy drawing this out.'

'I'm not sure they have actually tracked us. How could they? We've been ultra careful.'

'We'll discuss the how later,' said Joshua. 'Let's think about what we're faced with now. That's a fair few vehicles, potentially with a heap of people.'

'And they'll know they're being watched,' said Dingo.

'How would they know that?' said Bill. Maggie detected that scepticism in his voice again. Harsher this time, possibly, and more challenging.

Disappointingly, Dingo did not respond straight away. Instead, he poked his head outside and swept the flashlight around in a semicircular motion before pulling back in again. Bill repeated his question and Maggie could see his stance had changed slightly. It was not outwardly aggressive, as such, but it hinted at that underlying layer of toughness she had seen on the Voigt case. He was obviously not as trusting of Dingo as she was. *Perhaps he's a little bit jealous, Maggs. Perhaps he's sensed an attraction between the two of you and he doesn't like the thought of his mum being with someone else.* Maggie stamped her foot in irritation at herself for thinking such stupid things, particularly at a time of potential crisis. Joshua noticed it.

'What's up, Maggie? What's bothering you?'

Be professional, Maggs. It's the only way. Anyway, Bill's question is a good one. 'Is there something we need to know, Dingo?' she said as neutrally as she could manage. 'Something you've not told us?'

'I haven't been deliberately hiding anything from you, Maggie. Not as such, anyway.'

'Go on.'

'There is something I could have mentioned earlier, I suppose, but I didn't think it was relevant. Now I realise how serious this really is.'

'So you knew someone would come?' said Bill.

'Nah, not really. I had concerns which I shoulda told you about, but I didn't coz... well, it's complicated.'

'How complicated?'

'Look, it's best I show you. Come on; follow me back to the shelter.' He moved as if to head out into the night again, but stopped when Maggie laid a hand on his arm.

'Hang on, Dingo. We've been down there once already. What is it you want to show us that you didn't show us earlier?'

Dingo turned to look directly at her. It was hard to tell what he was thinking Rather than answer her question directly, he said, 'My old man was a bloke of very few words. But one thing he did say I have always remembered. I find it reassuring, particularly in difficult times such as this.'

'Oh?'

'Yeah, he said: Take care of the rooster before the storm and the old dog will look after the boiling pot.'

'That's a complete hash of several proverbs that makes no sense,' said Ben.

'Exactly. He used to talk a load of old bollocks did my dad. So when I cock things up, I just tell myself I'm just like him. I find that quite reassuring as he wasn't a bad bloke. I think I might have cocked things up here by not telling you everything, but I want to put it right now. Will you give me a chance?'

Maggie looked at all three of her companions and they all gave the same resigned shrug. She turned her attention back to Dingo. 'My old Nan liked proverbs too. She shared one with me on her deathbed.'

'What was that, Maggie?' asked Dingo.

'She said to me: "Always remember, Maggie," she said, "procrastination is the thief of time." Then she looked me in the eye and said: "I've been meaning to tell you this before, but I kept putting it off." Your dad's not the only family member who talked a load of bollocks. None of us are perfect.' Maggie ushered them out. 'Come on, let's go.'

The climb down the ladder was harder in the dark because, quite rightly, all their lights and those in the hatchway were switched off to avoid risking unwanted attention. As a result, Maggie had to feel her way down and it seemed like an eternity before she reached the bottom. There, she had to wait in almost pitch black until she heard the inner hatch close, at which point Dingo switched the lights on. He asked them to follow him as he made his way along one of the tunnels, stooping as he went. The other men had to do the same, giving Maggie a brief feeling of satisfaction that she did not need to; right up to the point that she bumped her head. It was at that stage that she looked back and realised they had been going steadily down a slope. The tunnel opened up into another chamber, smaller than the one they had left and a dead end. Except that it was not.

'Give us a hand with this, will you, fellas?' said Dingo as he crouched down by a hefty-looking slab of rock. 'My old bones can't shift weight like they used to.'

Between them, they moved the slab to one side. Maggie bent down and stared into the hole in the cave wall that it revealed. 'It's only a couple of metres thick and then we can stand up again,' said Dingo lowering himself onto his knees. There's a light switch on the other side. I'll flick it on. You okay there, Maggie?'

'Bloody marvellous, thank you, Dingo. I spent last night in a waste skip wearing an old boiler suit which would have been ideal for this. I finally get some new togs and here I am ten metres below ground in a bunker polishing the floor with the bottom of my dress. What could be better?'

She heard Dingo's deep throaty laugh echo as she followed Joshua through. Dingo was right; it was not far and she was soon on the other side. Using Joshua's offered hand as a prop, she pulled herself up and looked around. The light was limited so that, at first, she was fooled by the size of the chamber. She had expected it to be another small room, but, as they walked along and more lights came on, she realised that this was far bigger, in fact, enormous – the size of a school hall. They continued to walk on a gentle slope downhill into the centre where the ground flattened off.

'Surprised?' said Dingo.

From the look on the others' faces, Maggie could see they were as awestruck as she was. They were standing in the middle of a dome with yellow lights dotted around which gave the place a cosy feel, despite its size. The rock above her was red in colour, rough, exuding ancientness, sculptured over many thousands of years. The air had a 'tang' to it; not stale, just the impression that it had passed through many nooks and crannies, deep into the earth over a long period of time. It should have felt cold so far underground in such a deep space, yet there was surprising warmth to it.

Some markings caught her eye on the wall to the right and she headed straight over to it. She barely registered Dingo's cautionary warning to be careful where she stepped because of the unevenness of the floor. Having visited many historical sites over recent years, that was normally the first thing she watched out for, but physical safety lost its importance as the markings beckoned to her, inviting her to learn about the story they had to tell.

She had seen Australian Aboriginal art before. Whenever she had visited the country and gone anywhere vaguely touristy, it had been rammed down her throat. It could be gimmicky, tacky almost, but original art was different and the paintings she had seen in the Flinders Ranges near Adelaide were far superior to anything recreated anywhere else on the tourist trail. They had touched something inside of her which was almost primeval in nature.

She could remember looking at one section of rock art that the guide had said made references to the local version of the creation story. There were representations of adults and children, plus various animals and symbols for things like watering holes and

100

hunting areas. It had struck her as being not only a record of their lives but a practical roadmap that they might have used at the time. And here in front of her now was another section of history in action, very similar in lots of ways to what she had seen in South Australia, though a lot clearer, more defined. At Flinders, she had been hampered by the light in a couple of the caves. The morning was the best time to go and she remembered getting up incredibly early to catch the paintings at their most magnificent. Even then, many of the figures and symbols were hard to make out in the shadows. Here, though, she could see everything, even in the yellowy artificial light. She lifted up her glasses as she approached. Black lines and shapes had been drawn on the wall with such care and attention to detail it took her breath away. As she studied the wall, she could see a sequence to it, like a storyboard, but without the delineation of scenes by boxes. It was more akin to the Bayeux Tapestry, a copy of which she had been to see at the museum in Reading back home, except it ran across from left to right for a few metres and then continued down on the next line. She stepped back to get an overall perspective. At the start, she could see dark scenes indicative of the Dreamtime stories she was familiar with. They moved on to figures descending from the sky, gods, she assumed, forming the world. There were rivers, mountains, some colour in the form of rainbows and sunshine, and many unrecognisable animals which evolved into the more familiar eclectic mix of today. A regular theme was 'the hunt'; figures in various positions with spears and knives chasing their prey. As she moved through the sequence, there were more calming scenes; people sitting around fires or under trees, maybe sharing stories, eating, and nursing young ones.

She was completely lost in the drama, the culture, and the beauty of it all. She bent down to look at the last line and readied herself to complete the journey of life, so intricately and lovingly drawn out by the Iwelongas' ancestors. It was at that point she saw the picture of two youngsters talking into their Smartphones.

'Amazing, isn't it?' said Dingo over her shoulder. 'I didn't think the Sharpie pens would work on this rock, but it's pretty bloody good. I just hope we don't get a leak somewhere above it and it gets all smudged.'

'But...'

'I know. It's hard to express how you feel.'

'Who... what...?'

'Nelly and Sid's boy was done for plastering graffiti on the side of the bridge nearby over the river. He used to be a little bugger. She persuaded him to channel his artistic talents into doing this. It looks like the real thing, doesn't it? Except for that picture. It's Miley Cyrus, apparently. He's bloody infatuated with her, I'm told. I haven't a bloody clue who she is.'

Maggie was speechless. A magical moment had been ruined. She stood staring at the picture of Miley Cyrus for several seconds before rejoining the real world again and realising she did not have a bloody clue who she was either.

She was diverted by Joshua calling across to her and Dingo to join him. He, Bill, and Ben were on the other side of the hall examining a stack of crates.

'What's in these, Dingo?' asked Joshua.

'Ah, now that's what I've brought you here for. Before I open them up, I want to explain what this place is. I've already shown you the other section which will be the Iwelongas' place of safety. Most of that was adapted from an existing network of tunnels which goes back years. This chamber we're in now goes back even further in time The Iwelongas believe it was shaped at the beginning of humanity and used to hide all the riches of the first gods from man.'

Maggie, still smarting from being taken in by a kid's cartoons, could not suppress a sarcastic comment. 'When you say man, do you mean Batman, Spiderman, or Superman?'

'Maggie!' said Ben. 'I'm surprised at you. Where is your respect for their culture?'

'I'm sorry, but I'm not feeling particularly culturally aware having just been hoodwinked by the Iwelonga's juvenile answer to Banksy. Please continue, Dingo.'

'The tribe will often meet in here to decide on important issues. All their ceremonies are held in here. It's a special place.'

'So why keep these crates here?' said Bill.

'Security.'

'What are in them, then – spare felt tips?' said Maggie who was still struggling to let it go.

'I'll show you,' said Dingo unfolding a screwdriver on a Swiss army knife he produced from his back pocket. He set to work unscrewing each corner of the top crate. As he lifted the lid, Maggie caught a glint of something underneath as the light above

103

filtered through. Before the lid was fully off, she had worked out what was inside. A quick estimate of how many there were in that crate multiplied by five crates soon gave her a hint as to why there were unwelcome visitors parked up nearby.

~ ~ ~

Chapter 10

'Are all these crates full of diamonds?' said Maggie.

'Not full and not all diamonds. But, yep: there are a lot of diamonds here.'

'What's the quality like?' asked Joshua.

Dingo put an enormous hand in and scooped out what might have been construed as a bucket load. 'Take a look. Of the genuine diamonds here, the quality varies from good to excellent, but there's a mixture of other stones of a lesser value in here too. Every time they dug out enough of the real stuff, they sent it away to Brisbane to get polished, cut, and classified. The agents and specialists took their whack of course. This top case is kinda the dregs. The really good stuff is at the bottom.'

'How long have they been mining this for?' asked Bill taking hold of a piece offered to him. He held it up and shone his torch through it.

'Hundreds of years.'

'I'm no expert,' said Bill, 'but if this is an example of the less good stuff, I can't imagine what the rest is like.'

'It can't all be local,' said Joshua. 'It must be from all around the world. There's enough here to keep a medium-sized country going for a good long time.'

'That's about right. There aren't many diamonds left in the ground in Australia, none at all if you believe the Iwelongas.

Certainly, all that was around here has been mined. Parts of these caverns were dug out to form access tunnels for that mining. Other chambers have been formed naturally by rivers that used to course through here. This chamber is all natural. The Hall of the Gods, they call it.'

Maggie had picked out a larger diamond from Dingo's hand and was staring into it. It was the size of her little fingernail, huge by the standards of most others she had seen, bettered only by the one she had taken out of Taylor's luggage which was three or four times that size.

'No chance that Sid and Nelly's kid made it all from old beer bottles?' *Sarcasm, Maggie. Stop it.*

'Why would he do that when there's all the real stuff here?'

'Impressive,' said Joshua who was examining one of the diamonds using an eye-piece that Dingo had handed him. 'Look, Dingo: you brought us here, now tell us what you know, please.'

'It's a long story.'

'Make it one of your short long stories, Dingo,' said Maggie. 'Don't forget we've got visitors nearby.'

Maggie had listened to many of Dingo's stories before. He was a good raconteur, able to embellish the most mundane of occurrences so that they seemed like they were the main point of the story. Frankie had maintained that if Kenneth Williams and Muhammad Ali had met and been able (and so inclined) to have a baby between them, and then decided to bring it up in the outback, Dingo Derek would have been that love child. The fact that Dingo was white and had never seen a 'Carry-on' film in his life, did not, in Maggie's eyes, make the liaison any less credible. Because Frankie had a point.

For a start, Dingo had never been able to sit down when he told a story. It always involved a lot of waving around and other movements which could not be contained within the confines of a chair. He was also prone to exaggeration. Whereas Ali would always do it to exaggerate his qualities, Dingo would do anything to make the yarn more interesting. And for someone who sometimes went for months without speaking to anyone, he had, as Ben pointed out, an unusual and wide vocabulary, many words and phrases which would, no doubt, have surprised even Kenneth.

Maggie decided to sit down on a crate as Dingo began.

'So, about six months ago, I'm on a rare sortie over to Dyson's Creek to take a look at a knackered crane that old Pete the Crap has just got in. This crane is a good hundred feet high,' he stretched his arm above his head and stood on tiptoes, 'enough metal in there to build a dozen harbour bridges.'

Maggie saw Ben's mouth begin to open up ready to form a question. She raised a warning finger and he closed it again.

Dingo continued, pacing around as he spoke, his hands and arms gesticulating at any word or phrase that could possibly be gesticulated. 'Pete the Crap gets all sorts of stuff, most of it bloody useless, hence his name, but this time he's come good. I've paid him his four hundred bucks,' – he dealt out the imaginary money much like a croupier at a casino would deal a deck of cards – 'arranged delivery, and I'm about to get back into my plane when

107

I'm approached by a woman. She's dressed up in a smart suit, looking swankier than a wombat in a dickie bow.' Maggie didn't have a readily available wombat-in-a-dickie-bow image to compare with, but, had she had, Dingo's quick impression using his fingers to denote the bowtie and a wombat-like facial expression would have been right up there in terms of likeness, she reckoned. Dingo continued: 'Very unusual to see anyone round there not covered in dust or other crap, so she stood out. She asked me if I did tourist trips in my plane. I told her I did not. She said it was a shame, as she had clients who would be very interested. Then she asked if I had any dealings with the indigenous tribes in the area. "Nah," I said. "They keep themselves to themselves, just like I do." I shoulda' added "like you oughta", coz she then started twittering on, asking what I knew about the lie of the land, that I musta spotted all sorts of unusual features in the local landscape while I was up in my plane, and asked whether I'd heard any rumours about unusual happenings. In the end, I just got in the plane and buggered off. Before you ask: the woman was in her sixties, I reckon. A Pom, short and got a sour-looking face, like a Tassy devil sucking a gooseberry.' He put his hand at waist height and sucked his cheeks in before adding, 'Gave me a name: Fiona. Fiona Mapeland.'

'Are you sure that was her name?' said Bill.

'I didn't tattoo it on my arse, but I'm pretty sure.'

Bill and Joshua looked as worried as Maggie felt.

'What's significant about that name?' asked Ben cautiously.

'It's the alias that Sheldon used in the Service,' said Bill.

'If this was six months ago,' said Joshua, 'Sheldon was safely locked up in a secure unit then.'

If it was Sheldon, it was surprising that she had had the temerity to use a name similar to her alias. It was well known amongst Service personnel, and the surname had often been used by 'wags' in the office to sign off birthday and leaving cards. Sheldon would have been aware of that.

'I'm just passing on what she said,' said Dingo.

'Go on, Dingo,' Maggie said calmly.

'I head back home and forget about her. Until one day, about three months later, I hear a car stopping a little way down my drive. I look out the window and a bloke is walking towards the house. It's pretty hot and he's wearing a three-piece tweed suit and a deerstalker hat. He only needed a pipe, a cape and to be waving a ticket for the Orient Express to complete the picture.'

Ben opened his mouth again, no doubt about to correct Dingo's working knowledge of European detectives, but closed it before Maggie needed to remind him.

'I let him walk up to my door, greet him in a friendly enough manner, and ask him what the buggering hell he's doing on my property. He says nothing, just opens up a briefcase. Inside, on a velvet cushion, is a boomerang with the words 'Watch out' inscribed on it. I give him a *what the fu...* – sorry, Maggie – a *what the goodness is that* look, but he just closes the case and turns away, real smug, like an emu who's just won the New South Wales Miss Lovely Legs competition. The following day, I walk out the back for my morning coffee and there's a date written in the dirt:

109

24th November. I reckon, to start with, that it's the Iwelongas, maybe just giving me a gentle reminder about the end of the world. When I speak to Sid a couple of days later, he denies all knowledge of it.'

'So, since then, you've been expecting visitors,' said Bill.

'Sort of. Two unusual encounters in a short space of time. I'm pretty laid back about these things usually, but there are a lot of strange people around, which is why I'm happy with my own company generally. I figured the bloke was some crackpot.'

'You didn't tell the police?'

'Yeah, course I did. Miss Marple, our local copper, agreed with me. He said...'

'He?' Ben obviously could not help himself.

'Thinks he's some sort of great detective, hence the nickname. He agreed that it was either a crackpot or a boomerang salesman. If it was the latter, I should expect him to keep coming back, he said. Bloody hilarious is Miss Marple. Could be a threat of some sort, but if I didn't know anyone who would want to hurt me, then best forget it. So I did. It was only when you arrived out of the blue that it really got me thinking. I know what Maggie and Frankie used to do. And when those cars turned up, I thought things were getting jittery.'

'But we told you we were in trouble last night,' said Maggie. 'Didn't it occur to you to tell us about all this then?'

'Yeah, of course.' Dingo's eyebrows lowered. He was still clutching the fistful of stones, and he now emptied them carefully back into the open crate. Joshua and Bill returned theirs and

Maggie reached over to put her one back in too. Solemnly, Dingo closed the crate. 'Remember the newspaper article Maggie read and what I said about what the Iwelongas believe?'

'Yes,' answered Maggie. 'That when the last diamond was removed from the ground and taken off Australian soil, the world would end.'

'It's a sacred belief. The Iwelongas think that all these diamonds are important. They would never sell any of them, not even for a shedload of pizza. But that last diamond is the key. If that leaves, it means the gods have given up on them. While it is still here, they have hope. This is a big thing, believe me, to have shared this with you. I wasn't sure I shoulda.'

'We appreciate it, Dingo. You said, "they have hope". Is the last diamond still in Australia?'

'Yeah, but not here. A big bugger – a bigger bugger than the one you and Joshua had – in a cave down south. If that goes, we're all up Jacob's Creek without a corkscrew.'

'Does it have a name other than *bigger bugger*?'

'They call it the Jingdon – from the Iwelongan word for *star*.'

'The Iwelongas know where it is?' asked Maggie.

'Yeah, but they keep it secret. Only the elders of the tribe know. It's the last one ever mined, so they're not going to give it away. Bear in mind what they think would happen if they did.'

'Though they must feel it is in danger because they have a date when the world will end?'

'Yeah, guess so.'

Maggie could not help but feel them turning up like this was probably not helping matters in that respect. And there was something else bothering her. Something she had seen in Sid's kid's picture. She got up from the crate she was sitting on and walked back over to the far wall. The others followed.

'What is it, Maggie?' asked Bill as she started to examine the pictures again. She honed in on the section with the children on their mobile phones.

'What's Sid's kid called, Dingo?'

'Brian.'

She heard a snigger from Ben which turned into an embarrassed cough.

'Brian?' she repeated.

'Yeah.'

'Is that him on the phone?'

Dingo took some glasses out of his top pocket and examined the picture. 'I reckon it is.'

'Have the Iwelongas ever lost any diamonds?'

'I know where you're going with this. Yeah, they had their own little big bugger which they kept here. Although it's not the Jingdon, they cherished it as if it was; a symbol if you like. They believed by protecting the one here it would keep the Jingdon safe too. Unfortunately, the diamond here went missing six months ago. Probably brought on the prediction about the end of the world. I don't like to ask too much about it, to be honest, in case they're right.'

'Could be the diamond we exchanged,' said Joshua.

112

'Could be,' said Maggie. 'What do you mean by went missing, Dingo?'

'Disappeared. It should have been with the new leader. Each time the leadership changes, they have a ceremony in here to hand it over, and then the leader puts it somewhere safe, away from the others, in their own secret place. It went missing in one of Sid's weeks.'

'I'm surprised Sid has had another turn at being leader,' said Ben. 'Responsibility and accountability and all that. Sorry if that sounds a bit harsh.'

'They believe in fate. They trust the collective leadership to do their best to protect all of them, but if fate intervenes, well... that's fair dinkum. It's like the bigger bugger. It's still hidden, but if that goes, well that's fate too. The world will end.'

'Any idea of the value of the – what's it called – the Jingdon?' asked Bill.

'Don't think that one has ever been officially valued.'

'The one we got back from Taylor was worth millions,' said Joshua.

Dingo shrugged. 'The Jingdon is nearly twice the size. Worth a fair bit, I reckon then.'

Maggie, despite herself, was still intrigued by the pictures. 'Who is that other girl near Brian? Not the Milo Cyprus one.'

There was a cough from Ben; a correction to ignore.

Dingo leaned in. 'Ah, that's a girl from outside the tribe Brian used to hang around with. Helped him with some of the drawings.'

'Used to?'

'Yeah, Brian went on walkabout, part of the growing-up ritual before he turns eighteen, then they stopped hanging out as much. I'm... er... I'm not sure why. I should, but I... um, I don't.' Dingo seemed a little unsure of himself. 'Good kids, both of them,' he added hastily.

'How long was Brian gone?'

'About three months.'

'Did he start before or after Sherlock Poirot turned up with his gun?'

Dingo scratched his head. 'Ah, a few days after, I reckon.'

'And when did the diamond here... does that one have a name, by the way?'

'Nah. Little bigger bugger will do.'

'Okay. When did the little bigger bugger go missing?'

'A week or so after that probably.'

'Is Brian back?'

'Yeah, with Sid and Nelly. He'll be with them now.'

'Dingo...'

He raised a hand. 'Hold on a sec, I get it.' He took a deep breath in. 'You think that this Mapeland woman heard something about a hoard of diamonds in the area and decided to take a look for herself. When I was unhelpful, she got the bloke in the stupid hat to spook me. That didn't work so they got Brian to steal the little bigger bugger the tribes here and give it to Taylor. Taylor tried to sell it abroad, but you guys intercepted it. Mapeland's made a connection between Maggie and the diamond and is trying to get hold of it, pissing you about along the way with all these clues on

114

notes and articles. They're going to come barging in any minute and scoop the bloody lot, including the little bigger bugger which they think you've still got, and force the tribe to reveal the exact whereabouts of the Jingdon. The fact that the date the Iwelongas think the world is going to end is the same day as this Sheldon's birthday is a nice twist to add to the intrigue.' He took another deep breath and looked at each one of them, before finishing with, 'Am I right?'

Maggie was only aware her mouth was open when she spotted that her three companions had theirs open too. She shut it as soon as she twigged that Dingo was looking at her now. He had articulated all of her thoughts, all of her suspicions, and this had all been stated in one nice, surprisingly short, unDingo-like summary.

There was only one thing he had not covered and she was about to raise that very point when Joshua chipped in. 'If Dingo's right and Sheldon is behind this, how could she have been here six months ago organising it all when she was in prison on the other side of the world? We all saw her taken away to the cells in court.'

'Unless that wasn't her who escaped,' said Bill. 'I think it's possible Sheldon never actually went to jail. She could have done a switch with a double and that double has been serving her time.'

'Why would Sheldon be so brazen and see Dingo six months ago when she should have been in jail?' said Ben. 'Wouldn't she prefer to lie low so she could never be connected to the crime if it goes wrong?'

'If it is Sheldon, this is typical manipulative behaviour,' said Maggie. 'Playing games, showing off. She's got people like Taylor doing her dirty work while she controls things in the background. She'd love the fact that we're involved too – a perfect chance for revenge at the same time as making a fortune.'

Ben became suddenly animated. 'We've led them to you, haven't we, Dingo? We've put you and the Iwelongas in danger.'

'Possibly, but you weren't to know.'

'I'm not so sure,' said Bill. 'I doubt we've been followed. We took so many precautions to go undercover, you two especially.' He pointed at Maggie and Joshua. 'It's more likely, as Dingo said, that they've found us through someone in the tribe working on their behalf.'

'I didn't say one of the Iwelongas was working for anyone,' said Dingo.

'You said that Brian stole the diamond from Sid's hiding place.'

'Nah. I said that I reckon you all think that. I don't. None of the Iwelongas would do that. This is sacred ground you're standing in. These diamonds are sacred too. They would never give them away, just like they would never let on about the exact whereabouts of the Jingdon.'

Bill's expression was not the look of someone who had been convinced. 'Everyone has their price, Dingo.'

'Not the Iwelongas. I've always found them to be straightforward and honest.'

Two diamonds, together worth millions and millions, one Taylor had and was safely back in the hands of the authorities, the other also safe (for now) somewhere in a cave in the south. Add in the substantial stash they had just been looking at, it was no wonder that people were sniffing around. There were a few moments when no one said anything. There had been so many points raised and questions asked that Maggie had lost track as to who might be able to provide the answers.

It was almost a welcome distraction when the ground they stood on was rocked by a sudden ear-shattering explosion above their heads.

~ ~ ~

Chapter 11

Joshua tried to say something, but his words were drowned out by another huge bang. This time dust, like red snowflakes, started to fall from the high ceiling.

'Are you sure this place is strong enough to withhold this, Dingo?' Maggie spluttered as she inhaled part of the dust cloud that had started to form around them.

'Yeah, no worries. A tassie's fart couldn't touch it. This crap falling around is just the loose bits reacting to the explosion. That was pretty heavy stuff, but we'll be fine.'

'What about Sid, Nelly, and the others?' asked Maggie.

'They'll have made themselves scarce. They'll be alright.'

'Can our attackers get in?'

'Even if they find the entrance we came in through, they won't get be able to break open the hatches. This place is safe.'

There were two smaller explosions, and then it went quiet.

'They're trying to scare us,' said Bill. 'It's not an all-out attack – just a few warning shots.'

'So what do we do?' said Maggie. 'Sit here and wait it out?'

'Okay, well, we have options,' said Joshua. 'Option one: sit and wait it out. Option two: make a run for it. Option three: launch a counterattack. The first two options are the safest, presuming that option two is viable. I'm assuming, Dingo, there will be other ways out of here, if this network is as vast as you have indicated?'

'You assume right, Joshua. Apart from back the way we came through the hatches, we have a shortish way out which is a quarter a mile or so in that direction.' He pointed to the other end of the chamber through which they had come. 'Fairly straightforward that way, but comes out near the road you came in on. The other route is in the same direction, but longer.'

'How much longer?' Maggie asked.

'About a mile. Not easy either. Quite tight in places. Hope you're all alright with claustrophobia if it comes to it?'

Joshua and Bill did not, as Maggie would have expected for trained agents, react to Dingo's question about tight spaces. She was pleased to see Ben seemed okay with it too, so that did give them a viable alternative. The shorter route was dangerous since it would come out close to their attackers. They discussed the advantages and disadvantages of staying put and, although it did allow them to remain safe and possibly enable them to protect the diamonds, it seemed the least attractive alternative on the basis it did not move things forward at all, something they were all bought into, much to Maggie's satisfaction and pride. Maggie was impressed to hear Ben raising this exact point and dismissing the safer options. He had guts, no doubt about that.

It brought them onto the most interesting – and dangerous – option: the counterattack. Maggie was intrigued as to how, if at all, this might work with just the two guns they had between them against what, judging by the noise up above, had sounded like serious armoury. Bill voiced the same concern.

'But the good thing is that they won't be expecting any counterattack,' said Joshua. 'And we don't have to actually compete with them; merely threaten them so they think we could.'

'Scare them?' said Ben.

'Exactly.'

'How?'

'Dingo, did you put the shortwave radio back down here after you were fiddling with it last night?'

'Yeah, mate. It's working fine. I put it by the main entrance.'

'What are the chances, Bill, of them picking up any communication from us? I'm hoping none of their digital equipment would be tuned into shortwave?'

'So far they have been pretty thorough if these are the same people who have been threatening us,' said Bill. 'The chances they have compatibility with relatively outmoded communication interfaces are minimal. I would expect them to have been using some sort of interception software that configures to broadband and mobile data.'

Maggie and Dingo exchanged blank looks. 'Does that last sentence mean it's a yes?' asked Dingo.

'It's a maybe,' said Bill.

'We'll have to risk it,' said Joshua.

'What are you thinking, Joshua love?' said Maggie.

'Well, that depends on whether Dingo gives me the answer I want to the next question. The Iwelongas have shortwave too, Dingo, right?'

'Some. Six of 'em have shortwave radios. Wouldn't be without them. They use them to order their pizza at Big Al's.'

'So Al has access too?' said Joshua.

'Yeah and Pete the Crap. Psycho Simon uses his one occasionally. I'm sure they'd all be willing to help out.'

'Psycho Simon?' asked Ben. 'As in psycho meaning crazy?'

Dingo nodded. Ben looked like he was about to ask him to elaborate, but was interrupted by Joshua. 'I was thinking we could contact the Iwelongas to arrange some sort of diversion. Can they do it safely so they wouldn't be harmed, Dingo?'

'They'd do that, no worries. No one would get near them. They know every inch of this countryside. But I reckon the other blokes would want to do their bit too. They're solid fellahs and handy. Big Al can hit anything with a pizza cutter from fifty yards.' Dingo smiled to indicate the last part was a joke, but the way he spoke showed his apparent affection and loyalty towards these neighbours at least, if not some others nearby. Maggie was beginning to wonder whether he really was the recluse he claimed to be.

'They could contact the local authorities, couldn't they?' said Ben. 'Surely, attacking smallholdings is illegal?'

'No police,' said Joshua forcefully. 'Until we know exactly who and what we're up against, we can't trust the authorities.'

'There's an opportunity to be taken here,' said Maggie. 'This lot attacking us know quite a bit about what's going on. We need to speak to them, and I think I know how we can do that without getting hurt.'

It was a risky plan, but so were most plans Maggie had been party to in the Service. After she outlined her intentions and it was broadly agreed, they fleshed out the details. The counter manoeuvre would begin shortly, at first light.

Dingo would coordinate things from the chamber directly by the entrance where there was the best signal for the radio. Ben, despite his request to be more actively involved, would stay and assist him. Dingo knew the lie of the land and could judge and explain where people were. He also had the Iwelongas' trust, a vital aspect if the plan was to work. The Iwelongas would arrange a diversion. How they did it was up to them. This would enable Bill and Joshua to make their way out to the top via the other shorter exit to provide backup for Maggie. They would be armed and carry a small shortwave radio device to keep in touch with Dingo. For extra security, Dingo had suggested he communicate on a different band setting for the Iwelongas. It was hoped that they could create enough chaos to put their attackers on the back foot and enable Maggie to get into position to 'have a quiet word,' as she put it.

Maggie's role – information gathering – would put her close to or in the firing line. She had always liked treading that point between being safe and not at all safe. To be on that just safe side took a lot of skill. A misplaced word here or a misjudgement on timing there could result in disastrous consequences. Renowned for her guile, tact, stealth, and discretion, she had always prided herself on her ability to spot subtle nuances of character or behaviour that other colleagues might miss.

None of these skills would be needed today, however.

It was hard to be subtle and discrete if you were inside a tank.

In 1996, Maggie had spent three months as one of the Service representatives on the Multinational Division which co-ordinated operations in Bosnia. She was tasked with building a list of contacts who could tell her about the movements of militia gangs in the area. At one point, when leads went cold because of the heavy bombardments of the town where she was trying to establish those contacts, it involved some downtime and she was forced to withdraw back behind allied lines. It was a boring and frustrating time for her to start with. That was until – with the assistance of a kind-hearted sergeant in charge of armoured vehicle maintenance – she learnt to drive a tank. She had never forgotten how to do it, even though she had never had cause before to make use of that specialised skill. Now she could, providing she could get up into it.

'Sid says they're all set,' said Dingo as they gathered around the main entrance below the hatches. He pushed the button down on the mouthpiece and readied himself to make contact with Joshua and Bill to check if they were in position at the other exit. Maggie had seen the ancient-looking transmitter when Dingo had been trying it out in the house the night before. It had taken her back to the way they used to do things in the Service when, if she was lucky, she would have had a techie on hand nearby to deal with any issues. More likely she would have been out in the field on her own, trying to find a signal strong enough to make contact with base. Her own technical expertise back then extended to twiddling knobs and banging on it. She had tried the same technique on the iPad Joshua had given her. Lacking knobs, it was nowhere near as satisfying.

Joshua's crackly voice responded to Dingo's query. 'We're above ground, Dingo, ten yards from the hatch and in the shrubs you suggested. Tell us when Sid and Nelly have started their diversion. Over.'

'No need. I think you'll realise. Over.' Dingo changed the band setting and spoke again. 'Sid, Nelly... go when you're ready... Over.'

There was an eerie silence during which Maggie thought that maybe the Iwelongas had not received the instruction. That was until she heard Joshua's voice coming through again. 'I think we can safely say the diversion is in progress. I can see people moving to check it out. There's no one near your exit. Send Maggie out, but with caution. Over.'

Maggie needed no more telling. 'Help me up this ladder, Ben love, will you? That's it; give my backside a good shove. Don't be shy.' She heard Dingo confirm receipt of Joshua's message as Ben, with impressive gusto, put his shoulder firmly into a position where she had no other choice other than to go upwards. Within a couple of seconds, she found the top of her head was almost touching the hatch. She heard Ben press the switch and the hatch opened slowly. She whispered down. 'You can take your shoulder out of there now, Ben love... if you can. Ohh... that's it. Thank you. Close the hatch behind me, won't you?' She scrabbled out onto the ground and paused there to catch her breath. If there had been anyone threatening there, she was a sitting duck, but there was not. It did not take long for her to realise why.

In the breaking dawn, Maggie could make out the backs of figures as they moved away from Dingo's house on foot towards the road that ran at the end of his property. Even with her deteriorating eyesight, two things told her they were heading that way. One: she had not been attacked. Two – and this was the most telling – who would not be interested in checking out a huge neon sign on top of the only hill for miles around that was flashing alternately 'Fuck off out of it' and 'Big Al's Pizza Palace'? She could make out, too, the distant buzz of an engine, the generator she assumed that was powering the sign. Standing neatly on either side of the sign on the slopes of the hill holding spears above their heads were many silhouettes. There was another figure on top of the sign that was very actively jumping up and down, which, Maggie surmised from the erratic nature of it, had to be Psycho Simon. As Dingo had predicted, the Iwelongas, with the help of Pete the Crap and Big Al who, Maggie later found out, had helped drag the sign up there and were now waiting on the other side of the hill in two four-by-fours with engines running, had well and truly diverted their attackers.

She was so impressed that she failed to hear Bill and Joshua appear by her side.

'Looks like we weren't needed then,' said Bill. 'There's no one here. They've obviously scoped Dingo's place, seen it was empty, then been taken in by the little sideshow.'

The neon sign suddenly flashed off.

'Right,' said Joshua, 'hopefully that means the Iwelongas are moving to safety. Our visitors will either follow or some will return back here. Now's your chance to get the tank going, Maggie. We'll join you inside.'

They moved swiftly over to the tank. Maggie stared up; tanks – like top shelves in supermarkets – had looked so much more accessible back in her day.

'Right – son or great-grandson – which one of you has a shoulder with more padding on it than Ben's?'

Gripping a handle and putting her foot onto a step, she pulled up and then felt herself elevated onto the small platform next to the turret. Bill followed her up, opened the hatch, and then with a little more manoeuvring, she was helped down into a dark space.

'Dingo assures me it has fuel in it and it's working,' she said. 'Let's find out.'

Joshua located a switch that turned on the interior light and gave Maggie the view of the controls she needed.

'Can you drive it?' he asked.

'Between us, we'll manage.' She was amazed at how quickly it was coming back to her. How was it that sometimes she could remember obscure things like a crash course on how to drive a tank from years ago, and at other times she could not remember if she had paid the milkman the previous day?

'We might not be able to do all the fancy stuff like going backwards and forwards...' – she smiled at Joshua's sudden anxious look – 'but I reckon we can do enough to shake them up.

Now, this button here should start the wotsit, once I've pulled this thingamy up.'

'Don't get all technical on us,' said Bill sarcastically.

'Love this! Not a computer in sight. There!' She laughed out loud as the engine roared into life. 'They'll definitely know we're here now. Which one of you wants to go up and operate the gun from the turret?'

'I assumed you could do that from down here,' said Joshua. 'You said you could operate this thing on your own.'

'I said I could drive it on my own. My plan was to get it near them, stop and then have a chat. I'm not a bloody octopus.'

'So what happens now, then?'

'You two drive and I'll stick my head above the parapet when we get in a good position.'

'Joshua,' said Bill, 'you ever driven a tank?'

'On a game using a console, yes. I suspect this is different.'

'Now, if I'm right,' said Maggie, 'these early Steelhearts were still fitted with hydrodynamic transmissions in the double differential. So much simpler than the double differentials on the Panzers. Not that I've ever driven one of those, but I've heard that it was a right pain applying the brakes all the time to keep the idlers fixed.'

She took a moment to enjoy her relatives' blank looks. She loved them both dearly, but she had to admit she had enjoyed the last few days, being more in her comfort zone away from technologies she did not understand. It did no harm to keep the younger generations on their toes.

127

'Basically, press this to slow the left track down to make it go left, and that to go right. Both at the same time and it stops altogether. Remember to take your foot off the pedal to decelerate.'

'What pedal?'

'You'll work it out. Now, let me see if I can remember how the turret swivels.'

The low morning sun was in her eyes as she carefully poked her head through and above the turret. She was impressed at how quickly the boys had got the tank to move, and she was even more pleased that it was finally moving in the right direction towards the road and no longer towards Dingo's veranda. She had got a quick glimpse of the chair she had sat in just last night as they watched the sunset. She had enjoyed a moment of peace and reflection then. Today she was in charge of a tank. Only in the Service would you get such a contrast.

She could see now, with some relief, that the hill was devoid of people. She just hoped that they had all – including Dingo's non-indigenous friends who were perhaps less familiar with the geography of this part of the near outback –got away safely. Judging by the relatively low numbers of people making their way cautiously towards the tank from the road, a few of their attackers may have been sent off in pursuit. She could make out eight of them left now, spread out more or less in a line. All seemed armed, but there was no sign of the sort of weapon which would have caused the loud explosions earlier. That concerned her a little.

Below her feet, she was aware of Joshua and Bill fighting with the controls. She had forgotten how loud it was inside a tank. In addition to the engine, which reminded her of the clapped-out VW Beetle with a broken exhaust that she and Frankie once owned, there was the thunderous rumble of the tracks, made worse by almost unbearably loud intermittent squeaks. On her last go in a tank, she had been allowed up into the turret on strict instructions not to press any buttons or touch any levers. That had not stopped her from working out what controls might do what. It was fairly basic in principle, it had been explained to her, but took a lot of experience and practice to master; essential prerequisites if you wanted to get a gun pointing in the right direction and hitting the target. She had a moment to mull on this briefly as she started to do exactly what her instructor had asked her not to do, and found herself and the barrel, rather disappointingly – though maybe unsurprisingly – facing in the opposite direction to which they were travelling.

At the same time, the tank came to an abrupt halt and she was left staring down the right end of the barrel of a gun (for a change) at a solitary man, dressed in tweeds with his hands in the air. By his feet was a gun. Maggie took a glance around to find out how far they had travelled. They were still about a hundred meters from the house, but it was behind them now. To her left, fifty metres or so away was the long drive. The engine had stalled and all the noise had stopped; a blessed relief as she remembered now why tank operators wore earphones. She was left with an unpleasant ringing.

There was a nudge in her back as Joshua joined her.

129

'Ting-a-ling-a-ting-ting,' he said addressing the man.

'What did you say to him?' she said. The man in tweeds was static other than his mouth moved after Joshua had spoken. 'I can't hear you. My ears...'

Joshua repeated the sentence. This time he made her look at him as he spoke. 'I told him to ting-a-ling-a-ting-ling-ting.'

Maggie stuck a finger in her left ear and wriggled it. She then felt for her hearing aid in her right and fiddled with the controls. 'That's a bit better, I think. Repeat please.'

'I told him to tell his men to put their guns down.'

'Oh, right. Good idea. Have they?'

'Not yet. Bill?'

Bill clambered up past them and stood behind her on the front of the tank, his gun, like Joshua's sweeping slowly across the men at the front – a potential standoff until he repeated Joshua's instructions, loudly and with some force. There was a 'Do as he says,' from the man in tweeds on the other side of the tank which brought about the desired result. The men started to filter round to stand together, arms aloft, on her side of the tank.

Happy things were under control, at least for now, Maggie kept her eyes on her man. It was time for that chat.

One of the first rules about interrogation techniques that Maggie had learnt when she joined the Service was never to reveal any weaknesses that you, as the interrogator, might have, if solid information about the suspect and their activities was lacking.

'Make up something general about them or their associates, if you know nothing at all,' her trainer had said. 'The subject has to think that you are not desperate for information otherwise it might harden their resolve.' In this case, Maggie was one hundred percent sure this was Emanuel Taylor, the same man who had visited Dingo with the diamond not long ago. Thus, she knew quite a lot about him, but she had several theories about his role in all of this. These theories needed fleshing out so that the truth could be established.

The second rule on interrogation was to ensure that you put yourself in a position where you had good leverage over your subject. The third rule was connected to the second rule in that it stated that if the agent did not actually have good leverage, bluff it so that the subject thinks you have. Being behind the barrel of a gun belonging to a sixty-ton tank that was aimed at the subject met the second rule, she reasoned. The fact that Dingo had dismantled its ability to fire anything meant that she was now in the realm of applying rule three. There was also a rule thirteen which she hoped would not come into effect.

'What are you doing here, Tweedy?'

His voice was as posh as his tweed suit. 'Tweedy? What do you mean, Tweedy?'

'You prefer to be called Taylor?'

There was no reply.

'Tell us or that three-piece suit of yours will end up being in considerably more than three pieces, Mr. Taylor.'

Maggie had always been taught by her parents to treat people fairly and not be too hasty to make judgements. In the world of espionage, hasty judgements about character were exactly what were needed in many situations, and she did not have much time to weigh up Taylor now. But even if she had had a week to spend getting to know him, she suspected she would have come to the same conclusion: Emmanuel Taylor was a bit of a prick, evidenced by the way he spoke down to her now with a sneer that people who have a sense of entitlement tend to use freely.

'I am, indeed, Emmanuel Taylor. I've come to get my diamond back, plus any others that happen to be around this Godforsaken dump of a place. Make no mistake, old woman: we will do this, regardless of this little intervention of yours.'

Maggie ignored the jibe (and the urge to go below, start up the tank again and use the tracks to press his suit while Taylor was still wearing it). Instead, she asked, 'What makes you think there are diamonds here?'

'Don't play games. I know who you are, Agent Matheson. I know that you know what your friend is sitting on: it's an absolute goldmine.'

'Goldmine? I'm confused. Gold or diamonds?' Maggie had a quick check to the side as the group of men that Bill had rounded up came into full view, their hands on their heads. 'You're wasting your time here, Taylor. Your boss won't like that.' She was fishing for signs of Sheldon's involvement. Would he bite?

'My boss? I don't have a boss. I'm my own man.'

'I didn't lure you here so you could waste my time on these lies. I suggest you talk, or your tailor, Taylor, will be looking for a new customer.'

'Lure us here? What are you talking about? You didn't lure me here. I found you. I have means, contacts...' *Sheldon, in other words.* 'As I said, I am my own man.' *Definitely Sheldon.*

'Why the heavy artillery?'

'What?'

'Look around at the enormous potholes you've created.'

Before she could probe further, he changed tack. 'Why is your name on the back of the tank?'

'What?'

'Your name; it's on the tank'

'Is it?'

'With something else that I can't read. That's what I was walking up to look at before you turned that gun around.'

'Right, well...'

'This could be a trick,' whispered Joshua.

Taylor could well be playing for time, but still... Maggie had felt that small twinge in her stomach, that warning that something was wrong. 'Best check. Do you mind, Joshua?'

Joshua slid down the rear of the tank, keeping his gun trained on Taylor while Bill kept an eye on the others. He studied the back, looked up at Maggie, and nodded. He then looked down again and ducked in a little closer. His eyes widened, then, without hesitation, he jumped up onto the tank again, and said in a voice loud enough so that only they could hear, 'Back in the tank! Now!'

There were a few seconds when Maggie lost track of what was happening. Before she could react, she found herself being bundled back into the main body of the tank by Joshua, closely followed by Bill.

'Why did you stop me talking to Taylor? What's the rush?'

'We need to get going,' Joshua said urgently as Bill closed the hatch. 'Start her up. Quickly!'

Somewhat confused, Maggie flicked a couple of switches. With a roar, the tank burst into life. Joshua took hold of the controls and, with several jolts, they were rolling once more.

'Taylor was right,' shouted Joshua above the din. 'The tank does have your name painted on it... and a bit more.'

'What else did it say?' asked Bill as he checked the hatch was secure.

'In tiny letters, it said, "Take aim... Fire!"'

Maggie was now well into rule thirteen of interrogation techniques, which was applied across all regulations and areas of work. Rule thirteen basically reminded agents that whatever procedure they were hoping to follow could be thrown out of the window by unexpected, half-expected, or even expected events. In such circumstances, it said, rather unhelpfully, that the agent should apply common sense.

She wished she had applied rule thirteen earlier. As they talked to Taylor, Maggie was troubled by the fact that there was no sign of the heavy weaponry they had heard from within Dingo's shelter. As agents, Joshua and Bill would have been sensitive to that, which was probably why Joshua had acted so promptly after reading the back of the tank. It was apparent that the main threat was coming not from Taylor but elsewhere. Maggie was now inclined to believe him when he said he was his own man – his own man being manipulated by another woman.

All of this went through Maggie's head as the tank swerved its way this way and that across Dingo's not insubstantial property...

... until rule thirteen hit them squarely on the front end of the tank and threw it, and them, onto its side.

~ ~ ~

Chapter 12

It was dark inside the tank. Someone's elbow, by the feel of the shape, hardness, and neatness with which it fitted, was in Maggie's left ear. Her legs had someone on top of them, possibly the same person, but it was a little early to tell who. She felt the pressure come off her legs, indicating that either Joshua or Bill was okay to move about. If that was the case, she reasoned that they were soon likely to take their elbow out of her ear, unless – and she could not imagine why – there was a pressing reason to keep it in there. In her confused state, she summarised that, since the elbow remained in her ear, it meant that one of Bill and Joshua was unconscious.

'Mum! Mum, are you okay?' It was Bill. She could hear the tension in his voice: not panic, just worry.

'I think I'm alright. I'll find out when I move.'

'Thank goodness for that. Take care as you move in case you've hurt yourself.'

Maggie groaned as she tried to gently shift her head from underneath the elbow, then stopped, conscious that the arm she was under might be hurt, even broken. 'Can you help me? I think Joshua is on top of me.'

'Don't think I am,' said Joshua's voice from further away.

'Then kindly explain how your elbow is in my ear.' Wasn't that the title of a Lonnie Donegan song from the 1960s? *Note to self,*

136

Maggs: check if you have concussion. That's not a logical thought at this stage.

'Don't think it's mine either,' said Bill.

They were interrupted by a clang followed by a loud creak, and a shaft of light lit up most of the interior. It was enough, as Maggie eased her ear away from the elbow, for her to see that it was not an elbow that was the culprit, but a lever with a knob on. As the tank had fallen over, she had been thrown into a corner, leaving her head partly wedged up against the controls. As she wriggled about, she gulped as it dawned on her that she could have been much more seriously hurt had her head hit any of the controls directly. Judging by the angle they were all at, it was a miracle they were alive, let alone conscious.

She could not face getting up yet, even if she had been able to. 'What about you two?' she asked.

'I'm okay,' said Bill, closely followed by confirmation from Joshua.

Another voice – male – came from the source of light. It was not Taylor's; there was a thick accent to it, possibly French or Spanish.

'You come out. We 'ave lots of guns.'

Even if they could find their weapons, they were in a position that not even the Sundance Kid would have tried to shoot his way out of.

'Understood,' Joshua called back. 'We will come out peacefully.'

It was far from peaceful, as far as Maggie was concerned. Painful, awkward, and extremely stressful, would have been how she would have described it. For a start, she could not stand; it was far too disorientating with the tank being on its side, a problem compounded by the fact it was at a slight angle too. There seemed to be obstacles everywhere she looked. In the end, Bill, who she worked out must have fallen closest to her, managed to part drag and part carry her lengthways to the hatch and she ended up being passed through and out, before being lowered to the ground by other willing hands.

'I need to sit down,' she said the second she felt her feet touch the floor. She had lost one shoe and her head felt like she had been through a fast spin cycle at the laundrette. She knew what that was like as she had been put in one once – or something similar: a tumble dryer. That was a case she did not like to dwell on.

She began to slide down but was propped up again by two sets of strong arms.

'No, we must move away. Se tank might be an explosion.'

French, she decided as she part-walked, part-floated across the rough ground. The accent was from Monty Python and the Holy Grail, the final castle scene, she decided. Another random thought. It was possible that the recent exertions and excitement might have been getting to her because the next thing she knew she was sitting in the very chair she had sat in the night before on the veranda. This time there was no cold beer and friendly smile on offer.

Taylor pulled up a stool and sat down opposite Maggie. Miraculously, after several draws on the glass of water that had been thrust (reluctantly – she had had to play the 'old lady card' quite forcibly) into her hand, she was feeling not as bad as she should have done. Surviving rolling about inside a tank chalked off another of her ninety lives she had claimed from ten fictitious cats (Korky the Cat, Felix, Garfield, Top Cat plus any five from the Aristocats she needed to make up the numbers). Standing either side of her, two armed guards looked on as Taylor adjusted his seat awkwardly, flicking the bottom of his jacket from underneath him, frowning as the stool wobbled slightly.

Eventually, he said smugly: 'Now, what were we discussing before we were so rudely interrupted?'

She ignored the question. 'What have you done with Bill and Joshua?' Her concern was not purely operational. Having a son and a great-grandson working in such a dangerous line of work was not stress-free.

'They're being held until I have a chance to have a proper conversation with them, though that may not be necessary. I thought I'd start with you. See if you can give me what I want.'

That superiority (inferiority?) complex she had decided straight after meeting him was evident again. 'I'm right. Definitely a bit of a prick, this one.'

'What?'

'Sorry, did I say that out loud?' *Yes, Maggs, you did.*

'I'll ignore that, for now. But I suggest you don't mess with me, Agent Matheson.'

'I won't.' *You will, Maggs. You know you will, but easy does it.* Taylor was not the most threatening of adversaries she had come across. Still, she was not yet feeling one hundred percent, so she would need to be careful how she played this.

139

'Now, let's discuss these diamonds in more detail. I have some demands: firstly, give me back the diamond that you took in Singapore. Secondly, I know there is a huge stash somewhere around here. Tell me where the diamond and that stash are, and we can all pack up and go home.'

Maggie paused as she studied his features more closely. His file back in the UK had said he was forty-seven, but he looked older than that. There was no sign of the hat which Dingo had spoken about when he had paid him a visit, but the tweeds certainly gave him a 'distinctive' look. Dingo had not mentioned his moustache. Maybe he had not noticed it, which was understandable because it was pencil thin. He had thick swept-back hair, grey at the sides with specks here and there. His face was sallow and she wondered, because of it, whether he spent a lot of time out of the sun. Now and then, he used his finger and thumb to scratch either side of the fleshy skin between his nostrils. It was an unpleasant habit, one she decided to hold against him. The right eyebrow would lift occasionally, something she normally found attractive in men, but with Taylor, it seemed forced – a deliberate attempt to appear enigmatic. *Or constipated*, she decided spitefully. When he spoke, his head tilted back a little and he looked down at her. *You were right to call him a prick, Maggs: he does think he's better than you. He thinks he's better than everyone.* Without the annoying habits, and take twenty years off, he might have been handsome. He reminded her of someone famous, but she could not think who it was.

'Do you know anything about the threats to my family?'

'Ah, now that would be telling.'

'Telling is precisely what I'd like you to do.'

'Later, perhaps, if you tell me where the diamonds are.'

She was tempted. Anything to make sure they were safe, but there was a lot at stake here, including the future of the tribe. It was not her call, at this stage, so she went down a different route.

'Aren't you worried, Mr. Taylor?'

'About what?'

'That you're not in control. Okay, I see you've done your research... to an extent. This area is renowned for diamonds. You've visited the property to try to unsettle the owner. You've got an impressive gang of hoods who seem to do your bidding; no doubt enticed by riches you have promised them. You've been to London to sell a diamond and found a customer in the Far East who wants it. Maybe they've helped finance some of your fellas. You may even have people who can do fancy things with the internet; tap into... into...' Maggie searched for the word 'servers' in her brain, not realising that, although it might have passed through several times, it had resolutely refused to stop anywhere convenient where she could access it. '... things,' she finished, trying not to sound frustrated. 'I admit: you did a good job. Joshua and I thought we had done enough to lose you in Sydney, but we obviously hadn't. I thought, at first, that she had supported you. Given you access to certain systems. That you were in cahoots. But you don't know her, do you? She's doing it all without your knowledge. Am I right?'

'My dear woman, what are you talking about?'

Maggie paused for a second, and then blurted out: 'Leslie Philips!'

'What?'

'Leslie Philips. Did those doctor films in the 1960s. Smarmy character.'

'What about him?'

'You remind me... No, nothing. Ignore me.' She knew she was right though. He was the spit of him. 'You were as surprised as we were to see my name on the tank.'

'Yes, that was a bit of a surprise.' He turned his head to one side and gave her a strange look before touching his nostrils again and asking, 'So you didn't paint words on the back?'

'No. Why would I write "Take aim: Fire" inside a tank I was inside?'

'That's what it said? No wonder you left suddenly.'

'Exactly.'

'One of our chaps must have hit your tank.'

'Did you tell them to?'

A flicker of doubt. 'I had backup in position, ready.'

'With enough firepower to knock over a tank? Ask them.'

Taylor waved a finger and one of the guards drew away from Maggie, before disappearing round the corner of the veranda. She could hear questions being asked and the cackling sound of a radio coming back in response before the guard returned. He shook his head as he stepped back into position, gun still drawn, by his side.

'It appears, Mrs. Matheson, that you may be right. We have someone else on the scene.' The eyebrow went up again, slightly

142

haphazardly, before coming to rest back level with the other one. She thought she could see the left one twitching in excitement as if it wanted to have a go too. But gravity, a lack of left-sided dexterity, and the fact there was no way the right one was going to let it go anywhere in that direction without it, all contrived to defeat it.

'So, what next, Mr. Taylor?'

'Well, as I said, my first job is to persuade you and your buddies to tell me where all the diamonds are. After that, we will see.'

'I'm unlikely to even consider telling you that until I've finished interrogating you.'

'I'm interrogating you. The tables have turned.'

'Of course you are, dear. Now, tell me: how did you keep track of Joshua and me in Sydney?'

'I didn't. I flew into Sydney, got my people together, and then came here, based on information received. Now, stop asking me questions and answer mine.'

'Yes, yes. I'll do my best, of course. What would you like to know? Something about where all the diamonds are, correct?'

'Yes.'

'And you're not worried that someone else is trying to get hold of them too?'

'No... well, yes, but you're going to tell me first, and then we can leave.'

'Someone who managed to manipulate both of us?'

'I've not been manipulated. We had our eyes on this place before. I came here to check how the owner would react to a little provocation.'

'Yes, I heard. A boomerang? What was all that about?'

There was a tiny laugh that stuck in the back of his throat, an attempt at something evil, she decided, that he could not quite manage.

'Oh, just a little something to get him thinking.'

'Got him thinking what a prized prat you were. A boomerang is hardly scary, even with a vague threat engraved on it. Cost a bit too, I'd imagine.'

Taylor looked rather hurt. 'I thought it was a nice touch.'

'Did you do the date in the sand, too?'

'What date?'

'Never mind. You were plainly so intimidating that Dingo forgot all about you.'

'Dingo?'

'Dingo.'

'Who's Dingo?'

'Who's Dingo?'

'Yes, who's Dingo?'

'Dingo Derek.'

'Derek Parfitt?'

'Gosh, you are good. You got that name out of me so quickly.'

Taylor's eyebrows cooperated, in a rare moment of solidarity, with their colleague the brow, to put together a joint statement expressing their complete and utter confusion. 'But I already knew his name was Derek Parfitt.'

'As I said, you're good.'

'He's the registered owner of this place.'

'Dingo?'

'Stop saying Dingo.'

Maggie nodded. This was going okay, except she was still missing information. It was clear Taylor was acting separately from Sheldon and was as large a victim in this as she, the boys, Dingo, and, worryingly, the whole tribe of Iwelongas seemed to be. Taylor undoubtedly had firepower at his disposal. He was a gangster of some considerable wealth and resources, and he was not stupid. Well, not that stupid. Independently of Sheldon, he had found the location of a considerable source of diamonds – unless Sheldon had guided him to here too, which was a possibility – and he now had a degree of control of the situation. Except that he did not; someone else out there was calling (and firing) the shots.

The tank had been hit with something very sophisticated – something sophisticated enough to stop it, yet not destroy it. Something precise enough so that Maggie and Taylor could still carry out this conversation they were having. Sophisticated and precise enough so that Maggie would lead Taylor to where the diamonds were, at which point, the person firing and calling the shots, would, no doubt, pounce.

Taylor leaned forward in an attempt to up the ante. 'Tell me...' His face was only inches away from Maggie's. He was doing his best to act menacingly, but Maggie had seen too many films with

145

Leslie Philips in. A look of mild frustration at the fact the nurse had covered her body with a towel as she got out of the bath was as menacing as that actor got. And Taylor's attempt at intimidation didn't even come close to that.

'Look, Mr. Taylor. We're all in a bit of a pickle at the moment. You know that I know where the diamonds are. Most likely you know they are on this property somewhere. You've arrived a little too late to watch us, otherwise, you'd already have a rough idea by observing our movements. Why you haven't been keeping an eye on Dingo – sorry, Mr. Parfitt – all this time, I do not know.'

Taylor moved away and did Leslie Philip's rather hurt expression. 'We've been tied up in Singapore.'

'Where you aimed to offload the diamond to finance a larger operation. We both know that that didn't go well, did it?'

He swivelled round, his eyes burning with anger. But then he made the mistake of twiddling the end of his tiny moustache, and Maggie nearly lost it. She faked a sneeze to cover up her amusement and went to pull out a tissue from inside her sleeve. It drew a firm warning hand on the shoulder from the guard on her right.

'Enough of this!' Raising his voice a few decibels did little to increase Taylor's credibility as a rough, tough interrogator – a role that was already shot to pieces by the fact he wore tweed, and he was hopeless at it. 'Tell me where the diamonds are!'

'Look, even if I did tell you, you won't be able to get to them.'

'Ahh, so you do know.'

'Dammit! You finally got it out of me. You ought to do this for a living.'

Taylor did his this-isn't-going-well Leslie Philips face and ran his hand through his thick hair. He tried a change of tack.

'Maggie – can I call you Maggie?'

'I respond well to Maggie.'

He crouched down so that their eyes were at a similar level and gave a lopsided smile that had Maggie in a dilemma as to whether she might have to pretend to sneeze again. She managed to keep control and smiled sweetly back at him.

'Maggie. Tell me where the diamonds are... please.'

'Yes, dear.'

There was a pause that Taylor may have hoped that Maggie might fill with the information he wanted. When she did not, he said simply, 'Well?'

'Yes, thank you. You?'

While Taylor took a deep breath or two, Maggie was pondering a more pressing dilemma than whether to decide to laugh or sneeze again. Several, actually. She had all she was going to get out of Taylor, for now. Whoever was waiting for her to reveal the diamonds' whereabouts would probably realise she was unlikely to say. That could mean they may act very shortly, possibly with violence, then they would tear the place apart until they found them. She was not too keen on that. Dingo and Ben were safe for now; she, Joshua, and Bill were not. That needed to be addressed, fairly urgently. These people had considerable resources – more than Taylor – sufficient to set up this whole situation, which suggested they were either a country or, at the very least, a huge organisation. Or – and she kept coming back to this – Sheldon.

Taylor stood up and walked away. His finger and thumb had moved out of his nostrils up to the bridge of his nose and were now doing a fine job of keeping his tear ducts occupied by rubbing any residual snot into the corners of his eyes. Maggie refrained from saying, 'Dear... don't do that.' Instead, she said: 'Okay, I give up. Anyone who has gone to all that trouble to tie us to the top of a bridge deserves a reward.'

She waited for a reaction from Taylor, confirmation that he had done that, but he was giving nothing away, just a continued look of frustration. They were sitting ducks, ducks without prospects of waddling anywhere soon if they were not careful. It was time to move things along. Time to take a risk.

'Okay, you've wrung it out of me with your devilishly brutal interrogation tactics, Mr. Taylor. I'll show you where the diamonds are.'

~ ~ ~

Chapter 13

Joshua and Bill had been kept under separate guard in the lounge. With their hands tied behind their back, they were shoved onto the veranda and down the steps by two burly men to join Maggie, Taylor, and the two other guards. Joshua stumbled and fell as he was pushed, his shoulder and the top of his arm taking the brunt of the impact on the dusty ground as he twisted to avoid a face full of dirt. Maggie yelped in alarm, but Joshua reassured her he was okay as he was manhandled to his feet. It was a stark reminder that, as ridiculous as Taylor was, these were not nice people they were dealing with.

'Lead on, McDuff,' said Taylor glibly to Maggie. He had perked up as soon as she had indicated she would show him where the diamonds were.

'I've already said you can call me Maggie.'

'I was quoting from Shakespeare.'

'Then you would know that McDuff was the goody who prevailed.'

'Making me the evil Macbeth?'

'Don't big yourself up too much, Mr. Taylor, I suspect you are just one of the supporting characters.'

Maggie led them away from the veranda, all the while assessing the situation. To her right, the upturned tank sat motionless, a single armed guard standing by its side. There was no sign of

149

activity on the mound in the distance, but she could not fail to notice Taylor's men dotted around the property. The sun to the east was still low, yet it was already belting out more heat than she felt comfortable with. How Taylor put up with wearing the full set of tweed, she did not know. The white shirt was undone at the top, but surely that would provide little relief, accompanied as it was by the full set of trousers, waistcoat, and jacket.

'Is that Harris tweed you wear, Mr. Taylor? Scottish ancestry?'

'Actually, I'm from Bognor,' he said.

'Ah, Bognor.' Another piece of information – probably useless, but it all added up.

She turned right past the house, took another right behind the outdoor kitchen, and headed off at a forty-five-degree angle when she reached the other corner, acutely aware that a left turn from the veranda would have taken them in exactly the same direction. Taylor, walking alongside her, seemed oblivious to the fact. Both turns had given her an opportunity to suss out the lie of the land, but also to check on Bill and Joshua who were walking behind, guards on either side with another to the rear. All the guards had weapons drawn. Bill had caught her eye on the first turn and flicked his tongue quickly from one side to the other; a Service signal to indicate he was ready to back up whatever she had planned. She reciprocated with a slight shrug: a Maggie signal to indicate that the plan she had got planned may just this second have been scuppered. Unfortunately, she had forgotten that the tank – the original marker to find the bunker – was no longer where it had been and so she had no idea where the entrance was. Australian scrub looks largely the same wherever it is. Dingo's land, broken up by the many old vehicles, had a chance of being distinctive – if the many old vehicles that broke it up had not, in Maggie's eyes, all looked largely the same too.

She tried to get her bearings, relative to the mound which was directly in front of her again. She knew the bunker entrance was not far from the house, and that she had to be going in roughly the right direction, but precisely where it was, she was unsure. Dingo had done an excellent job at concealing the entrance. With no access inside, further action by the third party seemed inevitable, something that Taylor seemed not to have grasped fully as Maggie stopped and held her hand up for the others to do the same.

'Well?' Taylor said impatiently. 'And don't say, yes thank you, this time. What exactly are we looking for?'

She did have a plan – a very rough one – and it went something like this: rely on Dingo and Ben to have hidden the diamonds somewhere safe; find the entrance and open the hatch; take Taylor and some of his men down into it; expect third party to reveal themselves at that stage; expect third party and Taylor to be in conflict over diamonds; pick up pieces at the end.

She was not keen to expose the bunker and there was detail in there that needed thrashing out, but she did like its intent. In particular, it would draw out the third party into the open, hopefully with no collateral damage.

As she would shortly find out, her plan would indeed draw them out. As for the collateral damage, that had ideas of its own.

On her first mission back after retirement, Maggie had been hospitalised by a car crashing into Sukie and Sam's restaurant where she was about to enjoy tea and cake. As well as being struck by a pizza peel – Sam's shovel – she had also been struck by how slowly it all happened, a complete contrast to how she experienced what happened next at Dingo's place. She had just lowered herself onto all fours in preparation to see how long she could hoodwink Taylor into thinking she was able to track the location when there was an almighty screeching sound. There was no time to look up, but her brain registered danger. Being already close to the ground possibly saved her life. Joshua and Bill, they said afterwards, reacted instinctively, hitting the floor immediately as soon as the screech started. As Maggie collapsed onto her stomach, there was a *whump* followed by a horrendous slam, an ear-splitting shattering sound that made the Sukuel crash seem like the tentative first step of a baby's foot on a deep-pile carpet. (Or as Dingo later described it from below – 'Louder than a Pom's middle stump being ripped out the ground at the Sydney Cricket Ground.') Maggie passed out, which meant she was unaware that Dingo's house was no longer anything that could even loosely be described as a house.

~ ~ ~

Chapter 14

Unlike a lot of people, Maggie quite liked hearing about people's dreams. It gave her an insight into the narrator's character, a side of them they would never usually expose when they went about their daily business.

It was amazing how quick and easy it seemed to be to get onto the subject of dreams, often with the dream bearing no relevance whatsoever to the current topic. Sandra Burgess, Vice-President of Frampton bowls club (which Maggie had refused to join because it was full of people who complained about bad backs, yet spent all day stooped over, arguing about which bowl was closest to the jack) had once inexplicably opened up to her while they were waiting in the queue to use the cash point. They had been talking about the work being done on the seafront to the groynes when Sandra had, without preamble, said the stock phrase: 'I had a really strange dream last night...' What followed was an extraordinary ramble through her subconscious, involving – amongst other things – a talking cheese plant and a naked ride on a supermarket trolley through Horse Guards Parade. Maggie was baffled by what it revealed about Sandra's character, other than the randomness of a brain that could jump from sea defences to being gawped at by red-coated men on horseback wearing large black furry hats.

Had Sandra been there when Maggie woke up on this occasion and Maggie been willing to reciprocate, she might well have been impressed by the relevance of Maggie's dream to her current circumstances. Much has been written about Dreamtime in Australian Aboriginal culture, the time when life and the world were created. The Iwelonga's own dreaming – specific to them and their families – placed a huge emphasis on the diamonds, the story told through Brian's drawings. While Maggie was unconscious, her spirit could well have merged with those of the Iwelongas and their ancestors, as she was taken on a trip from the beginning of time and the formation of the earth, rocks, and diamonds, through to the present day when they faced an uncertain future. The fact she was naked in a shopping trolley for the entire journey was a detail that Maggie tried to dispel from her brain as she came to and Dingo's head loomed into view.

'What have you done to your face?' Maggie asked. 'Why is it so blurred?'

There was a snort of laughter and she felt a squeeze on her hand. 'Lucky you. Makes this craggy old mug much more bearable. Wish my bathroom mirror was as forgiving. Not that I need to worry about that any longer. Whole lot blown to smithereens.'

'Dingo, I'm so sorry.' Then, a sudden moment of panic as she realised who else had been with her. 'What about Bill and...?'

'The boys are okay,' Dingo interrupted, holding up a reassuring hand. 'Shaken; scratches and bruises, but okay. Tough fellas. They've stayed up top.' Maggie breathed a sigh of relief. They were in a dangerous profession, but the idea that either of them could be lost to her was too painful to contemplate. Joshua with his whole life ahead of him, and Bill – well, she just could not bear the thought of letting him go – again. 'You, though, Maggie Matheson,' Dingo continued, 'are going to need some medical attention.'

'Nonsense!' she said, shifting to her left, ready to prop herself up on her elbow. 'I'm fine... arrgh!'

'Stay still.' Dingo's blurred face morphed into an alarmed blurred face as his hand caught the back of her head and gently eased her back down. 'We think you've cracked the top part of your arm. It's all swollen up. Tracy, the Iwelonga's healer, is on her way.'

A cracked arm? Maggie had had her fair share of injuries in the past but never broken anything before. It had been one of her greatest fears as she aged that she would break something - a hip, or leg especially – and she would be incapacitated, dependent on others for the day-to-day tasks that had kept her just about sane since she had retired from the Service. Maybe an arm was not too bad, although in the current circumstances any injury was inconvenient. Talking of which, what were the current circumstances? The sharp pain she felt subsided, and, despite a desperate need to be up and involved in things, she decided to accept the fact that being horizontal was the best position from which to assess the situation, at least for the moment.

'What's going on, Dingo?' she said.

'You're safe; we all are for the moment. Some sort of missile hit close by. When we dug you out...'

'Dug me out?'

'Yeah – you were all covered in dirt and a few bits from my house. Sorry about that.'

'You're sorry? God, Dingo. Look what we've done to you.' Maggie had never considered herself to be the emotional sort – having a hard heart, to some extent, came with the job – but she felt awful.

'Don't worry about any of that. You guys scared the crap out of me and Ben. We really thought you were goners when we came up. Good job Sid and the others turned up to help. No sign yet of who or where the missile came from though. Probably a handheld rocket launcher, Bill reckoned. Same one that had a pop at the tank and us earlier.'

'We've messed up all your plans. For the Iwelongas too.'

'Nah, we'll be alright. We've covered up the main entrance and even if anyone finds it they won't get in. Our first job is to get you moving, if we can.' I don't suppose you'll want to hang around here waiting for the end of the world. You wanna drink?'

'A large gin and tonic, please. Plenty of ice and give the lemon a squeeze before you put it in.'

'Or some water, maybe? Here, let me help you sit up again, if you can? If I carefully hold you just there... Is that alright?' Maggie felt his arm ease under her right shoulder. With her good hand, she held his other arm and, with no obvious pain, sat up. The room did a couple of three sixties before settling into the familiarity of the great hall. She was sitting on some blankets, strewn across crates. At one end, where her head had been, was a rolled-up jacket – Dingo's, she assumed. The hall appeared empty at first, and then she noticed three or four people milling around in the opposite corner to where they had entered earlier that day.'

156

'That's Ben, Sid, and Nelly, making some calls.' Dingo sat down propped against her and offered up a plastic bottle, which she took and immediately started to gulp down. She had never felt so thirsty. It had an unusual tang, but it was wet and thirst-quenching. When she had finished it, she let the bottle fall to her lap and just sat for a moment while she regained her breath.

'Better?'

'Yes, much. Your face is clearer now, and you've stopped doing summersaults.'

'Good. Look, as I said, Tracy'll sort you out, but she's coming from the far entrance because we think it's too dangerous to go out directly above or via the other nearby entrance. We don't want to reveal ourselves. We'll try to meet her halfway if you're up to it.'

'I am.'

'Sid slipped a couple of doses of a pretty powerful pain killer in that bottle which will help until we can get Tracy to have a proper look at you. You've got a few cuts on your arms and legs too, but apart from that, all good.'

Maggie felt her arms. The swelling on her left arm was apparent and hurt when she touched it. She was not keen to examine that too closely. The other arm's sleeve was a little tattered, with a few plasters on display, and her knuckles looked like they had done a couple of rounds with a brick wall. She looked further down and could see some grazes on her knees. It could have been a lot worse, she decided.

'We've cleaned up the best we could with the first aid kit.'

'So, what's happening next? I'm a bit confused. My, oh my... what is in that water? It's got a kick.'

'Told you – something to help with the pain. Ben's over there with Sid and Nelly on the radio where they can get a signal. All the Iwelongas are accounted for, as are my mates. They've all made themselves scarce. Nothing more they can do for now. Taylor and his goons looked to be alright – alive anyway. To be honest we were more focussed on getting you and the boys out the rubble and you down here to safety before anyone else turned up.'

'You said Joshua and Bill were up top.'

'As soon as they knew you were going to be okay, they decided to stay above ground. They're with Brian.'

'Sid and Nelly's Brian?'

'Yeah. Joshua said they wanted to scope the area to see if there is any indication of who's been launching these missiles. Brian has special skills: particularly good at sniffing and hunting. They've got a shorty.'

'Have they? A shorty – that's good.'

Dingo had started to do facial gymnastics once more and her mind was struggling to keep up. Whatever Sid had put into the water was certainly doing a good job of keeping the pain away, but things were becoming decidedly fuzzy. She would have to park the word 'shorty' for the moment and also rely on Joshua and Bill to know what they were doing.

Besides, something else was nudging its way to the front of her – and she had to be quite honest about this – increasingly pleasantly, hammered out of her head mind. Something she felt was very important.

'Dingo,' she said, deciding that she liked the sound of the 'o' at the end so much that she was going to stretch it out for a good few seconds longer than necessary, 'I had a really strange dream...'

~ ~ ~

Chapter 15

Maggie giggled. It was a natural release from the intensity she had felt as she finished telling Dingo all about her dream. It was also a natural response to being stoned. While recounting it, she felt she had experienced the whole of man's existence again (the shopping trolley twist, she had decided, was a detail Dingo did not need), climaxing with what she now realised was a vision of what was going to happen next.

'It's the end of the world, Dingo. The diamonds are taken and leave these shores. Unless...'

'Unless what?'

The dramatic cliff-hanger was punctuated by another giggle she struggled to contain, followed by an equally sudden gap in her recall.

'Tell you what,' said Dingo, 'we'll deal with the end of the world as and when it comes. For now, let's get you sorted. Let's see if we can get you going.'

He started to gently ease her legs off the crate but stopped when she blurted, 'Flanders Ringe!'

'What?'

She could see the words she wanted to say, but it was an effort to get her mouth to say them. 'Flinders Flanders.'

'The mountains? Flinders Range?'

'Yes. That's where we should go. Will stop the world ending.'

160

'You sure?'

'Abslo-slutely. That's what I didn't dream. That's not what I didn't dream. That's... um... am I making any nonsense?'

'Plenty. Probably a side effect of the potion.'

'Tasted nice.'

'Right, well first we need to get you that medical attention, Maggie. Can you walk if I help you?'

The attraction of walking did not appeal. But the attraction of walking whilst being supported by a hunky outbacker did, so much so that the weakness in her knees as she slid off the crates could not be put down solely to her inebriated state or to the damage done to her arm. She giggled again as Dingo put his arm around her waist and guided her to the far side towards Ben and the others.

Ben looked relieved to see her. 'How's that arm?'

'Perrrr-fectly fine,' she said. *Who'd thought, Maggs, that elongating sounds in words could be such fun!* She enjoyed the 'er' so much that she repeated it.

'Errr?' said Ben.

'Yes,' she said. 'Errrrrrrr'

'Right, good.' Ben turned to Dingo. 'Is she alright?'

'She's pissed, mate.'

'S'true,' she said, smiling at the two Iwelongas. 'Pleased to meet you.' She held out what she thought was an open hand but turned out to be a fist. 'Are you Ira... Iwelonda. Iwe... are you with Dingo?'

'Maggie,' said Dingo, 'this is Sid and Nelly.'

161

'Nid and Stelly. I am so sorry,' Maggie said. 'For everything. And... I'm not usually like this. Carry on... please.'

'Sit down, for a sec,' said Dingo.

Much to her relief, she was lowered onto something which felt suspiciously like a rock. After much patting and bottom shuffling, she concluded that the reason she thought it felt like a rock was because it was, indeed, a rock. Very pleased with herself, she let out another giggle then crossly shushed herself to be quiet.

Ben touched her shoulder in concern and then spoke to the group. 'Okay... so, quick update for you, Dingo, and Maggie if you're able to take it in?' Maggie nodded what she thought was a wise and knowing nod, unaware that it had stopped being a nod the moment her chin touched her chest and remained there. At least, she told herself, she had a good view of everyone's shoes as Ben continued, 'I've been in contact again with Bill and Joshua on the radio. I always thought shortwave radios were there just to play crackly music, but actually it works pretty well.' He tapped a large box that was strapped to his shoulder. 'To pick up signals from down here is impressive.'

'You can rely on a shorty for sure,' said Nelly. Somewhere in Maggie's mind, one of the earlier questions she had, had been answered. If only she could work out which one.

'It appears Taylor's lot have survived the attack too, have pulled back from Dingo's property, but are still probably hanging around somewhere close. Joshua says he, Bill, and Brian have now got transport and have left the immediate area to see what they can find

162

out. They said to tell you, Maggie, that they'll be very careful. We'll meet up somewhere later.'

Maggie was just about following the conversation and wanted to chip in. All she could manage was, 'Flinders.'

'Yeah,' said Dingo. 'That's where she wants to go next: Flinders Range. Let Joshua and Bill know.'

'Will do,' said Ben. 'How will we get there? It's a long way.'

'Leave that to me. First, we need to get out of here. To confirm, we leave by the far exit. I'll help Maggie. You okay carrying the shorty, Ben?'

'Shorty Ben!' chortled Maggie.

Ben gave her a stern look. 'Yes, it's fine.'

'Tracy's already making her way to the far end,' said Sid. 'She's got her healing stuff with her.'

'Good. More stuff! I like stuff.' said Maggie, feeling overly positive about what she was now remembering Dingo had said was a taxing journey through the tunnels. 'Tell her to wait. I'll be with her in a jiffy.'

There was a pause before Dingo whispered in her ear: 'You can stop saying the e at the end of jiffy now, Maggie.'

'Right.'

'What will you do with the diamonds?' said Ben.

'They're as safe here as anywhere,' said Nelly. 'The two closest entrance points are double sealed but we'll tuck 'em away out of sight. You okay doing that while we make a start with Maggie, Sid?'

'You don't need to come, Nelly,' said Dingo.

'You might need a hand with Maggie and I know the route well. I'll be right back, Sid.'

'No worries, 'said Sid. 'See ya soon.'

Maggie was helped to her feet and guided towards Nelly who had turned round and was heading towards another hole in the wall, the exit from the great hall. As Dingo ducked down and helped her through, Maggie felt a pang in her stomach – a warning of possible danger ahead. After what she had just been through, her mind dismissed it as something perfectly normal...

...leaving the knot in her stomach to ponder its very existence if it was going to be simply ignored.

Maggie would never remember much about the next hour or so, which was a hard trek through some tight spaces and over awkward jagged rocks. It was towards the end of the hour, as she became aware of a sharpening pain in her arm, that she realised that the mixture Sid had provided had made her go completely limp and useless. She was being partly carried, partly dragged over rough terrain underfoot, difficult to make out in the wavering light from a torch.

There was a grunt that sounded like Ben from somewhere underneath her.

'You're awake,' said Dingo from somewhere else underneath her.

'I am. You can put me down now,' said Maggie, a little unsure what parts of her body were being used to support her weight.

'I think Sid overdid his doses,' said Dingo as she was gently lowered onto her feet.

Nelly, with the radio slung around her neck, came into view behind the torch. 'You were all over the place back there, Maggie. They've had to carry you most the way.'

'It was no problem,' said Ben breathlessly.

'Someone – Dingo – gave you the whole bottle of water,' said Nelly with an edge to her voice. 'You've had a triple dose of the painkiller in one go. I'm not surprised you were groggy.'

'Well, it was very nice, dear,' said Maggie. 'I would say I was happy to take a top up whenever convenient as my arm is starting to smart a little, but perhaps I shouldn't since I've caused so much trouble.'

'You haven't caused trouble, Maggie,' said Dingo. 'Anyway, sounds like I'm to shoulder the blame – literally, in this case – for getting you in that state.'

'Well, thank you, all of you. I've been a burden – literally, too – but I think I can stand on my own two feet now.'

'Is that water I can hear?' said Ben. 'Could do with a drink, if it's fresh.'

'Yeah, I think so,' said Dingo. 'That's a good sign we're nearly there. You sure you can walk on your own now, Maggie?'

'Yes, thank you. I'm okay.'

With Dingo supporting her good elbow, they tentatively moved forward once more. The tightness of the surrounding space, plus the dark and dampness made it a testing environment and she wondered how they had got her body – not one she had ever considered was designed for potholing – around so many corners. They turned another bend to find a shaft of light penetrating through a small gap in the rocks high above. It illuminated a stream with fast-flowing water, its silver tops flickering and dancing in the light, like mischievous elves playing under a full moon. For a second, Maggie was lost in the beauty of something so simple.

'You're doing great, Maggie,' said Ben leading the way over a last tricky part before the ground flattened out.

Not for the first time was Maggie impressed by this man, now her son-in-law after he and Bill had tied the knot a few months ago. He had demonstrated a great deal of pluck in the face of adversity on the last mission in Belgium and had thrown himself into things again here. It took guts – and stamina, bearing in mind the physical effort of helping to support her weight for the last hour. Everyone around her seemed to be the same. She barely knew Nelly and the other Iwelongas, yet they were prepared to take risks for her, as was Dingo whose quiet life she had royally messed up within twenty-four hours of seeing him again. Okay, she had not sought this mission, but she was complicit in it. She had brought trouble upon this community; to make matters worse, she was slowing them down now, all because of a stupid arm. If it was not broken and if there had been more space, she might have waved it and the other one around in consternation, Italian Nonna style.

'It doesn't feel that way, Ben. It's all of you that are doing great things. You're bombed and shot at then you have to carry an old lady through caves. Nelly, Dingo, Ben, you shouldn't be doing this. The thought of you Ben love, or any of you, risking yourselves anymore feels me with dread.'

There was a chorus of 'no worries,' one of which sounded suspiciously out of place in an English accent.

Maggie smiled her thanks, then asked, 'How much further do we have to go before the exit?'

'About the same again,' said Nelly, 'plus this next little bit. Easier on the other side.'

'This little bit?' asked Ben nervously.

'On the other side of what?' said Maggie.

'The wet bit.'

'The water?' said Ben.

'Yep.'

'And the boat is where?'

'There's no boat,' said Dingo. 'We need to get in, go under, swim through a short tunnel, and out the other side. It's not far.'

He pointed to the dark part of the stream which, like a monstrous black beast, was hungrily devouring whole the dancing, flickering mischievous elves Maggie had just been admiring. She had confronted most of the phobias the country had thrown at her so far, but they had tended to come in ones so far. Aquaphobia was not usually on her list, nor were any of them really, but it looked like a whole bunch were about to be served up in one go as she studied the tight, black void. *Concentrate on one thing at a time, Maggs.* It had held her in good stead for most of her career, as well as when trying to follow some rather complex Inspector Morse plot twists.

'Are you sure you don't need a hand finding your way back, Nelly?' said Ben with far too much hope and enthusiasm.

167

'Nah,' said Nelly with a smile. 'I'm fine.'

'Or perhaps I could help you find another route, one that doesn't involve black holes and water?'

'There's no other route,' said Nelly. 'Not that takes out. Plenty that keep you in, though, permanently if you don't know where you're going.'

'I know,' said Ben. 'I'm joking... sort of...'

'I know you'll do it, Ben mate. Here, hand me the shorty and I'll wrap it in this.'

'Can I put my hearing aid in with it?' said Maggie. The thought of trying to hear anything with a waterlogged aid was daunting. She was just so reliant on it these days. Before they left for Australia, Bill had downloaded some of her favourite songs onto her iPad. After much persuasion, he had finally got her to listen through earphones, a tricky thing to do with a hearing aid. One day, she decided to strap the iPad to the vacuum cleaner with a bungee so she could listen while she did the housework. Having eventually got the technology to work, she had a very pleasant half hour cleaning the flat whilst listening to Frank Sinatra's Greatest Hits, only to realise when she took the earphones out that she hadn't switched on the vacuum cleaner.

Nelly produced from a bag slung over her shoulder what looked like a piece of thick animal skin. Frayed around the edges, it was the size of a small tablecloth. Nelly immediately started to wrap up the shortwave radio and her hearing aid, expertly folding and folding again until it was a tight package.

'That's impressive,' said Maggie. 'Do all the Iwelongas learn skills like that?'

'Yeah, ancient arts.' There was a snort of laughter before she continued, 'Nah, I'm kiddin'. I used to work in a Mexican restaurant. Burritos, tacos, enchiladas... you name it, I folded it. Shortwave radios were my speciality.'

'Tell me that's kangaroo skin, at least.'

'Got it half price from Bunnings years back... some kinda plastic probably,' said Nelly handing it to Dingo. 'Bit knackered now but should do the job. Right... I'm off. When you get to the other side, it's much easier going. If it's okay with you all and you're okay, Maggie, I'll go and make sure Sid hasn't cocked things up. Stay in touch, Dingo, and look after that shorty, mate,' she added, nodding at Ben. 'Mind your heads as you go through the hole.'

Maggie heard a gulp from Ben as Dingo wished Nelly well. He followed it up with something in a language Maggie did not understand and then she disappeared.

When he turned to her, she asked, 'What did you say at the end there?'

'Ah, nothing much. Just an Iwelongan saying. A parting phrase. Right, let's do this.'

Without further ado, he put the radio on the edge of the water and jumped in. He disappeared for a few seconds, long enough for Maggie to share worried looks with Ben, before resurfacing with a broad grin on his face. The water came up to his chest, which Maggie reckoned meant the top of her head would be covered when it was her turn.

169

'Streuth! My knackers haven't been this cold since they got trapped in an esky at my brother's stag do in Tasmania. You ready, Maggie?'

Once again, she caught Ben's face forming itself into a look that reflected the fact his brain was trying to understand what was going on, this time for Dingo's knackers to have been subjected to freezing temperatures at a stag do in Tasmania. Hopefully, he was building up enough resilience now not to bother asking.

'Park your bum here, Maggie, and I'll help ease you in.' Dingo patted a flat rock. The flowing water was becoming less and less inviting by the minute. It was now or never. 'Best take off your shoes. You got somewhere to put them?'

'Like where?' Maggie asked easing first one shoe off with her toe on the heel, then the other, steadying herself with her stronger hand on Ben's shoulder. 'I'm not bloody Cinderella with Prince Charming following me around holding a cushion.'

'Dunno. You women seem to have bags for everything.'

She stared down at him. 'Dingo... I've driven a bloody tank, been captured by a gang of diamond thieves, blown up, drugged up to my eyeballs then carried through a mile of tunnels. Why on earth would I have a handy bag for my shoes on me?'

'What's an esky?' piped up Ben, his brain and face not as resilient as Maggie might have hoped. 'You said your knackers were trapped in an esky.'

Maggie grunted as she switched her attention to the second shoe. 'They speak a foreign language here, Ben. Some sort of fridge, I would imagine.'

'But, how on earth, Dingo, did you trap them in a fridge?'

'Cool box, actually. It's a long story. I'm lucky they're still with me to tell the tale.'

'Talking balls,' said Maggie. 'You're not the only Australian with that epitaph.'

'They'll be like a couple of raisins if we don't stop yakking. Come on; help her down, Ben... that's it.'

Thankful for the nondescript flat shoes she always bought these days, Maggie tucked them down her top and, with Ben's help, lowered herself to the floor. She winced as her injured arm took more weight than she would have liked, and then gasped as the freezing water struck her feet and up to her knees. It was cold, but she took a deep breath and reminded herself she had been on many a summer holiday in the UK and felt worse. Far worse.

'Right, Ben,' said Dingo. 'Do you want to take the shorty?'

'No, you take Maggie, I'll follow on with the radio,' he replied dryly.

Maggie scooped up some water and threatened to splash him. Just that movement, although with her good hand, hurt. Ben, seeing her reaction, obviously decided enough was enough, and with the prerequisite ohs and ahs of an Englishman entering any waters of any temperature anywhere in the world, slipped in to join Dingo.

Maggie kept her reaction to being immersed in the cold water to one word, but the 'er' part of 'bugger' lasted longer than any of the words she had said when under the influence of Tracy's concoction.

171

~ ~ ~

Chapter 16

Desperately, she took a large gulp of air; oxygen had never tasted so good. The sloped exit out of the water looked easier than the way they had got in on the other side of the tunnel. Still, she had to half-swim and half-walk, with Dingo's help, over rocks underfoot until she felt secure enough to stand up. For one awful moment, she wondered whether Ben had got stuck somewhere because there was no sign of him. Then she heard a cough and splutter and she realised he was just a little way behind, still holding the dripping package with the radio inside.

There had been an agonising ten seconds underwater when she had doubted whether she would, quite literally, ever see the light of day again. Before going under, she had been sorely tempted to turn back before Dingo had counted down for them to all take a deep breath together. She had held firm, just like Dingo's grip which pulled her onwards. Her life as an agent had put her into some daunting situations. She told herself this was just one more as the sparse light of the cave was soon replaced by the blackest black imaginable. The shock of that and the impact of the cold nearly forced her to take a breath, but Dingo had warned them both about that. After that, she was at the mercy of Dingo's swimming skills as he pulled her down and onwards into the abyss.

She had expected to be scraped and battered by rocks but felt nothing. And that feeling of nothingness had nearly been her undoing in that long, drawn-out ten seconds where they were swimming – breaststroke, Dingo had advised – along the very bottom. Because with only inches of water above their backs, then metres and metres of thick rock, the magnitude of what she was doing suddenly hit her. She had kicked out in panic and turned her head from side to side as she searched, in vain, for Dingo's face. Then she felt a squeeze on her hand and a jerk, and she was moving up towards a light. For a brief moment, she was back in the dreaming with hunters stalking prey, babies opening their eyes to bright sunlight, snow-capped mountains, sweeping bush landscape that seemed to go on forever, diamonds... flashing in front of her eyes.

Dingo – his strength and energy like that of a forty-year-old – clambered up a couple more step-like rocks and held out a hand to pull her up and out. They were in a ravine. Bright, pure blue sky zigzagged its way ten metres above her head with clumps of greenery clinging for dear life to rocks near the top. She knew that feeling. To one side of the water was a sheer face. The side where Dingo was heading was less steep and there might have been places where an experienced rock climber with the right equipment would be able to climb out to the top. Without crampons and ropes tucked down her sodden top with her sodden shoes, it looked like they would have to go on a little further yet to find somewhere accessible to the ground above. She pulled out her shoes, dropped them to the floor, and girded herself to squeeze her soaking feet back into them.

173

The gentle babbling of the water – back to its visually ethereal best now that the dancing elves, having survived a drowning, were back in party mode – could not compete audibly with the coughs and splutters of the three divers as they sat on rocks to recover. Maggie had given up trying to get her shoes on until Ben or Dingo became available to help. Both, wearing boots and having kept their footwear on, were emptying the contents between convulsions. Each phlegm-ridden explosion echoed off the ravine walls, making for a cacophony to rival any of Sharon's primary school Christmas concerts Maggie had attended over the years.

Predictably, Dingo was the first to get his breath back. 'It's a rite of passage for the young Iwelongas, that,' he said bending down to help Maggie with her shoes. 'They all do it at the age of eight. Both ways, starting the other side, surfacing on this, and then straight back.'

'Well, give me a minute,' said Maggie, doing her utmost to squeeze water out of anything that was vaguely squeezable, 'and I'll pop back again.'

'How's the arm?'

'Sore, but I'll live. You okay, Ben?'

Since the last mission when it was revealed that Ben was soon to become her son-in-law, Maggie had been on a private mission to persuade Ben to do something about his hair and beard which, in her humble opinion (as she was always keen to point out), had a tendency to be on the scruffy side. References to him as Robinson Crusoe or the hermit from Life of Brian, and throwing subtle comments into conversations about how cheap scissors were at

174

Boots or on the market, went largely ignored. Right up until the day before his wedding to Bill when Ben had surprised everyone by turning up at the registry office clean-shaven and with a crew cut. Bill had hated it, though, and since then Ben had been grooming his hair – in other words, paying it no attention whatsoever – back into its former 1970s-style status. He stood shivering, shoulders hunched, water dripping from every part of his body, hair plastered over his face. He now thoroughly owned the word *bedraggled*, claiming it from every dog or cat which had ever spent too long in a ditch.

'Ben?' Maggie repeated.

He kept his head down and said, very slowly: 'That was the dumbest, craziest, scariest...,' he looked at her and his eyes suddenly lit up, 'most exhilarating thing I've ever done.'

Maggie allowed herself a smile that turned into a grimace as she realised how cold she was getting. Dingo noticed it too. 'We need to get going. The ravine opens out a bit just up that way. There should be a corner where the sun sneaks into at this time of day. We can rest and dry out a bit there.'

Maggie wondered what time of day it was. Late morning, she guessed. It had been an early start and rather a hectic time, to say the least. She could add fatigue to her list of 'bothersomes' as her mum used to call worries. Still, Dingo was right to get them moving because she was getting no drier standing here. Their gasps and wheezes had died down now and the idyllic 'babbling brook' once more dominated the scene... to be quickly drowned out by the squelch-squelch of three sets of footwear trudging along a path the

175

Iwelongas had trodden along rather more quietly, no doubt, for hundreds of years.

With the benefit of daylight, this section of the journey, as Nelly had indicated, was much easier to navigate, a relief bearing in mind how uncomfortable and tired Maggie felt. With flatter ground, there was a clear path. Dingo explained that the Iwelongas used to regularly visit the ravine and go no further until they discovered the underwater tunnel they had just used which had then opened up a whole new area and the route into the network of caves near Dingo's place. She had to marvel at the bravery of the first person to have risked that journey through the tunnel.

No exit point meant that they had no choice other than to follow the stream which had widened slightly, along with the ravine. It was not long before they reached a wide enough section where the sunshine began to caress the rocks near the ravine floor. The height and angle of the sun confirmed her feeling that it was heading towards midday, and when they eventually found a suitable spot to sit in the sun, there was a real heat to it, such that their clothes soon began to steam.

She appreciated the warmth, although, unlike most of her elderly friends back in Frampton, she did not seem to feel the cold as much, and often had to sit sweltering inside the living rooms of flats or houses with the heating on full blast in August. Also unlike most of her friends in Frampton, she would not hold back on making her discomfort clear. Heating in summer was a needless waste of precious resources, she felt, so she would often start by removing an outer garment and hope they took the hint. Only once had she got as far down as her bra, before her host on that occasion, Irene, having been chatting about the fact she was still awaiting her first cataract operation, finally noticed.

They took their time, basking in the sunshine, occasionally returning to the stream to scoop up some water to quench their thirsts. Now and then, one of them would look along the route in the hope that Tracy might appear. A stab of pain in Maggie's arm reminded her that she was supposed to meet them halfway. The fact that she had not was either a sign they were not halfway yet or, worse, that something had happened to her. Neither was a pleasant prospect.

Ben unwrapped the radio and hearing aid and declared them both dry. That came as no surprise since it had taken him a good twenty minutes to unravel Nelly's handiwork. He and Dingo set about adjusting various knobs, hoping to contact Tracy while Maggie fiddled with her own on her hearing aid. After a fruitless while, Dingo suggested they should try Tracy again a little later, and set their minds to contacting Bill and Joshua. A crackly voice indicated success.

'Is that Bill?' said Dingo. 'Bill, Joshua, can you hear me, over?'

'Dingo, this is Joshua. I'm still with Bill and Brian. Your status. Over.'

'Wet, mate. But safe. Over.'

'Hello, Joshua,' Maggie said, getting in close to the mouthpiece Dingo had been holding. 'It's your great-gran. Are you all okay?'

'Over,' added Ben pointedly.

'Nonsense,' said Maggie. 'We don't need that. They know I've stopped talking because I've stopped talking.'

'It's protocol. Even I know that and I'm not a spy.'

'It kinda helps know when you're finished, Maggie,' Dingo agreed. 'Especially with shorties which are notorious for squeaks and cackles.'

'Are you telling me they're waiting for me to say, "over" before they answer?'

'Well, we haven't had an answer yet,' said Ben, rather too cockily for Maggie's liking.

Maggie snatched the mouthpiece. Instinctively, her finger pressed the button on the side to operate it, an action from a time long gone by. 'Joshua... it's Maggie. I said are you okay?'

'Ove...' said Ben before Joshua interrupted with a, 'We're fine, Maggie.'

'See, no need for *overs*, Ben.'

'Over,' said Ben.

'I didn't say anything more,' said Maggie.

'Joshua did. I'm correcting him.'

'He can't hear you.'

'It's a point of principle.'

'Give me that,' said Dingo, snatching back the mouthpiece. 'You two got bat shit in your ears? Joshua, it's Dingo again. What's going on, mate? Over.'

Maggie grumpily folded her arms, her adult brain warning that she was in child mode after then being sorely tempted to stick out her tongue at Ben. Her child brain warned back that if she wanted to stick her tongue out and fold her arms grumpily, there was nothing her adult brain could do about it. This was another one of her internal dialogues – one that her adult brain rarely won, although this time it claimed victory as both brains agreed to stop bickering so that they could listen to what Joshua had to say.

'You were right about Brian, Dingo. He is extraordinary. He smelt out where the missile was launched from and now we're at the location. Someone's definitely been here. There are tyre tracks and remnants of material from a rocket launcher. Fresh tracks indicate they're heading southwest towards Adelaide. Taylor and his people seem to have dispersed, not sure where. We've decided to head south to see if we can pick up traces of the launcher again. Over.'

Ben nudged Maggie and gave her a look, which she interpreted as saying that that was a long speech and they only knew it was over because he said, 'Over.' She gave him a look back which said that she still thought it wasn't needed, her child brain adding a 'so there' for good measure.

'Give us a moment, Joshua. Over.' Dingo moved the mouthpiece away. 'Flinders Ranges are southwest between my place and Adelaide. Maggie, you still feel we should head that way?'

'I do,' said Maggie thoughtfully.

'We've gone through a lot to get to this point,' said Ben. 'We nearly drowned. We could have gone above ground with Joshua and Bill and saved ourselves a soaking if we had followed them.'

'We didn't know it was safe then,' said Maggie.

179

'And you might not have experienced the dream about Flinders,' said Dingo.

'What dream?' asked Ben.

Maggie briefly recounted the dream she had had earlier, adding, 'You might not think we are following any logic here, but...'

Ben cut in. 'By following logic you mean acting on the basis of a half-cut elderly lady's hallucinations and a nose which can apparently sniff which direction people are going. The nose of an eighteen-year-old lad... called Brian, I might add.'

'Points well made and taken, but there is something in this,' said Maggie. 'I know we should be heading towards Flinders Ranges. Dingo, confirm with Joshua that that is where we are going... Over.'

'What?' said Ben. 'You can't say over now! You don't need to.'

Maggie gave him one of her 'innocent old lady' looks, often used when she either wanted a tradesman to do extra work for free or, as in this case, when she had wound up someone.

Dingo did as he was asked and then signed off.

'I hope you both understand,' Maggie said holding her arm which had started to throb quite badly, 'why I feel Flinders is the right place.'

'Yes, because of this dream,' said Ben. Like all of them, he had dried out quite a bit now. With his new lumberjack-style clothing looking less than pristine and hair sticking out at all angles, he had gone from wet and bedraggled to his more normal state of dry and bedraggled.

'Partly. Look, Sharon and the family have been threatened. They haven't chosen the life I chose, yet they're wrapped up in it now and are in danger. While people like Taylor and Sheldon are at large, they always will be in danger. I've got to see this out, got to somehow stop them doing what they're doing. If I don't, well...'

'And Flinders is definitely the place to do that?' said Ben.

'Yes, I think so. The big bugger diamond is there.' It felt a little disrespectful to call it by the name Dingo had allocated to it, yet somehow really satisfying. 'Sheldon, especially, will have her eye on the big prize. I think we need to check it out before anyone else gets to it if we can. Dingo, will Tracy know where to find the Jingdon if it is at Flinders?'

'She's an elder of the tribe, so, in theory, yes.'

'Good. So, Flinders it is then.'

'Let's hope you're right about this,' said Ben.

'Trust me. I feel it in my bones. Besides, there's one more thing: you know the paintings back in the cave that Brian did? One of the ones with Brian in it and that girl he liked had him holding a lunchbox. I thought it might have been a symbol showing the juxtaposition of modern Iwelongan life to the olden days when the tribe was dependent on hunting as their only means of food.'

'I remember that lunchbox now,' said Dingo smiling.

'What am I missing out on here?' said Ben.

'It had something written on it, didn't it, Maggie?'

'What?' said Ben, clearly frustrated.

'Another sign we should perhaps go there,' said Maggie. 'It said: I heart Flinders Ranges.'

181

~ ~ ~

Chapter 17

Like most mountain ranges, Flinders Ranges is a big area, but Maggie knew which part they should head for: the Aboriginal caves she had visited years ago. While Dingo contacted Joshua and Bill again to tell them to meet somewhere near the caves, and Ben listened in to check for the correct radio protocol, Maggie sat on the rock she had been on since they had stopped, and cogitated.

She reserved cogitations for special moments only, times when she had to delve really deep into her analytical brain to work things out. Different from her normal day-to-day thinking about solutions to problems – and certainly different from her musings which had tendencies to take her in all sorts of random directions – cogitations were a state of mind, similar to a meditative state. She had been taught the technique by a monk – well, he had said he was a monk, but she never got to the bottom of what or where he was a monk of – that she had met on her first holiday on her own, soon after she had lost Frankie.

Based in a small hostel on a tiny Greek island, it was supposed to have been one of those trips where 'you find your inner spirit.' Lacking any spirit at all – the hostel was dry and they were encouraged to drink only pure water or green tea – Maggie had hoped for some much-needed quiet time at the very least. But one of the instructors, Moby the Monk (Moby was his real name, he had insisted), had identified her as a person of 'low energy', and then spent most of the week unintentionally sucking out the little energy that she did have by fussing too much over her. He did, however, leave her with a gift; the ability to meditate – or, rather, go through the techniques required to get into a meditative state. Concentrating on the breath to help clear the mind worked for most people, apparently, but not for Maggie. Invariably, the part where Moby said that it was time to come out of the meditation and back into the real world was the time that Maggie realised she had been in the real world for the entire meditation, having spent half an hour thinking about things like how she could sneak in a massive gin and tonic, rather than drink the water and green tea that was on offer. With practice, though, she developed her own technique to clear her mind enough to concentrate on just the one thing – a semi-meditative state, which enabled her to blot out the other bothersomes and cogitate. Blotting out was no easy task since the very act of cogitating sometimes invited additional distraction, including enquiries from people like Ben who, having noticed Maggie was sitting on a rock repeating the word 'cog-i-tate' over and over again to help her cogitate, was wondering what on earth she was doing. But if she was in the zone, she was usually able to blot that out too in the hope that people like Ben would sod off and find their own inner peace somewhere else.

During this cogitation, Maggie managed to simplify the conundrum she and the others faced. It was now obvious that from the time she had boarded the flight to Sydney, she – they – had been manipulated. Taylor's role, the threats, the attacks, even the role of the Iwelongas and Dingo, all of these were being influenced

183

by a third party. Identify the third party and the case was solved. This case was complicated by the fact there were possibly two third parties: the Russian government (because of their interest in her last case which was never fully exposed) and Sheldon. It was feasible they could be working together, though her cogitation led her to believe that Sheldon working on her own was the most likely option.

Indications were that the Flinders Ranges was the place to be. The Jingdon diamond was there – in itself worth an absolute fortune – and the other parties would be desperate to get their hands on such a unique stone. The thought that she could well be leading them there was a concern. Then again, she felt that there was a fair chance they would find their way there anyway. And there was an upside from the perspective of the Iwelongas: it took the immediate threat, geographically at least, away from them. On the downside, it increased the threat of the end of the world if that diamond was allowed to get in the wrong hands and leave the country.

The threat to her family was what preoccupied her most. Were the operational decisions they were taking adversely affecting their safety? The answer to that, she decided, was no: the operational aims were to find and stop the diamonds from being taken. If that was done successfully, then whoever was responsible for threatening them would be behind bars and, consequently, her family would be safe. Able to live a normal life.

A successful cogitation, and it looked like they were on the right track. An unexpected bonus as she came out of her meditative state was the idea – via a brief tangent – to sew a pouch, like a wallaby's, into all her jumpers when she got home, so she had a handy place to keep her spare glasses and indigestion tablets. And shoes, if she ever needed to swim through an underwater tunnel again.

'At the risk of sounding like an eight-year-old on a trip to a local supermarket, Dingo, how much further is it before we can get out of this ravine?'

'Oh, not much further.'

'You've come out with exactly the same answer an adult gives to that eight-year-old, haven't you?'

'Never had you down as a whinging pom.'

Nor had Maggie, but she felt she had good reason to feel, at the very least, a little uppity. 'Feeling a little uppity' was another phrase her mother had used to describe her reaction to things as varied as worrying about losing a hair grip to how she felt when bombs were dropping all around their neighbourhood in London during the war. Maggie's arm was throbbing to the point of it becoming unbearable and, despite the rest they had taken, she was feeling very tired and, now, very hungry. Following the path of the stream, thirst had not been an issue; they had all taken regular handfuls of water whenever the need arose. However, this had caused another problem that Dingo and Ben had found easy to solve by hanging back to do what was required, and which Maggie had been metaphorically hanging back from doing because of feminine practical constraints. It was not that she was shy about the idea of doing it al fresco; it was more that she was shy about doing it al fresco with either Ben or Dingo in direct attendance. Because that was what would need to happen. With one arm now too painful to move, and the other being required to hold up a knee-length skirt, there was nothing to stop her from falling over as she squatted. Well-versed as a younger agent in having to take opportunities to go when out in the field – including on one particularly dodgy occasion when holding a Glock 25 she had just wrestled from an East German agent – things had been easier then because she had had strong glutes to help her balance when squatting down. These days, the only balancing she did with them was to hold a tray with tea and toast as she watched Bargain Hunt on T.V.

She was now seriously desperate, to the point that she had to either swallow her pride and ask for that help, or jump back into the freezing water and do the innocent face that everyone tries to do when they are relieving themselves in the sea. She opted for the former. While Ben walked on a little way ahead, she picked a spot and started to organise a reluctant Dingo into a position whereby he could help.

She had thought that helping to haul her through a network of tunnels while she was semi-conscious, and then guiding her through an underwater tunnel would be a much harder a task than supporting a lady to take a pee, but she was wrong. Dingo the brash outbacker immediately turned into Dingo the bashful back-outer, as he tried to wriggle his way out of being involved.

'Can't you just pull yer cacks down and prop yourself against a rock?'

'I tried that, Dingo. I'm not as sprightly as I was, even a year ago. I need help to lower myself down to a squatting position. With just one useful arm, it's then a question of angles and biomechanics. I can't get that same arm round to pull down my knickers on the other side if it's holding onto a rock.'

'Well, pull them down first, then lower yourself. Slide down the rock holding your skirt up.'

'And where is this smooth upright rock I can slide down? Plenty of jagged non-vertical ones. And incidentally, my pole dancing days where I slid up and down vertical objects finished some years back.'

'Tree?'

'Where Dingo? Show me a tree not covered in sharp things or bitey things crawling up and down it. Look, just do it, please. Here, grab my skirt while I pull my knickers down.' His face was a picture of dejection before, reluctantly, he held out his hand. 'That's it, hold on there. Right, keep hold of my skirt, and I'll grab hold of you to lower myself down. You might have to help me with your other hand, particularly when I get up again.'

'Jeez, Maggie. I don't wanna watch!'

'Well close your eyes then. There, that's it, bend down with me as I go.'

'Streuth! My back.'

With much grunting and the occasional yelp of alarm from both, Maggie clung to Dingo's hand and got herself into a position where she could begin to do what she needed to. There was an uncomfortable silence, broken when the floodgates opened.

187

'You could at least whistle or something, Dingo. I thought that's what you blokes did in situations like this.'

'Nah, never. I keep quiet, eyes fixed ahead, and concentrate on willing the ol' prostate to shrink, is my approach.'

'Are you alright back there?' Ben's voice sounded concerned. 'You've been an awful long time.'

'We're fine,' said Maggie, relieved that the Serengeti appeared to have, at last, hit a dry spell. 'Right, up now, please, Dingo. Careful of that arm. Just pull me up by my hand and I'll try to find some hamstrings to help things along.'

It was not a problem; Dingo was more than strong enough, and she was soon upright. He stepped back and turned away to give her a chance to adjust her clothing.

'Thank you, Dingo. I appreciate the fact that you had to step out of your comfort zone, helping an old lady like that.'

'It's fine. Happy to help. And I'll say it again: you're not old. Okay if I turn round now?'

'Yep.'

She was met by those piercing bright blue eyes. 'Funny situation this, isn't it? Guns, diamonds, caves... you and me together...' A shy smile formed through his beard. When her heart fluttered these days, Maggie tended to reach for pills. But on this occasion, she enjoyed the experience of a slightly raised heart rate in response. A slither of guilt about Frankie reared its head, a feeling she dismissed surprisingly easily. He had always wanted her to be happy, and generally, she was. Perhaps, if Dingo felt as she did in

188

that moment, there was a chance for the two of them to be happy together?

Perhaps. They stayed like that for several seconds, gazing at each other, totally lost in the moment, neither wanting to break off. With a babbling brook nearby and a shaft of sunshine suddenly breaking through the top of the ravine to bathe them in light, Maggie had good reason to feel a warm glow.

Dingo was the first to break eye contact and look down. He quickly looked up again 'Maggie... I...'

'No, don't say anything, Dingo. Just let us be for a moment.'

'Okay.' This time his eyes found points to focus on that were anywhere except her own eyes. 'Um...' There was a short pause, and then he spoke again. 'Maggie... I... I gotta say something.'

'Very well,' she said, irritated. 'What is it, Dingo?'

'Maggie... yer cacks are still around your ankles.'

'You took your time!' said Ben as they caught up to him.

'You're right, Ben,' Maggie said, glancing across to Dingo who had not yet got rid of his smirk. 'You can't hurry nature.'

'Or love,' added Dingo.

'Indeed, or, as Dingo says, love,' said Maggie in her most matter-of-fact voice. 'Phil Collins, nineteen eighty-something.'

Ben looked quizzically from one to the other. 'Are you both okay? You're acting very strange.'

'Are we, Ben love? I think I'm just relieved to have got that off my... um... chest. The next thing I'd like to get sorted is my arm, then grab a bacon sandwich and a nice cup of tea, before sitting down with my feet up to watch the telly somewhere. How far off are we from doing all that, Dingo?'

'Closer than you might think,' he said. He had taken the radio from Ben and started to fiddle with the controls again. It was not long before a crackly voice came through.

'Sounds like Tracy,' said Dingo, turning one of the knobs. 'Ah, that's better. Tracy, can you hear me? It's Dingo. Where are you? Over.'

'See? Over.' Maggie tried to ignore Ben's smug smile.

'Hey, Dingo, Dingo, can you hear me?'

'See? No over.' Ben tried to ignore Maggie's smug smile.

'We hear you. Over.'

'I got delayed. There was an incident...' The voice faded then cut in and out for a few seconds before they lost her again.

Maggie watched on as Dingo, his thick eyebrows propping up a patchwork of worry lines, adjusted various knobs and slider controls. 'I don't like the sound of that. Tracy, Tracy, can you hear me?... Tracy...'

Eventually, a muffled reply came through that Ben, his hearing possibly being stronger, repeated as: 'I'm right above you now.'

Then, a voice, not on the radio, called down: 'Look up, you daft bugger!'

Thirty feet directly above, a head appeared. 'I've been calling you for ages, Dingo. That shorty you've got is a pile of chicken shit.'

Dingo looked hurt for a moment but recovered quickly. 'Everything okay, Tracy?' he shouted back up. 'What's happened?'

'Nah, it's all good.'

190

'If it's all good, why don't we talk when we're a bit closer?' said Ben. 'The sooner we get out of here, the sooner I might be able to stop carrying this thing.' He tapped the bag with the radio. It was the first serious moan Maggie had heard from him. She wouldn't begrudge him that.

'I've got wheels,' Tracy said.

And drugs, hopefully, Maggs.

Tracy must have read her mind because she called down for someone to catch, which Ben, much to his obvious surprise, did. It was a small pot.

'Dip yer finger in and rub that in,' shouted Tracy. 'No more than a fingertip's worth, mind. That'll help you for a bit. I reckon you've got another twenty minutes walking and you'll reach the steps. I'll meet you there and sort you out good and proper then.'

Dingo gave a thumbs up while Maggie took the pot from Ben. She gave it back when she realised she could not even move her fingers on her injured arm to hold it while she opened it. Ben obliged, and immediately recoiled. The stench was awful.

Maggie took a sniff from a safe distance. 'What is it?' she asked uncertainly.

'Probably best you don't know,' said Dingo. 'Go on, take a bit and rub it in like she said. Or shall I do it?'

'No, it's fine,' said Maggie. She pulled her sleeve up and then reached over to the pot which Ben, with two fingers squeezing his nose, held at arm's length. She dipped her finger into the brown gooey contents and immediately her finger started to sting. She hesitated.

191

Dingo gave a reassuring nod. 'Go on.'

'Okay.' As soon as she spread it over her the swollen part of her upper arm, she felt the sting, then, just as quickly, the pain evaporated away. Redness and swelling were still there, but the discomfort had reduced to no more than a dull ache. The contrast was huge, reinforcing just how bad the pain had got.

Maggie smiled.

'Better?' said Dingo.

'Much,' said Maggie. 'So much better.' She looked up to thank Tracy, but she heard a distant door slam and the sound of a car engine starting up. 'She's some sort of miracle worker. Incredible.'

'Not a miracle. Just thousands of years of people breaking their arms and other parts, and needing help. You've experienced it yourself, Maggie: the dreaming. It's all connected. That stuff probably works better on you because you have a strong connection to the spirits. You're open to it.'

'Do you really think so?'

'You're like me, Maggie. You believe in the old ways, but still very modern and open-minded. Now, let's get goin' before those pretty little legs of yours get all wobbly and I have to carry you again.'

'Full of vim and vigour' was a phrase often bandied about amongst her friends back home, particularly after an operation or recovery from an illness. It was an anachronistic phrase, never used by young people who are usually brimming with the stuff, and largely wildly overoptimistically used by the likes of people like Maggie's friend, Alan. He used it to describe how he felt after his hernia operation, just before – to prove it – he tottered out of the hospital ward without his stick and staggered sideways into another patient who was tottering into the ward with his. But it was appropriate for how Maggie felt in the last mile or so. Tracy's ointment might have been the most disgusting thing she had ever smelt, but it had the opposite soporific effect to Sid's potion because Maggie virtually skipped her way out of the ravine. Dingo and Ben could barely keep up. Even the steps Tracy had mentioned – a natural rock formation that had been adapted to allow safe passage up and down a steep slope – were negotiated fairly easily, and they were soon at the top, looking back and down into the ravine they seemed to have been trapped in for an eternity.

Tracy was waiting for them at the top in a vehicle that reinforced Maggie's recent increasing propensity to believe that the world she was now immersed in was different. In front of her now was a Fiat 500, very similar to the car she and her friend, Marijke, had used to travel to Bruges in, and to the one that Joshua had driven onto the ferry at Harwich. If the gods were looking down and controlling the latter stages of her life, then the god of all things ridiculous was clearly suggesting they all have a bit of a laugh before Maggie joined them, as two men over six feet tall contemplated how they were going to squeeze into the back of an Italian sardine can.

The 'incident' Tracy had referred to earlier had, in the scheme of things, been relatively minor and had now been resolved. Tracy's explanation was lengthy and involved: something to do with a camshaft, an irate exchange between Tracy and Frank from Frank's

Fiats – *'No finer Fiats then Frank's Fiats!'* apparently – and a good whack with a very large hammer. She had explained all this, with Maggie desperate to ask her a vital question that could either support or scupper their plans as to where to go next. Eventually, she asked it: 'Tracy, do you know the location of the diamond, the last diamond?'

Tracy gave her a curious stare before looking to Dingo for some sort of reassurance.

'You don't have to say if you don't want to,' Maggie added.

There was a pause before Tracy looked Maggie in the eye and said, 'The Jingdon? Yeah, yeah, course I do.'

'It's at Flinders, isn't it?' Maggie said simply. 'Again, you don't have to...'

'Dingo's vouched for you. That's good enough for the tribe. And we trust fate. This is what's meant to be.' She nodded. 'Flinders. I'll know exactly where when we get there.'

'I don't want the diamond.'

'And you're not havin' it! But this is right. I feel it. This needs to be done.'

'Thank you,' said Maggie.

'So bloody polite, you poms. What's wrong with yer? Now, let's have a good look at that arm.'

Tracy confirmed that she believed the arm to be cracked. She applied more ointment, a different one, equally pungent, that she said would take down the swelling and help knit the bone together, then insisted Maggie join her in the front where her arm was unlikely to get knocked. As Dingo and Ben worked out how they

194

were going to squeeze into the rear seats – 'It's okay,' said Ben, 'I've got this. I've played a lot of Tetra.' – Tracy produced and handed round bags of potato chips and apples from the boot. Maggie was halfway through her second bag before she realised she had been using the hand on her broken arm to cram the contents into her mouth.

She had had her fill by the time she and Tracy had strapped themselves into the front. When the smell of the second ointment hit her in the confined space, she was nearly sick and felt close to passing out again. Ben and Dingo in the back may well have, as they were awfully quiet for the first five minutes along the very bumpy track. It eventually, led onto a slightly less bumpy one where Maggie no longer had to hold her hand over her mouth to keep her teeth in. After a short while with the windows open, the smell wore off and she felt more at ease.

Tracy had a casual approach to driving that did not require much visual interaction with the road, her eyes too busy either looking at Maggie while they chatted away, or pointing in the same direction as her lips as she blew smoke out the window from one of the many cigarettes she had on the go. Her hands shared the workload of steering, changing gear, and supplying her mouth with the lit cigarettes. It was a chaotic system which only just kept the car on course.

Dressed in jeans, flip-flops (or thongs, as Maggie had learnt to call them in Australia), and a yellow blouse that was pulled up over her belly button and tied across in a bow, Maggie would have put

Tracy's fresh unwrinkled face as being in its late-thirties, along with the rest of Tracy.

'I'm sixty-two,' Tracy revealed as she nearly steered the car around a particularly large bump. 'Six kids, nine grandchildren, and two great-grandchildren.'

Maggie gaped, at which point, as the car responded aggressively to the bump Tracy had not fully steered them past, her teeth did fall out onto her lap. She made a mental note to get something done about this rather annoying habit when she got home while, with Tracy in fits of laughter and the car veering in all directions, she attempted to put them back in via her nose and left eye. Tracy's throaty laugh suggested her lungs were at least sixty, even if the rest of her appeared not.

'It's another one of my potions, Maggie. Keeps me looking alright. I slap a bit on now and again whenever Sid has his urges.'

'Sid? As in Sid and Nelly?'

'Yeah.'

A direct follow-up question was about to pass Maggie's lips before she thought better of it. Instead, she tried a more subtle approach. 'Hope those two met up okay. Sid and Nelly. She seemed pretty confident of finding her way back.'

'They'll be alright. Sid and Nelly are like magnets. That's what marriage does to you, I guess.'

A very direct question hammered the inside of Maggie's lips, its hand raised like a kid in school saying 'pick me, pick me,' but was overruled by a muffled noise from the back which sounded like Dingo trying to say something. With Tracy's prompting, he

196

repeated it. 'Turn right onto the main road, Tracy. We'll head well away from my place.'

'What about your plane?' said Maggie. She had assumed they would somehow wind their way back in the hope that Dingo's place was no longer being observed. 'I don't fancy rattling across thousands of miles of desert in this tiny thing.'

'Too risky going there,' said Dingo.

'How will we get to Adelaide then?' said Ben from behind most of Dingo.

'By plane, but we'll have to nick one.'

'Not Molly's?' said Tracy. 'She won't like that!'

'No choice,' said Dingo. 'The sooner we get into the air, the better. Do you agree, Maggie?'

'I'm still worried about Sharon and the kids, so yes.'

They reached a T-junction at which, to Maggie's great surprise, they stopped. Tracy put on the indicator, lit another cigarette, and then looked both ways... several times. Maggie followed Tracy's lead, noting that there had to be nothing on the road for at least a hundred miles in either direction. After a pause, Tracy pulled out and resumed her laissez-faire approach, this time relying mainly on her knees to do most the steering, thankfully, on a better road with less lateral and vertical movement.

It was hot and uncomfortable in the front so Maggie dreaded to think what it must have been like cramped in the back. There were no complaints, but one of the two-litre bottles of water Tracy had shoved by Maggie's knees when they had got in was returned empty within a minute of Maggie passing it back.

'There's a couple more in the boot,' said Tracy. 'You sure about this, Dingo? Stealing from Molly isn't going to go down well.'

'She's hardly likely to just lend me a plane after you know what.'

Maggie could not help herself. 'You know what?' she asked.

'Nah, what?' said Dingo.

There was a snort of laughter from Ben. 'Hah! You've just been Maggied, Maggie.

'You know perfectly well what I meant by you know what,' she said, trying not to sound too prudish. 'What does Tracy mean by saying you know what? What is the what?'

'Ah, now, that's a long story which I don't have time to go into now,' said Dingo.

'We've got a little while till we get to her place,' said Tracy. 'Come on, Dingo. Don't be shy.'

'Shy?' said Maggie. 'Dingo... shy? Now, this I want to hear.'

There was a false attempt to clear his throat and Maggie imagined that had Dingo had space to shift awkwardly, he would have done so.

'I've... er... got nothing to be shy about. It's just that it's a long story.'

'And we all know what you feel about telling long stories, Dingo,' said Tracy, ducking her head under the steering wheel while she searched for the lighter she had just dropped. Maggie was relieved, at least, that she swapped steering with her knees and used her free hand instead. The road was incredibly straight, yet the action did not prevent Maggie from instinctively raising her hand at the ready. Again, it was her injured arm she used, with no pain whatsoever. The transformation was incredible.

Ben joined in. 'Come on, Dingo. We're about to steal a plane from this Molly. Personally, I always prefer to know everything I can about the victim before I steal their planes.'

'Well, okay, but it really is nothing big.' Dingo cleared his throat again. 'So, Molly and I go back a long way. A few years ago, we had a fling. Well, I say we had a fling it was more of a one-night stand... or two... several... quite a few, over a number of weeks or months... years, even. Nothing too serious. You know how it is.'

'No,' said Maggie at exactly the same time as Tracy said yes.

'As far as I was concerned, it was casual, a bit of fun, but I reckon she wanted it to go a bit further.'

'Was it the bride's outfit she turned up in at your place, Dingo, that made you think that?' Tracy took a large glug of water and offered the bottle to Maggie who shook her head. She was too engrossed in Dingo's previous love affair to think about drinking.

'That didn't happen! Well, it did, but it was a misunderstanding. This was over fifteen years ago! We'd been on the sozzle the night before and she reckoned I'd proposed and said we should get hitched straight away.'

There was a sudden loud raspberry, for which Ben apologised and then explained in more detail than was required that his right buttock was uncomfortable, so he had needed to swap, and while he did so his jeans had rubbed against the plastic seat and made the noise that sounded like he had broken wind. He had not, but, again, he was sorry that they all might have thought he had.

'Then why say sorry?' said Dingo. 'Bloody poms apologise for everything.'

'We have a lot to be sorry for,' said Maggie. 'And don't change the subject. So you didn't lead her on in any way, Dingo?'

Dingo sounded genuinely hurt. 'Nah, Maggie. I'm not that kinda bloke.'

Was that a hint, a reassuring statement directed at her? *Be careful, Maggs. Don't read too much into everything he says or does.*

'What could I have possibly said that would make her turn up dressed like that?'

'Let's get married tomorrow?' offered Ben helpfully. 'Wear something nice.'

It drew a loud guffaw from Tracy as she slapped the steering wheel. It seemed a timely and fortuitous reminder to her knees that they needed to hand back control to a part of the body that could actually help the car change direction. They were approaching the first bend since they had turned onto the highway.

'Definitely not. We'd had a few tinnies, I dropped her back to her house in the morning...' Maggie had half turned round so she could hear more clearly. Their eyes met as he said the word 'morning', at which point they both seemed intent on studying Tracy's head from their own unique perspectives before Maggie quickly found a window to look out of as Dingo continued. '...Still a little worse for wear. That afternoon, Molly turns up all ready to be joined in unholy matrimony.'

'So, what happened?' Ben asked.

There was another raspberry, followed by another apology from Ben as Dingo shifted position.

'She stormed off when I told her I wasn't interested.'

'She was far too young for you anyway, Dingo,' said Tracy.

'That was it?' said Maggie indignantly. 'That's all you said? No letting her down gently?'

'I find this type of thing difficult. Emotions and all that. What else could I say?'

'Well, I don't know... something along the lines of an apology might have been appropriate. I know you criticise the English for saying sorry, but it seems like it was the right thing to do in this situation.' She was angry with Dingo, for what, she was not sure. Was it the fact that he had been with another woman? If it was, what should she have expected? Should he have remained faithful to her, a good friend who was happily married to another good friend, on the off chance that years after Frankie had died, she became a spy again, got wrapped up in a complex case that meant she and Dingo would meet again in the middle of the outback, fall in love, and then... and then...

Whoa.. backtrack, Maggie! Fall in love? Is that what had happened? Had she – they – fallen in love? Was it possible at the age of eighty-two, and if it was, what did it mean in terms of how she was feeling about this Molly? *That you're jealous, Maggs. Simple as. This is what this is about: you're jealous of Molly.*

'I tried to make it up to her, tried to do the right thing, stay involved to an extent, especially after the...' His voice trailed off

'After what?'

'After... well, after all that. I tried to make sure they – I mean, she – was alright. I'm not a monster. She put the shutters up. Wouldn't let me anywhere near the place.' There was a pause before he added: 'I got hurt too.'

As he said those words, an image of a forlorn-looking Dingo when they had first met properly by the harbour in Tenerife popped into Maggie's brain. Back then, he had opened up to her about his feelings. He might do so again. And she might have encouraged him to if she had not been so busy analysing her own feelings... and trying really hard not to feel smug as she imagined them sauntering off in this harlot, Molly's, plane.

~ ~ ~

Chapter 18

If envy of her relationship with Dingo was not already enough for Maggie to dislike Molly, then jealousy of her huge Spanish-style villa that sat nestled in the middle of an oasis of green grass and lush brightly- coloured flora next to a lake was.

They were about a mile off the highway along a track that had challenged Maggie's teeth retention skills again. Ben had asked how long they had been travelling and whether he could, please, very soon detach the right side of his body which had, 'by a process of osmosis,' become part of Dingo's left side. Tracy had said they had been going for about an hour and it was not much further, at which point she screeched to an abrupt halt virtually outside Molly's villa. So keen was Maggie to get out of the car, she did not even bother to question why, if they planned to steal a plane, they had stopped in plain view of someone who she gathered would be reluctant to let them do so.

By the time the men had fallen out either side of the car and managed to get the blood running through their legs so they could stand up without support, enough noise had been made to add to the screech of brakes to attract the attention of the inhabitants of Perth, thousands of miles away. It, therefore, came as no great surprise to Maggie to see a figure emerge from the large oak door of the villa, make its way down the dazzling white steps onto the perfectly manicured lawn, and head towards them. It – she – moved with exceptional grace. Her long neck held her head up and back at a slight angle, and curved elegantly onto her bare shoulders. Dark hair, done up in the sixties beehive style Maggie had herself worn years ago, barely wavered as she slinked her way across the green grass in her bare feet. Her face – well, apart from the high cheekbones, pert nose, vivid green eyes, and lack of wrinkles, Maggie decided – had little going for it other than youth and perfection. It was only as she got nearer that Maggie realised that this vision of loveliness was a little older than she first appeared. In her late forties, perhaps. This had to be Molly, confirmed by the fact that she stopped short a few metres away, folded her arms, and belted out in as broad an Australian accent as any Maggie had ever heard: 'What the fuckin' hell you doin' here, Dingo, you stinkin' lump of bat shit?'

Entranced, no one had said a word up until that point. Maggie looked across at Dingo whose face had become more and more worried the closer Molly had got. The other two, like her, no doubt, were taken in by this remarkable figure and were now just staring at Molly who stood motionless, her eyes fixed on Dingo. It was obvious it was his turn to speak. There was a long pause, punctuated only by the slight movement of Molly's dress as she tapped her foot impatiently. She cocked her head slightly and raised a thin black eyebrow. 'Well?' she said.

Dingo exchanged a quick look at Maggie before drawing a deep breath and saying, 'We've come to nick yer plane, Moll.'

As Molly screeched and hurtled towards Dingo with her hands outstretched ready to grab his throat, Maggie noticed something, as an experienced spy highly trained to observe the world around, she really should have noticed before.

Molly's dress was a wedding dress.

Tracy's approach to dealing with Molly's attack was almost as casual as her approach to road safety. Maggie had no doubt that Dingo would have coped with Molly's attempted strangulation, yet she could not help but admire the way that Tracy deftly stepped in front of Dingo at the very last second with a raised palm to intervene. Maggie caught the look of confusion on Molly's face as she realised her own hands were likely to make contact with the top of the head of a small, smiling, black woman, rather than the middle of the neck of a grimacing, tall, white man. She lowered her arms which allowed her perfect, angry face to slap into Tracy's surprisingly sturdy unyielding hand. Tracy shrugged as Molly collapsed into a heap on the ground.

'Sorry about that, Moll,' she said. 'I don't want anyone hurting him.' It was said in such a way that the jealous part of Maggie's brain immediately took the opportunity to hunker up next to the part of the brain that was naturally forgiving and innocent to quietly suggest that its approach to life, in this case, was wrong, and together they should delve into whether Dingo and Tracy had had some sort of relationship too. But there was no overt reaction from Dingo, other than to bend down to check on how Molly was, so she decided to leave it... for the moment.

Hair ruffled, dazed, and bewildered, Molly had lost some of her earlier glow and elegance. Maggie could not help but feel a little sorry for her.

'Why don't we just ask her if we can borrow her plane?' she asked no one in particular.

There was a growl from the floor. 'You ain't borrowin' any friggin' plane of mine!'

'But...'

'And who the hell are you, anyway?' Molly's pale blue eyes held Maggie as she took Dingo's proffered hand and got to her feet. 'You his new Sheila? Or, rather, old Sheila?' she added with a sneer.

'My name is Maggie Matheson.' She replied much more formerly than she intended. 'And, no, I'm not his or anyone else's Sheila.'

'Why are yer cheeks flushin' then?' Molly suddenly turned on Tracy, an arm raised. 'And you, you bitch...'

This time Dingo did intervene. His hand shot out and grabbed Molly's wrist. 'Calm down, will you, Moll? I knew you would be like this. There's no point asking about the plane coz you'd say no. But, look, we need it. This is an emergency. So let's not waste any more time. Get yer tantrum over and we can all get on with the important stuff.'

Molly snatched her hand from his grip. Maggie half-expected another attack but, instead, Molly smoothed down her dress and adjusted her hair.

'What important stuff? What's more important than explaining why you left a girl danglin' at the aisle?'

'I've told you countless times, I didn't leave you danglin' anywhere, Moll. You turned up at my place in that...' Dingo held out a hand, apparently unable to finish the sentence.

'It's a dress, Dingo. A wedding dress. It was a wedding dress then, and it still is.'

'Why are ya still wearin' it, Moll?' asked Tracy. 'After all this time.'

There was a cough, an intervention from Ben which worried Maggie. His interventions tended to require further interventions from someone else to put right.

'What?' said Molly turning towards him.

'Er, it's displacement theory.'

'Who the hell are you?'

'I'm Ben.' Much to Maggie's relief, he had the good sense not to follow through with the twitch of his hand which might have resulted in the offer for her to shake it. She imagined Molly might have taken hold, whirled it and him several times above her head, before dumping him on the floor. He continued: 'Displacement theory would suggest that your disappointment at not marrying Dingo has been concentrated into – displaced onto – that dress, an obvious symbol of the terminated marriage.'

'The marriage was not bloody terminated!' said Dingo loudly. 'Something has to start to be terminated. I never agreed to marry you, Moll. You bloody well know that.'

There was a sniff and Molly turned away, head down with one hand holding the skirt of her dress which she gently swished from side to side. After a moment, she addressed Ben. 'I don't know

207

who you are, young man, but you certainly know a great deal about the effects of unrequited love on a spurned woman such as I.'

'Jeez, Moll,' said Dingo. 'You might have the dress, but for Chrissakes stop suddenly talkin' like bloody Miss Haversham.'

'Clearly, she feels she is Miss Haversham,' said Maggie, now over the shock of recent events and suddenly feeling a touch of sympathy for the woman. She was also keen to get on and sensed an opportunity to get things back on track. 'My dear,' she said in her best *can I convince you to give me a discount on these flowers, young man, if I let you unload all your problems onto me about running this stall in the middle of winter* voice. 'Why don't you and I have a nice cup of tea inside this beautiful house of yours and you can tell me all about it?'

Tea solved most issues. Not only was it a comfort, it was also something that took only a little time to make and then enjoy. The ritual of offering, making and drinking had lowered the guard on many people she had shared tea with. In her heyday as a spy, Maggie had negotiated the release of prisoners at an East German prison; persuaded a Columbian drugs baron to stop trading in heroin because his mother would be ashamed of him; convinced a minister in the foreign office to own up to his wife about his affairs, and secured a pay rise and better working conditions for workers in a factory when she was working undercover in a textile house. All done over a nice hot cuppa. She knew how to do tea, both how to make it the best and how to make the best of it. A nod towards Dingo as she had ushered Molly back to her house had been enough, she hoped, to indicate he and Tracy should track down the plane. As she predicted, Ben followed her and Molly inside. He had rarely, if ever since she had known him, refused the opportunity for a cup of tea. He might be handy to have around; Molly had quite clearly been impressed by his 'displacement theory' theory.

Anyone with great expectations of the house from the outside would have been disappointed when they went inside unless they were an actual fan of Dickens' Great Expectations. Molly's front door led straight into a dark and dingy lounge which continued the Miss Haversham theme. Cobwebs in the corners were so voluminous that it turned a rectangular room into a curved one. Maggie was not at all interested in meeting the spiders that wove those webs. The curtains at each end of the room were half-drawn, each side hunched up like boxers in a ring who had just been pulled apart yet were raring to get at each other again. What little light there would have been was blocked by net curtains, a pointless claim on privacy, in Maggie's opinion, since Molly's place was miles from anywhere else. Piles of books and magazines were scattered over the floor and across what would have been a luxurious sofa had it not been covered in cats, all of which had enjoyed raking their claws across it, judging by the holes and thread hanging down. One or two looked up as they entered the room, but the rest – and Maggie counted at least seven on the sofa with more bundles of fur lounging about on mantelpieces, occasional tables, and various threadbare rugs covering parts of the wooden floor – carried on the very important business of draping or lolloping. The humming, she realised, was the sound of numerous

209

lazy cats and not the encouraging distant sound of a light aircraft being started.

'Don't mind Tiddles,' said Molly as she deliberately pulled up a captain's chair, placed it in front of the window, and completed the effect by moulding herself into a Miss Haversham silhouette.

'Which one's Tiddles?' said Ben as Maggie tried to spot a door that might lead to tea.

'They all are,' said Molly. 'Jeez, do you think I'd remember all the names of these filthy ratbags?'

'Ratbags? Why keep them if you don't like them?'

'I thought you were supposed to be the Sigmund Freud round here. You tell me!'

Maggie, sensing that Ben's honeymoon period with Molly might have come and gone – an analogy she was not going to share out loud, bearing in mind the circumstances – perched on the edge of the wing-backed chair near Molly and put her 'tea' face on. 'Go and find the kitchen, Ben love, and put the kettle on. I'll do the rest in a minute. Now, Molly,' she said turning to the bride not to be. 'What's this all about?'

Twenty-five minutes later, Maggie and Ben were sitting behind Dingo and Tracy in a red and cream bush plane, bumping along at sixty miles per hour along the rough terrain, the wheels currently refusing to do what the wings (and Maggie) most wanted, which was to travel the bulk of the several thousand miles to Adelaide in the air. Maggie turned round to return Molly's enthusiastic wave as they sped past her house. She had changed out of her wedding dress, and was now sporting light brown khaki shorts with a T-shirt to match, plus a sturdy pair of walking boots which she had told Maggie she had never worn. 'I used to be a real bush girl,' she had divulged. 'Loved the open spaces.'

As the plane finally gained enough lift to hop, skip and then jump into the air, Ben shouted above the rattle of the engine noise: 'Um, does anyone know where we are going?'

'Flinders Range,' said Maggie.

'I know that. What I mean is, does anyone know how to get there?'

'Go up, turn right a bit, and head south,' said Dingo. 'No navvy in this.'

'Navvy – sat nav?' said Ben sounding rather pleased with himself.

'Got it in one, mate,' said Dingo. 'Can't risk outside interference, so good job there's no high-tech stuff on board anyway.'

'And up, right a bit, and south is specific enough, is it? I guess Australia's not that big a place so the margin for error is small.'

'Sarcastic bugger, isn't he?' Dingo commented to no one in particular.

'Everywhere's connected,' explained Tracy. 'Look, down there.'

Maggie and Ben both looked out their respective side windows. There was not that much other than a lot of brown now as the plane gained ascendency and landmarks faded.

'What are we supposed to be looking at?' asked Ben.

'Lines... can't you see them?' said Tracy. 'When you're down there, you can only feel them. Up here, you can really see them. It's how we find our way around. They'll take us to where we want to go.'

Maggie believed her. She had heard of ley lines back home and guessed this was the same principle. How they worked, she had no idea, but she was quickly learning that the Iwelongas were remarkable people. She was very happy to be in Tracy's capable hands; after all, she had worked wonders with medicating her.

'That's quite a transformation there, Maggie, with Moll,' said Tracy, cutting off the opportunity for any more questions Ben might have had on the subject. 'She'd gone proper troppo. Now looks like she'll be apples.'

'Proper what?' said Ben, picking up on a new line of questioning. Although coming across sometimes as being impatient with Ben's interventions, deep down, Maggie loved that about him – always curious, and not shy to ask the questions others might not dare to, even if it resulted in having the micky taken out of him. She imagined him as the kid at the back of the class who always put his hand up, willing to go against his impatient peers who would want him to shut up so they could go out for break time. No doubt, the persistence and thick skin he showed stood him in great stead over the years when faced with people all around him challenging him on his sexuality.

'Troppo – crazy,' Tracy repeated.

'Oh... and she'll be apples, will sheee...!'

Ben's voice dipped and whined in response to the plane unexpectedly doing the same. There was a throaty roar from the engine which lasted as long as Ben's 'eee' until Dingo stepped on the gas to return to a level.

'No dramas,' he said coolly pointing to the expanse of blue that now surrounded them. 'I've not missed the sky yet.'

Having travelled in many small aircraft on various escapades in the past, Maggie remained calm and tried to make light of it. 'No dramas, troppo, she'll be apples... We seem to be in the middle of an Australian soap. Flying Doctors, maybe?'

There was a snigger from Tracy. 'Streuth, Maggie! That's goin' back a bit.'

'That's coz I go back a fair bit myself, Tracy. I'm not one for insisting on the Queen's English, but some sort of English might be helpful for us poms.'

'Ah, fair Dinkum, Maggie,' said Tracy with a broad grin. 'I'm just sayin', Ben, that Molly went from crazy to calm very quickly. What d'ya say to her?'

'We just had a little chat, that's all. Sheila to Sheila.' There was the faintest of twitches from Dingo. The mischievous part of Maggie half hoped he would be worried about what they had talked about – a sign, perhaps, that he cared about what she thought of him – though she had nothing too tantalising to reveal. 'She unloaded, I think the modern term is. Said she had wanted to be the trouble and strife but couldn't Adam and Eve it when Dingo said 'no' to the old Otis Reading. Since then, she's been in a right two and eight.'

Tracy's 'What?' could barely be heard above Ben's loud guffaw.

'If you want to play confuse the pom with your Aussie slang,' Maggie said, 'I have a whole load more cockney rhymes I can unleash in revenge. Anyway, Molly said she'd found life rough: unsupportive family around, a daughter she hardly ever sees, no proper relationships since she was dumped...'

Dingo tried to interject, but Maggie stopped him. 'I'm not apportioning blame, Dingo, just seeing things from her perspective. I asked her what she hoped to achieve by wearing the wedding dress all the time, which got her thinking. I suggested she spent more time living in the moment. Lord knows, some of us haven't got many moments left, and Molly's no spring chicken either. I went through what I'd been up to the last 3 days or so. Life is out there, I told her. Just got to grab hold of it by the balls.'

For a few moments, no one said a word. The engine had quietened now that they had levelled off. Maggie stared out the window at the vast brown landscape some way below and reflected on her own counsel. Since Frankie had died, she had done her best to grab hold of life by the balls. But to start with, after she retired from the Service, life had winced and politely suggested it would be less painful all round if she stopped squeezing so hard and used her hands instead to control the TV remote. Coming out of retirement last year had changed all that. International espionage was not what Molly craved, but neither was moping around in a wedding dress all day. Molly's was a remarkable transformation, and Maggie, using her own experience, had been very happy to help.

214

And here Maggie was now several thousand feet in the air flying over the Outback into another adventure. She would keep grabbing those balls at every opportunity, although, for now, she would make do with holding something more accessible as she reached forward and caressed Dingo's shoulder. In response, he flicked a switch on the console and returned her touch with what had now, conveniently, become a free hand.

~ ~ ~

Chapter 19

Maggie was awoken by the sound of loud snoring. She opened one eye to blackness outside and Dingo with his head slumped forward, out for the count... at least he was until, alarmed, she shouted out his name. Dingo reacted as if he had been electrocuted. Ben next to her jumped and hit his head on the side window with a loud thwack which, in turn, made Maggie cry out again. Tracy with headphones on was the only one who did not react... which was just as well as she was actually flying the plane now. It was at that point that Maggie remembered the effort in the confined space that Tracy and Dingo had gone to swap places shortly before Maggie had dropped off.

'Jeez, Maggie,' said Dingo. 'What the hell's got into you?'

'I'm sorry... I... I forgot where I was for a moment. Is everyone okay?'

'I was,' said Ben rubbing the back of his head.

Tracy lifted a headphone from her right ear. 'We're not far off now,' she shouted behind her in response to a thrust from the engine as they made their approach to what Maggie hoped was a safe and comfortable landing spot. Tracy's voice suggested otherwise. 'Best buckle up and hold on tight. I can't see a bloody thing.'

Maggie nodded and concentrated on trying to slow her heart which was still elevated after the shock of seeing Dingo not being in control of the plane. There was a time when she used to thrive on that adrenalin rush. The energy and increased alertness that came with it had got her out of many a tricky situation. Nowadays, she was conscious that a racing heart could be a potential precursor to something much more final and damaging. *There are worse situations to go out on, Maggs,* she reflected. *Could die alone in bed.*

They hit the ground fairly hard, several times, before eventually rattling to a halt. Tracy flicked a couple of switches and there was a last judder as the engine cut out.

'Thank God, I can have a ciggie now,' she said, extracting a cigarette and lighter from somewhere about her person. 'I never smoke and fly. Bad for you.''

'I must admit, I'm relieved we're down,' said Ben. He picked up the radio from the floor, placed it on his knees, and began to rummage around with his right hand into what Maggie quickly realised was her left buttock.

'I don't think that part of me will release your seat belt, Ben love. Try something with a bit of plastic around it.'

'Sorry.'

Tracy opened up the door on her side, lowered the step, and clambered out, followed by Dingo. Once both she and Ben were decoupled from their belts, Maggie, with the necessary 'hups' that all people over a certain age make when getting up, started the process of decoupling herself from Ben. There was a plop sound as contact was broken, made by Dingo's finger flicking the inside of his cheek while he stood on the step waiting to assist her down.

217

She raised an eyebrow at his grinning face as he held out a hand. 'How's that arm?' he asked, the grin tapered at the edges by concern.

'It's okay.' Though, in truth, she felt a little wobbly and was grateful for Dingo's presence as she negotiated the three steps down.

The sky was lit up with stars, a truly inspirational sight – and, Maggie realised, an essential aid to Tracy's ability to land – but she felt a chill in the air, whipped up by a gathering breeze as they waited for Ben to disembark.

'Thank you for flying with Bumpity-Bump Airlines,' Tracy said in a mock English accent. 'Have a pleasant onward trip.' She grabbed a duffel bag and a large torch stowed in a compartment in the front of the plane and slammed the door shut. There was a brief moment of darkness, save for Tracy's cigarette end and the stars, as the plane's interior light went out before she flicked the torch on. 'Right, let's check out the bar and karaoke. Who's for cocktails?' She shone the torch towards a building which, at first sight, made the dunny at the petrol station look like the Taj Mahal in comparison.

'That's where we're staying tonight, is it?' said Ben as they approached what could loosely be described as a door. 'I'm glad someone booked ahead, , we might not have got in.'

'It'll do us,' said Dingo. 'I've slept in worse.' There was a loud creak as the thing that could loosely be described as a door revealed itself to be exactly that when it almost came off in his hand. 'Here,

218

give us that torch, Tracy. Bill said there should be a couple of gas lamps.'

They waited outside while Dingo stepped in. There were a few bangs and clangs, and a 'Bugger, me head!' before the space inside was lit up by first one, then another lamp, the latter suspended from the ceiling and the likely source of Dingo's complaint. Tracy doused the torch and they followed Dingo into what was a surprisingly spacious and un-hovel-like room.

There were two large benches cum beds on either end, each with plastic mattresses on, and a stove in the corner with a gas bottle underneath. The kettle on top gave Maggie's 'cuppa radar' cause to swing from side to side, and it made loud beeping noises when Dingo revealed that the sealed plastic Tupperware box in the little cabinet next to it did indeed contain teabags. The two metal mugs and a five-litre bottle of water in the opposite corner completed what would have been the makings of a perfect hot drink had the milkman's round extended that far outside of Adelaide. The chocolate bars Tracy produced from the duffel bag were, Maggie decided, more than an adequate substitute in the circumstances.

Earlier on as dusk had descended over the outback, the shorty had come into its own once again, when, a thousand metres above sea level, they had received from Bill the coordinates of somewhere they could land, rest, and even refuel. Discrete enquiries had been made through Joshua's contact – a friend of a friend of a friend, a network the right agent in the Service would be good at exploiting – which resulted in them being led to this shack, a local hunter's bolthole north of the Flinders Range. Permission from the hunter had not been sought for obvious reasons, so there was an outside risk he might turn up in his own plane. If he did, he would be in for quite the surprise, thought Maggie.

She would have put up with Sheldon and the Russians arriving with a fleet of fighter jets, so long as she could still drink the cup of tea she was now cradling. The drink, the chocolate bar and the fact she was no longer rattling around in vehicles was plenty of reason to be thankful. The stopover to recharge batteries after what had to be one of the longest days of her life, even by her standards in a career full of long days, was much needed.

They couldn't be that far away, by Australia's vast geographical standards, from where Sharon and the family were in hiding. As tempting as that might be to check on them tomorrow, she would have to resist that. People had gone to a lot of trouble to keep them safe. Hopefully, no one other than Bill, Joshua, and the contact were aware of their whereabouts, but she was not about to risk leading anyone to them, even though she had confidence they were still effectively off-grid. Tough, stressful decisions. For now, though, with a cup of tea in hand and another slap of the potion Tracy had just applied to her arm, she felt she could cope with anything.

Especially with the warmth of Dingo's body propped up against her next to her on the bed.

Maggie was awoken by the sound of snoring. She opened one eye, ready to berate the villain before she realised she was alone in the shack and was the only possible source. Frankie often complained

220

about her snoring, though he was just as bad. They would often argue over who woke up who. It was the only thing they ever argued about.

She took a moment to get her bearings. It was morning, evidenced by the shaft of sunshine that shone through the large gap that remained after Ben had tried to secure the door the previous night. It was warming up already; she could feel the heat radiating through the walls. She had been quite cold overnight, she remembered, until Dingo had suggested she lie flat on the mattress next to him and wrapped his enormous arms around her, spooning her, just like Frankie used to. She convinced herself the act was purely practical, a needs-must situation – particularly when Tracy did the same to Ben on the other bed – but she could not deny how comfortable and safe she felt with Dingo.

There were sounds outside – reassuringly the voices of all three of her companions who seemed to be preparing the plane. Judging by the snippets of conversation she could hear, they were debating whether to move the plane closer to save hauling fuel cans over to it. Quite how many cans this mysterious hunter whose shack they had commandeered had stored nearby, she did not know. She supposed she also ought to haul her lazy self off the mattress and go outside to look, but she could not bring herself to do so for fear of finding out exactly how much of her body hurt after yesterday's exploits. Another couple of minutes would do no harm.

Except that it could, of course, as she remembered about Sharon and the possibility that Sheldon and others seemed to be putting a lot of effort into making Maggie's life difficult. She was lucky to

221

have people around her prepared to go out of their way to help her. In return, she should assist them, and she would... in just a minute, as soon as she gave her eyes a little rest. *Definitely time to get on with things, Maggs... definitely...*

The dream was so vivid.

Frankie was beckoning her into a small cave. Naturally, she followed. The walls were covered in pictures, similar to the ones in the bunker at Dingo's in that they were designed to tell a story, but these, she realised, had the same story repeated over and over. They were old – ancient. She knew that because they were faded and simple, with stick-like figures in different poses. The scenes varied: in one they were dominated by three tall people, presumably adults; in another, there were more figures, of different sizes, possibly to differentiate the ages. Each story ran vertically, top to bottom before the next story began at the top alongside. Events also varied in the middle sections with some involving a journey – just like Brian's drawings back in the great hall – others a gathering or a hunt, but they all started similarly with two figures sitting back to back on either side of a pole or tree trunk atop a simple structure that, if Maggie did not know otherwise, was a bridge.

Slightly disconcerting was that the final two frames of every story were the same. The penultimate scene showed a hole in the ground, next to a pile of rocks or stones, possibly diamonds. A semi-circular line was drawn over each scene, denoting, perhaps, the roof of a cave. The final scenes below that, though, were what caught Maggie's – and Frankie's – attention. Each one was split in

222

two; on the left side was an idyllic scene with a river running next to three trees of ascending height going left to right. People and animals congregated next to the river and the sun was high in the sky in the background. The one on the right had the same trees and river, but no people or animals. They had been replaced by small flames.

The end of the world.

Then the screams started.

'You alright, Maggie?' Dingo was there, leaning over her, his eyes wide in alarm. 'That was quite a holler. Nightmare?'

'Yes... what... where...?' It took a moment to realise it was Dingo and not Frankie. She could have felt disappointment, but she did not. 'Oh, Dingo, that was awful.'

'You're alright,' he said softly. 'You're with me.'

'Yes, yes, I am. Thank you.' And it did feel okay. 'I was just about to get up. I must've dropped off again.'

'Yeah, that's what Tracy wanted. You need your rest, Maggie.'

'But we have to get on! Sharon... the kids, Sean... Bill, Joshua...'

'Are you gonna make a list of everyone you know?' Dingo said fondly. 'We might be here for some time if you are.'

'No, course not. But we do have to show some urgency. Sheldon could be...'

'This Sheldon woman could be anywhere, but most important at the moment is to make sure you're okay. You needed that sleep after the day yesterday. And the drugs you imbibed.'

Maggie eased herself up and put her feet on the floor at the same time as gently swinging herself upright into a sitting position. Dingo hovered nearby, hands ready to support.

'Easy, girl,' he said.

'Thank you, Dingo, but I am not a horse.'

'No, but you snore like a bloody donkey. Jeez, Maggie!'

'I do not snore!' she said huffily, aware she was throwing him the same glare she might have given Frankie during one of their many conversations on the matter.

'You do. How's the arm?'

She gave the affected area a rub. There was no pain. 'Better,' she said.

'Tracy hoped it might be. The extra salve I put on while you were asleep should have done the trick.'

'I'm fine. Now, can we please go? I've delayed us already.'

'It's barely seven thirty, Maggie. Time enough to get on our way. The plane's ready.'

With that, there was a throaty roar as the engine shot to life. Maggie got to her feet feeling, for the first time in a while, her old, albeit, old, old self.

'Get this down yer,' said Dingo holding up a mug of water. 'Gas has gone so no tea this morning.

'Thanks.' She was thirsty. 'Is there enough? Have you all had some?'

'Yeah, plenty. More or less cleaned the guy out though with that, and used up all the jerry cans of fuel he might be planning to use next time he's here. Hope the fella'll be alright.'

As with the clothes she needed in Sydney when she wanted to change her look, this was technically theft, albeit in the name of Her Majesty's Government. She felt a pang of guilt; hopefully, recompense could be made swiftly as and when things were resolved. They had desperately needed this overnight stop and they desperately needed fuel. For the moment, guilt would have to take a metaphorical running jump.

She glugged back the tepid water, smacked her lips for no reason whatsoever, and then marched out the door, leaving Dingo in her wake. She was met by blue skies and a sun shining brightly just above a large area of bushes and small trees to her left. She waited for her eyes to adjust before taking in the rest of the scenery they had not seen last night. In the far distance to the south were shapes that could have been clouds or mountains. The rest of the nearby terrain was a mixture of scrub and trees, interspersed with a good many hillocks and clumps of rocks. It was not the flat area she had assumed it was. Through it all, Tracy had managed by luck, skill, or both to negotiate them safely to the ground in the dark without major drama. From the cockpit of the plane which had been moved closer after the discussion, Tracy caught her eye now and gave her a cheery wave. At the same moment, Ben appeared looking rather sheepish from behind the shack, which in daylight looked every bit as decrepit as she thought it did last night.

'Just had a wee,' Ben announced, stooping to pick up the shorty by the corner of the shack.

'Well done,' said Maggie, giving him the same encouraging smile she reserved for her grandkids when they were younger. 'Did you leave the loo seat up?'

'Er, there is no loo seat. There is no loo. I just went round the back so no one would know.'

'Then told us where you'd been and what you'd been up to,' said Dingo walking over to the plane and picking up the two jerry cans that were standing at the rear. 'You need a piss, Maggs, before we fly?'

'Not right now, but thank you so much for your delicate enquiry.' Despite the tea last night and the water, her bladder seemed to be in go slow or no-go-at-all mode. 'I'll go on the plane if I need to.'

'Is there one on the plane?' said Ben looking rather offended that he had not been told.

'Yeah,' said Dingo dumping the cans back into a wooden box attached to the side of the shack. He pushed the lid back down and dusted his hands off. 'The stewardesses don't tell everyone because people get up and use it, and then get in the way of the drinks trolley when they bring it round.'

Ben shook his head before clambering up the steps to join Tracy. Maggie gave Dingo a nudge in the ribs.

'He's a good man. Do you need to tease him so much?' she said.

'Nah, I know he is,' said Dingo rubbing his ribs. 'And yeah, of course, I need to tease him. He's a pom.'

The battery on the shorty was very low with no means of recharging it. They all knew the importance of reserving what was left for what could be important hours ahead, but still, there were things they needed to find out. Up in the air, the reception was marginally better than when Ben had tried from the ground, but it was a very crackly and short exchange with Joshua, from which they ascertained they were 'on their way'. Dingo had tried contacting other members of the tribe, as well as Pete, Al, and Simon, to no avail. No news, they had to assume, was good news.

She felt contact with third parties was inevitable. It would happen – had to happen – at some stage, but by staying below the radar for as long as possible, it would more likely be on their terms. They had put so much effort into it so far. Tracy and Dingo had tried to keep it that way by deliberately not flying in a direct line the previous day, avoiding habitations – apart from a remote 'one-kangaroo town', as Dingo described it, to refuel where they paid by cash Tracy had. Hopefully, it would be enough. Maggie hated to think that the struggles out of Dingo's shelter through the caves and the long plane journey here had not been in vain. But she was also conscious there was a chance they had been.

With the course set for Flinders – 'Fly up, do a U-ee (U-turn, Ben before you ask) and bear left' – it was time for a brief cogitation once more. The strange dreams Maggie had had, including the recent weird one with Frankie and the stories in the cave, were not prophecies, she knew, but more her mind reacting to the circumstances and settings around her. That made sense: Frankie was rarely out of her thoughts; diamonds had been a thing recently (to put it mildly), as had the real experience of her and Joshua being tied to the top of a bridge. Add to that the fact she had, in the past, visited Flinders to see similar (but real, unlike the ones at Dingo's) cave paintings, the nature of that last dream this morning was hardly surprising. Nor should she be surprised at the way the stories in the cave paintings finished up showing fire. They lived in a violent world dealing with violent people. All very logical, her old, experienced, analytical spy brain told her. Therefore, should she take the dreams as further validation that they should head to Flinders? Well, in many ways she already had: instinct, dreams, feelings had undoubtedly influenced their decision-making so far, as had Brian's drawings and his lunchbox which she had taken as a sign. Overriding all that, though, was the fact there was a huge diamond there tempting dangerous people. Very dangerous people... *What on Earth are you thinking, Maggs*? They should go straight to Adelaide, speak to the authorities, and call the whole thing in. Surely, not everyone was corrupt.

Except, she knew they could not do that. If this was Sheldon they were dealing with, she had worked her manicured fingers into many pies before, and there would be plenty of people out there still who would be willing to bake for her again, particularly further up the chains of command. They had no alternative other than to keep going. So, when Dingo announced they were as close to the caves as they were going to get unless they expected him to land on a pile of rocks, she was cogitated out, and her mind was firmly set once more on finding out what they could at the caves.

~ ~ ~

Chapter 20

A loud click on the radio, followed by a lengthy high-pitched warble stopped the discussions between Dingo and Tracy about the precise spot to land. Dingo took down the revs to quieten the noise of the plane slightly, while Ben concentrated once more in his increasingly expert role as 'shorty knob-twiddler' as he had named it earlier. There were a few more cackles before a faint voice came through. All, except Dingo as the pilot, leaned in to listen. It was a female voice.

'Hello, it's Nelly. You there? Over.'

'Hello, Nelly,' said Maggie. 'We're here. You okay?'

'Big Al's had a hand-written message delivered to the restaurant. I'll read it out. It says: "Maggie. I have your family. If you doubt this, remember the Smarties business. Diamonds – all diamonds – will be exchanged for their lives by the tank on Parfitt's property at ten this morning. My people will be there. No police, or else. Taylor." That's it. Over.'

Ben asked the message to be repeated, which Nelly did while Maggie listened with increasing dread. Joshua had said the family was safe. The thing she had feared the most had happened: her family had been found. She felt numbness setting in, but she was shaken out of it by Ben.

'Hang on, Nelly. Over,' said Ben. 'Maggie, what does it mean by Smarties?'

'What? Oh, Smarties, yes.' *Maggie – you're needed. Focus!* 'Taylor's asked Sharon for something memorable to confirm he's with her. When she was six, she ate five boxes of Smarties in one sitting. The results were spectacular and difficult to forget, unfortunately. We called it the 'Smarties business'. Taylor's got them, for sure.'

'Shit,' said Tracy. 'What do we do?'

Taylor was not to be underestimated. He had managed to recover from being nearly hit by a missile, located her family, and got to them. In usual operational circumstances, her analytical spy brain, to understand her adversary better, would be trying to work out exactly how he might have achieved all that. But these were not usual operational circumstances; family was involved. Emotion could dictate operational thinking; she must not let it.

'He said ten. Tracy, isn't there a time zone difference between New South Wales and South Australia?'

'Half hour behind here, so exchange would be at nine-thirty our time.'

'So he still doesn't know where we are.'

'Which means we have a chance to rescue Sharon before the bastard wipes his arse.'

'Yes, I guess that's one way of putting it, Dingo.'

'It's just gone seven forty,' said Ben. 'Less than two hours.'

'They're round here somewhere. We need to contact Joshua to find out where. Push the button again, Ben... Nelly, can you hear me?'

'I can hear you, Maggie. Before you go on, the tribe has decided we will do the exchange. Over.'

'But what about your diamonds?'

'A few diamonds for life – no contest. We can spare enough to think they've got the lot and still keep plenty. Over.'

'I don't know what to say.'

Tracy grabbed the microphone. 'The answer's yes, Nell, if we need you to, do the exchange. We have a plan which hopefully means you won't. We'll be in touch. Out.'

With a finality that brooked no argument, Tracy handed the microphone back to Ben and faced back to the front. She folded her arms. 'Right, you've all heard how long we've got. Contact Joshua, then we'll head down.'

Dingo had taken them east of the mountains and found a remote road, barely wider than the plane, on which to set down. The doors were flung open as soon as the plane stopped to avoid any of them being cooked, but they remained inside with a cool breeze whipping through the cockpit, while they waited for Joshua. Astonishingly, he said they were close by, which meant that all were in the vicinity of where Sharon and family were being held.

Maggie was feeling the nerves. 'Tracy, Dingo, when Joshua and Bill get here, you should stay with the plane or head back or something. You too, Ben love. I've put you all in too much danger.' She continued to marvel at the bravery and commitment of people around her. Dingo, Ben, Tracy, the tribe, all were going to extraordinary lengths to help, as were Big Al, Psycho Simon, and

231

Pete the Crap, friends of Dingo she had not even met. But enough was enough. 'I can't expect you, any of you, to do this any longer,' she continued. 'This is my problem and it's my family. I can't...

'And my family by marriage,' interrupted Ben,

'Yes, but still...'

'And you and Frankie have always been like family to me,' added Dingo.

Maggie caught his blue eyes, momentarily diverted by how they could be so steely in one moment and soft like a baby's in the next. 'I know, Dingo, but...'

'And this is our tribe's battle too, anyway,' said Tracy. 'We're as wrapped up in this as you. They're our diamonds, remember.'

'I know that. But...'

'But nothin', Maggie,' Tracy continued. She had a very serious side to her laid-back persona, which was now on full display. Twisted round in her seat so she was facing Maggie and Ben in the back, her face showed a determination that had to be typical of her tribe. These people knew how to survive. Their ancestors had lived in harsh conditions for thousands of years, overcoming hurdles that Maggie could not even begin to imagine. What was happening now was just another one to jump.

'We need to stick together,' Tracy continued.

'Yes, I understand, but...'

'And if you say "but" one more time, you'll find my size threes halfway up your actual butt. Bloody poms... if you're not apologising you're trying to act all pious. Oh, I want to do this all on my own. Oh, I've put you all in too much danger.'

'Is that supposed to be me?' On a scale of one to ten of Dick Van Dyke English accents, it was in the high nineties.

'That's exactly how you talk, Maggie. Exactly.'

Maggie opened her mouth again and, faced with an eyebrow that shot up, closed it again. There were not many things that could silence Maggie, but Tracy seemed to have found a rare button that worked.

'You need help,' said Tracy, 'and that's the end of it. And we need to do this soon. If we give Taylor the diamonds, he might not fulfil his side of the bargain. Might not be pretty for your family, Maggie.'

Bluntly put, and a point that had occurred to Maggie; a point she did not want to think about it too much. 'I know. Okay. Thank...'

'Don't say it! We don't need your thanks. We do need you to be on the ball. Okay?'

'Yes.' She had needed that straight talking. 'Right, well, Joshua said they had been taken to a safe place.'

'House,' corrected Ben. 'Aren't they called safe houses?'

'That's different,' said Maggie. 'If it was a safe house, they'd be a lot safer than they are right now. Those places really are impossible to find.' Having been bamboozled by a street numbering system that only the enigma machine could crack, she had always thought anywhere in Basildon would be ideal for a safe house.

'So, that's decided: we hook up with the others,' said Tracy, 'and go rescue them. Simple!'

'Yes, Tracy,' Maggie said emphatically. She was pleased she had these people around her. As much as she worried for them, there

233

was an element of safety in numbers. With Joshua, Bill, and Brian on their way, their merry band was about to be boosted.

~ ~ ~

Chapter 21

'I reckon that must be them now,' said Dingo standing up and leaning out over the plane door. He pointed at a cloud of dust heading towards them from behind a line of trees.

'Is that the same truck we had?' said Ben leaning forward to stare through the space vacated by Dingo.

'Whatever it is, I hope it's big,' said Maggie who, as grateful as she had been for the loan of Molly's plane, had had more than enough of being squeezed into tight spaces.

As the vehicle neared, it became apparent that they did indeed have the same pickup truck from Coffs Harbour. The back seats and an open area behind would provide ample room. They screeched to a halt metres from the nose of the plane and got out. Brian, Maggie noticed, was driving, and from the look on his face had been enjoying himself. He must have had his foot permanently to the floor to have got them there so quickly.

As they converged on the road between the truck and the plane, Joshua got straight down to business by asking for a quick debrief. Maggie spoke on behalf of her group, mainly to stop Dingo from coming out with his usual liberal smattering of metaphors and also to stop Ben from asking what those liberal smattering of metaphors meant. Naturally, she started with the worrying call from Nelly. Tracy chipped in with what her role had been before Joshua and Bill filled in the gaps from their perspective.

The boys had had a journey too. 'Quite the ride,' Bill commented with a sideways glance at Brian. As Joshua had intimated, Brian had sniffed out the direction the missiles had come from, ascertaining that they had been fired from the south. It was thought very unlikely indeed that Taylor had been responsible since he and his people had approached from the north, plus the fact that it would have meant Taylor had been firing missiles at himself which was just not at all credible.

'Impressive work, Brian,' said Ben.

'It's a seventh sense I have. I'm able to smell unusual things in the air even better than our top hunters. You gotta do that when you're on walkabout to survive.'

Maggie did not ask what the sixth sense was – she half-expected Ben to – but she could take a guess that it was most likely connected to that feeling of fate, expressed by tribe members. Instead, she asked: 'So you found the site, you said. Any useful information you haven't already shared?'

'It was close enough for a rocket launcher to be used,' said Bill. 'There were tracks: a large vehicle, plus one other smaller vehicle.'

'Not a heavy presence,' Joshua added, 'but enough to cause serious damage. And it did. Sorry, Dingo.'

Dingo shook his head dismissively. 'It's a wonder no one was killed. Let's be thankful for that.'

'Easy to transport that kind of equipment along public roads without raising suspicion too. I would imagine,' said Maggie.

'Exactly,' said Joshua, 'and not a problem even if you're stopped, if you've got the local police under your control.'

236

There was a moment of silence while that was reflected upon, before Dingo asked, 'What did Taylor do after we left you? It looked like some of them might be struggling.'

'We didn't hang around for long after we met up with Brian. We had to make a decision to stay and maybe intervene or find out the missile launch source. We know this thing has to be bigger than Taylor, although I regret that decision not to follow Taylor now.' Joshua looked at Maggie in concern. 'I've underestimated him. Aunty Sharon and the family wouldn't be in this mess now if we'd stayed on him.'

'We've all underestimated him,' Maggie said supportively. 'You were outnumbered and also you had to find out what else you could. So you've driven straight down to here after finding the missile site?'

'Virtually non-stop.'

'You were quick,' Dingo pointed out.

'Brian's a maniac driver, capable of going all night,' said Bill. 'We tried to take turns, but he wouldn't let us have the keys.' In response to the comment, Brian, who was perched on the massive silver bumper, shrugged and rattled the keys playfully before gulping down some cola from a large plastic bottle. Dressed in tight black jeans, a white T-shirt, and blue and white trainers, he showed no signs of wear and tear after the long drive. Joshua – and Bill, especially – looked a little ragged. Joshua was still in his outlandish – now ripped and filthy dirty – outfit that he had picked up in Sydney, and Bill in his lumberjack gear was looking like he had

237

been attacked by a large dray of squirrels, intent on revenge for him chopping down their tree.

'We've been trying to keep tabs on you as much as possible,' Bill explained, 'aiming to meet you somewhere near the caves. Knew you were in the area but pure luck we spotted the plane in this huge expanse.'

'Our ancestors guide us,' said Brian between glugs. 'And sustain us.' Another glug. 'Thanks be to the god of caffeine... full-fat version, of course.' He wiped the opening on his T-shirt and offered the bottle up. 'Any takers for the dark liquid that bubbles brightly in the morning sun and injects us with that which awakens us to the world.'

'Love some,' said Maggie. Brian nodded and smiled as she took the bottle from him and had a couple of swigs. It was slightly warm, but it would help give her a much-needed boost.

'Blessed be the great god, Caff,' Brian added with a finger pointing to the sky, then to the ground with a mock confused look, before taking the bottle back and making the sign of the cross. 'Amen.'

With no other takers, Maggie watched him swill back more. He could not have been much older than seventeen or eighteen, yet there was something of the wise hippy in him. Carefree, yet quietly capable. She had a soft spot for hippies, having dabbled as being one herself, both undercover on duty and off duty in the 60s and 70s. Thus, she should have immediately warmed to Brian, but there was a cockiness there that slightly put her off. Still, he had been instrumental in helping to get them all together now, and he had helped locate the missile launch site. Those things had to count in his favour. A quick look at Bill's guarded expression as he watched Brian place the cap back in the bottle suggested he might share her concerns.

Up to speed now, Joshua started the discussion on the next steps. They went through the contents of Taylor's message again to be sure of timings. 'Just over an hour and a half till the exchange,' he said. 'We need to be in and out by nine-thirty to be sure. The earlier the better. Are the family definitely still together?'

Maggie said they were not able to say for sure, but assumed they were. She felt a little ashamed that she had not thought so much about Sean. Her focus had been on Sharon and the girls.

Joshua dismissed her worry. 'We'll assume Sean is there with them and they're still in the place my contact put them into.'

'The same contact who found us the shack?' asked Ben who, since they had met up again, had been standing protectively right next to Bill. Maggie could hardly blame him. She realised now she had virtually become Dingo's third leg as they each sought reassurance from people they relied on.

Bill spotted her looking and mouthed, 'You okay?' She nodded. 'You?' Both checking in, both making sure the other one was okay. It was a warm moment between them in what had been a manically dangerous couple of days, the sort of mother and son moment she had been searching for – possibly too hard – since they had been reunited.

Joshua confirmed it was the same contact. In fact, the family's no longer hidden hideout belonged to a relative of the contact. 'It's a pre-fab on top of a hill not far from here.'

Not far. Maggie felt a sudden flutter of hope.

'A small place. I can't see how Taylor will have a lot of people inside it or around it.'

'How Taylor knew about it is the concerning thing,' said Tracy.

'Agreed,' said Joshua. 'I've got to say though that my contact has been reliable so far. Done everything we've asked.'

'I don't doubt you, Joshua mate,' snorted Dingo dismissively. 'but the tweedy git has found them somehow.'

'True.'

'What are you thinking, Dingo?' said Maggie.

'It has to be an inside job.'

'One of us?' said Ben.

'No one in the tribe,' said Tracy defensively.

That had been raised before, Maggie recalled, back at Dingo's, and been dismissed sharply by Dingo. Was he suggesting it now? There was a slow shake of the head from the big man. 'Well,' he began slowly. 'You know more about this sort of thing than I do, Joshua, Maggie and Bill, but I guess it depends on how, what, or where the job is that you're inside of.'

Maggie was right with Ben, for once, as he gave his trademark 'Huh?' look.

She stepped away a little from Dingo and placed a hand on his chest in encouragement. 'Go on, Dingo love.'

'Well, I reckon Taylor's found out from someone on the inside where they are. If it's not us, the Iwelongas, and we accept Joshua's contact as valid... well, that only leaves one other group of people with a potential insider.'

Maggie caught up with Dingo's reasoning at about the same time as Joshua and Bill, she guessed from their faces.

'You mean...' she began.

'Yep,' said Dingo. 'Exactly how well do you know this bloke of Sharon's?'

It had not even occurred to her. Sean? Sharon's Sean? He had always been a good host, a doting husband, and a caring father, as far as she could tell. Australian by birth, Irish father, English mother, Sean met Sharon when she was in her last year at university in London while he had been on a gap year from medical school in Sydney. They had fallen in love, and she had not hesitated when he asked her to join him back in Sydney to see how she liked Australian life. She liked it very much, so when Sean proposed to her six months later, Maggie had, of course, given them her blessing, as had Frankie. Sean had had a few months to go on his finals and was already talking about specialising in cosmetic surgery in Adelaide. Since then, Australia had been their home.

So Maggie knew Sean through occasional visits, but did she know him well? Truth be told, not really. However, not being emotionally close to a son-in-law was one thing; assuming that the same son-in-law was involved in criminal activity was another. Yet it could explain a few things. Sean would have known in advance about their plans to travel to Australia. As a member of the family, he would have had contact details for herself, Joshua, Bill, and even Ben. Thinking Dingo might be a useful contact, Maggie had told Sharon about him when she had moved to Australia, so Sean even knew about the big man who lived in the Outback. And, of course, he knew of Sharon's whereabouts because he was with them now. But it did not explain a motive, and there was no connection established between Sean and Taylor or Sean to anyone else significant for that matter.

All of this went through Maggie's head in double-quick time, quick enough for her to respond to Dingo's probing question about how well anyone knew her son-in-law with: 'Well, he's a doctor, vice-president of a sailing club, and a member of the Adelaide Chamber of Commerce... but I'm thinking you're not impressed with those as credentials, are you, Dingo?'

'Nah.'

'Never trust a thirsty gecko,' Brian chipped in. 'They'll bite yer nipples as soon as look at you.'

Maggie noticed Tracy and Dingo nod sagely at Brian's contribution. She avoided Ben's gaze. 'Well, yes, I see what you're saying, Dingo and, er, Brian. It's certainly a consideration.'

'Bill and I only know him through the bit of Facetime we've done with you, Maggie,' said Joshua, 'so we've not got a lot to go on.' It was part of the reason they were going – to get to know the family better. 'We can't discount it.'

Maggie was suddenly feeling her favourite word, if not her favourite feeling, that word being, 'discombobulated'. (She liked to

242

deliberately throw the word into conversations specifically so she could watch those people who did not know what 'discombobulated' meant, look discombobulated). Her head had been trying to deal with all the nuances of a complicated situation and mainly, so far, failing. Maggie considered herself to be an excellent judge of character. Had she judged Sean so wrong? Perhaps, but likely not, yet she would deal with it at face value. It was apparent Joshua – and from the look on his face, Bill too – was doing exactly that.

'Let's assume that someone is leaking information,' Joshua continued, 'and act with caution.'

'Especially when we approach the target,' said Bill. 'Taylor and his people are not suspecting we're going to do this.'

'That's good, isn't it?' said Ben.

'On the one hand, it is. But we know catching animals by surprise can be dangerous. Just be wary. And we need to spread our resources. E.B.B. and all that.'

Before Ben could ask, Maggie chipped in: 'Eggs, basket, buggered. Don't put all your eggs in one basket, otherwise, well, you're buggered.'

'E.B.B. agreed,' said Joshua. 'I need to speak to my contact again. He needs to know the safe... not so safe place has been compromised. I also want to flag up for possible backup when we get this sorted. I'll keep an open mind about him and his true loyalties too.'

'Do you wanna borrow the shorty?' asked Dingo.

Joshua and Bill both looked puzzled.

'Shorty is short for shortwave radio,' said Ben sounding slightly impatient. 'Everyone knows that,'

'No. We've used Morse code so far,' Joshua said.

'Really?' said Dingo. 'That high tech? And I thought I was out of date!'

Maggie smiled. 'The old ways are the best. Good on you, Joshua. Does that old trick through public phones still work? We used to call it phone tapping before phone tapping was a thing. Literally, phone up and tap out what you want to say with the handset.'

Joshua nodded.

'Well I'll be jiggered,' said Dingo. 'Proper spy stuff.'

'Can't beat it!' said Maggie proudly. 'Though we'll need a phone box, of course.'

'Closest one,' said Brian, 'is about seven miles, that way.' He pointed down the road past the plane.

'How'd you know that?' asked Ben, impressed. 'Is it instinct? Something to do with ley lines?'

'Nah. Pokemon Go.'

'What?'

'You played it?'

'No!... Well, yes, actually.' Ben coughed. 'Maybe once or twice. You need a mobile.'

'Nah, don't need that. I play it with blokes from tribes all over Oz. We've got our own version over the shorty.'

'Dare I ask how this Poke your mum works?' asked Maggie.

Brian chuckled. 'It's called *Pokemon*, Maggie. You could, but aren't you lot wantin' to get a wriggle on?'

244

There were several nods around the group and an actual wriggle from Ben which he thought no one had spotted... until Maggie caught his eye.

'Then, trust me. There's a Pokemon hotspot with a phone box outside of Dez's Barbers, seven miles away.'

'Let's go,' said Joshua. 'All in the truck.'

'You mentioned you wanted to let your contact know what the plan was,' said Maggie as they started to move. 'Have you got one?'

'Not yet, but I will have by the time we get there.'

'What about Molly's plane?' said Maggie.

'I'll deal with it properly later,' said Dingo. 'Give us a hand to push it off the road.'

Maggie, well experienced in women being disadvantaged in all manner of ways over the years, was very happy to let the men be macho and take charge of this particular dusty and back-breaking task. She and Tracy watched on critically, arms folded, until it was a few metres from the road, before walking over to the pickup to claim another advantage over the men – first choice on inside seats.

As Maggie got into the truck, she said to Joshua, 'Hope this won't take long. I know seven miles isn't far but we've got to get to Sharon too, remember? How close is she?'

'Very. Place called Othello,' said Joshua, grabbing the front passenger seat. 'About seven miles away.'

~ ~ ~

Chapter 22

Time was of the essence so they did not even try to stop Brian from taking the wheel. Bill squeezed into the rear seat with Maggie and Tracy, while Dingo suggested that 'the blokes with the biggest knobs' jump up onto the cargo area at the back. Ben looked a little flummoxed at first before realising Dingo was suggesting it was the two of them. Maggie, with her arm beginning to ache again, was relieved to be sharing the space with Tracy and Bill, the slightest of the men (apart from Brian who was 'scrawnier than a Polish pole dancer, partially pole axed round a beanpole,' according to Dingo).

Maggie distracted herself from her arm by worrying about Bill instead. Since they arrived in Australia, Bill had gone about his business with little fuss, largely separate from her. Joshua had taken control when Maggie was not busy rushing headfirst into situations, dictating how they work, and Bill had been in the background with the odd sage comment or showing he was ready to act and support. Prior to Australia, she and Bill had tried to spend as much time together since she had discovered he was her son. There was nothing important that he had not told her about his life, nor she told him about hers. Yet, she sensed there was a barrier still between them, caused by the years apart, for which, having given him up, she felt responsible. Maybe he still begrudged her decision? She hoped not, but something to bring them even closer would be good. Something along the lines of a quiet cup of tea with cake and a long chat. Failing that, she thought, maybe the tried and tested method of stopping a diamond heist while saving their family from a violent international gang. The danger of that, of course, was that if they failed, it might drag them apart again.

She looked across to Tracy who gave them both a thumbs up. Bill returned it with one of his own, followed by an encouraging smile, ruined slightly by worry lines around his eyes. It was a reminder that there was a sister and nieces in danger here, not just a daughter and grandchildren.

Just then, Brian took a bend designed to be taken at thirty miles an hour at a speed approaching double that. It induced a double clunk in the cargo area followed by two muffled double obscenities. Joshua turned to look past Maggie out the back window.

'They're still there,' he said calmly. 'Though Ben's now put his arm through Dingo's.'

'Such a flirt,' said Bill dryly.

Maggie tapped Joshua's arm for attention. 'You said you'd have a plan by the time we got to Othello. We must be nearly there by now. You thought of something?'

'No.'

'But...'

'I said I'd have a plan by the time we got to Othello. I didn't say it would be my plan. You're the senior spy here, what do you think we should do?'

Having spent the last few miles thinking about her relationship with Bill, Maggie was taken by surprise. But, as was often the case, while she had been busy unpacking her emotional baggage, the analytical part of her brain had been getting on with planning out schedules for day trips, assessing the best places for breakfast, lunch, and dinner, investigating bingo sessions, and ensuring they had the strongest team available for quiz night.

'I'd like to split into two groups after you've made your call, approach from two sides, if possible, you and Bill one in each group for cover. You do still have weapons?'

'Yes, one each.'

'We don't exactly know what we're up against, so will have to act on instinct, unless your person can give any more info?'

'I'll ask, but might prove tricky on specifics with Morse code.'

'After the rescue, Dingo flies them back to the shelter at his. Safest place for them, for now. Brian and Tracy, as much as we value you, I...'

Tracy jumped in with all the force of an elephant wielding a wrecking ball plastered with bright pictures of rhinos. 'Don't even raise that possibility again!'

There was a 'Nah, don't' from Brian.

'Anyway, you might need my knowledge at the caves.'

'And there won't be enough room in that plane,' added Brian.

'Well, let's agree to keep that part of the plan fluid for now.' There was a huge temptation after what had gone on to never allow her family out of her sight ever again. 'After the rescue, some of us...' – she tried to ignore the glare from Tracy – '... do what we came down here for which is to check out the caves in Flinders Ranges.'

'Are we counting on Sheldon – and let's assume it is her – are we counting on her being at the caves?' asked Tracy.

'Whoever it is will head in that direction at some point. We have to get there first.'

'And what exactly do we do when we get there?' asked Joshua.

Now, that was a point no amount of cogitating had sorted out yet. 'I'll know when we arrive,' she said with more confidence than she felt.

There was another bang from behind and a Ben-like squeal as Brian negotiated a left turn on a t-junction by taking the hypotenuse of the triangle rather than bothering with the sum of the two sides.

As the truck settled back down onto four wheels, Maggie gave Tracy's arm an affectionate cuddle. 'You're risking a lot here. Are you sure you...'

'Enough! You bloody poms!'

'If you spend much more time with, us, you might turn into one.'

'No chance,' Tracy responded with an open smile. 'Would I make a good pom?'

'Definitely not.'

'Nah, thought so. I don't whinge, can't stand tea... and I like my cricket teams to win.'

On the way into town, they passed a sign saying, '*WELCOME TO OTHELLO, pop. 276*'.

It was no surprise to Maggie that with only the one obligatory dusty Australian town road in, the run-down shops, and the one bar on display, some wag had tried to scrawl out the Os and the T in the place name. What was left was '*HELL*', not a place she hoped she would end up in. *Not yet, anyway, Maggs!*

It did not take long to find the barbers and phone box right at the other end of the street. While Joshua made his call to his contact, they radioed Sid and Nelly with an update on their movements. Both reiterated how they would willingly give up the diamonds if needed, with Maggie saying she fervently hoped that would not be necessary. Asked about whether they were worried they might lose the diamonds, Sid pointed out rather dryly that they had dealt with far worse – a missile attack, for example – and were still smiling. Maggie made a point of asking them to pass on their thanks to Al, Pete, and Psycho Simon who, though excellent at making a nuisance of themselves, perhaps should not be encouraged to apply those skills to the more delicate matter of the *diamonds being swapped for lives* scenario. Psycho Simon, in particular, Dingo said, would be rubbish at that sort of thing.

The contact had, disappointingly, suddenly gone quiet, Joshua said emerging from the phone box, a worry that none of them could shrug off easily.

'Do we still go ahead?' said Dingo.

'We have no alternative,' said Joshua. 'It's time to split up.'

Ben was still sticking to Bill like glue, so Maggie said she would go with them and Dingo, while Joshua teamed up with Brian and Tracy. Maggie's group would be dropped off and would approach the house from one side of the hill on foot, after which Joshua and the other two would double back in the truck through town via the phone box to try again. They would then drive up the other side, culminating in a pincer movement in exactly – Joshua and Bill set their watches – twenty minutes.

It only took a minute to drive to a heavy plant yard on the edge of town, a point far enough away from the house where Sharon and the family were being held with hopefully enough cover for them not to be seen as they approached. The house was half a kilometre up a track which started behind the yard. As they got out, Maggie looked up above the ten-foot boundary fence to see a skyline dominated by tall cranes, below which were buckets of cherry pickers, rather spookily spying on them from over the top. At the entrance, twenty metres on, a battered wooden blue sign read, 'Dirty Dicks Plant Higher' in faded white lettering. Judging by the dodgy lettering, spelling, and punctuation, Maggie guessed that Othello's welcome had never extended to professional sign writers. The obligatory dust – a feature of Australia in areas which were either not indoors or made of water, it seemed – swirled around them in what was building up to be quite a stiff, and increasingly hot, wind.

Caution was the watchword, Joshua had said before he and Brian drove away.

'Knackered' was a more appropriate watchword, Maggie thought as they set off in the opposite direction to the plant entrance to take them round and up beyond the back of the yard. The combination of the heat and the wind blowing dust into her nose and eyes quickly contrived to sap away at energy levels that had not started at a high point that morning. *You're eighty-two, Maggie. Remember that,* and she was feeling every day of those eight decades and a bit.

251

Bill picked up on her low mood. Over sixty himself, he was not a youngster by any means, yet he had an aura that suggested otherwise. She was relieved to feel his reassuring hand on her elbow.

'You alright, Mum?'

'Keep calling me that and I'll be fine.'

'We'll all be fine,' he said, 'including Sharon and the girls. How's that arm?'

'Surprisingly okay. Just an ache.'

They rounded the corner of the yard and followed the line of the fence. There were no sounds of movement or work from within. A late start to the day, maybe. She glanced at her wristwatch several times before she realised she was only checking freckles.

'It's gone,' she said dully.

'What has?'

'The watch Frankie gave me. It's gone, and I've only just noticed. Even after you and Joshua set your watches, I didn't realise.' A pang of guilt prodded her. Her head was all over the place – for good reason – yet that was no excuse.

Dingo pointed out a break in the trees to their right which was a continuation of the track that led up the hill through the woods to the house. Bill acknowledged Dingo with a wave, and then said to Maggie: 'Are you talking about that little dress watch you said he used to wear on special occasions?'

'Yes.' She was pleased he had remembered it. 'Your dad loved it. I had a new strap put on it before we came out to smarten it up a little. I was going to give it to Sharon. Why was I so stupid to wear it on a long journey all the way to Australia?'

'Did you not anticipate when you put it on that you would be dangling from bridges, driving tanks, and crawling through caves?'

'Obviously not, but I should have taken more care. The point is I've only just realised that it's not with me anymore.'

She looked up at Dingo who was a few yards ahead with Ben at a point where the path turned sharply to the right. He waved them into the tall scrub to the side. Maggie was grateful for the small piece of shade and the shelter from the wind. 'Looks okay up there,' Dingo said, leaning out.

'Plenty more foliage for coverage,' said Bill checking. 'But the track loops back and forth, I reckon, so we'll have to listen out as well as keeping our eyes peeled. Can't see the house which is a good thing because it should mean they still can't see us.'

'I'll take point,' said Ben. 'I've no idea what that means, but I've heard it in movies. Always sounds so reassuring, so I thought I'd give it a go.'

'At the back, Ben,' said Bill with an affectionate smile. Maggie was grateful she was with Bill. He often had a habit of making things sound alright and normal, even when they were not. Frankie, she reminded herself, was the same. They set off again with Maggie having to force herself to get her legs moving forward. If it wasn't for the thought that her daughter and grandchildren needed her, she might quite happily have found a comfortable spot in a bush – bitey beasts and all – lain down and gone to sleep.

She vented her frustration on the missing watch. 'Infuriating,' she said as they set off again. 'I told Frankie I'd look after it.'

'There's nothing you can do now,' said Bill soothingly. 'He wouldn't be cross with you for losing it.'

'But I am cross for losing it.' A twist in her stomach – the warning sign – added to the anxiety which was building at a rate she was struggling to cope with. Every other situation she had been in before, both recently and in her time as an agent, she had felt as if she had at least an element of control. Why the sudden drop in energy and motivation? This was her plan, her idea, yet the sense she could positively influence what was going to happen was slipping away. As the path steepened and her breath quickened in response, the feeling got worse. She looked down at her feet, willing them to go forward. On the toe of each shoe, as she placed one foot in front of the other, the face of one, then the other grandchild appeared: Alice, Emma, Alice, Emma. Bill continued to hold her arm, but she was aware that he held more of her weight now. Without him, she could well have ended up face down in the dirt.

'I need to stop again for a sec,' she said.

'Lean against here,' Bill said easing her towards a small tree that threw out enough shade to shelter under. He produced a bottle of water from the drinks holder on the side of the rucksack he had slung over one arm and handed it to her. All the while his eyes roamed around, his hand firmly on the handgun he was carrying. 'Do you need to sit down?' he asked.

Maggie took a long slurp from the bottle. 'Yes, but I'm worried I might not get up again. I don't know what's wrong with me.' She took a couple more sips and handed the water back.

'Don't be so hard on yourself,' said Dingo. 'It's tough goin'. We're all feelin' it.'

'Me more than others.' She looked at her empty wrist again. 'What have I done?' she said under her breath.

'It's a watch,' said Bill. 'Yes, it held memories of Dad, but it's still only a watch.'

'It's not just the watch. My stomach is doing tumble turns. I'm putting us all in danger with this crazy plan. How are we going to overcome a potentially heavily armed gang? And what on earth are we doing here to start with? All this so I can stop some crazy woman who has got it in for me from getting her revenge. Why don't I just give myself up to her? The rest of you would be better off.'

'Because it's not about you,' said Bill. 'Not exclusively. If she wanted her revenge, she would have had it by now. She wants power and wealth. She's always wanted those things. Remember that I knew her well when I was working undercover on the Bruges operation. She trusted me, but only because I fooled her into thinking I wanted the same things as her, convinced her I was as ambitious as she was. The things I had to say and do to prove I was as power-hungry and ruthless as she was... well, you're an agent; you know what it's like. We don't always do the right things but we should always try to do what's right. That's what you're doing now: what's right. This is for Sharon, the girls, the future of the

Iwelongas who would be under constant threat if we didn't tackle this now and, remember too, for your country. These are dangerous people – arms dealers, thieves, people who lob missiles at innocent people. Sheldon, Taylor, people like them have to be stopped. You're going to be the person to do it.'

It was as much as Bill had said to her, ever, in one go. And she could not have felt more uplifted if he had finished with the opening lines to Jerusalem (or anything by Michael Bublé whose voice always sent a shiver down her spine). She put her hand out to squeeze his and then withdrew it as she realised that hand contained the gun. Instead, she dropped her head into his chest. She felt a gentle squeeze as his other hand come around her shoulders.

'I feel better,' she said, withdrawing. 'Thank you.' She looked at Dingo and across at Ben who had taken 'point' very literally and was standing some way back. 'Thank you to you two, too. I couldn't do this without you.'

'I couldn't do without you either,' said Dingo, before looking away, slightly embarrassed.

It took a moment for that to sink in, but when it did, Maggie smiled. Shaking her shoulders, she lifted her chin and stepped out of the shade.

'Come on then,' she said. 'You bunch of slackers.'

'By the way,' said Ben, oblivious to what she and Bill had been talking about, 'I've been meaning to give you this.' He held up a small object. 'You asked me to put it in the bag with the shorty to protect it when we went underwater in the cave. I keep forgetting I'd got it. I'm surprised you didn't ask me for it earlier.'

Maggie tried – and failed – to not catch Bill's eye as, sheepishly, she took the watch and attached it to her wrist. 'I'd forget my own head if it wasn't screwed on.'

The track flattened out and the trees thinned a little as they got higher. They were in danger of being exposed, so Bill said he would go on ahead to check out the situation. In less than a minute, he was back.

'Problem,' he said. 'The track curves round slightly and after that is a fifty metre run up to the front door of the house. Though I'm very confused. It's not a small pre-fab as Joshua described it.'

Maggie could not hide her concern. Joshua had been convinced this was the right location. 'We're definitely at the right house?'

'Have to be. It's the only one at the top of the hill, as Joshua's contact said. Hill slopes away again on all sides.'

Could his contact have been wrong about the description? Interpreting information over Morse Code could be tricky. She doubted it, though. This had setup written all over it.

'What do we do?' asked Dingo. 'Should we wait for Joshua and the others?'

'We should check it out,' said Bill. 'Find out whether they are there or not. We are time-limited and this is all we've got for the moment.'

There were nods all around, so Bill continued. 'The place is a one-storey bungalow with a large front garden set out behind a front fence and hedges to both sides. A straight driveway to the right leads up to a double garage. Large amount of space to the rear.'

'Desirable area,' chipped in Ben, 'decent schools nearby, and only three hundred miles to the railway station puts this property high on any discerning buyer's wish list.'

His contribution was met with a glower from Bill.

'Sorry,' said Ben to Bill. 'I'm quite nervous.'

'Look, Ben, you don't...'

'I said I'm quite nervous, not that I didn't want to be involved.'

It earned a hefty pat on the back from Dingo. 'Good on yer, Ben.'

'Can't see any sign of life at the front,' said Bill. 'Windows are too far away to see in properly. There's only one vehicle on the front drive. I suggest we track around the left-hand side and find somewhere to work our way into the back garden if it looks safe. Split into two subgroups initially: Maggie, you're with me. We'll go on ahead, suss it out. Ben and Dingo, wait a minute then follow on behind. I've still got one of your guns, Dingo. You want it?'

'Nah. If I need a weapon, I'd prefer something more flexible.' He stepped into the wooded area just off the track.

'Good idea, grab a big stick for me too while you're there,' said Ben.

'I'm not after a stick,' Dingo replied over his shoulder before disappearing behind some bushes.

There was the sound of twigs cracking and the rustling of leaves, followed by a stifled, 'Gotcha, you little bugger!'

He emerged a few seconds later, slightly red in the face, his hair tousled. In his hand was the head of a snake which judging by the open mouth and loud hissing was not too keen to find itself taken away from its usual pastime of hunting and swallowing crocodiles whole, or so it seemed to Maggie whose only real experiences with snakes was through watching David Attenborough watching snakes doing precisely that. This snake was only about two metres long, though it was hard to be precise since the rest of it was coiled tightly around Dingo's arm.

'What you got there?' asked Ben in a voice that Maggie had come to recognise as his *brave but I don't feel brave* voice.

'It's a snake.'

'Yes, I can see that,' said Ben taking the same number of steps backward as Dingo was taking forward towards him. 'What type?'

'A yella one. I was hoping to find a green one but this little fella will do the job. I never can remember whether it's the yella or green one which has the more lethal bite. Think it's the green one. This'll do though – will kill a hippo in less than two minutes.'

'A hippo? Do you get many of those in Australia?'

'It's a metaphor,' said Dingo rather defensively, while doing his best to unwrap the snake from an arm that was looking bluer by the second.

'And the green one?' said Ben looking around nervously. 'It's more deadly than that?'

'Think so. Or is it the green one that's not deadly?'

'I expect there are more than one type of green and yellow snakes, aren't there?' said Maggie helpfully.

'God knows. I'm crap with snakes. Hate the buggers.'

'Yet you have a head of one in your hand.'

259

'Yeah. Thought it might come in handy. Scare the shit out of anyone we come across.'

'It will certainly do that,' said Maggie.

The snake let out another loud rasping hiss, and Ben jumped back in response.

'Do you still want a stick, Ben?' said Bill.

'Not if it means going into those bushes to get one.'

'Well, we're going to need to go through those bushes in any case,' said Bill. 'That's the direction we need to go in so we can circle round to the back. You can pick one up on the way if you like, Ben. Leave the shorty behind. The battery's virtually gone and it'll only get in the way. We can come back for it afterwards. Right, Maggie, you ready to go?'

'I'm ready.' She set off after Bill as, gun to the fore, he traipsed through the gap Dingo had made. 'Don't drop behind too much,' she said raising a farewell hand to the others.

'We'll be right behind you,' Dingo said acknowledging her wave with a comical wave of the snake's head. 'Won't we, Mister Snake?'

Maggie chortled as she left with Ben stood frozen to the spot. 'I'm sure Dingo'll find you your own snake if you can't get a decent stick.'

Bill was accurate with his assessment of the bungalow. The small wood they walked through had recently had some thinning done on it, judging by both the ease through which they got through it and the stumps left behind. It was just as well there was a hedge inside the boundary of the property – a very well-kept hedge, Maggie noticed – that started a few metres from the edge of the wood, otherwise, they could well have been exposed. It was looking like a perfectly normal bungalow. The fact it did not look like the place they were expecting it to be was just another thing to add to their list of 'unresolved solutions' as she liked to think of it when she was in a positive frame of mind. And she was feeling more positive now. She pulled up her sleeve and looked at Frankie's watch. It was eight-thirty. Ten minutes before Joshua and the others should arrive on the other side. The sense of security the watch gave her helped; the realisation that time was ticking by did not. She took a deep breath and ploughed on.

Another minute or so and Bill came to a stop. They had travelled along the side of the property and were about to turn to the right to head along the back. With the wood continuing its line onwards, they were now in the corner where the rear of the garden's boundary was much less distinct as it went off at a right angle. It meant they were more exposed, so they tucked themselves behind the end of the hedge. From there, they had a full view of the back of the bungalow. It would have been an excellent view had it not been so far away, a good fifty or sixty metres in the distance. A low two-barred wooden fence, interspersed with bushes and ornamental trees, was all that stood between the back of the garden and the scrubland that dipped back down the hill towards the town. On the opposite side was a similar hedge to the one they had just been along.

At this point, Maggie thought something she did not recall ever thinking on any previous mission: *'Blimey, what a lovely lawn!'* It was vivid green and immaculately kept, stretching off away to their left into the distance past the bungalow and straight back where they had just walked on the other side of the hedge to the front of the property. Flower beds meandered along the borders, and the lawn was broken up with different shaped flat and raised beds, all of them packed with colour. A water feature with nymphs cavorting around a large naked godlike man sat against the hedge a few metres to their right, accessed by a redbrick path that snaked pleasingly towards the large patio by the bungalow. A stream spanned by two small Japanese-style blue and red bridges ran through the centre of the garden. Slightly to the left between them and the bungalow was an enormous greenhouse, behind which sat a large composting area. It reminded her of a stately home.

'Surely, this can't be right,' said Maggie.

'Well, it meets at least one of the criteria for a safe place in that it's not an obvious safe place.'

'Having been to many safe houses all over Europe and South America, I'm used to places that don't need an army of gardeners to maintain them.'

Bill grunted a laugh. 'It is what it is. We need to get across that lawn to the bungalow and suss out what's going on inside.'

'If we wait long enough there might be one of those little trains that do tours of the grounds.' She looked back into the woods the way they had come. 'Where are the others? They weren't supposed to wait too long before following.'

Bill took a few paces back where they had come, stopped, and listened. 'Not sure.'

His attention was diverted by the distant sound of a sliding door opening. They peered round the hedge again and watched as two men dressed in suits stepped out onto the patio. There was the sound of murmuring as one offered the other a cigarette and struck a match for him, before lighting his own.

From his pocket, Bill produced a small spyglass on a key ring and directed it towards the men. 'Two men, one very large, the other enormous. In their thirties, I would say. From the bulges, both packing sidearms in holsters under their jackets.'

'Not gardeners, then.'

'I don't suppose carrying weapons like that is normal in these parts. This could be the right place after all, though no sign of Sharon...'

He was interrupted by the sound of a telephone ringing.

'I want that ringtone when we get back home,' said Maggie. 'That's so loud.'

'There's a bell on the wall to the right of those patio doors, probably hooked into the main telephone.' In response, the larger of the two men threw down his cigarette and stamped it out, before going back inside. The other took a few more puffs before doing the same and following him in. 'Bill glanced at his watch. 'Eight thirty-five. We need to make some sort of move fairly soon. Any sign of Joshua?'

'No. We need him. Two blokes there,' said Maggie. 'There will probably be more.'

'No doubt. I'm concerned about Ben and Dingo. Maybe we shouldn't have split up.' There was an uncharacteristic hint of worry in Bill's voice.

'Usual Service protocol, Bill, and you know it.' Just as they had split into two groups earlier, splitting again spread the risk of capture and also gave different eyes on the target. Usually, they would be backed up with radio contact. Being off-grid definitely had its disadvantages.

'This place is bigger than we expected and we are under-resourced, not enough weapons. I'm tempted to find out what we can and re-evaluate.'

'Agreed, although don't underestimate our resources. There's also Dingo's snake and possibly a stick if Ben's found one.' Maggie was aware she was being flippant, the last thing that was needed in a dangerous situation. Yet she could not help it. *Nerves, Maggs. Cut yourself some slack... then shut up, so Bill can concentrate.*

'I'm going to try to get closer. You stay...'

'Don't you even dare finish that sentence, young man. I'm not staying anywhere.'

Bill looked levelly at her. 'I would say that it was worth a try, but I know it wasn't. If we can get to the greenhouse, we might be able to loop around from that side and get a better look at what's going on. I'll lead, Maggie, you follow.'

'Mum.'

'Mum feels daft from an operational point of view.'

'Okay, then call me Dark Hunter or something. I don't like it when you call me Maggie.'

'Okay, are you ready, Dark Hunter? The greenhouse it is. Let's go while those two heavies are out of sight.'

It was the turn of Maggie's heart, rather than her stomach to dominate proceedings as, keeping as low as they could (Bill, anyway – at her ever decreasing height, keeping low was not an issue these days) they broke cover and scuttled across the lawn to the back door of the greenhouse, with Maggie doing her best – and failing – to keep the Benny Hill theme tune out of her head. She was aware her state of mind was flip-flopping drastically. One minute she was exhausted and lamenting the loss of a watch that she had not lost, the next she was imagining herself and Bill being chased around the garden by scantily-clad women in bikinis, a scene that neither she nor Bill would remotely wish upon themselves. Throw into the mix the occasional visit to the dream world of the Iwelongas and her psyche would make a very interesting case study, to say the least.

They arrived at the backdoor to the greenhouse – surprisingly rough looking with peeling white paint – and Joshua turned the wooden knob, wincing as it squeaked. The door opened into a small alcove attached to the main greenhouse. Now they were inside, the greenhouse was enormously deceptive in terms of how deceptively enormous it was, its length stretching on towards the bungalow a good twenty metres or more. It seemed packed with every plant, vegetable, and fruit imaginable. They hid behind a rather large and attractive poinsettia in the alcove as they planned their next move.

265

'It's much longer than I thought,' whispered Bill. 'Goes quite close to the bungalow. We might be able to get a good idea of what's going on from the other end.' He peered through some tomato plants stacked in a line on a rack in front of the window to the side. 'Still no sign of Joshua. Never mind. Let's stick with what we said and focus on what's in front of us for now.'

What was in front of them, as Bill carefully led them round the poinsettia into the main stretch of the greenhouse was a good opportunity, with so much cover, to make their way down to the main doors without being seen. What was also in front of them, unseen initially because of the amount of foliage around, was the back of a flowery gardening smock, topped by a wide-brimmed straw hat, tailed by a pair of knee-length red shorts and sandals, and accessorised by a pair of secateurs in one hand with what looked like a gin and tonic in the other.

The figure turned round with a look of genuine surprise. 'Oh, it's you!' it said.

~ ~ ~

Chapter 23

As was often the case, before she could stop it, Maggie's mouth said the first thing that came into her mind when she saw the face. 'Tina Sheldon, what on earth are you wearing?'

Under any other circumstances, Maggie might have laughed at the way Sheldon was dressed. Her outfit was so un-Sheldon-like, it could only have been surpassed had she been wearing a pair of tight-fitting Lycra cycling shorts, a yellow cagoule, and a pink beret – a combination that Maggie herself had worn at the last Women's Institute monthly meeting in response to Sheila Barnes-Foley's suggestion that members who turn up should demonstrate a certain level of decorum.

Bill's gun was already raised by the time Sheldon had fully turned round. As Maggie studied the somewhat surprised look on Sheldon's tanned face, Maggie's first thought was how well, her former boss looked. Prison life had either suited her very nicely, or there was the other possibility – much more likely – that, as Bill had theorised earlier, Sheldon had never actually gone to prison. She was about to ask outright when the back door to the greenhouse opened behind them and through it stooped what Maggie assumed was the larger of the two heavies they had seen earlier. When he stood up to his full height, his head disappeared into the fruit of the vine that dangled from the roof. His gun, however, was on full view, and with the appearance of his

267

colleague on the other side, their plan to sneak up, suss out and scarper had been scuppered. Outmanoeuvred and outgunned, Bill was forced to surrender his weapon.

'Do forgive my casual attire, Maggie, and the G&T,' Sheldon said recovering from her initial shock. 'Bit early, I know, but I'm in holiday mode. I always am these days.'

With that Sheldon took a couple of sips from her drink, turned her back on them, and started to clip away at a plant which, judging by its dilapidated state, was used to being picked on.

'Still making swathing cuts whenever you can, I see, Tina,' said Maggie in an attempt to unsettle her. 'Plants, government departments, innocent people's life expectancy... is there no end to your talents?'

There was silence as the snip-snip-snip faltered momentarily before Sheldon continued her pruning. Despite their predicament, Maggie took a little solace from the fact she could still wind up her old boss so easily.

'Tina Sheldon: the woman who put the haughty into horticulture.'

'Can't say I've missed your wit, Maggie.'

'And you're not missed at Delton Park Prison?'

She turned and raised an eyebrow. 'Delton Park?'

'You got a double to do your time,' said Bill.

'Oh, you are so clever, Bill. I feel your talents are wasted working for the good guys. Yes, a body double, set free now to live her own life as she chooses. Like me, she can sit back and relax, enjoy the good things.' She leant down to smell a flower.

'Still sticking your nose in places you shouldn't be, I see,' said Maggie.

Sheldon suddenly stood upright and clicked her fingers. 'Oh, I think I might know what you're doing here. It must be connected to the information that just came through. Perhaps you're acquainted with a certain Mr. Taylor?' She tucked the secateurs into a pouch in the front of her smock and shoved her hands into pockets at the side. 'Apparently, some tribesmen are giving him some diamonds in exchange for the release of your family members? You're here because you think your family is here.'

'Where are they, Sheldon?'

'I really have no idea,' said Sheldon, taking a gulp from her drink this time. 'Not here, that's for sure. I leave others to deal with that sort of thing.' With that, she finished her drink and removed the pink gardening gloves she had been wearing. 'I must say: it is so nice of you to visit.'

'Don't play games, Sheldon,' said Bill. 'You knew we were coming.'

'Did I?' She put the gloves into one hand, stepped forward, and tapped them playfully against his chest. You know, I'm very upset with you, Bill. You double-crossed me.'

'That was business,' said Bill. 'That's what spies do. You know that, Sheldon.'

'True. I set up enough of those kinds of situations myself in the Service. Enjoyed that aspect of the work. Guess it was the nasty, conniving side of me. I was very disappointed in you, though, Bill. Very disappointed.'

269

'I imagine you would have been.'

She stepped back and gazed quizzically at both of them for a moment before settling on Bill. Her eyes flicked up to above their heads. The follow-up nod was almost imperceptible. The crash of the gun butt on the back of Bill's neck was not, and he fell to the floor like a sack of potatoes, an irony that Maggie – given the location – might have appreciated had it not been Bill. Startled, Maggie stumbled to her right and was en route to joining Bill until she was steadied by the enormous hands of Bill's attacker. She tried to stoop down to check on him but was pulled roughly back by the same pair of hands.

Sheldon laughed, a hollow cackling sound that reminded Maggie of what a nasty piece of work her former boss was. 'I'm sure there must be some plant or other full of healing powers in here that'll help with the headache he'll wake up with, though I don't much give a toss. Why don't we leave him in this gentleman's capable hands while you and I go and have a little chat indoors, Maggie? I find that after some serious pruning and my morning G & T, I need a little sit-down.'

There was a low moan from Bill which Maggie tried to respond to directly before she was forcibly wheeled round and marched away behind Sheldon. As she made her way towards the door, Sheldon let her hand drag lazily across the plants. Maggie half expected them to wilt and die at her touch.

As she trailed behind, with the huge shadow of the first man looming over her, Maggie found herself trying to work out how

270

things had gone so badly wrong. A trap had been set and they had fallen into it. Though a trap set by whom? Not by Sheldon, apparently who had seemed genuinely surprised at their arrival and, if she were to be believed, unsure about the location of Sharon and the girls. Distracted by Taylor and her obsession with getting to Flinders, Maggie just had not expected to come across her so soon. *You're losing your touch, Maggs. No... you've lost your touch.* With one last concerned look towards the greenhouse and Bill, she followed Sheldon through the patio doors.

To her surprise, she found herself in a large lounge packed with all the paraphernalia one might expect in a normal family home. There was a large flat screen TV in the corner, a couple of sideboards with photos and ornaments, occasional tables, and a large three-piece suite with a floral fabric cover that clashed hideously with the stripy blue and red carpet. Unbelievably, it was outdone by the Greek tragedy dominating the room that was the Clash of the Curtains. Two sets complemented each other – in as much as a rendition of the Sex Pistols' Anarchy in the UK might complement Vivaldi's Four Seasons. One long pair in luminous green framed the doors they had just walked through, the other, a shorter, though no less impactful, vivid multicoloured chiffon mess hung either side of a large window at the front. Maggie gazed around in disbelief. Had Jackson Pollock woken up from a psychedelic dream and told his people he wanted to dabble in soft furnishings, he might have produced something like that before her now.

'Nice place you have here, Tina,' Maggie said in a neutral voice. If she could get her talking, it might lead to some information about the circumstances of what Sheldon was up to and, more importantly, where her family was. *Let's face it, Maggs, you don't have anything else to offer in terms of a strategy.*

'You like it?' said Sheldon. 'I have more time to spend here now after all those annoying court appearances a while back.' She had been there for the trial, then, or at least some of it. 'Then there was all that business of lying low for a while in London after we did our swap before sentencing. Now though, well, I'm a free agent. If you'll excuse the pun.'

Maggie would love to find out how Sheldon had done the swap, but it was a diversion away from the immediate matters at hand. It was enough to know that she had been at large for some time, presumably planning and putting into place what could be the largest acquisition of diamonds ever. Except that she did not have them... yet. A considerable proportion of them was still in the possession of the Iwelongas, hopefully hidden deep in the tunnels that led off of Dingo's shelter, and the one she and Joshua had swapped should be in safe hands. And did she know about the Jingdon diamond?

'No, of course I don't like it,' said Maggie simply. 'But, we all have our own tastes, don't we?'

Sheldon looked genuinely hurt. 'I'm particularly pleased with the wallpaper.'

Maggie, having been too busy taking in the rest of the room, had not noticed the wallpaper. She did so now, before averting her eyes towards the least offensive spot in the room, which happened to be, unbelievably, Sheldon and her tasteless smock.

'That's unusual,' she said referring to the wallpaper. 'Astronauts...'

'Yes,' said Sheldon.

'Yes,' Maggie said. 'Look, I'm here because...'

'Diamonds? Something to do with diamonds? I like diamonds.'

'Yes, as does Taylor. What is your connection to him?'

'Connection?'

'Look, he says he's got my family.'

'Really? Are they a little tied up at the moment?' That awful laugh again.

'So, you do know.'

'What I know and do not know is of no concern to you.'

'It is because it's my family.'

'Yes. You're a big one for family, aren't you? Bill, Joshua, Frankie...' The sound of Sheldon saying all those names felt like an affront. 'Your family have caused me no end of trouble, as have you.'

'Where are they, Tina?'

'Oh, it's Tina now, is it?'

'Sharon, Sean, the kids. They're being held where?'

'Not here. Kidnapping and that sort of thing is no longer my area of expertise.'

'You're lying.'

'Now, lying is more my area of expertise. But in this case, I am telling the truth. My turn for a question: how did you find me? I'm intrigued.'

'You don't know?'

'Would I ask if I did?'

What was going on here? Sheldon's behaviour was strange: the garden and gardening, the decor in the bungalow, the fact she was not properly engaging... she seemed distracted, out of the loop. Different. This was not someone presenting as being on top of an international plot to obtain diamonds. Yet she seemed aware of diamonds and knew Taylor. Was she playing ignorant or just plain ignorant?

Maggie needed a few moments to work out what to do. Sitting down, under any circumstances, would help her do that.

'I'm desperate for the toilet,' she said. 'And I don't want to ruin your lovely carpet. I don't suppose...'

'Through the kitchen,' Sheldon pointed to a door, 'and it's at the other end.' Maggie made towards the door but was stopped. 'Maggie... now you've joined us, I'd hate for you to think you could just leave.'

'I won't.'

'Good. No funny tricks then?'

'Oh, I don't have the bladder control to do the funny tricks I used to do.'

'John will show you the way.'

'Why, does he know how to do funny tricks?'

Good banter, but it was not helping a chaotic mind desperately trying to take in recent developments.

The Jackson Pollock hanging on the wall above the washing machine was another distraction she did not need.

Hoping John the guard knew what a Paddington stare was, Maggie slowly closed the toilet door giving him her best one, and turned her attention to a – happily – much less busy room than the lounge. It was a simple wet room in fact, with a toilet round the corner in a small alcove, a basin, and a shower curtain... behind which, much to her great surprise, was Dingo with one finger on his lips and the other hand still clasping the snake.

'Shush,' he said rather too loudly and rather pointlessly, Maggie thought, bearing in mind their situation which so obviously required they make no noise.

She shushed his shush, realising immediately she was no better. There then began an awkward few seconds when Maggie was torn in three different directions. Her first, and her overriding instinct, since the snake, close up, was even less attractive than when Dingo had first captured it, was to pull the curtain back across the shower. The other option was what she most wanted to do which was to give Dingo a big hug, so pleased was she to see him. This, alas, was not viable because of the snake. The third option was the one she went for, which was to find a way to communicate that did not involve shushing each other too much. Most would think whispering would be a standard, given attribute as a spy, but in truth, she had never been that good at it. She blamed that on the

275

fact she had not had tonsillitis as a child and therefore never been forced to do it – and she had long accepted that as a practical limitation to her skill set. Moving in circles during the latter years of her life where the very opposite of whispering was the only way most of the people she knew could hear what others were saying, had not helped her either to prepare for the situation she was now in. Which was why she reverted to mime.

Poor at whispering, but she was good at mime. Because of the aforementioned circles, she had needed to be. Essential communication phrases like, *'Tea, two sweeteners, just a splash of milk, don't squeeze the teabag, let it brew naturally,'* were meat and drink mimes to her and her friends at crowded social occasions when orders were being taken above noisy conversations, often generated around topics such as actual meat and drink, tea, of course, and how noisy it was. When she used to drive, the odd mime was also useful. *'I've only gone onto this yellow hatched area because I thought the car in front was going to move further on than it did,'* was a challenge, but Maggie had tackled it with aplomb more than once to explain her situation to irate drivers who had, until that point, been hoping to turn right at a T-junction.

(Once, this had been backed up by a more difficult mime to a driver who had continued to rant when she had acted out using only hands and facial expressions that at least she was trying to explain the reasons for her error, rather than sitting staring resolutely in front pretending she was not blocking a line of traffic, like the driver who was ranting at her now probably would have done).

This time to Dingo, she started with: 'Where are the others?' – a straightforward mime involving a shrug of the shoulders, a splaying of the hands out front, followed by a rotation of the right finger at head height, lasso style.

Dingo's answer was to mime the look of someone who was very confused either by the question or by the answer to the question. He shrugged. She could have sworn the snake, despite the lack of shoulders, did the same.

'How did you get in?' was her next question, a good one, she thought, because it might illicit a plan for an escape route out. Maggie fell back on her stock mime again – shrugging her shoulders, splaying her hands out in front – but this time she finished it by pointing down at the shower floor with both fingers from either hand. There was a pause when both Dingo and snake once again looked confused, followed by a too loud an 'Oh!' of realisation from Dingo, which she tried to smother with another, 'Shush.' He took the hint and pointed towards the alcove where the toilet was. She peered round at the tiny skylight above the toilet, before looking him and the snake up and down, and miming, 'Really, you got through that little hole?' just with her face. He understood that one and nodded.

'Hurry up in there,' came the sound of John's gruff voice from the other side of the door.

Maggie put her finger to her lips before replying, 'Won't be a minute,' in her best public ladies' cubical voice.

The next mime had to be quick, decisive, and explicit if they were to make their escape. Fortunately for both, it was so blindingly

277

obvious what was required that all Maggie needed to do was point at Dingo, herself, then the skylight to indicate he should give her a leg up and out.

She omitted a role for the snake, which it seemed to take as a sleight because it slid off Dingo to do its own thing.

Breathless, Maggie waited as Dingo hauled himself up and out through the skylight to join Maggie on the flat portion of a roof of the garage attached to the side of the house. Having lifted and pushed Maggie through, Dingo had had to stand on the toilet seat, step onto the cistern and then jump up, at the same time using his arm strength to pull up through the opening. Scrabbling to his feet, he helped Maggie to hers and they stood there looking at each other for a moment before – following a quick visual check from Maggie that the snake wasn't there – falling into each other's arms.

They kept the embrace brief. 'Joshua's out front,' said Dingo. 'Caught a glimpse of him in the far corner to the front of the house when I shinnied up the drainpipe.'

Maggie's mind was awhirl; there was yet more to take in. The fact that Joshua was around was good news. Quite where Brian and Tracy were, Dingo did not say. Then there was Ben... Dingo's quick update raised all sorts of questions, the least important of which was the one she could not help but ask: 'You shinnied up a drainpipe?'

'Yep. Been a long time since I've done that.'

'With a snake?'

'Nah, not done it with a snake before. No need to.'

'I mean, Dingo, you're over seventy. How are you doing these things?'

He shrugged. 'I keep myself in shape, I guess. That and a bit of determination to make sure you're okay.' He smiled shyly.

There was a crash from below. 'That's the door, 'Dingo said. 'Guess your man got a little impatient. We best get moving.'

There followed an expletive that not even Maggie would use. 'Sounds like a man who's found a snake,' she said. There followed a yelp and a thud. 'And that sounds like a man falling onto the floor after being bitten by a snake.'

'Deadly bugger, after all, I reckon.'

'Deadly? I thought you were kidding. You had it round your neck!'

'Come on,' Dingo said with urgency. 'We can't stay here any longer. Maybe we can find Joshua and regroup.'

'Sharon and the kids aren't here,' said Maggie as they made their way over the flat roof to the front of the garage.

'I guessed that,' Dingo said.

'How?'

'You wouldn't want to leave if they were.'

He was right, and he was right about regrouping. Her plan had failed miserably. Far from regaining her family, she had lost another one of them in the form of Bill. From now on, she vowed, she would leave all the decision-making to Joshua. But in the short term, she had to concentrate on negotiating the garage drainpipe that Dingo was already halfway down.

Like Dingo, she had done this sort of thing before – both up and down, many, many times, often at a much greater height. Ignoring the creaking joints, she tackled the most painful part which was to get on all fours level with the top. It was about a twelve-foot drop, a chunk of which was ticked off as soon as she got her stomach on the edge and her leg swung over with her foot searching for the drainpipe. Instinct – and gravity – did the rest and, in a couple of seconds, she was on the ground next to a startled Dingo who had his arms up, ready to ease her down.

'We can't afford to hang around,' she said. 'That exchange is still supposed to be done. We need to make sure that plan B goes ahead.'

Just as she said that there was a roar of engines and the thunder of tyres on dirt tracks, forcing them to duck behind the front end of the Range Rover parked on the drive in front of the garage door. Two black saloon cars screeched to a halt on the road barely twenty metres away. Maggie was only too aware that with the arrival of those cars and the likelihood that Sheldon would now have the rest of her entourage out looking for her, they were in a desperately vulnerable position.

With one eye on the corner of the plot to the side of the garage, they kept low down. Doors clunked and there was the sound of a man's voice giving orders. Orders were given for a couple to stay with the cars, while the others – how many, Maggie could not see – were to follow their leader to the front door.

'Best give ourselves up,' said Maggie. 'I don't want you hurt.'

Slowly, with hands up by their sides, they started to stand up... to be met by an anxious-looking Joshua. He waved them back down again.

'Where's Bill?' he hissed.

'Sheldon's got him,' said Maggie.

'Sheldon's here?'

'She appears to be running things from this place.'

'Sharon and the girls? Sean?'

'Not here. Don't know where.'

'Taylor?'

'Don't know. Not here either, as far as I could tell. I think he is being played by Sheldon. I could have stayed to find out more but...'

'We've been led here, some sort of setup. Either someone has got to my contact, or he's been giving us the run-around. It's clearly not safe here, so let's get back to the truck. Brian and Tracy are with it, just to the left, out of sight. We'll get away and have a rethink on strategy.'

'What about Bill?' said Dingo.

Joshua made a tough call. 'We need to leave now. Without him, if necessary.'

'And Ben?' said Maggie with sudden realisation. 'Where is he?' Dingo's shocked expression did little to appease her concern. 'Ben was with you, Dingo,' she said.

'He was hanging back a bit because of the snake. Sorry, I shoulda kept a better eye on him. When I saw they'd got you, I had to help.

Spotted the flat roof as a chance to get in and just went for it. Didn't check.'

Joshua took control. 'Look, we have to prioritise. Right now, the priority is Sharon and the girls. Hopefully, Ben is safe somewhere in the woods still. We'll look out for him as we drive down. Bill will have to look after himself, for now.'

Joshua had taken over the decision-making, which was what Maggie had hoped for, so she was in no position to complain, despite her reservations. Besides, he was correct: in the world of espionage, it often came down to a numbers game. Bill was a trained operative and needed to be sacrificed for the moment. Trying to rescue him with so many people around was not feasible, as much as it pained her to accept that. Ben's absence was more of a concern, but Joshua could be right and they might come across him as they left. It was little consolation, but she knew that Bill would have suggested the same had his and Joshua's positions been reversed.

Reluctantly, she nodded. On Joshua's say-so, they followed him down the side of the car, headed right across the corner front lawn to the hedge where Dingo made a Dingo-sized gap more than big enough for them all to get through. From there, Joshua led them diagonally left across the road towards a dilapidated shed covered in brambles. Maggie had not done so much crouching in such a short space of time for many years, but she found herself doing so again now as they peered out to check on progress. The group of men was fanning out now along the front of the bungalow, some making their way round the side of the house where they had just been hiding. None, fortunately, were heading in their direction.

'Brian and Tracy are in the truck parked up just along there,' Joshua said pointing. 'Not far. Use the trees and bushes as cover. Ready?'

Four knees cracked – none of them Joshua's, she guessed – as they stood up again and followed Joshua directly away from the bungalow. The cover was not great, but their luck held out as they reached a clump of bushes, behind which was an empty building plot and Brian in the truck. They clambered through the back door which opened as they neared.

'I'm too old for this sort of thing,' said Dingo breathlessly falling in behind Maggie onto the back seat. She did not respond. There had been no sign of Ben and now there was no sign of Tracy either.

A quick, 'You alright?' from Brian was followed by the sound of their rear door closing then the passenger door opening and closing as Joshua joined them. 'Where's Tracy?'

'She went off,' said Brian. 'Dunno where.'

'Went off? Why? Did she say anything?'

'Something about Ben but I'm not sure. She just jumped out a minute or so after you went.'

'I told you both to wait in the car.'

'I couldn't stop her.'

Maggie looked around frantically. 'Perhaps they're close by.'

Joshua ran a hand through his hair. 'We can't stay around here much longer. Far too many to deal with.'

'But...'

'Maggie, listen to me. We have to get away. We're no good to anyone if we're caught.' He looked at his watch. 'And we're too late now to rescue Sharon, even if we knew where they were.'

Maggie looked at hers. Five minutes to go to Taylor's deadline. 'I've messed up.'

'No, you haven't, said Dingo, his voice reassuring. 'They'll be alright. Sid and Nelly will do the exchange.'

'And we can rely on Taylor releasing them? I don't think so.'

'We'll have to,' said Joshua decisively. 'In the meantime, we've no other alternative other than to head for Flinders.'

With just four of them, one gun and not even a snake now to use as a weapon, Maggie had her doubts as to what they could do. Still, once again, they were faced with few choices. They had to push on and hope that the fate the Iwelongas so relied on was on their side.

With strict instructions from Joshua to Maggie and Dingo to keep low and for Brian to drive as fast as he could, they skidded around a pile of bricks and a skip, over several planks of timber, and out onto the road that led down and away from the bungalow.

Any relief they might have got away was utterly squashed by Maggie's concerns for those not with them.

~ ~ ~

Chapter 24

After a minute or so, Joshua indicated it was safe for Maggie and Dingo to sit up. They were heading out of Othello, Brian having been instructed by Joshua to take a right off the main road. Four pairs of eyes continued to scour either side on the lookout for Ben and Tracy as Brian expertly swung back and forth around the bends. They were too far out now to have any hope of seeing them.

'This is all my fault,' said Maggie glumly.

Joshua turned to face her. 'The situation is retrievable.'

'You're supposed to say something comforting like: there, there, don't blame yourself, Maggie.'

'I might say that to my great grandmother, but right now I'm talking to Agent Matheson. Reality in the field is what's needed. No time for sentiment. It was my contact that fed us false information by sending us to Sheldon. I agreed to the plan. If there is any blame to be apportioned, then I'll take it. However, that's for another day. For now, we need to move forward with what we've got.'

Yet again, her young great-grandson had stepped up. His words were much more comforting than any platitude he could offer. It had a galvanising effect and she soon found herself giving a succinct, emotion-free debrief of what happened at Sheldon's place, slipping out of professional agent role only once as she commented on Sheldon's appalling taste in decor. Dingo chipped in with what had happened to him, repeating how he'd watched Maggie being taken from the greenhouse to the main house. Touchingly, he reiterated how there was no way he was going to leave Maggie stuck there.

'So, Flinders it is then?' said Maggie, acknowledging Dingo's act with a squeeze of his hand.

'Yes,' said Joshua, 'as I said, no choice. My contact can't be relied upon, which means we have absolutely no chance of any backup at any point. Ben has the shortwave radio so we can't contact the tribe.'

'That was left in the woods,' Maggie interjected. 'Bill said the battery was nearly out.'

'Okay. We have to assume, for now, an exchange of diamonds will be done.' He glanced at his watch. 'Has been done – and that the family will be released. If that hasn't happened, we still need to solve this case. Nothing's changed in that respect: we head for Flinders.'

'What do we do when we get there?' asked Dingo. 'Do we try to locate the Jingdon? If that's the plan, we haven't even got Tracy to help us.'

'True. It's maybe best that's kept secret, in any case. Anyway, that was never the main reason for going. We're there to engage with the third party or parties, There will, I strongly suspect, already be other people heading that way, as we speak...' Joshua paused and adjusted his position ever so slightly, his hand at the ready. Maggie doubted anyone else would have spotted the movement, but she knew: he was preparing for something. He waited a moment before turning his head to stare directly at their driver. 'Isn't that right, Brian?'

In an instant, his gun was out, the barrel at Brian's temple.

'I dunno what you're talkin' about, mate.' The laid-back tone in Brian's voice was gone. His eyes flicked up to the rear-view mirror and met Maggie's, before hastily settling down on a point in the distance of what was another long straight stretch of Australian road. The sentence and the look told Maggie everything she needed to know. They had found their mole.

'Turn left here and pull over by those trees,' said Joshua, 'and keep your hands on the steering wheel where I can see them.' They took the left and drew up fifty yards into a dirt track. 'Good. Now, be very clear that as I get out and come round to your side, I will not hesitate to shoot you through the windscreen if you try anything.'

Dingo's expression had turned into one of extreme shock, and Maggie could hardly blame him. The fact that Joshua seemed fully prepared to splatter Brian's brains throughout the insides of the truck was an aggressive side of the young agent he would not yet have seen. The determined expression on Joshua's face left no doubt in Maggie's mind that Dingo was right to feel nervous, at the very least. The engine was still running as Joshua got out his side and made his way round to the driver's, all the while the gun trained on a spot, Maggie guessed, that was somewhere between Brian's left eyebrow and his right. He opened the door.

'Get out,' he barked. 'Keep your hands above your head.' Brian, shaking extensively now, did as he was told. 'Dingo, Maggie, get out too. Dingo, switch off the engine and grab the keys on the way. That's it... slowly does it, Brian. Right, face the car, both hands on the roof. Maggie, search him.'

Dingo leant in to switch off the engine and get the keys while Maggie went through Brian's jean pockets and patted him down. All the while, Brian remained silent. He was scared, she guessed, but this was not a time to feel sorry for him. Joshua had to have a good for making this call.

'Check the well of the truck,' said Joshua, 'under his seat.'

It did not take long for Maggie to be convinced Joshua had probably made the right one. 'A phone,' she said.

'You didn't want to tell us about that, Brian?' said Joshua, his gun raised and his eyes drilling into the back of Brian's head. 'I did ask you to ditch it when we met up at Dingo's yesterday... Nothing to say? Check the call list, Maggie.'

'Let's change roles at this point,' Maggie said. 'I'm more acquainted with that F88 you're holding than this phone.'

Joshua nodded and they swapped positions. The gun felt surprisingly comfortable and familiar in her hands.

'Passcode?' Joshua demanded as Dingo joined him in scrutinising the phone.

'Go fu...'

Maggie stepped forward and twitched the gun slightly. 'I wouldn't finish that sentence if I was you,' she said. 'I am very particular about young men and swearing. Joshua, ask him again, but nicely this time, please.'

Joshua gave her a 'must I really?' look and repeated the demand, this time with a please at the end. As he did so, Maggie turned the barrel just a fraction to remind Brian it was still there. It did the trick.

'Twelve, eleven, sixteen.'

'Good,' said Joshua. 'That's worked.' A couple of swipes and clicks later, he had the call list up.

'A lot of recent calls there, Brian,' said Dingo looking over Joshua's shoulder, 'all to unknown numbers.' Maggie could hear the sense of disappointment in his voice. This had to be tough for him, one of the tribe he was so connected to, apparently willing to put them all in danger.

Brian remained silent.

'Text history has been cleared,' Joshua noted, 'but it looks like you were less careful with the calls, Brian. Who are they to?' Silence. 'There are five here to the same number. One of them was made round about when I left you in the truck near Sheldon's. Who to and what did you say?'

In response to Brian shrugging, Joshua stepped in, grabbed the barrel, and prodded it hard into the back of Brian's head several times. This was an old Service tactic Maggie had used herself with a partner on one or two extreme occasions. It was dangerous since the gun could go off, which was why Maggie released her finger from the trigger. The victim was not to know that, however. It was a variation of the good guy, bad guy act, with two bad guys; one holding the gun and the other seemingly not caring whether it went off or not.

289

The tactic may well have worked if they hadn't been interrupted.

They heard the cars in the distance before they saw them, which gave them some time to react. Joshua grabbed Brian by the scruff of the neck and threw him onto the back seat.

'Dingo, give me the keys. I'm afraid you're with Brian in the back. Give his balls a squeeze if he causes you any trouble. You ride gunshot, Maggie, from the front. Keep that gun on him every second you can in case Dingo gets tired of ball squeezing.'

'Got it,' Dingo and Maggie said together.

Within seconds they were off again, this time with Joshua at the wheel. It turned out that Joshua could be Brian-like in terms of his commitment to driving. With a screech of wheels and acceleration that pinned Maggie to her seat, they set off, continuing down the track they had turned into.

With some difficulty, Maggie managed to turn and place the barrel of the gun through a small gap in the headrest so that it was pointing towards the back. She had put the safety catch on before they got in, which was just as well as with all the erratic movement, there could have been several sets of brains splattered within the car by now. She tried to wedge her backside against the dashboard so that she could be in more control of the weapon, but even that proved impossible with every bump and turn of the vehicle.

'This isn't going to work,' she said to Joshua as, in response to the first of the cars turning into the lane, he shifted the automatic gearstick into sports mode. There was another burst of acceleration.

'No worries,' said Dingo as she extracted her backside from the front well. 'I've got this.'

With one hand holding on to the safety handle above the door, he used the other to pull Brian's head towards him and then place it securely around his neck, so that it was nestled awkwardly in his lap. Because of the angle, Brian's knees and feet lifted and ended up squashed against the other door, giving them both some stability. It was more stability than Maggie had as Joshua suddenly swung left onto another bumpy dirt track, this one even dirtier and bumpier than the one they had been on.

Joshua launched Brian's phone out the window as they passed over a river. 'We can't risk being tracked,' he shouted back by way of explanation.

'Shouldn't have done that,' said Brian. 'It's not them I've been in contact with.'

'Who, then?' But Brian went quiet again.

'Get your belt on, Maggie,' shouted Dingo above the thumps of the car hitting the track and the roar of the engine.

With extreme effort, Maggie turned so she was facing the front. The next job was to get strapped in. These days, she always had trouble with seatbelts, as did most of her elderly friends whenever she was out with them. Getting the strap over her body without it continually locking was only half the job. The real challenge was to locate the buckle it went into which was invariably tucked somewhere beneath her, or someone else's, backside. When the buckle was found, several minutes of wild stabbing would ensue before someone would say, 'I think that's my one,' which after more stabbing would, hopefully, result in a successful connection. At which point the strap would lock so tightly that breathing became difficult, and she would have to start all over again... once she had found the release button.

It appeared that it was a lot easier doing it at sixty miles per hour while being hurled around like a marble in a cement mixer, because, on this occasion, she did it the first time.

She was grateful for the security as Joshua began an unguided tour of Australia's roughest roads. Untreated potholes made big news in the Frampton-on-Sea Gazette and the local hack would have had a field day with the ones Maggie and her co-passengers were encountering. So far, Joshua seemed to be evading more of them than their adversaries who had now turned into jumping fleas when she looked in the wing mirror. After about ten minutes of being shaken and stirred, they eventually turned onto a tarmac road that had been crossed off the local council's maintenance programme, with Joshua able to declare that they had lost their pursuers.

The interrogation of Brian would continue on their way to Flinders.

They were safe, for now, but a little lost.

'Which way do we think?' Joshua asked as they came to a crossroads. 'Left or right?'

'Head for the mountains,' Dingo piped up from the back. 'There, to your right.'

'Which mountains?' Instinctively, Maggie put her fingers to her face to pull her specs down so that she could peer over the top to look, before realising she had no specs to pull down. Jay, her local optician, had recommended her latest pair, commenting on their robustness and how the tightness of the bridge would help secure them firmly to her face. Not robust or firm enough to survive its owner swimming through caves or being rolled over in a tank, apparently. They likely had not been on her for quite some time.

The road was busy: two tractors, a lorry, and three cars – none of which were black in colour or threatening – in the twenty minutes or so they travelled along it before turning off onto a smaller track again. They used that time to ask Brian more questions. To start with, he held out, until the part of Maggie's stomach that dealt with its primary function – food –reminded her she was hungry, as, no doubt, would be Brian. In the glove compartment, she found a packet of Tim Tam cookies and a multi-pack of Mentos which she distributed around. 'We got hungry on the way down,' explained Joshua, slightly embarrassed perhaps at what was available. A large bottle of water, now they were on smoother ground, had extricated itself from its hiding place under Maggie's seat.

Dingo allowed Brian to sit up to eat; the combination of a less empty stomach and not having Dingo's forearms around his head loosened Brian's tonsils enough for them to glean some facts, the most important of which was that he admitted he was working for Taylor. And, no, he could not confirm whether the diamond exchange had gone ahead. Someone had thrown away his phone.

Brian had not, as Maggie suspected from earlier conversations in the bunker at Dingo's, spent all of his time on walkabout walking about. Though he pointed out, it had still been a spiritual experience, just of a different kind. Much of the time had been spent in the bar next door to Pete the Crap's place at Dyson Creek, with – which came to no surprise to Dingo – Pete the Crap, amongst others. In one particularly heavy spirit-laden session, he had blabbed to the three people in there at the time how his tribe was sitting on a substantial amount of diamonds. Pete the Crap would already have been aware of this. One of the other three, the tax official who was on a grand tour of all the bars in that part of the state making sure the owners were fully compliant with excise legislation, was inebriated, having spent all day testing the bar's measures were accurate. The third person was Taylor.

'Thought he was a nice guy,' explained Brian. 'A bit up himself, but he bought me a couple and before I knew it he was telling me all about his playboy life on the international scene. That sounded kinda attractive for a young lad like me whose tribe spends most their time either on walkabout or eating pizzas.'

'Attractive enough for you to give away all your tribe's secrets?' said Dingo disgruntled. 'One's they've kept for hundreds if not thousands of years.'

'Let him talk,' Maggie interjected gently. 'What did you tell him, Brian, and what did you stand to gain?'

Brian looked down at the Mento he had been twiddling between thumb and forefinger for the last minute. He spoke softly, eyes fixed on the sweet. 'Not much at that point. Just general stuff about our beliefs and how important diamonds were to us. But I agreed to meet him again, on the basis that he said he had access to institutions that could help the tribe.'

'Help? In what way?'

'Well, make sure all the diamonds were properly safe, not just kept in some old bunker in the middle of nowhere. No offence, Dingo.'

'Plenty taken,' Dingo retorted stiffly.

'Dingo...' Maggie warned.

Brian continued, 'He said he could guarantee the diamonds would never leave Australia. If he had control of our stash, he'd keep them in safe deposits throughout Australia. Money could be made as investors would pay him to look after their investments.'

'So, he'd sell them?' said Dingo.

'Yeah, but they'd still be here. Like gold deposits, used as collateral or something. While my tribe had them, there was always the danger people would find out about them and nick them. Take them anywhere in the world. This way the diamonds would stay and the world wouldn't end.'

Joshua had been listening in intently. 'And Taylor and yourself, presumably, would make a few dollars in the process.'

'Yeah, well, I s'pose.'

'What went wrong?' Maggie asked. 'The diamonds are mainly still at Dingo's.'

'I couldn't see a way to persuade Sid and Nelly or the others, so I went quiet on Taylor. He started to get impatient, nasty, and that's when...'

He paused, struggling to finish.

'Brian,' Maggie said, 'suck on that Mento you've been holding. I find sucking a sweet a very calming experience.' Unlike chewing toffees which, with her teeth, were a much more stressful experience. Not that it had ever stopped her chewing toffees.

Brian looked up and popped the Mento into his mouth, a childlike action which reminded Maggie that they were dealing with someone who may look, drive – and drink, for that matter – like a grownup, but who was, in fact little more than a boy. On top of that, here was someone who had lived a very sheltered life. It was no wonder the bright lights Taylor offered were attractive.

'Better?'

He nodded, then continued: 'Yeah, well, Taylor started leaning on me more heavily as to the exact quantity and location of the diamonds. He'd text mostly – short ones with threats about what he'd do to me, the family, the tribe, if I didn't give him what he wanted.'

'What was it, exactly, that he wanted, Brian?' asked Joshua.

'He wanted me to find out how many diamonds were in the bunker and to find out from the elders in the tribe where and how much diamond stock there was elsewhere.'

'And you did that?'

'Yeah, as well as I could. Had to guess at the diamonds elsewhere. Told him there was some...' He looked up, embarrassed. 'Told him about the Jingdon.' It brought a loud tut from Dingo.

'And you stole the diamond that Sid and Nelly were looking after?'

296

'Yeah.'

'And gave it to Taylor?'

'Well, not directly. Someone collected it. Took it to him in London, I think. But, yeah, I stole it.'

'And I said no one in the tribe would do that!' said Dingo. 'Jeez, you're a...'

'Dingo!' said Maggie. 'Go on, Brian.'

'After the explosion yesterday, Taylor contacted me again. He wanted me to earn your trust because that was the best way to get to the diamond at Flinders as well as the stuff in the bunker.'

There was a Maggie-like harrumph from Dingo. 'Trust? You don't know the meaning of the bloody word.'

'So you've been feeding information of our whereabouts to Taylor,' said Maggie ignoring Dingo this time. 'What else have you been doing, Brian?'

Brian shrugged. 'Nothin'... much.'

Maggie thought about the pictures in Dingo's bunker. 'Who's the girl, Brian?' said Maggie.

'What girl?'

'The one you drew in the caves. You drew a picture of yourself with the mobile phone and a girl.'

'Ah, you know about that?'

'Who is she, Brian? She's not just some girl you fancied, is she?'

'Fancy her? No way!'

Dingo had stopped harrumphing and started coughing. In Maggie's experience, coughs usually meant one of four things: one – the person who coughed had a cough. Two: the person who

297

coughed wanted to say something. Three – the person who coughed didn't want someone else to say something. Subtlety of tone normally told her which one it was.

'Dingo?' Maggie said. 'What is it that you don't want Brian to tell us?'

There was another cough – number four – the embarrassed cough. 'Um, nothing... Maggie. Well... nah, nothin' that important, anyway.'

'Dingo?' He looked down. 'Brian, then?'

Brian looked at Dingo, who glanced up and gave a subtle nod.

'Well,' Brian continued, 'the girl's my sister – half sister.'

'Right. And...'

'And...' Another glance at Dingo who, this time, found some mountains to look at. 'And... Dingo's daughter.'

'Dingo's daughter?' Maggie said. 'You have a daughter, Dingo? I assume you knew you had a daughter?'

'Yeah. Ahem, with... erm... Molly.'

With Molly! Had he tried to tell her when they had talked about how they met? 'Well, of course, it's none of my business but, well, anyway... hang on. This girl, is... she has a name, by the way?'

'Flo,' Dingo and Brian said together.

'Flo is your daughter, Dingo, which means that Brian is... could be... I don't want to assume... but since he's Flo's half-brother, does that mean that Brian is your son?'

'Yeah.' Again the response came as one – a father and son duet.

'Me and Nelly,' said Dingo. He held up a hand. 'And before you have a go at me, it was before Sid and Nelly got together. It was a

298

brief fling. Sid and Nelly became a couple before Brian was born and Sid, good on him, insisted on bringing him up as part of their family. Both had had kids from a previous relationship. I thought it was best for Brian, so I agreed.'

'Okay, so I'm just working that one through, Give me a sec.' Her mind felt like her body did when it was being battered about in rolling tanks, fast-flowing water, and jumping cars. This new fact – two facts – were confusing, and surprising, but were they relevant? Dingo had two children she did not know about and he had not disclosed it. So what? He had no obligation to tell her. It was none of her business what Dingo got up to – had got up to. He had had relationships with Molly and Nelly. He was a grown man – he could do what he liked, and she should not feel in any way jealous. It was not as if he had been two-timing her. And, she reminded herself, it was she who had turned up unannounced and thrown his relatively stable – if a little hermit-like and slightly tank-dominated – life upside down (along with said tank).

Joshua threw in the grenade. 'You and Flo have been working together?'

'Dunno, can't say,' said Brian.

'If they were, that's news to me, I'd like to point out,' said Dingo.

'He's right,' said Brian. 'He knows nothin' about it.'

'Dingo knows nothing about what, if you "dunno, can't say", Brian?' It turned out that Joshua could not only do a passable impression of Brian's driving skills but also a passable impression of Brian. It elicited a scowl and a shrug.

'If Flo...' Maggie began, '...how old is she?'

'Fifteen.' The double act response again.

'If Flo's been involved in criminal acts at that age – or any age, indeed – then that's a serious matter,' Maggie said.

'I guess so.' Brian was beginning to sound unsure. A breakthrough, Maggie hoped.

'How did she get involved?'

'Well...'

'Brian!' He was pushing her patience and she was struggling to stay in good-cop mode.

Surprised at the change of tone, his response was hurried. 'Something to do with Sheldon.'

'How does Flo know Sheldon?'

'Um, well...'

'Well, what?'

'Well, Sheldon's her aunt.'

The father and son duet was replaced by a three-piece combo as all, except Brian, let out a collective, 'What?'

~ ~ ~

Chapter 25

Yourambulla was the specific site in the Flinders Ranges that Dingo had said was the tourist destination and the one Maggie had been to. They would head for the two peaks where the caves were situated, a trek and a climb from a nearby car park. If there had been any doubt as to whether it was the right place to head for, they were dispelled by Brian eventually admitting, 'Taylor'll be there, for sure. I told him way back that was where you lot were headed.'

'And, as a result,' said Maggie, 'so will Sheldon.' Of course, she would be. She had taken full advantage of the bizarre coincidence of the man who had had a relationship with her sister being also the longstanding friend of her archenemy. Staying in touch with developments from there would have been a doddle.

'And Taylor knows, after the attack at Dingo's, that there's definitely someone listening in on what he does,' Brian continued. 'He might not know who, but he's suspicious. I wanna be real clear that I've been working only for Taylor. I have nothing to do with Sheldon. And... if it helps... I'm sorry. I'm feelin' guilty about what I've done. I wanna help you guys if I can.'

'Good. A little bit of contrition,' said Maggie. 'Takes after his father. Sorry, Dingo, I didn't mean that you should be contrite. You have nothing to be contrite about. It's perfectly okay to have babies with whoever you like, whenever you like, and however you like. Well, maybe not that last one. Although... Anyway, it doesn't

301

bother me.' *You're gabbling, Maggs.* 'I didn't mean either that he takes after you in that you would work for someone like Taylor.'

'Would you like a shovel, Maggie?' said Dingo with an eyebrow raised.

'Another one?' she said. 'I get through so many.' A brief image of Sam's shovel in Sukuel's swaying dangerously popped into her head before it actually popped, with considerable force, *onto* her head. 'What I meant about being contrite is that it's good if he is like his dad in that regard, because contrition is a good quality – not that you need to show it, Dingo – but if you did, you would because you're a good man who would show it... if you needed to. But you don't.'

Dingo smiled. 'I'll take that as a compliment, Maggie. And good on yer, Brian, for showing contrition, I guess.'

Joshua got them back to the matter in hand. 'Do you think Taylor will already be there, Brian?'

'He didn't say, but I wouldn't be surprised. He has a lot of guys at his disposal.'

'As will Sheldon,' Joshua said before pausing and continuing thoughtfully: 'You know Tina Sheldon better than me, Maggie. Did she ever talk about a sister in Australia?'

'Not that I can remember. She was never one to chat much about nice things such as family. Was she involved in Molly's and Flo's lives much, Brian, as far as you know?'

'Flo never talked much about her. Don't know Molly that well.'

'What about Molly, Dingo?'

'Well, Molly and I were never that close.'

'Close enough at least once, otherwise, Flo wouldn't be around.'
Don't tease, Maggie. Poor man.

'Moll wouldn't let me anywhere near Flo after she was born, that was for sure. She was always more concerned about herself to bother talking about family. Certainly never met Sheldon.'

'Except at Dyson's Creek.'

'Yeah, and I had no idea who she was.'

'Sheldon knew who you were when you met her. She had done her research. I don't suppose she would have been too happy with how you treated her little sister, though.'

'Maggie, I swear...'

'Oh, stop it, Dingo.' She felt down the side of the seat for his knee and gave it a squeeze. 'I'm only kidding.' *Kidding maybe, Maggs, but don't push it.* Dingo might have presented as a tough bushman type, but underneath she knew him better than that. She liked the underneath vulnerable side of him as much as the rest and wouldn't want that to go.

Brian's latest comments had been revealing; it looked like the situation was heading towards there being a showdown between Sheldon, possibly Taylor, and themselves, as Maggie had guessed it would do, even wanted it to do. Would there have to be some sort of trade-off, an exchange, if her family were still under threat? If so, what could they exchange? Well, the fact that neither Taylor nor Sheldon had the Jingdon diamond meant there were still things their adversaries wanted, and Dingo's connections to the Iwelongas meant they were in a position to influence that. And they were still free. Maggie escaping had not been part of anyone's plan. *You,*

303

Maggie. Sheldon wants you, remember. Something, or someone, else to use as a bargaining tool. They were hardly in a strong position, but they had some leverage, at least.

They were well into the Flinders National Park by now. Having skirted round the nearby small town of Hawker, they located the tourist car park that Maggie remembered they had used many years ago when they had visited, and then deliberately avoided it to find a more discrete spot a mile away to park up. They were all well aware these precautions were probably pointless. They could well be being watched, but while they were free, they had the comforting feeling of some control and choices.

'We're not best placed,' Maggie said when they stopped. 'There's only three of us...'

'Four!'

'With all due respect, Brian, it's positive that you regret your actions, but it takes a while to build relationships. You've got a way to go in the trust-building department.'

'Let me start now. Let me help you.'

'We'll see,' said Joshua. 'Taylor doesn't know you've been exposed. That could – and I stress, could – be of benefit to us. But my experiences with people who keep changing whose side they're on, they are difficult to manage.'

Maggie nodded her agreement. Double agents were hard enough to handle. Triple agents – persons on one side, pretending to work for the other side who were actually working for the first side – were even more difficult. A lot of checks, assurances and reassurances needed to be carried out before the Service would consider working with someone in this role, followed up by a great deal of monitoring to ensure their stated loyalties were as they said they were. Brian was not a professional – he was a kid who had been tempted over a few drinks to do a job. If he had not been found out, he might still be working for Taylor. That was hardly a strong CV.

Dingo had something on his mind. 'Don't take it to heart, Brian, part of this is my fault. Sid's done the dad-job the best he can in my absence. He's brought you up like he has his other kids, and up until recently, you were a solid part of the tribe. As your real dad, maybe I have no right to be disappointed in you because I've not been active enough in your upbringing. But, I can't help it; I am disappointed. I care about the tribe and I care about you. Getting rat-arsed and following some fancy stranger who said he would look after your tribe's diamonds was not clever, to say the least. Then not having the bloody balls to tell Sid and Nelly, or anyone else, that he'd turned nasty and was putting the pressure on you – well, that makes you one special dickwit. So, you're gonna have to prove yourself if you're going to earn back our trust, and that of Sid and Nelly and the tribe.'

In his own way, Dingo had articulated his love for his son, and, hopefully, once this was all over, they would be closer, as a result. Expectantly, Maggie looked at Brian, a boy desperate for the love of his real father, perhaps? A boy who had made a mistake. A big one, but still a mistake.

Quietly, his voice full of emotion, Brian said, 'How am I gonna do that?'

'Dingo?' Maggie said gently. A few words of encouragement now could be the start of the healing process between father and son.

Dingo paused before placing a hand on Brian's shoulder. 'Well, son, unless Joshua says different, I suggest you keep that huge gob of yours tightly shut and stay the hell out the way.'

They set off for the Yourambulla peaks and the caves, not knowing exactly what or who they would meet. It was not an ideal situation. Joshua was the only one of them who was armed. If the situation merited him having to use the gun, Maggie suspected they were doomed. A gunfight was not something they sought.

The car park half a mile away looked empty. Maggie remembered there was a walking trail that led to the caves from there – about thirty minutes on foot, she recalled, to the base of the cave, from where there were steps up. When she had last been, they had just built a viewing platform which was used to look at the caves and the paintings. It was not possible to get close – fences prevented idiots who might like to add to the artwork. The other nearby caves were similarly protected. But there had been an aura to the whole place, despite the restrictions, and she could sense that now. The feeling of being somewhere old, important, spiritual.

The heat was more of an issue today; dry, still and oppressive. They had finished the water and the approach they were going to take from the opposite side to the car park provided no shade. Maggie was in familiar territory, and not just because she recognised the area. The knot in her stomach was warning of danger ahead.

Proceeding with caution, they picked their way over the stony ground towards the peaks. In theory, they were arriving out of sight of the main drag, though again, the situation meant that if anyone was here already, they would probably know all about them. The best scenario they could hope for was that they were slightly ahead of the game and had arrived before anyone else, allowing them to suss out the lie of the land. So far, the land was not giving much away. Hopefully, the caves themselves would be a little more forthcoming.

They walked in a line with Dingo at the front, then Brian and Maggie behind with Joshua at the rear, the gun by his side ready to use, if necessary. As they got close to the base of the peak where the cave was situated, Maggie was conscious that their general demeanour – two pensioners and two young lads, one of whom was packing a gun and all looking slightly worse for wear – put them on the wrong side of 'Happy to help' should any tourists mistake them as park rangers. They were hardly inconspicuous.

'It's quiet,' said Joshua as they stared up at the steps to the cave. 'I don't like it.'

'It's steep,' said Maggie, looking up the steps. 'I don't like that!'

'There's no one about,' said Brian sniffing the air. 'No one close, anyway.'

Had her friend, Eileen, arriving with her at the village hall for a hoedown sniffed the air and stated categorically that there was no one about (as had happened), Maggie would have been sceptical (and rightly so – the hall was packed and there was country music blaring out from the windows). But this was Brian – and Brian was part of a tribe which – unlike Eileen – did this sort of thing.

'You sure?' said Dingo. 'No bullshit now, Brian.'

'No bullshit. I'm as sure as I can be.'

'Well then,' said Maggie. 'Let's get these stairs done while I'm still standing.'

'You okay, Maggs?' said Dingo.

'You called me Maggs,' she said as she put her foot on the first step.

'Sorry, I mean Maggie. I know not everyone calls you that. Only Frankie and close friends.'

'No, I like it, Dingo. Call me Maggs if you want to.'

His face – his rather attractive, kindly face – broke out into a broad grin which she returned with a coy smile of her own.

'Shall we?' he said placing her arm through his and his size twelve boot onto the same step as her foot.

It was a casual gesture in the circumstances, but if Brian's instincts were wrong and there were people around, they were sitting ducks anyway, so Maggie nodded. To be honest, she wondered if she would make it up steps without him.

'If we're being formal,' said Joshua, 'then let me offer to lead the way. Come on, Brian. You can be my partner.'

Maggie and Dingo stood to one side to allow them past and then followed them up. Maggie was panting slightly by the time they finally reached the platform at the top, but the motivation to complete the last few steps was provided in the form of the shade the cave would give. When it came, the temperature drop was dramatic and welcome, though the transition from bright sunlight to semi-darkness took a while to adjust to. Gradually, in the comparative darkness, she began to make out first shapes in the rocks and then some of the paintings.

The paintings were as she remembered; beautiful, powerful, evocative, clearly designed to tell stories and depict things that were important to their creators. She was aware of the respectful silence as they all stood on the platform taking in the scene around them. She glanced at Brian who, having created his own versions back at Dingo's, seemed particularly affected. Dingo too seemed pulled in, while Joshua's eyes flicked nervously from picture to picture until eventually settling on one particular drawing to Maggie's left that she had not noticed. Once again, Maggie reached for glasses that were not there as she leant forward over the rail to get a closer look. It turned out she did not need them to see the picture that Joshua had been so drawn to; it was the clearest of all the paintings in the cave.

A shaft of sunlight illuminated it just as Maggie nudged Dingo in the ribs to get his attention. He looked at it and then nudged Brian. The four of them stood there rooted to the spot for a few moments staring in disbelief. Eventually, Brian broke the silence. His voice was calm and quiet, a whisper almost, but it still produced a faint echo. It made the question sound eerier than it otherwise might have, which was probably apt for the circumstances. The picture – and the situation – was frankly as eerie as it came.

'Maggie,' Brian asked pointing a finger at a figure on the left-hand side of the picture, 'is that you?'

It was. Of that, there was no doubt. Maggie had her own place, prominently sitting on a rock in the foreground to the right overlooking a montage of remarkably familiar scenes. There were five scenes in chronological order, each bordered by a rough rectangle of silver dots. The first showed her on a baggage belt, knitting and all, a line of suitcases behind. The second was an aerial shot of Sydney Harbour Bridge. Without her glasses, Maggie could not make out the detail, but she would not have been surprised if what looked like two smudges of colour in the centre were her and Joshua tied to the girders. Scene three was quite abstract and took a little more deciphering. The rectangle was filled with white wavy lines, one on top of the other running horizontally into a vertical thick black line. It was only after Maggie looked at the fourth scene – much less abstract with a tank being confronted by a group of people with guns – that she realised what the lines might depict.

'That's where we went off-grid,' she said to no one in particular. 'Radio waves hitting a brick wall.'

The fifth was a tank, in the background an explosion.

The last scene was the simplest and most revealing: two large sparkling diamonds.

'One must be the Jingdon, the last mined diamond,' said Maggie. 'The smaller one is the one we had, Joshua.'

'Nah, these drawings are supposed to be *both* the real ones.'

Maggie pulled her eyes away from the cave wall to look at Brian. '*Both* the real ones?'

'The Jingdon and the one I stole.'

Joshua stiffened slightly and his right hand twitched, Maggie noticed, a trigger movement pre-empting an actual trigger movement on the gun which was, for the moment anyway, still by his side. 'The one you stole and we got back from Taylor, you mean?' he said.

Brian took a deep breath, then stated simply, 'Nah.'

'For Chrissakes, boy,' said Dingo, 'explain what you mean.'

'The one you got back was a fake. Taylor was putting me under pressure to get the diamond, so me and Flo made up a plan. She said she knew someone who could get a good fake. It would get Taylor off my back. The one I gave to Taylor was that fake.'

Maggie was now wondering why she had gone to all that trouble at Singapore airport. 'So I took Taylor's fake and replaced it with a fake?'

Brian nodded. 'Reckon.'

'Where's the real one, Brian?' Joshua said tersely.

'Oh, I did steal that one.'

'I know you did. Where is it?'

'I gave it to Flo.'

Maggie was in the process of framing another question when they were interrupted by a young girl's voice. 'That was daft of you, Silly Bollocks.'

They looked around.

'Flo?' Dingo said. 'Is that you?'

311

'Full marks, Einstein.'

'Where are you?'

'Under your noses, you stupid galah.'

All four leant out over the platform railing. Ten feet below was the top of a girl's dark-haired head which turned into a round face as Flo looked up at them. The cave was artificially lit so Flo's features were clear to see. It was basically a young Dingo with plaits, though as Flo turned her eyes towards Maggie and held her gaze, she could see the same fiery green in them that Molly had displayed when she had tried to launch herself at Dingo. Flo held her ground directly below, waiting, Maggie assumed, for someone to say something. Maggie, never one for long silences – or indeed any – during conversations, obliged.

'Nice to meet you, Flo. Are you going to come and join us? We'd like to ask you some questions.'

'I'll stay right here.'

'Okay, well, I'll speak to you from up here.'

'Nah. Now, I'm gonna want you to stop talking so that you can listen to what I've got to say.'

Maggie knew she could be bossy if the situation so required, but this girl seemed to know exactly what she wanted and was going to make sure it was clearly communicated. She had come across many people in her time who were bossy; it was the nature of the job. Villains, leaders of spy rings, Sheldons – they had all tried to boss her and others around. Maggie's approach was often to respond in kind, an approach which took most of the bossy ones by surprise as they were usually under the misapprehension – and often,

312

apprehension, until that point, anyway – that they were the ones in control. She was sorely tempted to switch to boss-mode but because of the young age of the girl and the delicacy of the family connections with Dingo and Brian, the situation merited a different response.

'We're listening,' she said simply.

'Wait there; I'll be up when I've finished this final picture.'

With that, she took out a packet of permanent markers and drew another rectangle on the cave wall, bordering it with stars before setting to work on its contents.

Maggie was not sure how long they stood there watching the back of Flo as she worked on the next scene. She was aware that there was plenty they could have done in the meantime to intervene, but the bizarreness of the situation stopped her – any of them – from doing so. All they could see was the back of Flo and the six scenes – soon to be the seventh – plus the painted Maggie to the side. Like the real Maggie, her image seemed to be watching as the final scene was being drawn. Maggie drew her arms around her body in response to a slight chill which, as soon as she noticed it, sent a shiver done her spine. All the while, save for the occasional distant plip-plop of water from somewhere deep in the cave, Flo worked away in silence on the ancient stone.

Eventually, the girl stood back to examine her work. She nodded once, turned to look at the gallery, and then stepped to the side. Maggie stared at the last scene, trying to take in its implications. She took a deep breath, about to say something, when there was a

313

childish giggle from below, and all the lights went out. They were plunged into blackness.

'Stay calm,' said Joshua. 'Your eyes will get used to it in a second.'

Dingo expressed the confusion Maggie felt. 'What the hell was that all about?' Maggie had no answers to that at this stage. 'And what's happened to the light from the entrance?'

'It's been covered,' said Brian. 'I don't know that, by the way, in case you think I've got anything to do with what my crazy sister is up to.'

'This is the crazy sister that you've been in cahoots with,' Joshua said impatiently.

'Yeah, well... I'm just sayin'.'

'Saying what, exactly, Brian?' Dingo said. 'That's serious stuff Flo's drawn there. You sure you don't know what she's up to?'

'I'm sayin' that this isn't what we agreed. All I wanted was for her to help me get Taylor off my back. That...'

He paused to point, Maggie assumed. It was a pause that she would have expected Ben to fill with a comment about the pointlessness of pointing in the dark. And then she remembered that he was one of the many people she felt responsible for who was not there.

Brian continued: 'That painting is just weird. I mean, I had no idea she could draw like me for a start. Then to have done stuff that's been going on and finishing like that. Streuth!'

The 'that' in the scene they had watched Flo paint was still very much going through Maggie's mind. Apart from the scene with the

314

diamond, it was the simplest one; a cave – the cave they were in, assuming the marks on the wall were the same paintings they had just been looking at – in the foreground of which were two prostrate bodies. One was long and male; the other was much shorter, female. There was no doubt who they were supposed to be. Nor what state they were supposed in; she and Dingo looked very dead.

She flinched as she felt a touch on her arm.

'Don't worry, Maggs.' In other circumstances, she might have taken comfort from Dingo's words, at least the tone, if not the 'don't worry' part. As far as she was concerned, there was plenty to worry about, the least of which was Flo's obvious intention to kill her and Dingo, and the effect that was going to have on her ability to save the rest of the family. The darkness made that prospect all too real.

'Flo?' she said loudly to what felt like nothingness. 'Flo, what's this all about?'

A faint echo then silence.

'Flo love?'

Still no response.

'Let me try,' whispered Dingo.

'Don't bother.' Flo's voice was nearer now, behind them, wherever behind was. It was no less dark, despite Joshua's earlier hope their eyes would get used to it.

'And I'm not your love,' she added from a different direction this time.

'What do you want?' said Joshua.

315

'Not you. You're surplus. Not Brian either. You're not supposed to be in here, Dumbo.'

'You want us,' said Maggie. 'Me and your dad.'

'Yep.'

There was a sudden loud yelp from Brian. 'What the f...?' and then what sounded awfully like Brian falling to the floor.

'Be warned: I am armed,' said Joshua. His voice was calm, but there was an authoritative edge to it.

'Fire away!' said Flo. Again, her voice had moved. Was she to Maggie's left? Possibly, and not that far away, it seemed. She spoke again, definitely somewhere to the left but lower down this time. 'See who you hit. It won't be me.'

She was clever, staying on the move, varying her height as well as location. She knew some tricks – *Service tricks?* – and had to have a mechanical aide of some sort, infrared possibly, to help her see. The air rippled and there was a subtle movement to her right, the sound of feet on the gravelly floor. This, Maggie realised, was Joshua rotating slowly.

The opportunity for Joshua to act did not present itself. A surprised 'Ah!' and there was the sound of another body collapsing to the floor.

'Joshua?' Maggie said, not expecting a reply. 'Dingo? You still there?'

'Right here, Maggs. Excuse the language, Maggs, but Flo: what the fuck you playin' at?'

'Oh, I'm not playin' at anything... Dad.' The last word was laden with sarcasm.

'So, this is about me, is it? Some sort of game to get back at me?'

'As I said: I'm not playin'. This is no game, Dad.'

'I get it. You feel I've not been there for you. Is that it?' He didn't wait for a reply before he went on. 'You know that's what your mother wanted, don't you? I wasn't allowed to be part of your life. You know that.' He had to be waiting for a response, but there was none. 'Flo? Are you listening to what I'm sayin'? I wasn't allowed to be your dad. I wanted to. Desperately wanted to.'

The voice was closer this time, not close enough to locate, but Flo had moved, possibly to within reach. Not that it helped because Maggie still could not see a thing. 'That shouldn't have stopped you carrying on tryin'.'

A chink, at last, not of light, but understanding for Maggie as to what was motivating this remarkable young girl. Remarkable because it seemed she had been involved in the whole sequence of events from start to finish. From the diamond switch and the warnings that led them to go off-grid, through to Taylor's involvement and even Sheldon's role, it looked like Flo may be behind it all. Why? Well, in part, it seemed, because she blamed her dad for not being there for her. But more than that, she had beef, on a cattle-sized scale, with Maggie, proved by the paintings and her actions now.

'I did try,' said Dingo. 'Yer mother's stubborn.'

'So it's her fault?'

'Not totally, but it was... difficult.'

A little bit of bossiness was called for, now, Maggie decided. 'Whatever your feelings, Flo, you shouldn't be going around hurting people. What have you done to Joshua and Brian?'

'Would you be upset if I said I'd killed them?'

'Of course. Have you?' Despite the rising anxiety, Maggie tried to keep her composure. She was very aware that she was not only dealing with someone who was highly capable, there was more than one sign to suggest that Flo was unstable. She was not unlike Sheldon, her aunt in that respect. A lot of Molly in her, too.

'Nah. Brian's my brother. He's dumb, but he's alright. As for the other bloke, Joshua, I'm tempted because I know it would upset you.'

'So, what have you done to them?'

'It's a jab. Aunty Tina's. Don't know what it is, but it knocks people out.'

Some relief, but Maggie still had a lot of work to do if she were to avoid the last scene and the implications that might have for her family.

'So, you got the jab from your aunt? She's putting you up to this, is she?'

'Nah, she hasn't a clue.'

'What do you mean?'

'Do you think this the part of the film where the good guys get the bad guys to reveal how and why they're doing all these dastardly deeds, just before the bit where the good guys somehow defeat all the odds and overcome the bad guys? That ain't gonna happen, coz it's just us. I can see you, but you can't see me. I also have a gun.'

Maggie nearly died on the spot in response to a tumultuous crack, the sound of a weapon being fired in a confined space. She quickly realised she had not been hit, but what was of great concern was that Dingo may have been. He let out a loud moan and she was nearly knocked over by his arm as it reached out for her. She flailed around and managed to grab hold of some part of his clothing, but his weight was too much and he slipped to the floor.

'For God's sake,' she cried, any semblance of calmness gone now. 'You've shot him. Get some lights on. Quickly!'

She heard some shuffling around nearby, a click, and then the lights in the main part of the cave with the paintings came on. It was not a lot of light, but it was enough for Maggie to take in the scene around her: three bodies on the ground – Brian, Joshua, and, right next to her, Dingo.

Maggie looked up to see Flo standing a few metres away, wearing infrared goggles which she removed with one hand. In her right hand was a gun, pointing to the ground.

'It wasn't supposed to happen like this,' she said. 'You're both supposed to be down there, next to the paintings when you die.'

Maggie got down on her knees and felt for a pulse on Dingo's neck. There was a faint something there. 'You shot him?' she said as she desperately scanned his body, looking for a wound.

'Didn't. I fired it in the opposite direction to scare you.'

'Well, you did that!' She checked his pulse again, this time on a wrist. There was definitely a beat which was a good sign. She felt his forehead. It was clammy and his breathing sounded like he was struggling. 'He needs a doctor. I can't do much here. Flo... Flo!'

319

She looked at the girl again. Her features were not clear in the subdued light, but, as Maggie had thought when she had seen her below, there was a lot of Dingo in the strong jaw and high cheekbones. Plenty of Molly, too – she was a stunner.

'Flo, are you listening? He's collapsed. He needs a doctor.'

'You'll have to drag him down to the main part of the cave.'

'What?'

'It's supposed to happen down there. I shoot both of you there. He's not supposed to die here.'

'You're mad!'

'It's gotta happen like in the drawing I've just done. You saw it: you and him, down there in front of the other paintings. Get up.'

'Flo...'

'I said, get up!' The gun was pointing directly at her now. 'The stupid idiot has messed it up. What's wrong with him? Why has he collapsed? He needs to be down there below the gallery on the cave floor. Not up here.'

Her voice wavered. She was angry; again, something – a lot – of the Molly in those features. *This could go one of two ways from here, Maggs,* she told herself. An out-of-control adversary was unpredictable; she had learnt that in the Service through bitter experience. One of her colleagues had lost his life right in front of her when he had tried to tackle someone he thought had lost it. It turned out the other man had indeed lost it, but only at the point when Maggie's colleague tried to disarm him. He panicked and shot dead her colleague. It was established afterwards that the man had had no intention of killing anyone, had never killed anyone before, and would have probably given up.

Every situation was different, but the principles were the same. Slowly – there was no other way these days – Maggie got to her feet. Dingo was alive, for the moment at least, but if he had had a heart attack, he might not be for long.

'The others...' she began.

'Sleeping – little while yet.'

They were all alive. That was something. *Keep it that way for as long as you can, Maggs, until you can do something to change the situation.*

'What do you want, Flo? What do you hope to achieve?'

'I told you· I want you and him down there... on the floor... dead.'

'Why?'

'Because I've painted it that way.'

'I saw that. But why do you want us dead?'

'You trying to delay me again? I told you: this isn't a movie.'

'Naturally, I'm trying to delay you. I'm eighty-two, I haven't got that long before I naturally die so you'll probably understand why I'd like to stretch out what time I do have left for as long as possible.'

'That isn't much.'

'So I gather. But if you try to make me move this big lump that is Dingo down there, that'll be two of us collapsed in a place you don't want us, believe you me.'

The girl was thinking, a good sign that she was not panicking, at least. It could also be a bad sign that she might just shoot her dead on the spot and be damned with the painting. Maggie needed to keep her talking.

'Why is it so important you want us dead down there?'

'Coz that's what I painted. Like the ones Brian did at Dingo's, these paintings have to tell the story. These ones tell my story.'

'And what is your story, Flo?'

'What do you mean?'

'What's the story you're trying to tell? What is it that you want to say?'

'Well, it's obvious.'

'A story of revenge for the way you feel your dad has treated you and your mum?'

There was no reaction.

'Revenge against me because...' She left the sentence hanging. Maggie assumed it was because of her history with Sheldon, but Flo was not talking... not at the moment. Maggie waited. There was nothing else she could do really, but she was very aware that every second that passed could be vital for Dingo.

Eventually, Flo spoke, more quietly than before and Maggie had to strain to hear. 'Not revenge against you. All I need to do is beat you.'

That was an answer Maggie had not expected. 'Beat me?'

'Do what my aunt, the great Aunty Tina, couldn't. Do all the things she couldn't or wouldn't. I'm gonna beat you, and I'm gonna be there for my mum. She wasn't. She couldn't give a shit about her younger sister, nor me. Too busy spying. Then busy being a failed international criminal.'

'I don't understand.'

'I wanna be better than her. She failed; I won't. She wasn't around when he...' She paused to glance at Dingo. Maggie did the same, noting that his breathing was becoming more laboured. '...wouldn't marry mum. My mum went through hell for years after because of him, having to cope with bringing me up all on her own. Through it all, my caring aunty sat on her arse. Well, I'm gonna show her that I can do the lot: I can beat you, look after my mum, and put Dingo in his place for the pain he caused her.'

Maggie had witnessed some of that pain at Molly's place, seen that she had been hurting for a long time. They had flown away, hoping she could move on. Whether what her daughter was doing now would help with that was another matter. This was a girl who, like her mum, bore grudges towards Dingo and, apparently, Sheldon.

'He'd be friendly towards me when he saw me hanging around with Brian and the like, but he never committed to me. Mum told him she didn't want him to once he rejected her, but he shoulda seen through that... If you love someone enough, you'd do anything for them. Right?'

She was right about that, at least: that was why Maggie was here now. That was why she was desperately trying to work out how she could turn this situation around, and save Sharon and Sean, the girls, Ben, Bill... Dingo. Anything for those you love. She said nothing because the girl was talking freely now.

'I did my research on my aunt. I read about the trial, the things she did. Then, out of the blue, she wrote to mum saying she was free, living in South Australia, and wanted to meet up, after all that time of nothing, No contact, nothing at all.' The bitterness cut through her words. 'Mum refused to have anything to do with her, but I decided to see her on the quiet. Told her I wanted to be close to her, that I forgave her for not supporting Mum, that I wanted to learn from the best. She fell for it. All the while I was learning how she did things, the tricks, the cock-ups she had made. I let her boast, but inside I was thinking about how stupid she was. To be outsmarted by you – a retired spy in her eighties... She made so many mistakes. Her contacts were easy to find. She kept details on her phone – how stupid is that? E-mails, texts, easy for me to hack. She was so easy to impersonate virtually.'

'Virtually? Nearly impersonate?'

'Online. Jeez, you oldies are so ignorant sometimes. I became her, made contact with her contacts over here, in the UK, US. All the ones who were expecting rewards from her cyber operation you were involved in stopping in Bruges. Some of them were mentioned at the trial, others weren't but were easy to follow up.'

'Flo – that's impressive.' It was; the girl had out-Sheldoned Sheldon. 'You've done all this on your own?'

For the first time, there was a trace of a smile. Flo was proud of what she had achieved. 'I wanted to prove to her that she was wrong to have ignored us. Show her what she had missed. That I could do everything she could do and more. I set up the whole thing. Taylor was easy – he's just your typical greedy, slimy con. Aunty Tina knew loads of those types. I let him do most the dirty work...' Maggie was right about Taylor being manipulated, but she had got the wrong person doing the manipulating. 'Did things through him so that it wasn't too easy for you to work out who was doing what. Then there were the contacts she had in the Ozzie Service. God, people are so gullible and so easy to bribe. Offer them a few dollars and they'll do anything for an international criminal – even a failed one. Only needed one knowledgeable nerd in their security department to be bent and he did the rest. Security cameras, flight boards, phones – it's scary what the state controls – told him I wanted you and the others taken out and that's what he did.'

'And you knew I would end up at Dingo's?'

'Hoped. You did, so that was okay.'

'You knew about our connection in the past?'

'The great Maggie Matheson! You used to be a spy. You of all people should know they know everything about you.' *They* being the Service, of course. More specifically, *they* being Sheldon. Maggie thought she was beginning to understand what was going on here. She let Flo continue. 'Course, I couldn't believe my luck when I found out about you two. Hadn't believed you'd be this close though.'

'This close?'

'Come on, Maggie. It's obvious.'

'Is it?' She could feel herself blush. Apparently, it was. 'You put me and Joshua on the bridge? The ransom note?'

'Taylor wasn't happy about the diamond switch, so he didn't need a lot of motivation. I got the port authority to turn a blind eye, planted the idea into Taylor's stupid head via a well-placed meme or two,' – Maggie's inner Luddite was shouting out *meme?* but she managed to ignore it – 'of similar stunts on bridges. He did the rest. He's a very greedy, gullible man with a huge ego, as you can tell from those stupid suits he wears. It's been easy to get him to do things and let him think it's all his own idea.'

'Like the threat to Dingo with the boomerang?'

'Taylor used a boomerang? What an utter drongo!'

'The date the world is supposed to end, written in the dirt the following day?'

'That was me. Bit of fun. Aunty's birthday, too! Nice.'

'So Taylor did kidnap Sharon?'

'Eventually. Messed up at the start, needed a little help at the end to find your *lovely* family.' Cynicism was obviously a Sheldon family trait. 'They took some finding, but my aunt's resources stretch wide.'

Joshua's contact – was it the right time to push on that? Instinct told her to wait, despite her desperation. Build her up, keep her talking. Somehow turn her round.

'The article about the Iwelongas...'

'Planted by a helpful, bribable member of Airport Security. A little nudge to get you thinking about the Iwelongas.'

This girl was clever! She had thought of everything. *Possibly, Maggs, possibly. Keep thinking while she talks.*

Flo continued: 'Hadn't expected you to go off-grid so successfully, but you turned up in the right place in the end.'

'And the missile attacks on Dingo's place, on the tank – that was all your doing?'

'Yeah. The people who did it thought they were working for the amazing Tina Sheldon. They're going to be so pissed when they find out it was some gangly fifteen-year-old from the arse-end of nowhere.'

'I imagine they would be. I'm quite surprised myself.' Flo's smile was broader this time. She liked her ego to be massaged. *Just like her aunt.* 'You are an incredible young lady.' Again that smile. 'So the idea is to beat your aunt and get revenge on your dad.'

'And blame the lot on her.'

'It's a setup.'

'Yeah! Nice, isn't it? Mum and I'll keep the diamond that you thought you had swapped. Go and live somewhere nice. Europe somewhere, I reckon. She deserves a new start.'

'What about the rest of the diamonds?'

'Well, the Jingdon, if it is here, can stay for all I care. What's left of the stash at Dingo's belongs to the tribe. They can keep all that. I'm not greedy!'

'They'll come looking for you, eventually. Taylor, your aunt... They must know where we are now.'

'Taylor'll go anywhere I want him to. Despite his fancy suits and fancy talk, he really is as thick as wallaby shit. He's about to head off to Hong Kong to chase diamonds, as we speak.'

'But Brian said he'd told him we were going here.'

'Brian's telling you things that I want him to tell you.'

'What about Aunty Tina? She won't let you get away with it.'

'I think she will. Didn't you notice?'

'Notice what?'

327

'How my dear aunt was when you met her. Did she seem with it?'

Maggie thought back to her conversations with Sheldon. The experience had been slightly surreal. Her look of surprise, the perfectly manicured garden and her interest in plants, the strangely decorated bungalow. She did seem distracted, vague, unsure about what was going on. Yet...

'Aunty Tina is losing it. Come on: that awful decor! She thinks she's in control, but she's not capable of organising a piss-up in a kanga's pouch. Her brain is going.'

Getting Flo talking was one thing; following her logic was another. 'If she's losing her mental capacity, why set her up for killing us? Why not just leave her to her own devices? If she's as bad as you think, she might not even be aware what you're framing her for.'

There was no smile now. Instead, Flo's eyes were burning. 'Right now, she's with it enough to think she's some sort of super criminal. I want her to feel good now so that when she is stitched up for your murders, it hurts all the more. She thinks she's got everything she wants. A bit of power, nice house, bunch of ugly heavies to protect her.'

Maggie nodded. 'I met them.'

'Credit to you for finding her.'

Credit for finding her? So Flo was not aware of everything that was going on. *Don't raise that yet, Maggie.* There was more to find out. 'We had cars chasing us...'

'Not my doing. Hers. Angry bitch. Brian got you back on track, though. Got you here.'

328

Once Brian came round from whatever Flo had jabbed into him, he was in for a good talking to.

A whimper and a deep breath from Dingo distracted them. Was that a look of concern from Flo? Her tone suggested not. 'Enough talk. You need to move him down to my painting so it looks right. Then we can finish this.'

'To be clear: you want me to haul him down there, just so it looks right?'

'Yeah. I can't do it because I'm holding the gun.'

'You've just incapacitated two blokes who would have been much better at that sort of thing.'

Flo shrugged and then raised the gun.

'You can point all you like, young lady, but there is a physical difference in size, as I've already said, that makes it impossible.' Was that a flicker of doubt on Flo's face? A crack in that wall of stubbornness? It looked like it. *Now's the right time to challenge her, Maggs. Now.* 'You know, your painting is wrong; it's not what's supposed to happen.'

'It is what's supposed to happen.'

'I asked you to tell me your story of the paintings and you have, but you've got the ending all wrong.'

'I've got everything right so far.' *Not quite everything, young lady.*

Her hand was steady, but Maggie detected something in her voice that was not. There was doubt there, uncertainty. For good reason. 'You think your aunt's lost it?'

'I know she has.'

329

'Has she? What if she's the one fooling you? Allowing you to do all this, thinking you're getting one over her, but all the while she's the one in control.'

'Nah. I've spoken to her enough times. I know she's lost it. I've been all over her systems and she's not batted an eyelid.'

'Well, she wouldn't, would she? Not if you were doing exactly as she wanted you to.'

'She's on medication because she can't cope with everyday life. Right from when we met, I knew she wasn't right. Speech was slow, she lost track of what she was saying. It was so easy to hack into her stuff.'

'You know about her trip six months ago to meet with Dingo, then?'

Flo looked at her. Her silence spoke volumes. A vital piece of information she knew nothing about. *Got you, young lady. Got you.*

It was true; Sheldon had seemed not quite with it. But what if she was not quite with it enough to be across all the detail, yet still with it enough to know what she wanted? What would she do then? The answer was straightforward: get someone else to do it. Maggie was convinced that what she suspected all along was correct: Tina Sheldon was still in control. Very much so. Only Sheldon would have originally known about the connection between Dingo and Molly and the one between Dingo and Maggie. That was the basis for the whole scheme. Sheldon's idea, her scheme. Flo was being well and truly used.

The girl shook her head.

'Think about it, Flo.' *But not for too long*. Dingo was getting no better. 'You're hungry for revenge, but who has the greatest hunger? Your aunt hates me, hates us. Me, Joshua, Bill, even Ben. We're the ones who ruined all her plans. What better way to get her revenge than getting us over here, making us jump through hoops, then disposing of us, while at the same time getting access to the largest haul of diamonds in the world? And she hardly had to lift a finger – just allow her highly intelligent niece to take all the risks, to do it all for her. She may not be quite the old Tina Sheldon, but, from what I saw, there's more than enough in that head of hers to be pulling the strings.'

'Nah – not possible. I'd have known she was doing that.'

'Would you? Would you really? I'm telling you, I know her very well, better than you. God, I worked with her long enough. The Tina Sheldon I recently met may not have the moves to play the game, but she doesn't need them. She dictates the strategy; you do all the moves. It's not all gone to plan... for either of you. Your story has had to be adapted as it went along, hasn't it?' Maggie was taking a gamble; she was letting her mouth and stomach – her instinct – take over, and hoping, as had happened many times before, they would get her out of trouble. 'In the plus column, Taylor has served you well, you've had us running around like blue-arsed flies, and you're both very close to getting what you wanted. In the negative column, it's taken longer than either of you had hoped for because we've stayed at large longer than you expected.'

'If she's controlling me, then why isn't she here now?'

331

'Because the story's not finished. She wants you to kill us. She wants you to do what you'd planned to do. Once that's done, she'll pin the blame on her mad niece and force someone like Brian into getting access for her to all the diamonds the Iwelongas have. Job done. Classic double-bluff. God knows she's done enough of them.'

'No, that's not true. I...'

'Flo, it is true. Think about it. As good as you are, could you really have set all this up without some background help? Someone gently facilitating things?'

'Yes, I... I have... You're just trying to... to...'

'To what? To tell you the truth, is what I'm doing. This may not be the story you set out to tell, but that doesn't matter. Change the ending... change it to a good one.'

She took a step and bent down over Dingo, not caring now whether Flo would stop her. Even in this light, he looked pale, but his chest was moving. She stroked his forehead, adjusted his open shirt which had rucked up round his neck. Flo was watching her, thinking... deciding. *Ram the point home, Maggs. You've nothing to lose.*

'Look, Flo. You've proved everything you possibly could by getting us to this point. You've done amazing things, but, right at the end, you're in danger of being beaten by your aunt.' She waited a moment to allow that to register before continuing: 'You can still beat her if you do the right thing now.'

The gun twitched again. 'No, don't. I know what you're up to.'

'What I'm up to is trying to make this right for you, for all of us. Dingo's your father. He may not be perfect, but he does his best. We all do. Most of us, anyway, including you. You're angry, hurt, sad, but you'll feel a lot worse if you don't give Dingo the chance to be the father you want him to be. He's not to blame.'

Flo started to interject, but Maggie was in full mother/grandmother/great-grandmother mode and raised a finger to silence her. 'No, he isn't, Flo. Your mum has to take some responsibility and so, it has to be said, should you. You could have reached out, yet you chose to go down the route of revenge. Why? Do you really want to be like your aunt, wrapped in hatred? Is that really you? The only way to be better than her is to not be her.'

Maggie stopped. She had said all she wanted to say. Now she had to see if it made any difference. She maintained eye contact and waited. Flo's eyes narrowed, then her lips pursed. Maggie wondered if she had gone too far because there was a definite tightening of the finger on the trigger, but then, abruptly, the gun fell to her side. Her whole face changed from looking like a dangerous young adult to looking like a vulnerable young girl, which was what Maggie knew, deep down, she was.

Maggie breathed a huge sigh of relief... a sound which coincided exactly with the sound of the blackout curtain being raised.

333

~ ~ ~

Chapter 26

It was not obvious, at first, who the person was who barged through the curtain, but they could not have been that familiar with barging in on dangerous situations through curtains, or indeed dangerous situations without curtains, otherwise, they would have been much more circumspect. So, without even seeing a face, Maggie quickly concluded that it had to be Ben. It prompted Flo to raise the gun again, and she might have fired had she not been distracted by a second figure barging in, giving Maggie the opportunity to shout a loud, 'Don't shoot, Flo!'

That other figure was Tracy, a familiar one to Flo it seemed because as soon as she spotted her, she started to crumble. Tracy rushed over and caught her before she fell and held her in her arms. The gun dropped to the floor as Flo buried her head deep into Tracy's shoulder.

'It's alright, honey,' Tracy cooed. 'It's okay. Whatever's happened, you're okay.'

'Ben love,' said Maggie, injecting urgency back into proceedings, 'I'm glad to see you two. Surprised, but very glad. Go and tuck back that curtain; we need more light.'

The additional sunlight helped Maggie to see but did little to revive her spirits. Judging by the pallor of Dingo's skin, he was still in a bad way. 'Make sure Joshua and Brian are okay, will you, Ben?' she said, trying to sound more in control than she felt.

334

'I'm on it,' said Ben, and Maggie took comfort from the fact that he would be. 'Where's Bill?'

'Um, no... Sorry, I'll explain in a minute. I just...'

'That's fine. Concentrate on Dingo.'

Maggie bent forward and whispered in Dingo's ear: 'Dingo, Dingo, can you hear me?' Then louder: 'No, he's out of it.'

'Joshua seems okay,' said Ben. 'I'll check on Brian.'

'Well done. Tracy, can you help here?'

'Flo?' Tracy said pulling back from the girl. 'I'm gonna see to Dingo, ok?'

Flo nodded and stepped away. Tracy gave her an encouraging smile before walking over to kneel beside Maggie and Dingo. Maggie rocked back onto her heels to allow her the space she needed and left her to it as she watched Ben put his head on Brian's chest.

'Breathing okay, can hear a heartbeat... I think he's alright too.'

'Should be,' said Flo, looking on nervously from the side. 'The jabs were nothin' powerful.'

'Let's hope so, 'said Maggie. 'Just Dingo, then.' She needed a distraction. 'What happened with you and Tracy, Ben?'

'Oh, well, Dingo went on ahead with his bloody snake and we got separated, so I went back to near the spot where we split up and waited. Tracy spotted me. Bless her, came straight over. It all got a bit hectic with scary people around. We stayed low, then watched you lot drove off. Knew you would head here so we followed on when we could.'

'Sorry about leaving you. We did look out for you. Um, Bill's still at the bungalow.' Another worry, but one that she could do nothing about at the moment.

'You buggered off without him too?' Ben said with a lopsided grin. 'I expect he'll be along in a minute, knowing Bill.' He gave Brian a businesslike shake of the shoulder. 'Brian? Brian, can you hear me?'

There was an 'ugh' sound which Maggie took to be another good sign. She turned her attention back to Tracy and Dingo, hoping for similarly positive news. 'What do you think, Tracy?' she asked tentatively.

'We need to get him to a hospital. Even if I had a potion with me, there's nothing much I can do. Looks like he might have had a stroke or something.'

Ben stood up. 'We have a phone from the Land Rover we stole. Tracy, give us it, will you? I'll see if I can get a reception outside.'

The issue of trusting authorities after all that had gone on had to be shelved, Maggie realised. Dingo could die without medical help. Even if Sheldon had suddenly appeared with a dozen of her thugs, Maggie felt like she would have taken the lot down so that Ben could make that call.

'Be quick,' she urged Ben.

Tracy reached into her back pocket and threw Ben the phone as he passed by them towards the exit. 'Good catch. It's zero, zero, zero for emergency services,' she added.

Ben nodded and barged back out through the entrance with as much gusto as he had barged in.

'Have you got any water?' Maggie asked Tracy.

'No. We came straight here. No time to get water.'

'I've got some,' said Flo, her eyes puffy and red. 'Give me a sec.'

There was a sound of scrambling down some rocks as she went back to the cave floor before she reappeared with a rucksack. 'Here,' she said pulling out a bottle and handing it to Maggie. A jacket followed. 'I'll put this behind his head.'

Gently, Flo lifted Dingo's head and Maggie tucked her arm underneath as she put the water to his lips. His eyes remained closed, but his lips responded to the moisture and opened slightly to take in some of the fluid. She waited for him to swallow a few times before carefully placing his head onto the jacket.

'Not too much,' Maggie said. 'We'll wait to see what the medics say... if they get here. They will get here, won't they, Flo? Before anyone else?'

'Yes. I'll make sure of that. But I'll need to use my phone. Make a couple of calls.'

She stared into the girl's eyes, looking for an indication that she really did want to change the end to this particular story. There was something there, maybe... hopefully. Was there any other choice at this stage? The answer to the next question might give some validation.

'My family, Flo...where...'

'Taylor should have released them as part of the diamond exchange. He had no reason not to.'

'Can you check?'

'I will. I'll need to go outside for reception.'

'There's not much more we can do for Dingo,' said Tracy. 'I'll go with her. She trusts me. We've spent a little time together when times have been tough, haven't we, Flo?'

The girl nodded and they left together. Maggie watched them leave then looked back down at Dingo before grabbing hold of his hand. She did not let it go until the air ambulance arrived thirty minutes later.

That half hour was a blur. First Brian, then shortly afterwards, Joshua, came to. Both woke with a start, Joshua the more active of the two as he scrambled to his feet to put himself into the familiar fighting stance position that Maggie had first seen him in, back at Sukuel's restaurant in what seemed like a lifetime ago. Brian's rise to consciousness was less dramatic as he sat up, blinked several times, and looked around.

As soon as Joshua was able to take in information, Maggie updated him on the imminent arrival of medical help and the fact that Flo was on her phone in the process of trying to buy some time. With Joshua still feeling a little drowsy, it took a little while to explain the turnaround. He nodded his understanding throughout, but Maggie suspected she could have suggested they needed to fly to Mars and he would have gone along with it.

Brian too was not quite with it. He tried to say something to Maggie but stopped with his mouth half open when she gave him a stare. 'I suggest you take a good look at your dad, pray to whatever gods you believe in that he survives, and that you have the chance to speak to him about that word trust we spoke about before.

338

Okay?' Brian nodded. 'Now, stay out of our way until you have something useful – and truthful – to say.'

Another nod and she never heard another word out of him, not even when Dingo was strapped into the pod on the side of the helicopter to be whisked away to a hospital heading for a specialist stroke department in an Adelaide hospital. A stroke, as Tracy had suspected, was the initial diagnosis from the paramedics. Maggie had desperately wanted to go with him, but, as worried as she felt to be apart from him, she had unfinished business.

After Dingo had been taken away, she and Joshua perched anxiously on a rock outside the cave and watched from a short distance as Flo sat on her own rock, still on the phone. There was an occasional check to a tablet she had produced from her rucksack. At one stage, she pulled out a wire and connected the devices. It was taking a while, but there was little else to do but wait, and hope Flo delivered. Ben sat quietly on the other side of Maggie. She took comfort that he was there; none from the fact that he would be as worried as she felt for Bill who was still stuck at Sheldon's, as far as they knew.

Now and then, Flo looked to Tracy, who was standing nearby, or to Maggie, as if she needed reassurance. Tracy responded with an encouraging nod; Maggie remained impassive, concerned that if she responded in any other way, her true worries and emotions would flood out.

Eventually, after what felt like hours, Flo put the devices down on a rock, indicated that she had finished, and walked over to rejoin them.

'How did you get on?' said Joshua as she approached. He seemed more with it now.

'Your family is definitely safe, Maggie,' said Flo, addressing her directly. 'Taylor's released them before leaving the country.'

'On a plane somewhere with a crate of our diamonds, no doubt,' said Tracy. 'Still, it's worth it.'

Maggie felt like crying; the relief was so great. *Don't Maggs. There are still things to sort out.* She focussed on what the Iwelongas had given up to enable this to happen. 'Tracy, I...' she began but was interrupted by a raised finger.

'Don't say sorry, whatever you do.' Tracy softened the rebuke with a smile.

Joshua spoke again. 'The family is okay. That's the main thing. We'll have to sort out Taylor later. What about Sheldon?'

Flo paused before replying. For a split second, Maggie thought she had let them down, so it was a relief when she said, 'Maggie was right; she had people on standby just down the road, probably ready to come in on me once I'd disposed of Maggie and Dingo. I've sent them an order to return to base which they will think came from my aunt.'

'Good,' said Joshua. 'So, that was how long ago?'

'Ten minutes or so.'

'That gives us time to move away from here and...'

'You won't need to do that,' said Flo. 'It's sorted.'

'What's sorted?' said Maggie, her suspicion aroused again.

'The situation and my aunt.'

'How?'

340

'I realised that there's another way.'

'Another way? What do you mean?'

'I'm going to scare the shit out of her. Make her understand her little niece is not going to be pushed around and do everything she wants.'

Maggie stared at Flo. The girl stared back. No amount of staring was going to get more information out of her, it seemed, and so Maggie continued, 'Tell us, Flo, in clear understandable words, exactly what you've sorted.'

They – Maggie, Tracy, Joshua, even Brian who had been standing rather moodily on the sidelines up until that point – leant in while Flo explained what she had done. 'I used one of her contacts in the Ozzie Secret Service to arrange a visit from Special Services to a certain property in Othello.'

'This is the same Special Services from my day which used to perform – I can't put this any other way –special services?' Maggie asked.

'I guess.'

'It will be,' said Joshua. 'I reckon this is the same people who were firing from rocket launchers at Dingo's.'

'Correct,' said Flo. She pulled out her phone. 'Should be done, just about now, I reckon.'

'What's been done?' Maggie could sense her stomach frantically telling her ears that they weren't going to like the sound of this.

'Her house is going to suffer an explosion which is going to blow her ass to kingdom come... Well, not quite that. ' She smiled. 'Give Aunty Tina one hell of a fright!'

Before Maggie could answer, there was a bleep on Flo's phone. She pulled it up and smiled again. 'It's done.' Another bleep straight after wiped the smile away. 'It says... um... it says the target is flattened.' She looked up, aghast. 'Wow, shit! That wasn't what I wanted. I told them to target an end of the house with no one inside.'

Maggie's stomach went ominously quiet. Her mouth could only manage a whisper: 'The whole house? Sheldon's house, flattened?'

The girl's wide eyes said it all.

'Bill was there.'

'Bill?' said Flo. 'Your Bill?'

Maggie grabbed Joshua's elbow to steady knees that were feeling decidedly unsteady.

'Let's not panic,' said Joshua. 'He might have escaped.'

There was another bleep. Flo read it out in a quiet voice, her head down. 'Target destroyed. Comprehensive.'

'Comprehensive?' said Ben urgently. 'What does that mean?'

At this point, whatever control Maggie liked to think she had over uncooperative body parts failed as her whole body seemed to collapse in on itself. She knew exactly what comprehensive meant.

She took a few sips Joshua offered from a bottle the paramedics had left them and then handed it back to him.

'I'm here,' said Joshua, crouching down before her.

'I know you are, Joshua love.'

The physical reaction she had just experienced was very unlike her. Priding herself on her inner mental strength, she had generally been able to maintain at least a semblance of control, even in the most difficult of situations. Even when dealing with the worst news possible. 'Curtains,' Frankie had always said to her. 'You're like magic curtains – always able to pull yourself together.'

'Bill would have found a way, Maggie,' Joshua said lifting her chin up with his finger. This remarkable young man was hurting as much as she was, yet still, he had the strength to support her. 'It's Bill we're talking about here. There's always hope.'

She wanted to be strong, just like her great-grandson; she really did. But to say the last few days had been a chaotic and emotional experience would have been an understatement. She had been physically and mentally pushed to the limit, and that limit had just been passed with the news that her son – her long-lost son for many years – was likely to be lost to her permanently.

'Yes,' she managed. 'It's Bill. As you say, perhaps he survived.' But her stomach, like the rest of her, just did not believe it. A few moments passed before she looked up and around. 'Ben? Where's Ben?'

He was sat on the ground a few metres to one side, hands clasped around his knees, head down, his long hair obscuring his face. Tracy was kneeling next to him, a hand on his shoulder.

Their eyes met as he looked up. He should be angry with her for getting them into this mess, but his eyes showed no blame, no anger – only hurt. She shook her head slightly. *What do you say to someone who has just lost their husband, Maggs?* She should know with so many of her friends going through a similar experience but she could not form the right words in her head. For a moment, she floundered... before instinct kicked in and she realised she would deal with it the only way she knew how, the way Frankie would have wanted her to.

Pulling herself together, she got up and steadied herself, before walking over to Ben. 'We'll get through this,' she said gently, 'as a family.' She held out her hand, encouraging him to his feet.

Then, drawing him in and reaching up to ease his head onto her shoulder, she stood firm as she allowed her son-in-law to sob his heart out.

~ ~ ~

Epilogue

Maggie had been by Dingo's bedside for three days and nights in a row. The patient was doing okay, conscious, and making good progress, likely to make a full recovery. Though the medics declared that he was not quite to full fitness yet, his self-assessment was as obtuse as ever: 'I feel as chipper as a wallaby with Vegemite between its bollocks.' She would stay at the hospital until he was able to stand on his own two feet unaided – or at the very least propped up at a bar with a large glass of amber nectar in his hand. After that... well, there were a lot of things to think about, for them all to think about.

Maggie was not as exhausted as she might have been; the hospital had provided her with a comfortable camp bed, they had been inundated with visitors and, best of all, there was a constant source of tea from the nurses and ancillary staff who popped in regularly to check how things were. Some of her friends stuck in one-bed flats on their own for weeks on end without seeing anyone would have bitten off her hand – bitten off their own, if necessary – to swap places. Physically she was in surprisingly good health. Emotionally, with the loss of Bill, she was finding it hard. Fussing over Dingo was a welcome distraction.

The doctors confirmed that Dingo had suffered a minor stroke, brought on by some sort of shock. Maggie had wondered along with them what that shock might have been since they had been having such a lovely time with family visiting the caves up until the point he had fallen ill. Though matters were considerably more secure than they had been, it was best not to say too much, Joshua had said. Loose ends were being tied up, but with the security breaches on both sides of the world, there was work still to be done.

Joshua's 'reliable' contact had well and truly disappeared, leaving a huge gap in the audit trail. A solid colleague in the Australian Secret Service, Joshua had trusted him first to get Sharon and the family to safety, then to provide other assistance such as arranging the overnight stop at the shack. He had delivered on those things, yet had leaked information to Flo (and, as a result onwards to Taylor) about the true whereabouts of the family, and at the same time led Maggie and Joshua, literally and metaphorically, up the garden path to Sheldon's bungalow. Someone not affiliated to any of the known parties was a cause for concern and it suggested, worryingly, that other forces were in play; 'manipulating the manipulator manipulating a manipulator who was being manipulated,' as Ben rather unhelpfully put it.

Maggie had forgotten all about the injury to her arm, and it was Ben who reminded her to get it checked out. Since Tracy had given her the balm, she had had little trouble – no swelling, no pain. An x-ray revealed a hairline crack which showed evidence of recent healing. It was a diagnosis that only deepened Maggie's connection to the 'magic' of Dreamtime. She hoped that connection would give her strength as she dealt with the blow of losing Bill again.

She had sought comfort with Sharon, Sean, and the girls who had turned up shortly after Maggie reached the hospital to be with Dingo. Three thugs invading what was supposed to have been a place of safety had been a traumatic experience, but they were unharmed physically. Sean was as friendly and as concerned as could be, and had been a rock throughout, Sharon explained. Maggie felt bad for ever doubting his loyalty, a thought she kept to herself and concentrated instead on how proud she was of the resilience her family had shown. She and Sharon would have to tap into that resilience to deal with the sad fact that her daughter would never meet her brother.

Ben had been at the hospital almost as much as Maggie had, during the day at least. He, Joshua, and Brian had been staying at a hostel just around the corner. Brian had agreed to remain there and cooperate with investigations. He had already attended one interview with Joshua's counterpart in the Australian Service. There would be more. Whilst Joshua had been preoccupied with dealing with the fallout of two houses a thousand miles apart being blown to bits, along with the security breaches, Ben had been... well... Ben: supportive, considerate, and – Maggie had needed this most – positive. Despite the initial emotional shock, he was never going to give up hope that Bill had somehow survived, and neither should she.

The explosion at Sheldon's had been truly catastrophic. Flo's misconceived plan to frighten her aunt by arranging an unoccupied section of the house to be blown up had gone badly wrong. It had coincided with a real gas leak, and the result was that very little remained in one piece. DNA evidence was proving impossible to gather. Maggie wanted to share Ben's optimism, but the last time she had seen Bill, he was unconscious on the floor in the greenhouse. Nothing was standing of that structure either. Still, she responded to Ben with as many reciprocal positive vibes as she could muster, all the while having in the back of her mind that if Bill had survived, he would already be with them in the hospital, telling her and Ben what a soppy pair they were for even contemplating he might have been caught up in such a thing.

As for Flo, she had been taken away by the local social services as soon as they landed in Adelaide. Before they were all picked up at the caves, she had had the wherewithal to share with Joshua the contacts which had been used to plan and carry out this extraordinary operation. This enabled Joshua to 'sort out the wheat from the chaff' as Maggie put it, and get to the point now where he had a solid enough network within the UK and Australian Secret Services he could trust once more. Flo's cooperation at the end would stand her in good stead, but, as Joshua pointed out, she had broken the law many times. A mental health assessment and ongoing support would, Maggie hoped, help her move forward. In the short term, Tracy was with her acting in a guardian role until the complicated relationship Flo had with Molly was worked through. Maggie had her doubts on that front; they were strong characters, both volatile in different ways.

The diamond Flo had got Brian to steal was returned to the tribe – some recompense for the one crate of diamonds they had given up to Taylor. He had gone underground, Joshua explained, but would be brought to justice, of that he was confident. 'Can't be too many idiots swanning round in the heat and humidity of Hong Kong wearing tweeds,' he had joked.

On the fourth day into Dingo's – and Maggie's – recuperation, she was awoken from a nap by a quiet tap on the door.

Dingo was awake. 'Don't come in,' he called out. 'We're naked.'

'Dingo!' Maggie said, coming to abruptly. 'There's only so much bad behaviour you can explain away by saying it's coz you've not been well. Now, behave yourself... Come in,' she added as sweetly as she could manage.

The door opened a crack. 'It's Joshua,' said a quiet voice through it.

'Yes, come in, Joshua,' said Maggie. 'We won't bite. Neither of us have our teeth in.'

'I didn't want to wake you.'

'You won't do that, Joshua, love. You know me – always alert, always on the lookout.' She said it with a cheeriness that she did not feel. The look on Joshua's face took away even that need for the pretence.

'Um, we have an issue.'

'Is it Bill?'

'No... no, sorry. Still no news on that front.'

Maggie did not know whether to feel happy or sad. *Stay pragmatic instead, Maggs. That's all you can do.*

She felt the comforting grip of Dingo's hand and was grateful for the sound of his voice. 'Go on, Joshua mate.'

'Best show you.'

He produced his phone and handed it to Maggie who took it, then adjusted the length of her arm and squinted several times before looking back up at Joshua. 'What am I looking at?'

'You'll have to zoom in.' She adjusted her eyes into what she hoped Joshua would interpret as a withering look. Joshua took the not very subtle hint. 'Sorry, let me...'

Reaching over, he moved his finger and thumb until what came into view was... a finger and thumb, this set holding a diamond in between. He zoomed out again to reveal the finger and thumb's owner.

'Brian?'

'Lemmie have a look,' said Dingo pulling himself up.

They crowded around the phone as Joshua adjusted the view all the way out and back in again, finishing on a shot of Brian in profile holding the diamond outside the Yourambulla cave they had been at just three days earlier.

'That's not the Jingdon diamond?' said Maggie.

'It's big enough to be.'

'What's he playing at? I'll bloody kill him!' Dingo started to pull his covers back. This time it was Maggie's turn to provide a calming influence as she placed a gentle hand on his shoulder.

'He's not at the hostel and he's missed his second interview with my colleague,' Joshua explained.

'What are we saying here?' said Maggie. 'That he's gone back to the caves and somehow got hold of the diamond? I thought it was well hidden and only the elders knew where it was.'

'Not sure. Early days,' said Joshua shrugging. 'I got this through twenty minutes ago, via Flo. Did Brian say anything to either of you? Any indication at all that he was unsettled in any way, that, maybe he was still under some sort of pressure?'

'Not at all,' she said. 'He was here only yesterday saying how he would stop all the bullshit, as he put it, and do what's best, like his dad.' They had even joked how he shouldn't completely stop all the bullshit, otherwise, he would not be like his dad at all.

'It's a worry, what with my contact disappearing too and Taylor still on the run.'

'And what about Sheldon? You don't think somehow...'

'We don't see how that's possible. Indications from Flo were that she was inside when the explosion happened. As you know, there was nothing much left of the house... well, nothing much left of anything... ' His voice trailed off, obviously tuned in to how difficult that was for everyone.

'Perhaps Brian's been forced into this,' she said, aware that the straws in the water sitting on Dingo's bedside table would be much easier to clutch. 'Perhaps he was scared?'

'It's hard to tell just from the photo.' Brian's expression was neutral; neither gloating nor showing signs of duress.

Dingo started to sit himself up again. 'I'll give him bloody scared when I catch hold of him!'

'Lie back down, Dingo love. This is doing you no good at all. We'll sort this out... somehow.' But in truth, she was so tired, deep down tired, that she was struggling to even sort out fresh underwear to put on in the mornings. Despite its challenges, Brenda the Bag's

351

relatively simple life in Sydney had its attractions over the ups and downs she had endured. A big part of her wanted to find a skip to sleep in and stay there.

'I'm a dad with two kids,' Dingo sighed, 'both of them diamond thieves. How did that happen?'

Ben's outlook was rubbing off on her. 'Look on the positive side; there are two diamond thieves who have a wonderful dad.'

'I've not been wonderful, Maggs. I shoulda been there more.'

'You have been there, Dingo. It's a two-way billabong.'

He snorted. 'Good one!' She was pleased to hear his throaty chuckle. It was a sound she was growing rather fond of.

'I'll keep you in touch with developments,' said Joshua, stowing the phone back into his pocket. 'I'm sorry to have to bring you more difficult news.'

'I'm eighty-two, Joshua. I didn't get to this age without being able to live with difficult news.'

'Eighty-two!' chipped in Dingo. 'My very own cougar.'

Maggie appreciated his efforts to remain upbeat. 'I'd be inclined to call you my toy-boy if you weren't such a sugar daddy to all those women.'

'Ouch!' said Joshua wincing. 'I'll leave you two lovebirds to your bickering.' He laid a comforting hand on Maggie's shoulder before heading for the door. Half in, half out, he turned. 'Um, one more thing.'

'Yes, Joshua?'

'Bill... um... well, he's my granddad.'

'Yes, I know that, love.'

'I need to remember that more... Being an agent is... er... it's tricky sometimes, isn't it? Emotionally, I mean.'

'Yes, Joshua, it is. All we can do is keep going.'

A nod of the head and he slipped out.

That was the wording on her gravestone right there: *Here lies Maggie Matheson. She kept going. Until she didn't.*

'You okay, Maggs?' asked Dingo placing his hand on hers.

'Yes, yes. I'm okay... Worried, but okay. You?'

'You know me. Well, if you don't, I'm hoping you'll have lots of time to do so, from now on.'

'Very presumptuous, Derek Parfitt. Listen, can I ask something?'

'Whatever you like.'

'Have you got any cash?'

'Doubt it. Why?'

'Well, you remember I told you about that nice policeman who interviewed me after Joshua and I came down from the bridge in Sydney?'

'Yeah. What about him?'

'Sergeant Capelli, his name was. He lent me ten dollars. I promised I'd pay him back.'

Down Undercover

Acknowledgements

I write because I like it, but it's uplifting to have encouragement and support, a source of which is my family. Thank you to them, but I want to give specific thanks to others who have read early versions of this and the previous book, and given feedback.
These lovely, patient people are:

Wendy Bottero, Angela Cairns, Paul Olsen,
Lily Broom, Chris Dulake, Terry Hayward,
Kirsty Harrison, Tim Carter,
Angela Clarke and Matthew Young.

Other books by Ian Hornett

**Maggie Matheson: The Senior Spy
(Book 1 in the Maggie Matheson Collection)**

**Maggie Matheson: Last Orders
(Book 3 in the Maggie Matheson Collection)**

'The Quarton Trilogy'
**Quarton: The Bridge
Quarton: The Coding
Quarton: The Payback**

Sci-fi to die for...

All available on Amazon in paperback and as an e-book

About the Author

Ian is a retired teacher and former customs officer. He is also an ex-professional footballer, cricket international, and world-renowned golfer.

Some say he has an overactive imagination.

Ian very much enjoys writing, which is just as well as he spends an awful lot of time doing it.

Do tell Ian what you think of this book. His social media links are below. Or why not leave a review on Amazon or Goodreads?

Follow Ian on:

Website   www.ianhornett.com

Facebook   @ianmichaelhornett

Tiktok   @authorbuzzian

Instagram   @ianhornett

Made in the USA
Monee, IL
22 August 2024

64349493R00197